Ardagh sat alone in the quiet night, studying the small amulet and, strand by delicate strand, working out the weave of its Power.

Try it! the prince scolded himself. *You have all the words, the gestures, fixed in your head.* But he just couldn't seem to begin. With a little shock, Ardagh realized that now he was afraid, he was genuinely afraid!

His sudden shiver had nothing to do with physical cold. How could he ever forget that terrible moment of banishment, when every Realm-crossing spell had been torn from his mind? Since then, what had there been to do but try creating some new version? *Out of what? the bits and scraps of spells to be found in this magic-poor Realm? Amazing I managed anything at all!*

Ardagh grimly began. A corner of his mind felt the tiny bit of Power in the amulet rouse, and knew a thrill of hope.

"Open! Open! Open!"

He saw the shimmering in the air, he saw the Doorway beginning to form, he knew with a wild blazing of hope that this time it would work, this time he would leave the human Realm behind and—and— he couldn't hold it, there wasn't enough Power, he couldn't hold—

With a great rush of air, the Doorway snapped out of being. As the spell gave way, Ardagh's strength went with it and he fell forward on the cold earth. The backlash of unspent Power from his failed spell aching in his mind, he thought with bitter weary humor, *This Realm . . . must like me. For no matter what I do, it just : will not . . . let me go.*

Baen Books by Josepha Sherman

Prince of the Sidhe:
The Shattered Oath
Forging the Runes

A Strange and Ancient Name

King's Son, Magic's Son

Bardic Choices: A Cast of Corbies
(with Mercedes Lackey)

Castle of Deception: A Bard's Tale Novel
(with Mercedes Lackey)

The Chaos Gate: A Bard's Tale Novel

FORGING THE RUNES

JOSEPHA SHERMAN

FORGING THE RUNES

A Baen Books Original

Baen Publishing Enterprises
P.O. Box 1403
Riverdale, NY 10471

ISBN: 0-671-87752-6

Cover art by Ruth Sanderson

First printing, November 1996

Distributed by Simon & Schuster
1230 Avenue of the Americas
New York, NY 10020

Typeset by Windhaven Press, Auburn, NH
Printed in the United States of America

ACKNOWLEDGEMENTS

The author would like to thank Dr. Susan M. Shwartz for her help in answering such questions as "Would he be an ealdorman or a thegne?" The author would also like to thank Diana Paxson for help in separating the runic wheat from the chaff.

Old Storms and New
Chapter 1

Ardagh Lithanial, exiled prince of the Sidhe—green of slanted eye, tall, elegant and almost too blatantly Other to be passing for human as he was—sat a horse on a hill in this human land of Eriu, and stared out at devastation. The wind was strong enough to scream in his ears and whip his long black hair stingingly about his face, but it was an ocean-borne wind, cleanly scented and no more than natural. The forest that lay before him had been torn apart by a force far greater than that, trees thrown aside like so many broken spears.

Arridu, the prince thought, remembering that demonic force nearly crushing the life from him, and just barely kept his hand from rubbing newly healed wounds. *Arridu and Gervinus. Bishop Gervinus, human lie though that title was. Ae, let the demon rend him forever!*

Ardagh's horse stirred restlessly, calling a rumbling greeting to another. A second rider was coming up the hill, a solidly built man, no longer quite young, at least as humans rated such things, his red hair streaked with silver: Aedh mac Neill, High King of all Eriu. Reining in his horse beside Ardagh, Aedh looked out over the ruined forest and drew a shuddering breath.

"Dear God." It was said with soft, fervent horror. "Dear, loving God." The king shook his head as though trying to deny his own vision. "Each time I dare to think, no, the damage couldn't be that bad, and then . . . Eriu has

1

always been storm-racked; we're surrounded by sea, after all. I've seen my share of tempests, and some of them monstrous enough to seem truly sorcerous. But . . . I have never seen anything to match the fury of . . . that."

"Nor are you likely to see such a storm again," Ardagh said, and felt Aedh's keen grey glance turn his way. "Not if I have any way to stop it."

"Are you *expecting* another sorcerer?" the king asked sharply. "Yes, and since when has a prince of the Sidhe developed such concern for a human Realm?"

"No, to the first. And since he's had to take shelter here, to the second." But then Ardagh stretched wearily in the saddle. "Ae, that's not the whole of it. King Aedh, this can never truly be my homeland, we both know that, but I have . . . grown fond of it. I would not see it harmed."

Aedh snorted. " 'Grown fond.' I wish you could have been fond enough of Eriu to keep that—that storm demon from—"

"I did what I could."

"And nearly got yourself killed in the process. Yes. I know."

The king turned away, looking out over the ravaged land again. "I'm not accusing you. You saved us all from God only knows what further horror. And if it were simply this one forest devastated, och, well, we could all say, 'Was that not a terrible thing?' and go on with life. But I'm beginning to think that the whole land's been changed!"

"Surely not—"

"Surely yes! You've heard of the island of Fitha? No? Our tour hasn't included it, but there've been enough witnesses to swear that the cursed storm tore it to shreds! And so many people slain . . . *my* people . . ." Aedh's face was rigidly impassive, but he could not keep the anguish from his voice. "Over a thousand dead in Corca-Bhaiscinn alone." He glanced at Ardagh. "How can you look so composed?"

"My brother," Ardagh said softly, "once went to war with a traitor." He could not keep the bitterness from his voice. "A genuine traitor, not someone betrayed by false courtiers into only seeming an Oathbreaker. The war didn't last long; magical battles seldom do. And Eirithan was, of course, the victor. When he was done, the traitor's lands looked . . . far worse. Nothing ever grew on them again."

"*This* land will recover," Aedh said, almost defiantly. "I don't think I would like to see your people's idea of war. Or peace."

"Ae, no, there are long periods of tranquillity, of beauty that would, I think, make even you weep. As for a Powerful war—you saw it, or at least a hint of it."

"Ah." Aedh looked out again at the ruined forest and shuddered. "That was more than enough of—ha, who is this?"

A horseman was riding frantically up the hill. "News, King Aedh," he called out, "foul news!"

"What, worse than this?" the king retorted. "Then we are sorely pressed, indeed!"

But he signalled to the messenger to approach.

Ardagh glanced subtly about, recognizing this man, that. The audience chamber here in Fremainn, Aedh's royal fortress, was walled with stone, one of the few buildings not of wood, and crowded now with men: advisors, courtiers, all of them murmuring like an angry hive of bees. Ardagh sat among them with total Sidhe stillness—which meant that the humans around him had nearly forgotten his presence—but he, too, was feeling a sympathetic stirring of anger as he watched King Aedh. The king, too well schooled in regal ways to pace, fairly blazed with rage, nearly blinding to Ardagh's Sidhe sight.

"Leinster dares attack us now, *now*! Does King Finsneachta think us broken by the storm?"

That brought a roar of denials. Aedh held up a hand for silence and continued, "He is obviously blind to Eriu's

pain, or so jealous for power that he doesn't care about
the wrecked land, the ruined harvest—he would starve
his own people to attack us! What shall we do about this,
eh? What shall we do?"

Clever, Ardagh thought. *They can hardly fail to shout
for war. And I—I cannot help this time but agree.* Pitching his voice to carry over the turmoil, the prince said
(feeling his neighbors flinch in surprise at his sudden
coming to life), "It seems to me that the only choice of
honor is to take the fight to Finsneachta—but after he
has made the first move."

"Wait?" shouted someone.

"We cannot wait!"

"We dare not wait!"

But Aedh held up a hand again, and the shouting
gradually died back into silence. "What would you have
us do, Prince Ardagh?"

"I will not pretend to fully understand your" *human*
"ways. But it seems clear to me that Finsneachta did,
indeed, mean to catch you with your guard lowered."
He glanced about, seeing every man watching him
intently. "Very well, then, let him start on the march.
Then *he* is the aggressor, the one in the wrong, not you.
Gather a force, not just of your own men but of those
from your vassal kings as well, to show that all Eriu is
outraged by his action."

From the light blazing in Aedh's eyes, he'd already
decided on that. "Exactly! Laity and clergy both shall
meet him on the field of battle—and it shall be *our*
choice of battle, *our* choice of field!"

"Not the clergy!" protested one voice. "The Church
has no part in this!" It was Fothad mac Ailin who spoke,
Aedh's Chief Poet and Chief Minister. Wise Fothad, with
his clear gaze and deceptively ordinary face. *Fothad,*
thought Ardagh, *father of Sorcha, my Sorcha.* "You must
not involve the Church!" the poet continued to protest
as they all began filing out of the audience chamber.

But the others were too mad with battle-hunger to

heed. And only Ardagh, the prince thought, even heard him.

Eithne, queen and wife to Aedh mac Neill, stared bitterly up into darkness and told herself this was no different from all the other times she'd lain awake beside her husband, hearing him sleep and knowing he would ride out tomorrow. Ride out into battle. Ride out and maybe not return—

"No," she whispered, softly so Aedh would not hear, "gods above, gods below, no, not that."

Aedh had no idea that his wife held this one secret from him, Aedh had no idea that Eithne still belonged to the old religion, the ancient faith. And he most certainly had no idea that she practiced the smallest, weakest but very real magics.

Eithne reached out a tender hand to stroke her husband's bearded cheek and heard him murmur her name in his sleep. "Whatever magics I possess are for you, my love," she whispered.

If only they were enough! If only they could wrap Aedh and their children, their Neill and little Fainche, safe forever . . .

There was no such thing as "forever" for mortals. And she'd known when she'd wed him that a High King must almost always be at war. Eithne shivered, wriggling closer to Aedh for warmth. He murmured again, wordlessly, and an arm, heavy as a log, fell across her. Eithne squirmed into a more comfortable position under the weight, feeling the heat of his body, smelling the familiar scent of him.

Mortal, she repeated silently, and that brought her to the next thought: Prince Ardagh, who knew nothing of the word. Prince of the Sidhe that he was, he should, were there any justice, bear magic enough to Ward all this land. But in this mortal Realm, he had little more Power than she.

I've kept your secret, Eithne told the prince silently,

never quite sure if he might actually hear her. *And you've kept mine. Our pact remains. I'll work what spells I can to keep Aedh safe—but you, och, you, too, must do what you can.*

With the softest of sighs, Eithne burrowed her head against Aedh's broad chest. Let the night pass, and the following day. Let the battle come and go and let Aedh win and be unharmed.

Let it be so. Let it be so. Let it be so.

"*Cadwal.*"

No, ah no, *Dewi Sant*, not this dream, not again. Cadwal ap Dyfri, leader of the High King's mercenary band, groaned in his sleep and fought to wake. And yet the voice called to him:

"*Cadwal,* cariad, *Cadwal.*"

The voice was so real, the endearment so familiar.

"*Cadwal, dearest heart, hear me. Know me. Cadwal, you must hear me!*"

"Gwen?" he asked softly. Now Cadwal knew for certain it was a dream: His Gwen, his Gwenith, was dead these many years, falsely accused of sorcery and put to death. Murdered. All for having fought off the lord who'd tried his hand at rape. Cadwal had slain that lord, his own liege lord—and in the process gotten himself thrown into exile. His only comfort in all these years since had been the surety that Gwen was up there with God and His holy ones. And: "Och, Gwen," Cadwal said with a dreamer's certainty, "you can't be here. Your soul is safe in Heaven now."

But the voice continued, as he knew it would, as it had continued these three nights running: "*Cadwal, no. I am not safe. I am not safe. Come to me, Cadwal. Free me. I beg you, love, save me. Free me.*

"*Free me . . .*"

Cadwal woke gasping, sitting bolt upright in his lonely bed, then swore, harshly and steadily. He was that rare thing, a mercenary of middle years, and he hadn't made it to this age by allowing weakness of body *or* mind to steal into him. A dream, curse it, this was nothing more than a dream! And why he was letting the thrice-damned thing haunt him—

Because it felt so real, so very painfully real, Gwen's enslaved soul calling for his help . . .

Pw, what nonsense! *You're a warrior,* Cadwal snapped at himself, *head of the High King's mercenaries—yes, and a fine bit of good you're going to do Aedh letting dreams get the better of you.*

He shot to his feet, fiercely splashing his face with water from the pitcher at his bedside, letting the icy water shock him fully awake. Still dark out there, still a good way from morning, but Cadwal knew he was not going to sleep again this night.

Aedh, now. Aedh mac Neill had always dealt well with him, treating Cadwal not like an exiled mercenary, but like a man of honor fallen on difficult times.

"And damned if I'm going to betray that trust!"

Throwing on his clothes, Cadwal stalked out into the night. A walk would stir the blood, get him back to— to reality. Away from . . . dreams.

"No," Sorcha said and, "no," again. "Ardagh, no, you can't mean to go—"

"I can. I will." Sidhe vision keen even at night, Ardagh glanced down at his human love with her fierce face and lovely deep blue eyes, then turned sharply away. No one dared say to a prince, *you must not do this thing,* certainly not a mere human—

Save this one. "What else is there for me to do?" Ardagh asked, still not looking at her. "Return to my own land? I would most dearly love to do that. But thanks to my oh-so-suspicious brother and his oh-so-treacherous court and that one necessary spell they stole from my mind, I cannot. These folk have given me sanctuary. What else is there for me here but to aid them in turn?"

"As what? Ardagh, you're not a-a warrior! And I thought we—"

He whirled back to her at that. "Ae, 'we!' What is there of that? You know I've sworn a vow to harm no one here—and thanks to that vow and your people's code of honor, I cannot even exchange more than chaste words or a few stolen kisses with you! Anything more would harm your honor, and that would hurt you." *And you are human, short-lived human, and I—I—will not think of that.* Despair feeding his anger, Ardagh continued, "And if any suspected we walked together alone at night like this—ae, I can imagine the outcry then! Prince I may be, Sidhe, yes—but in the eyes of these folk I am nothing more than a *cu glas,* a grey dog, a landless, clanless exile—"

"And do you think it's so easy for me?" she snapped. "Do you? I'm a widow, not a simpering maid, I'm a thinking, feeling *person,* not just the daughter of Fothad mac Ailin, I'm not just some ridiculous symbol of honor or purity or-or—"

Her strangled little gasp of anguish stabbed through him. "Sorcha . . . I'm sorry." It didn't come easily. "I tend to forget that I'm merely a . . . visitor here, while you've been trapped in this society's rules all your life. You know I would not hurt you."

"But you are! You're hurting me because you're hurting yourself!"

"I . . . it's simply that I . . . cannot find my way and . . ." Ardagh paused, hunting for words that wouldn't reveal too much. "Sorcha, I am afraid," he finally admitted, "sorely afraid not so much that I will never be at home in this land—but that I may."

"Ah . . ." It was the softest exhalation. "Ardagh, no. A hawk caged is still a hawk. You can no more stop being what you truly are than—than the trees could fly off into the sky. Give me something I can do, something that will help you."

"Ae, Sorcha. There is nothing." He saw her eyes

suddenly turn suspiciously bright, and touched her face with a gentle hand. "Forgive me. I don't wish to seem like some self-pitying fool of a—"

"Human. You were going to say 'human,' admit it."

Ardagh had to grin at that, and saw a reluctant little smile twitch at her lips as well. He bowed. "I yield to my most perceptive lady." But as he straightened, Ardagh let his grin fade. "Yet I am going, Sorcha."

"Into battle. Against men with iron swords."

"I've fought against such before, yes, and survived unscathed."

"You can't expect such luck every time!"

"Hey now, grant me a *little* skill!"

But this time he couldn't coax even the smallest of smiles from her. "You are a prince, not a warrior," Sorcha said coldly. "And I expected more from one of the Sidhe than this sudden mindless need to kill."

"Give me strength against this woman!" That had erupted in his native tongue. Switching quickly back to the human language, Ardagh added, "I do love you. I do. But do not presume on that love too far. I am what I am, Sorcha, as you remind me, and human has no part in it."

"Go, then," she said flatly. "Go. Fight. Kill. Only return, alive, unharmed. That's all I ask."

That's all I ask as well! Ardagh thought. But he would not say that, and he could find nothing else.

Cadwal ap Dyfri let out his breath in a wary, soundless sigh as the prince and Sorcha ni Fothad went their separate ways. The last thing he'd intended was to be trapped in a corner like this, hiding like someone in a silly tale and horribly embarrassed lest the prince's keen night sight spot him. He most certainly hadn't wanted to be an eavesdropper.

But then, Cadwal thought with a rueful shake of the head, he doubted that either of the two would have noticed, lost in the heat of their lovers' quarrel as they'd been, if he'd paraded them painted all in blue woad.

"Fools," he said, but so softly it was no more than the faintest whisper. "Ah, fools. Don't they know?"

No, of course not. They had no idea, they *could* have no idea, how frail a thing was love. . . .

Cadwal realized suddenly how he was clenching his fists and very deliberately forced his hands to relax. He would *not* be ruled by memories. Or . . . dreams. (Gwen, his Gwen, calling, *help me, Cadwal, help me*—)

No. Ridiculous. Gwen was long dead, and dreams were . . . only dreams.

Even if they hurt so fiercely.

"*Damnio*," Cadwal muttered and started blindly forward. He knew why Prince Ardagh burned for battle, even if Sorcha did not; he'd felt the same madness. It was all too easy for an exile to fall into a frenzy of despair, to act with a wildness that said, clear as words, *what does my life matter?*

It mattered to Sorcha. The prince should remember that. But then, *cu glas* as Prince Ardagh was, what hope was there on that point? *Pw*, his own people had their codes of honor, of course they did, but these folk of Eriu had more such codes than any sane man needed!

"I must be at the king's side," Cadwal said to the absent prince. "I can't watch over you, too."

Still, Prince Ardagh was a more than decent swordsman, and he'd been training now and again with Cadwal; for a prince, someone who hadn't needed to fight for his life—at least not with a sword—he wasn't a bad warrior. Besides, there was that uncanny grace and speed of his, a definite asset.

Uncanny.

Cadwal stopped short, uneasily considering the word. Uncanny, yet. And what, specifically, had he overheard amid the quarrel? Something odd, something of magic . . .

Nonsense. He'd once drunk with Prince Ardagh when

the weight of their respective exiles had burdened them both beyond solitary endurance. Yes, and they'd gotten a little drunk, too, talking like old comrades fully half the night. Nothing uncanny about that!

"Nonsense," Cadwal repeated aloud, and turned his mind grimly to the forthcoming battle.

It was a fine, bright day. A good day for a combat. Aedh had chosen the site well, forcing King Finsneachta's men to fight uphill, the sun in their eyes.

For all and all, Ardagh thought, trying not to pant, it wasn't shortening the fight. *Sorcha was right. This is* not *my battle.* The prince fiercely parried a sword cut meant to take off his head, feeling the shock of blade against blade shudder all the way up to his shoulders. *This is not my land.* He twisted aside to let a second blow whistle past, very well aware that his armor was of leather while everyone else—including this cursedly enthusiastic foe— was clad in iron; no way around that liability, not for one of the Sidhe. *This is not even my* Realm, *curse it!*

All around him, the clash of sword on sword and the roar of men's battle-mad voices tore at the air. Powers, how long was this battle going to last? Finsneachta of Leinster must surely know by now it was hopeless; Aedh had mustered far too many allies against him. And yet, Leinster fought on.

Oh yes, and I went into this stupid human fray with equally stupid enthusiasm. Though why I ever wanted to—

Ae, time enough to scold himself when he was safely out of this tangle.

If ever he was. By now, Ardagh's swordarm was brutally weary, his head pounded, and his side ached from someone's direct hit on that barely adequate leather armor. Only Sidhe reactions, swifter than anything human, had kept him unhurt so long. And now, somehow in the crush of bodies, he'd gotten himself separated from King Aedh.

Ardagh spared a second's glance to hunt and (with a little surge of relief) find Aedh mac Neill, there on a slight rise, fighting with the zeal and strength of a much younger man, iron helm hiding his silver-streaked red hair, and apparently totally unharmed. Yes, he'd brought this battle to the rebellious Finsneachta to teach that underking some humility. But no such serious motive could have been read from Aedh's face; he was very clearly enjoying the fight.

Hastily refocusing on his foe, Ardagh parried a new slash, then cut at the man, left, right, left again, trying to find an opening in that cursed iron mail. He didn't dare glance away again, but a part of his mind noted that it wasn't very long since the matter of the late, villain-ous Gervinus; Aedh was probably delighted to be fighting a battle that didn't involve sorcery.

No need to worry about the king, at any rate. Even if Aedh hadn't been so fine a warrior, Ardagh knew that at his side was Cadwal ap Dyfri; no joy of battle in Cadwal, only a grim and very professional efficiency that had kept the man alive so long.

It's his job, keep the king safe. Does it well, too. It's not my job though, and—

Suddenly his hair, admittedly far too long for battle, tore free from its thong, sending a black wave across Ardagh's face, nearly blinding him. He sprang back, clawing frantically at the strands with his free hand to clear his sight, struggling to parry at the same time, just barely managing both.

Damn and damn! It was sworn in the human tongue; the Sidhe language was too elegant for raw words. Still half-blinded by his own hair, Ardagh lunged savagely forward, driving his startled foe back and back again, hoping the human would slip on the wet, grassy slope. But now a second foe was trying to close with him as well. Ardagh sprang aside with inhuman speed, hearing the two humans crash into each other—and hopefully spitting each other on their

weapons—only to find himself facing a new swordsman.

He looks as worn as I feel. Fortunately.

At least he'd finally gotten the hair out of his eyes. But
without warning Ardagh felt the first blaze of iron-sickness
burn through him. He staggered back, reminded—as
though he really needed reminding—just how much of
that cursed metal was around him. A small amount of
iron was no problem, but there were limits—and his body
had clearly just reached its. In another moment, Ardagh
knew, he was going to have to flee or be ignominiously
ill—and get himself killed during the latter. Did he care
if the humans thought him a coward?

Not a whit!

Ardagh lunged to give himself room. The human drew
back, expecting a charge, and Ardagh turned and fled
the battlefield. His legs gave out halfway down the slope
and he collapsed under a scraggly oak, struggling with
nausea, struggling to draw new strength up from the
native Power of the earth. If any stragglers found him
here, helpless, he was dead. A stupid, stupid way for a
prince of the Sidhe to die, even a prince who was,
through no fault of his own save stubborn honor, trapped
in exile in this human Realm.

Ardagh looked up with a gasp, suddenly aware of
someone standing over him, and saw King Aedh, his mail
stained but not so much as dented, his face still fierce
from battle.

"Iron?" the king asked succinctly, too softly for any
human to hear; Aedh knew his Sidhe guest's keen senses,
and a disconcerting bit of his weaknesses as well.

Ardagh nodded, but before he could say anything,
Adeh added a curt, "You're lucky to be alive," and turned
away, shouting commands to his men and his allies,
working order on chaos by sheer force of voice and will.

Victory, the prince thought. *Of course victory.
Finsneachta didn't have a chance.*

By ancient law, any king who'd been defeated—as

Finsneachta of Leinster clearly had, could be deposed. But Aedh would hardly want to replace a known but at least temporarily cowed threat with an unknown, and possibly greater, menace; the High King, clever man that he was, had almost certainly already worked out some nicely convoluted treaty by which Finsneachta could keep at least a good part of his honor, and he—or at least his heir—could keep the throne. It would take some time to get the living sorted out into their respective royal armies, but soon enough everyone but the dead and the badly wounded would be riding back to their fortresses, and peace would once again fall over Eriu.

For the moment. Ardagh rubbed a weary hand over his face. These humans were more volatile than any nobles at his brother's court, and Aedh had more reason to be constantly on his guard than ever did Eirithan.

And what in the name of all the Powers did I think I was doing? "Lucky to be alive," indeed. What was I trying to prove?

Ardagh sighed. Difficult at times to be of the Sidhe, unable to lie even to one's self. For nearly two years of mortal time now—a mere instant by Sidhe standards but tediously long when one was living through it—he'd been trapped here, with not the slightest sign of a way out of exile. Unable to go home, unable to live here, unable to wed or even bed his lady—no wonder frustration had blazed out into battle-rage!

But . . . the very existence of such frustration and rage was a foreign thing, a . . . human thing. Why should he be . . . how could he be . . . Even as he staggered to his feet, tying back his wild hair with weary hands, Ardagh felt a chill stealing through him. A human thing, a human emotion . . .

I am not human. I cannot be human. But . . . what am I? What have I become?

As he watched Aedh's men sorting themselves out, tending to the wounded, counting the dead, the prince could not pierce the veil that seemed to have fallen between himself and them. He had lived among these humans, eaten with them, laughed with them, but right now all he could see were alien folk, so very alien. . . .

Ae, enough. With a great effort, Ardagh tore himself from what he knew could too easily turn to blank despair, and went to join the others. He had no great Power, not in this all-but-magickless Realm, and he couldn't risk showing those gifts he still possessed, not and keep up the convenient fiction of being a human prince from Cathay. But he could subtly ease pain here and there, speed up the organizing of the aftermath. The sooner matters were settled here, the sooner they were away from this cursed place, and—

Ardagh froze, suddenly still as a stalking cat. He had just sensed . . . what? The prince dropped to his knees beside a dead Leinster warrior, staring. About the warrior's neck hung a small clay amulet—and it bore Power.

Hands shaking slightly, Ardagh cut the leather thong with a quick slash of his dagger, closed his hand about the amulet. Yes, ae yes, the small thing did hold Power, just the faintest, faintest traces, but Power nonetheless. From where? No skilled sorcerer, surely; that would have left a definite psychic trace. Besides, Ardagh thought, opening his hand to study what he held, any sorcerer worth the name would be ashamed of such crude work. No, whatever self-claimed magician had created this had accidentally blended a touch of the earth's natural magic with the protective spells he'd cut into the amulet.

The not quite accurate spells. Ardagh glanced wryly down at the dead warrior. *They didn't do this fellow much good.*

Still, it was Power, no matter how slight. More important, it was solid, tangible, *fixed* Power. And what might not happen if he combined it with a spell? With one of the many, so far useless, Doorway spells he'd gleaned from human tales?

Ardagh's hand clenched shut. Though he had never guessed it, *this* was why he had entered the battle, not out of some foolish imitation of human frustration but from some arcane sense so faint he hadn't even known it. This was what he'd been seeking.

I dare not hope. But I do, Powers help me, I do indeed!

Foreign Politics
Chapter 2

He was Egbert, son of the late King Elmund—for what good, he thought, that proud Kentish lineage did him. He was Egbert, a tall, fair-haired young man, no more than that, once of Wessex but now just an exile in these Frankish lands, this royal court of Charlemagne.

He was also, being an exile, fair game for these bored young Frankish nobles. Cornered against a plaster wall brightly painted with scenes of Charlemagne's ancestors, he listened, perforce, to their witty jibes about "Saxon fools" and "landless idiots" and fought back the angry words that sprang to his lips. *No,* Egbert reminded himself fiercely as he had for all these years. *No reaction. Smile and bow. Play the innocent. Never once let them know that anything but docility lies behind the bland eyes and slack face.*

It worked, as it always did. Of course the nobles couldn't do anything worse than so cleverly insult him; they might think him an idiot, but he *was* of royal blood, not to be touched. Instead, bored by his lack of response and their own wit, they strolled away down the palace's frescoed halls as though he didn't even exist.

And he didn't, Egbert thought, not according to Saxon or Frankish law, because not even the great Charlemagne in whose palace he lived here in Aachen could decide what he should be: exile, certainly, of royal birth, certainly—but someone who'd never actually inherited a throne or kingdom.

Ha, I doubt that Charlemagne even remembers I exist. Particularly since the man seems to spend more time out conquering others than he does here at court. And now he's off to Rome to be crowned emperor by his pet pope.

Not that the royal absence made it any easier to escape this place. Egbert glanced about, seeing nothing but the brightly painted walls, knowing his apparent privacy was illusion. The guards had their orders: he was not to leave the main hall without escort, let alone do something daring such as go for a solitary stroll. After all, Egbert was here by command of King Beortric of Wessex, son-in-law of the late Offa, who had been Charlemagne's close ally in Albion. A convoluted political chain, this, but quite sturdy.

Egbert shook his head. Since he had no choice about matters, wiser to seem harmless, surely, even if it did mean watching every word and gesture. Even if it did mean smiling and smiling, letting everyone think him simpleminded.

God, he was tired nearly to death of smiling!

No. If he had learned anything in all these long years of exile, it was patience. Yes, he was Egbert of Kent, yes, his father had been king and as such had left him in the direct line for the Wessex throne—and made him, therefore, Beortric's foe—but right now his safety lay, as it had lain for nearly sixteen years, in being no one. Just another face at the Frankish court. Allowed good food, good clothing, even (since no one expected him to ever be able to use it) a good education in sword and spear, but no more than that. Fair game for idle nobles—damn them!

Again, no. Egbert forced his face to relax into its usual blankness, forced his fists to unclench. He had never blamed the Witan, the Wessex council, for having ruled against him; he'd been only a boy at the time of banishment, barely more than nine. The ealdormen had all surely been weary of the bloodshed that had followed the death first of King Sebright (slain by Cynewulf) then of King Cynewulf (slain by Sebright's kin). Not surprising

after that chaos that the Witan had chosen Beortric to
rule them. No matter that his claim to the throne wasn't
half as strong as that of Egbert: he was what Egbert
hadn't been—a mature and settled man.

A complacent man. Egbert shook his head. Whether
the courtiers here realized it or not, over the years they'd
taught their captive prince a fair amount of political guile.
One befriended as many nobles as was feasible—but one
didn't hesitate for a moment when it came to removing all possible rivals.

*While I'm certainly glad that Beortric let me live, in
his place I never would have been so weak!*

Of course, Beortric had never expected a boy, alone
and friendless, to survive exile, let alone grow to man-
hood. Let alone vow to return.

*Yes, but how, curse it? I don't have men, I don't have
supporters—even if I somehow managed to escape this
soft prison and found my way back to Wessex, alone, it
would be as good as committing suicide.*

Osmod. The name came without warning to Egbert's
mind. Osmod. He frowned. Now, who . . . ? A Saxon
name. Yes . . . one of the ealdormen, surely. But which
one? He had the vaguest memory of a pleasant face,
cheerful blue eyes, golden hair: Osmod.

*I haven't heard the name for sixteen years. Why
should it come to me now?*

For that, Egbert had no answer.

Ah, what difference did it make? An exile alone and
frustrated, Egbert, son of Elmund, stalked grimly
through the halls of his elegant prison and tried not to
notice the guards who forever trailed him.

King Beortric of Wessex rode out through the early
autumn forest with his hunting party, standards flying
bravely, hounds baying: the very image of a royal hunt.

It would be a great deal more impressive, Osmod
thought, *if Beortric was actually able to hit something
with that spear he's waving about.*

Beortric, solidly of middle years and grown just a touch too soft in the sixteen years of his reign, was— for him—dressed almost plainly, although his dark red hunting tunic was frivolously edged with priceless silk and gold glinted from about his throat; the man had, Osmod knew, picked up some extravagent tastes from his late father-in-law, Offa of Mercia.

Yes, but now Beortric was glancing his way. Osmod smiled and dipped his head. Polite and charming as always. But then, being the noble ealdorman, the trusted royal advisor he was, he could hardly be anything *but* polite and charming. Osmod knew he made a pleasing picture: pleasant-faced if not truly handsome, with not a sign of aging, his eyes still clear blue—merry eyes, Beortric had once called them, and most folk seemed to agree—and hair bright gold untouched by grey. They wondered at that, did the courtiers, even made jests about "ageless" and "undying," and Osmod had laughed with them: how ridiculous, those jests, how patently impossible.

A sudden blaze of sunlight through leaves just beginning to be touched with red and gold caught him by surprise, and Osmod threw his head back to it. Ah, what a pleasant day! Charmingly warm for this late in the year, but with the faintest touch of sharpness to the air, charmingly dry and calm—perfect.

"A pleasant day."

Osmod snapped his head down at this echoing of his thought, and found himself meeting the earnest young gaze of Ealdorman Worr, who'd brought his horse next to Osmod's own. Ah yes, Worr, Beortric's favorite: honest and trustworthy and handsome. And, some scandalous rumors hinted, more than merely the king's political favorite.

Ask Edburga what she thinks about that. Ask Beortric's spiteful queen. See what happens—

No. Not yet. Osmod smiled, charmingly, dipped his head ever so slightly to Worr, and rode on.

Green as grass, that one. Almost too innocent to be a courtier. His blood would probably run out thin as water.

Not that Osmod planned to find out; no need stirring up trouble. Again, not yet. Beortric was complacent as only a man who'd ruled for sixteen years and never fought a war could be, but he was a king, and for the moment there was no reason to change that fact.

I certainly don't want the throne! Aside from the inconvenient little fact that I haven't a drop of royal blood, I would rather be the secondary target, thank you, the power behind the throne, rather than having to be perpetually on my guard.

Bah, as though he wasn't already! It was difficult enough as it was to balance the two worlds of power and Power with no one suspecting; it would be almost impossible to add a crown to the mix.

As for Beortric, well now, a king without ambition did give one status and wealth, yes, and a certain amount of freedom to experiment with—*be honest,* he thought with a wry flash of humor, with Power beyond what might be known even to a king.

A king without ambition, though—there was the thorn that pricked. Oh, granted, Osmod admitted that he never could have properly honed his abilities were it not for the chance sixteen years of peace and noninterference had given him. And while powerful King Offa of Mercia had lived, neighbor to Wessex, Offa who had been the rival in might of Frankish Charlemagne himself, ambition on the part of Wessex would have been national suicide.

But Offa was dead these six years now. A far weaker heir sat the Mercian throne. Now was the time for action on the part of Wessex's king—

Osmod snorted. Not the smallest chance of that. Beortric would never be remembered as a conquerer, a great ruler, one fit to be mentioned in the same breath as Charlemagne or his late father-in-law.

A perfect chance, perfect political ties—and even I can't rouse him!

A man could only be content with lethargy for so long. *Egbert,* Osmod mused, *Egbert the exile.* A younger man than Beortric, certainly, but by now no longer a boy. A man, and one with, it could be argued, a stronger claim to the Wessex throne than the current occupant. Ambitious without a doubt and, judging from what the runes had told Osmod, half-mad with frustration. Willing, most certainly, to help anyone who helped him.

Ah yes. For one glorious moment, the ealdorman let himself surrender to fantasy, to images of other lands, maybe even all of Britain, bowing down before Egbert, *King* Egbert, and his oh-so-faithful advisor—

But the dogs had begun to bay in earnest, the sound of hounds who'd started up a quarry. The hunt exploded into a storm of blaring horns, shouting men and the drumming of hoofs on ground, and for a time Osmod let his horse run as it would, surrounded by others' excitement without it touching him. The so-called thrill of the chase had never appealed to him; he preferred a more personal hunt.

A hunt, eh? *Why not?* Osmod thought. A small one, perhaps, just a . . . tidbit. In the excitement, no one would notice his absence. He turned his horse aside, forcing it through the underbrush, pretending to anyone who might see that it was the horse who was in control.

Yes. Here was a likely spot, this brushy little glen. Osmod dismounted, tying the wild-eyed horse firmly to a tree; the animal never had accepted his doings, and he was not going to risk having to walk home like a peasant.

Now, to work. No one had ever guessed that the pouch at his waist might hold more than coins any more than anyone knew he wore the nine-knotted cord about his waist under his tunic; reaching into the pouch, Osmod drew out a small square of bone on which was carved the doubled runes of Sigel and Cen. Of course runes in themselves had no magical powers; only idiots believed otherwise. They were merely a convenient form of writing. However, when certain runes were drawn under certain ritual circumstances—which he had performed—and with a certain amount of will—which he possessed—they could lose their mundane function and became very potent focuses of Power.

Potent, indeed. Osmod smiled slightly. Foolish, perhaps, to use so powerful a Binding Rune for so trivial a purpose as this, but again, every skill did need practice. As he muttered the proper words, he felt a faint but familiar tingling race through him: Power rousing within him. Osmod looked about the underbrush again, more carefully this time, listening, sniffing, aware that, thanks to the runic Power, his senses were now ever so slightly enhanced.

Not enough. Never quite enough. Whoever told those wild tales of ancient sorcerers and vast magics was drunk, lying, or a fool.

Still, some Power is better than none.

Ah, look. There was his prey. No need to waste more than the merest scrap of Power now. Osmod slipped the rune safely back into his pouch, whispering a Call, whispered it again, then watched the rabbit squirm out of the underbrush, its nose quivering, ears flicking in confusion.

"Pretty thing," Osmod told it, and drew his knife. The rabbit came to startled life, leaping for shelter, but Osmod was swifter. Cutting the rabbit's throat with one quick slash of the blade, he drank.

Ah, delicious the taste, delicious the tiny rush of life energy. Odd, how quickly a man could overcome his revulsion. Particularly when Power was involved. Of course, invoking the rune had used up almost more of that Power than he'd gained, that was the frustrating way things worked, but at least there was—

A gasp made him glance sharply up. Worr sat his

horse, staring down at Osmod with eyes wide in stunned disbelief. For one quick moment, Osmod knew how he must look to the young man: wild-eyed, face stained with blood, a dead rabbit still at his mouth.

Damnation!

He threw the rabbit aside, fumbling in his pouch for the right rune, frantic that Worr might escape, hastily judging by *feel* . . . there. He caught the unmistakable spark that was the carving of Stane, hopefully bound to the second rune of—

No time to worry about it. "You saw nothing strange," Osmod hissed, fixing Worr's stare with his own, hurling all his will against the other. "You saw nothing. Nothing. You saw nothing strange, Worr. Nothing strange. Nothing."

Worr blinked, rubbed a hand over his eyes, then rode away without a word. Osmod stood staring after him, then crumpled to one knee, gasping, fighting the sudden waves of weariness surging over him. Maybe sorcerers in those stupid ancient sagas could work their phenomenal feats without getting tired, but he certainly couldn't; he doubted anyone could. But Worr—had it worked? Lords of Darkness, had it worked?

Of course it had. Worr surely would have said or done something if his will hadn't been overcome. He wouldn't have ridden off like a blank-faced puppet. No, the youngster wouldn't remember a moment of what he'd seen.

And yet, and yet . . . Osmod shuddered, wondering after the fact if he hadn't sensed just the faintest spark of resistance gone unquenched. That would be all it would take, one unconquered spark, to let memory return. Controlling something as simple as a rabbit was one thing; controlling the human mind was another matter entirely.

Ach, nonsense. If they'd been returning to the royal hunting lodge, that might have been a problem; it was impossible to work anything useful while crowded into such a small space with so many potential witnesses. But of course the season was already too late for the lodge. All he needed to do, once they were back in Uinta-caester, the king's city, was reinforce matters with something stronger than a rabbit's life.

He certainly couldn't stay kneeling here like some mindless, bloodstained predator. Osmod hastily set about cleaning his mouth and hands, then scrambled to his feet, catching his terrified horse by the bridle and swinging back into the saddle, fighting the animal till it obeyed him. He'd known the risks of his chosen path from the start. As for Worr . . .

If I fall, Osmod promised Worr silently, *I take you with me.*

The hunt had, Osmod mused, turned out to be a good one after all. The king had somehow managed to bring down a fine stag, and Osmod (careful as ever not to outdo his ruler) had felled one almost as fine. More, Worr was his usual earnest, perfect self, showing no sign that sorcery had been worked on him. Yes, and—a petty thing, perhaps, Osmod thought, but it was most satisfying to note—the young man had missed his mark completely.

In every sense.

They came out of forest into cleared farmland. Ahead lay the city, safe within its ancient stone walls, "the old work of giants," as the common folk claimed, and Beortric suddenly raised his arm and ordered a gallop.

With horses already weary from the hunt, Osmod thought. *And with the crowded city ahead. We must have our dramatic gesture, mustn't we?*

Wagons on the road ahead were being frantically dragged out of the way. People were scurrying for cover. The hunt came sweeping through the gates and into Uintacaester, which brought them, perforce, back to a more sensible pace; the High Street might be wide enough for a gallop, even though it would mean trampling pedestrians, but the side streets, with their closely packed wooden houses, were just too narrow for anything more than a walk.

Osmod shook his head, glancing about. All this wood, with never a gap. No one had learned anything from the fire some . . . what was it? . . . thirty years back, had they? But then, how many ordinary folk could remember something thirty years back?

A good many in the crowds were yelling polite cheers. Osmod raised a startled brow. Well now, listen to this: some of the cityfolk were actually calling *his* name. The ealdorman smiled and courteously dipped his head as he rode by. It never hurt to show yourself friendly to the common folk; you never knew when they might prove useful.

Besides, Osmod admitted to himself, he liked these people, so busy and industrious. Loyal servants of their complacent king who would easily shift their loyalty to whomever else sat the throne so long as he left them alone. And to whomever stood beside that throne, as well.

Osmod glanced to one side, to where the great wooden bulk of Uintacaester's cathedral towered over the common houses. Another reason why he had no desire for the throne: the Church would *not* support a sorcerer-king, and no king could rule a Christian realm without the Church. Bishop Cynbert was a civilized, politic man, but there were, Osmod thought wryly, limits. Cynbert was off in Rome—as well he might be, what with the coronation of the mighty Charlemagne drawing a good many prelates to the holy city.

Ah, Charlemagne. Things could be worse. I could be at his court. Even the strongest of sorcerers would be dwarfed beside the arrogant power of that man.

The ealdorman shrugged. Even when the alliance between Mercia and the Frankish realm had been alive, Charlemagne had made it clear that he had no interest in Wessex or the rest of Britain; no need to worry on that front now that the alliance was as dead as Offa.

A flash caught his eye. The massive bulk of the royal hall loomed before him, every bit as splendid as the cathedral, the lofty roof taller even than the surrounding palisade. Its gilded shingles glinted in the sunlight like something magical, something out of the sagas, and Osmod smiled anew.

What a perfect day, indeed.

plans and trials
Chapter 3

It had been a wearying ride back from the battle with
Leinster and the victory over Finsneachta. But now at
last Fremainn lay before them: Fremainn, royal fortress
of the High King of all Eriu. Ardagh glanced up at the
high earthen rings through which Aedh and his men
were riding, and felt the by-now quite familiar little pang
of dismay.

Fremainn. Ahead, encircling the great mound within
the rings, stood a wooden palisade, ridiculously plain and
primitive to someone used to the elegant, spun-silver
walls of the Sidhe. Within that topmost wooden ring, he
knew, lay not some breath-catchingly beautiful estate
(flash of memory: his own quiet, airy mansion, his own
lovely gardens ablaze with flowers—no!) but nothing
more grand than a wide, grassy field set with simple
houses of stone or—more commonly—wood and thatch.

Ae, Powers.

Tolerate these folk, even rather like these folk though
he did, he would never be able to accept that this, *this*
was the finest palace in all the land.

But now they were all at once racing up through the
palisade's gate and out onto the grassy field. The prince
let go of his dismay, realizing that he was, to his surprise,
doing just what every other returning warrior was doing:
scanning the gathered crowd for one special face.

Why, you romantic idiot! he jibed, amazed at himself. *You refugee from a bardic tale!*

Aedh was already leaping from his horse, arms open, as Eithne his wife came running to him like a girl, laughing, her chestnut hair flying out behind her, her eyes wild with relief. Ardagh alone knew that the queen must have been spending all her time till now secretly weaving protection spells to shield her husband; Eithne was no great sorceress, but she did have that touch of Power. Aedh swept her into his embrace and gave her a passionate kiss that made the crowd cheer.

But there, ah there . . . Ardagh froze, forgetting his self-mockery, all at once—just as the bards sang—hearing nothing, seeing nothing but one face. "Sorcha," he murmured.

Sorcha ni Fothad stood just as still, her face sharp with mingled joy and rage: only she, Ardagh thought with an inner smile, could have managed such a mix. Her eyes in daylight were the deepest blue of the midnight sky, her hair was dark red flame slipping free of its braids, and Ardagh suddenly found himself abandoning control as thoroughly as any human.

So be it.

Imitating Aedh, he flung himself from his horse and caught his lady in an embrace.

In the next instant he wondered if that had been such a wise idea; Sorcha was hardly the sort to be submissively swept off her feet. But for one endless, splendid moment, Sorcha's lips were fiery against his own. Then she pulled back, gasping, "You're not hurt? You're safe?"

Ardagh chuckled at the human ability to ask obvious questions. "Quite safe."

"Good!" Sorcha practically snarled that out, her voice suddenly sharp as a slap. "Don't ever frighten me like that again. If a sword had cut you—iron—"

She stopped short, choking on her anger, knowing as well as Ardagh that she dared not continue this train of thought where others could hear; as far as Sorcha knew, only she, in all Fremainn, was aware of his true Sidhe nature.

The truth's not that much greater, Ardagh thought.
*Aedh knows as well, and—our secret, hers and mine—
Eithne.* "You're right," he said before Sorcha could
regroup. "You're truly, totally right. I had no business
taking part in that battle. It was a stupid thing to do,
and I'm incredibly fortunate not to be hurt. Just let me
bathe and rest a bit," he added, voice dropping to a sleek
purr, "and then I will . . . more properly tender my
apologies."

That startled a laugh out of her. "Ardagh," she murmured, for his ears only, "och, Ardagh. Maddening, no,
no, totally infuriating though you are, I do love you!"

Her hand rested gently on his cheek for a heartbeat.
Then, still trailing laughter, she scurried off into the
crowd.

And I, Ardagh thought, watching her go, *I love you,
human though you are. I love you.*

And what, I wonder, is to become of us?

The humans had given him a fine little guest house
when he'd first arrived in Fremainn: small but clean and
quite comfortable, even though it contained little more
than a feather bed, a table and a chair. More to the
point, at least to Ardagh's way of thinking, it was set a
bit apart from the other buildings; it gave him some
much-needed privacy. Particularly since, eccentric though
the idea might make him seem to the humans, he
refused to have a servant share the house with him.

Right now, the prince was very glad of the solitude.
There had been, understandably, quite a feast to welcome home the triumphant king and army, but by now
the last revellers had staggered to their beds. Ardagh sat
alone in the now blessedly quiet night, keen-sighted as
all Sidhe in the darkness, studying the small amulet he'd
taken from the dead Leinster warrior and, strand by
delicate strand, working out the weave of its Power.

Such as it was. Ardagh straightened with a sigh that
turned itself into a yawn, arching his back to get out the

stiffness, thinking with regret of the magically hot baths of his homeland.

Ah well. He was here, and if this ridiculously weak amulet was all he had to work with . . .

And yet he hesitated. This one thing he'd kept from Sorcha, this one thing he'd held to himself . . . why? If he did, indeed, manage to open a Doorway home, what then? Did he mean to leave at once, without so much as a glance behind?

Did he mean to leave Sorcha?

No, Ardagh realized. *Never that.* Whatever else might happen, he would not merely abandon her.

What, then, was bothering him? The prince searched his thoughts with Sidhe honesty, but found nothing but vague uneasiness.

Now isn't this ridiculous? Why worry about What Might Be when for all I know the amulet is going to shatter the moment I start a spell?

"Enough," Ardagh said, and set to work.

The hour was much later than it had been when he'd begun. Ardagh stood alone in what was surely the darkest time of the night, sagging slightly with weariness and looking down at the amulet in his hand, *feeling* it tingling ever so faintly with Power. At this late hour, no one would be about. And no eyes but his could pierce this moonless darkness.

Then why was he hesitating anew? He was tired, yes, longing for that soft feather mattress, but he'd been much more weary and yet successfully worked far more intricate magics.

Try it! the prince scolded himself. *It was ridiculously easy to compose the spell; it should be ridiculously easy to cast. You have all the words, the gestures, fixed in your head. You're not that weary. Go ahead! Work it!*

But he just couldn't seem to begin. With a little shock of that total Sidhe honesty, Ardagh realized that now he was afraid, he was genuinely afraid!

His sudden shiver had nothing to do with physical cold. How could he ever forget that terrible moment of banishment, that more terrible yet moment of realization that every Realm-crossing spell had been torn from his mind? Since then, what had there been to do but try creating some new version?

Out of what? The bits and scraps of spells to be found in this magic-poor Realm? Amazing I managed anything at all!

There had been so many almost-successes so far, so many tantalizing hints, glimpses of a Gate, of Faerie glory beyond—

So many heartbreaking failures.

You idiot! Suppose you finally have the right spell? Are you going to trap yourself here because you're too frightened to use it?

No. Ardagh grimly began, staring at the little amulet, using it as his focus. This newly minted spell required little more than his own will and a quiet incantation, which was good, because the original spell had been simple as well. A corner of his mind *felt* the tiny bit of Power in the amulet rouse, tingling, and knew a thrill of hope, but Ardagh could not let anything distract him. He continued chanting softly, willing more and more strength into the spell, willing more and more of the amulet's Power awake, willing the spell and the amulet and the full force of his longing into one magical call:

"*Open! Open! Open!*"

There, ah there, he saw the shimmering in the air, he saw the Doorway beginning to form, he knew with a wild blazing of hope that this time it would work, this time he would leave the human Realm behind and—and—

—and he couldn't hold it, there wasn't enough Power, he couldn't hold—

With a great rush of air, the Doorway snapped out of being. As the spell gave way, Ardagh's strength went with it. He fell forward as though his legs had been cut out from under him, landing full-length on the cold earth.

Alone in the darkness, too worn for self-control, too worn to do anything else at all but despair, the prince wept.

But the ground was just too chilly for such weakness. After a short while, Ardagh caught his breath and forced his emotions back under control. Shivering, the prince pulled himself slowly to his knees, but could get no further. He huddled like that for what seemed half the night, head resting on one upturned knee, trying to find the strength to stand, the backlash of unspent Power from his failed spell aching in his mind.

But . . . was someone watching him? With a great effort, Ardagh struggled back to his feet, staggering with exhaustion, trying to identify who . . . Cadwal . . . ? Yes. It was the mercenary whom he'd sensed standing nearby.

He straightened. How near? Had Cadwal seen anything of what had just happened—or rather, not happened?

Impossible. Human eyes were all but night-blind, and what was left of the night was still very dark. The man could have seen nothing. Staggering, Ardagh headed back towards his small guest house, his home in Fremainn. Falling across the bed, too weary to undress, he thought with bitter, weary humor, *This Realm . . . must like me. For no matter what I do, it just . . . will not . . . let me go.*

Cadwal stood where he had been standing still as stone ever since seeing Prince Ardagh collapse. His first impulse had been to run to the prince, see if he was hurt. But something inside him had said, clear as words, *no.* It wasn't right to intrude on a man's private grieving, be he prince or commoner.

Yet . . . there was more here than an exile mourning his lost land, much more, though Cadwal couldn't quite have put his thoughts into clear speech. He hadn't quite seen, the mercenary told himself, not in all this darkness, he hadn't quite heard, either. But surely before he'd fallen, Prince Ardagh had been chanting in his strange, beautiful native tongue, whatever it might be. And just for a moment Cadwal could have sworn there had been something more than . . .

Than what? He felt a little shiver run up his spine, in that moment for all his years of war nothing more than a child of his homeland, of often-mystic Cymru. Had he really seen something other than the mundane walls of Fremainn? Something more? Had there been just for that bare heartbeat of time, a hint of something very splendid, indeed?

Och, idiot! And are you going to start believing in Faerie at this late date? Are you going to add that to— to whatever it is that's driving you to wander about like a lost soul?

That last question was far too easy to answer: Dreams drove him—

No, Cadwal corrected himself, not dreams, only one dream. *The* dream. Gwen, so real he could almost touch her, Gwen pleading with him, *Help me, save me, free me.* It couldn't really be her, of course not. And yet, and yet . . . he had heard so many stories in his youth, tales of souls held from rest, souls held captive in little cages. . . .

No. There are no such things as soul cages. No such things as ghosts, either. With all the battlefields I've seen, there should have been at least one someone reluctant to leave life behind. But no. You're dead, you're dead. Your soul goes on to heaven or hell. You do not hang about pestering the living like an unwanted guest.

And why couldn't he believe it? And why couldn't he banish the dream? Feeling rather foolish about it, Cadwal had gotten himself some holy charms from Father Seadna, the High King's own priest, and worn one charm about his neck and spread the others all about his bed. Feeling even more foolish, he'd said a few rhymes dimly remembered from his Cymric childhood, things that the old women had taught him would chase away all uneasy spirits.

And yet the dream refused to be banished. Every night: *Save me, Cadwal, cariad, free me.*

"*Iesu Crist,*" he muttered, not quite in prayer, not quite not. Not much of a choice here, and neither very pleasant: either it really was poor Gwen's trapped soul—or he was going mad.

A Bit of Conversation
Chapter 4

The new day was bright and cheery as though there'd never been a battle from which to recover. Praise God that he could recover, Aedh thought, flexing a still-stiff swordarm, wincing at the pull on bruised muscles. Eithne had wanted him to stay in bed this day while she rubbed her herbal mixtures into his sore skin.

A pleasant thought, that, though I suspect we'd have spent more time rubbing those herbs off than on—ah well.

He'd refused, of course. Let the word spread that the High King was incapacitated, even for a day, and they'd all be having him ready for his grave. True, Aedh admitted, he was no boy to fight so fiercely one day and be untouched by strain the next. But he could still more than hold his own. The moment he stopped being able to lead his men like this—och, that day hadn't yet come, nor, God willing, would it come soon.

So, now. They'd come through the battle relatively unscathed: surprisingly few losses, while most of the wounded seemed, at least so far, likely to recover. *Looks like a good time to make some nice, pious public statement about God being on our side. Which I suppose is true enough,* he added with a wry little glance to heaven, *since we won. Besides, it won't hurt to let the clergy have something good to say about me.*

Aedh lowered his head to look about his royal "conversation house"—stone walls to the small house, guarded door, slate roof on which no spy could perch. In short, thought the king, this was the one place in all Fremainn that he knew was secure from prying eyes or ears. The only other person in here with him just now was Fothad mac Ailin, and Aedh let the man wait and worry a bit longer before quoting sardonically:

"The Church of the living God, let her alone,
    Waste her not.
Let her right be apart, as best it ever was."

He watched Fothad's slight wince, though at the same time Aedh caught the faintest glint of delight in the minister's eyes: the poet's involuntary joy that, no matter the circumstance, his words should have been so well remembered. *Can't separate the poet from the man, can we?* Aedh thought. *Never could.* He asked aloud, "Well?"

"I had to compose the poem. You know that."

"Did you have to recite it within everyone's hearing?"

Fothad reddened. "I wasn't thinking clearly."

"So I noticed. So everyone noticed."

The redness deepened. "I'm sorry for that, truly. You know I'm not usually so . . . well . . . impolitic."

"Good choice of a word, that. Impolitic."

"Aedh, please. I didn't mean to make things difficult for you, you know that. It's only that . . ." The poet shook his head helplessly. "The ancient bards were right about this: The words come when and where they will, and I don't always have a chance to control them. Besides," he added defiantly, "you know I was right. It was one thing for you to call up a full muster of Eriu's men to battle Leinster; that was well within your royal rights—"

"Thank you so much for reminding me."

"Och, well . . ." Fothad hesitated, not quite meeting the king's gaze. He and Aedh had once been tutor and pupil (with Fothad, who was not that much the elder, scared nearly foolish by the responsibility), but the poet was very obviously reminding himself that this wasn't an erring pupil but the High King.

"You are Aedh Ordnigh," Fothad continued at last, ignoring Aedh's impatient wave at the obvious statement, "Aedh the Ordained, proclaimed rightful High King by the Church, and yes, of that I do remind you. When you wished to involve that Church in secular matters—"

"Where they've certainly been before," Aedh snapped.

"Yes, but in this case involving them could not have been justified by any stretch of political maneuverings. And yes, yes, they might have joined in if you'd ordered it—but then again, they might not. And how would *that* have looked?"

"Embarrassing. Awkward. I agree on that point, and yet—"

"Aedh, please, listen: We both know that you've had quarrels enough with the clergy since the very first days of your reign. They don't care for your independence—"

"And I don't care for their meddling."

"Yes, but we both know that without the clergy's support, no king is going to rule for long. That is the way it is, like it or not. And High King or no, you cannot afford to antagonize the Church again!"

You always could cut right to the heart of arguments. And win most of them. "Enough, Fothad. Enough! That poem of yours was damnably convincing all by itself. And," Aedh admitted reluctantly, "you are quite right." There were too many years of friendship between them for him to need to add more than the simplest of warnings. "Just don't embarrass me in public like that again, agreed?"

Fothad, mouth half-open to defend himself, shut it again, reddening. "Ah. Indeed," he said awkwardly.

Aedh accepted that for the apology it was. Besides, he thought, suddenly amused, Fothad's outburst of poetry hadn't done either of them any real harm; folk expected bizarre behavior from poets, and forgiveness to those poets from kings. "Onward."

"Onward," Fothad agreed with blatant relief in his voice. "What of King Finsneachta?"

Aedh knew his grin must be downright predatory. "He has given me the usual hostages and pledges of good behavior. More importantly, since he is that unfortunate paradox, a defeated king, Finsneachta has suddenly discovered a religious vocation."

Fothad raised an eyebrow. "How convenient! That leaves . . . wait, now, if memory serves, he *has* no son to inherit."

"That's right. And don't give me that dismayed stare. I'm very well aware that his unfortunate lack means I'm going to have to split his land between his two nearest kinsmen. Yes, Fothad, just as I needed to do with the two royal sons in Meath three years back. And yes, I'm very well aware that splitting a land between two ambitious young men means trouble in the future—but as with Meath, there's no other solution short of murdering one or both of them. A nice thought, but hardly politically wise."

Fothad, who knew as well as Aedh that the king's ambitions stopped short of the downright ruthless, added flatly, "Or morally proper. Nothing ever gets truly settled, does it?"

"Not in Eriu!" Aedh held up his hands in a wry shrug. "But then, when has governing this realm ever been easy? Come, enough of Leinster. Tell me how the repairs are going."

Fothad glanced down at his scrolls. "You know that the . . . ah . . . storm, the one in which Bishop Gervinus . . . ah . . . died, did terrible harm to Corca-Bhaiscinn."

"Over a thousand folk dead there, God rest them, yes. And the island of Fitha is permanently split apart."

"Into at least three pieces, yes. Of course there's also been a sizeable loss of trees and flooding of coastlines. But aside from Corca-Bhaiscinn and Fitha, Eriu does seem to be recovering." Fothad opened another scroll, then another. "The harvest isn't going to be as good as we'd like—"

"No surprise there! I'm amazed that anything is left growing."

"We were lucky. But unless we're faced with another storm of that terrible force—the good Lord deny—no one, except in Corca-Bhaiscinn, is going to face genuine hardship."

"Mm. Make notes to send wheat there should they request it. Go on." Aedh forced out the next words from a suddenly tight throat. "No Lochlannach raids while I was away?"

"No. You seem to have stopped those Northern thieves."

"Hah!"

"Or at least thrown some fear into them."

"Again, hah. One little defeat of one little raiding party isn't going to frighten that lot. If the traders' stories are correct, the Lochlannach actually *enjoy* the thought of dying in battle. Such a death sends them, their pagan priests claim, straight to a warrior's heaven."

"Let it be straight to a warrior's hell," Fothad snapped.

"Amen to that." Aedh hesitated, wondering how to word what he wanted to say. "Your mistimed poem wasn't the only reason I sent for you."

Fothad frowned slightly. "The Lochlannach?"

"Exactly. They worry me, Fothad, they truly worry me."

"But they're nothing!"

"Well now, we seem to have swung completely about, haven't we?"

"I don't . . ."

Aedh held up a hand. "If I recall, it was originally *you* who tried to put worry into my mind about them, and *I* who scoffed."

"True, but—"

"But I've had a chance to actually face them in combat since then."

"And I have not," Fothad admitted. "Yes, granted, and

granted that from everything I've heard from everyone the creatures are fierce enough—but they're still nothing more than seafaring thieves!"

"No. Think. My spies and loyal vassals give me warnings of trouble from any not-so-loyal vassal, and I have no doubts I can control each and any would-be traitor. But how can I possibly defend Eriu against sea raiders? Raiders who can strike without warning anywhere along our coast and be away again in those incredibly swift ships before we can so much as take up arms against them?"

"But . . ." Fothad began hesitantly, almost as though embarrassed, "the last time, Ardagh and I both received a warning from—"

"Ardagh is hardly a saint." Aedh nearly strangled in the sudden, unexpected effort not to laugh. *God, no! A Sidhe saint?* "And neither, my friend," he added hastily, before the unseemly laughter could break loose, "are you. How or why you two received that ghostly warning of the attack, well, we'll never know the truth of that." *Unless our Sidhe prince admits it.* "But we can't expect . . . ah . . . Heaven to send us a warning every time."

Fothad grinned ruefully, agreeing, "No. Alas. But you still aren't catching my point. Yes, the Lochlannach are a danger, no, their attacks can't always be predicted—but they are hardly organized enough to be a true threat."

"Not yet. And not in such small numbers. But we don't know just how many discontented, loot-hungry Northerners actually exist. We don't know where to find their home base or bases. Yes, and what happens when some ambitious, charismatic fellow turns up among them? What happens when he unites them into one force?"

Fothad snorted. "I've yet to see a charismatic Northerner."

"Hey now, we wouldn't look so pretty or smell so sweet either after a long sea voyage! Remember their

elegant swords and axes and those lovely, deadly ships:
the Lochlannach may be pagan thieves, but they're
hardly primitive. Don't underestimate them."

Aedh broke off, trying not to see the dark image that
his mind was all at once insisting on conjuring. "And
what happens," he added slowly, "when the Lochlannach
learn how badly the storm has hurt us? What better time
for them to launch a raid or, worse, a series of raids on
Eriu? What better time for those thieves to join together
against us? Savage fighters without any Christian sense
of morality, and very probably, judging from what we've
heard of their homeland, with an equally savage lust for
land."

"Och, they wouldn't . . ." But Fothad fell silent, eyes
widening.

"You see the same vision I do."

"Devastation." It was a whisper. "Conquest or devastation."

"Indeed. The Lochlannach will come again, Fothad.
That is as sure as the turn of the seasons. And I quite
honestly don't know what we can do to stop them.
Except," Aedh continued thoughtfully, "this. We have
someone among us who studies issues from angles
neither of us would ever imagine. Yes, and solves problems from weird perspectives as well."

Fothad's eyes glinted with instant comprehension.
"Prince Ardagh."

"Exactly. Have him summoned, if you would. I suspect
our far-travelling prince may well give us a new view of
this problem. And—who knows?" Aedh added with a
grin. "He may even come up with a solution."

The Sudden Ambassador
Chapter 5

Ardagh just barely stifled a yawn. King Aedh seemed to have an unerring knack for sending a servant for him at just the wrong time. After the full backlash of his failed spell had hit him, the prince had collapsed into a dreamless pit of sleep, but that sleep hadn't been quite long or deep enough. And the shadow of last night's despair still lingered, there at the back of his mind like a chill mist. He had very much wanted to do nothing but spend the day doing . . . nothing.

But the servant was watching him earnestly, looking like a nervous bird about to dart into the air, and the prince sighed and said, "Yes. I'm coming."

Aedh and Fothad both were waiting for him in the royal conversation house, the usual table piled with scrolls set between their chairs; a third chair waited. The two humans looked disgustingly alert and aware, watching him with identically keen stares, and Ardagh bit back the impulse to snarl something rude and thoroughly human at them and forced himself instead to bow politely.

"Please, Prince Ardagh," Aedh said, "be seated."

So formal? "Do I look that weary?" Ardagh asked.

"A bit, yes. You *are* recovered from the battle?" The delicate emphasis on the king's question made it clear that he referred to the bout of iron-sickness.

"There's been no lasting harm," Ardagh countered, just as delicately. "I merely had a less than restful night. King Aedh, what would you?"

43

"We were pondering a problem, Fothad and I, one that we thought you might help us solve."

What bizarre test was this? Prodding his still sleepy brain, Ardagh hazarded, "The Lochlannach," and saw by the humans' slight starts that he'd guessed correctly. "Yes, of course that's it. You fear that they'll return in greater numbers, and you don't know how to stop them."

Aedh's smile was wonderfully sly; he must be suspecting Sidhe magic at work. "No magic," the prince told him dryly, "merely logic. You would hardly have summoned me over something as trivial—your pardon, good Fothad—as my relationship with the lady Sorcha. Bishop Gervinus is most certainly dead, and the storm is ended. As far as I know, no other underking is foolish enough to mount a rebellion." *Yes, and no one,* he added silently, *witnessed my failed Gate-opening spell, so it can't be about that.*

"Neatly summarized." Aedh studied him speculatively. "We were wondering if you, being who and what you are"—a glint almost of mischief flicked in the king's grey eyes—"remarkably far-travelled, I mean, of course, and from such a foreign culture—"

"Of course."

"—might not have some unique view of how we can stop the Lochlannach." Aedh's voice hardened. "Preferably forever."

"I doubt you could ever totally stop them," Ardagh countered. "Not without mounting a massive attack on their homeland. That, I take it, is out of the question?"

"Quite," the humans answered almost as one. Not surprising: Eriu had hardly struck Ardagh as a naval power.

"Besides our lack of warships," Aedh added, "there's no evidence that the Lochlannach come from any one kingdom. There are a good many hidden corners of the Northern lands where they could be breeding."

"Ah. Awkward."

"Very."

Ardagh cocked his head in Fothad's direction, seeing the hint of wondering in the poet's eyes. "I'm afraid not," the prince said. "We can't hope to receive a warning from . . ." the prince paused almost imperceptibly, dodging falsehood, "from the Other Realm before every attack." Worded this way, it was quite true; the last warning they had received, though Fothad hadn't realized it, hadn't been from the human Heaven but from the Sidhe Realm.

"A pity." Aedh's tone was ever so slightly cynical. "But here we are at the point where Fothad and I got mired. Since we can't mount a frontal attack or sit back and beg for Heavenly intercession—what would you do, Prince Ardagh?"

There was no hoping that Aedh could muster all the kingdoms into a coastal patrol; Ardagh had already seen that the natural way of things here was for each king to be at war with the next.

No. Anything useful was going to involve some strong equivalent to the Ard Ri of Eriu. "What if," Ardagh began warily, "the next time the Lochlannach come raiding, they find not one isolated community but an alliance? One powerful enough to block their ships, deny them landfall no matter which way they turn."

Fothad blinked. "Are you speaking of a political alliance? With other kingdoms?"

He sounded so incredulous that Ardagh just barely bit back a sharp, *Powers Above, man, what else did you think I meant?* "Yes, of course," the prince said with great restraint. "Eriu can't be the only land in danger from the Lochlannach. I should think any kingdom with a coastline would be glad of a chance to stop those raiders."

"Prince Ardagh, you wouldn't be aware of this, not being native to this land, but no king of Eriu has *ever* tried an alliance with another power."

"That can't be right! Father Seadna told me once that it was Eriu's missionaries who spread your faith through Britain!"

"Oh yes," Aedh interjected, "over the last two centuries or so, the good friars have turned many a pagan Sacsanach into a proper Christian. But friars are hardly political emissaries."

"In all our recorded history," Fothad continued, "we've never had nor needed an ally."

"Not a human ally, at any rate." Aedh raised an eyebrow at the startled prince. "And no, Prince Ardagh, I'm not getting mystical; I'm speaking of the sea. It's kept Eriu nicely isolated all these years. It protected us, for instance, back in the old pagan days when the Romhanach armies were swarming over the mainland and conquering everyone else. The sea protected us again when those armies were followed into Britain three centuries later by the Sacsanach hordes."

"I gather," Ardagh commented blandly, "that neither of those groups were seafarers. The Lochlannach undeniably are."

"There is that."

This is like wandering through mist! "Then what's the problem with an alliance? Granted, you always need to be cautious: too weak an ally is useless, too strong an ally is perilous, but—" Ardagh stopped short. "Am I missing a point? Is there some law that out-and-out forbids alliances?"

Fothad's gaze went remote; he was clearly searching through mental archives. "Och, no," he said at last. "At least not so far as memory serves."

Ardagh stretched weary muscles. "Then I fail to see why you're both being so reluctant. 'Because it's never been done before' just isn't a convincing argument."

He didn't like the sudden smile on Aedh's lips. "I assume," the king said, "that you aren't expecting us to jump blindly into the political sea."

So that's the way the wind blows, is it? "Why, King Aedh," Ardagh purred, "you've thought this all out already, haven't you?"

"Why, Prince Ardagh," Aedh purred right back, "of

course I have, long before this meeting. An alliance is *not* going to be a popular idea with my advisors. I can win them over—but only if they're sure that I'm not involving Eriu in something we can't control."

"Go on," Ardagh said flatly. "There's more."

"I think we'd both agree that the only way I can get everyone's approval is not to do anything too dramatic, but to simply send out someone as an informal, or even an unofficial, ambassador."

Ardagh raised a slanted eyebrow. "Someone doing nothing more suspicious than sending innocent greetings, I take it, one king to another? And in the process seeing how things stand? May I remind you that I'm not one of your subjects?"

"That's exactly the point I was about to make." Aedh leaned forward in his chair, grinning like a wolf. "I think that our unofficial minister *can* only be you. With your permission, of course."

Ardagh's first thought was a quick, panicked, *No! I don't dare leave Eriu, not when the Doorway home lies here!* But then the prince snapped at himself, *And what good does a so thoroughly sealed Doorway do you? Or are you waiting like a dog at a locked gate for Eirithan to throw you a scrap?* Besides, a new land just might mean new spells. . . .

Ardagh kept his face Sidhe calm, but he could feel his heart begin to pound. "Why me?"

Aedh's smile never faltered. "Prince Ardagh, please don't take offense at this, but you are a man of honor who can yet be as cunning as a rogue and smooth-tongued as any bard. You can talk almost anyone into or out of almost anything. What's more, as a foreigner, you have no awkward political or kinship ties to anyone at any . . . ah . . . western court. Besides," Aedh added, "if you can't manage to snare us some aid with your sleek words, then no one can."

"That," Ardagh said in genuine admiration, "is the most convoluted and backhanded compliment I have received since my days at my brother's court. King Aedh, I salute you." He bowed in his seat, received Aedh's ironic little dip of the head in return.

"Then you agree. You are the only choice."

"Perhaps." Ardagh glanced slyly sideways. "And is that relief I see on your face, Fothad mac Ailin? Are you that glad at the thought of separating me from your daughter?"

"You know that's hardly true."

"And if I was anyone but *cu glas,* you'd welcome me into the family."

"Yes. No. I—that's an ugly way of putting it, but—" Fothad stopped short, shaking his head. "A smooth talker, indeed!"

"One does what one can," Ardagh said sweetly, and turned back to Aedh. "And of course, since I *am* a foreigner, you have another advantage: If something happens to me on my mission, why, I'm none of yours, so you need do nothing but say, 'What a pity' and go on with life as before."

Aedh smiled but did not deny it. Ardagh mirrored that smile, thinking that he could hardly take offense at something so beautifully, cold-bloodedly, practical; it was almost as properly devious as a Sidhe plot! "And of course you know that since I never lie, when I say I won't just . . . run off and not return, there's no danger of my abandoning your cause, either." *Or rather, of abandoning Sorcha.* "So, now. Where is your most informal and smooth-tongued minister to go?"

Was his easy acquiescence surprising Aedh? The well-schooled royal face showed no sign of it. *You think I've turned into your obedient tool,* Ardagh told him silently. *You have no idea I'm using you as well.*

"Now that," the king mused, "is an entirely new problem. We can eliminate one ruler under the 'too powerful for safety' category: the Frankish soon-to-be-Emperor Charlemagne. Trading with the Franks is one thing; we don't want that ambitious fellow sniffing at

Eriu's borders! No, let him play his political games on the mainland. At any rate, the Franks haven't been threatened very much by the Lochlannach."

"Yet," Fothad muttered, bent over a scroll.

Ardagh straightened. "Is that a map you're studying?" As Fothad nodded, unrolling it fully, the prince got to his feet to lean over the poet's shoulder, pretending a casual interest but actually trying to make sense of the inked-in lines without revealing his ignorance of the human Realm beyond Eriu. "There, now," the prince said, guessing wildly. "Is that not Cadwal ap Dyfri's homeland, Cymru?"

Fothad glanced up at him. "Of course."

"It seems to lie relatively near Eriu, without too much water between. Mm, yes, and it has quite an extensive, if convoluted, coastline. Why not—"

"Because there's no such thing as Cymru," Aedh cut in. "No one such thing, rather. The land is sliced into several small, often warring kingdoms—Cadwal would know the lot of them," he added offhandedly. "None are strong enough to do us much good, and there's no one High King to unify them." Contempt tinged his voice. "Besides, that convoluted coastline is far too rocky to suffer many Lochlannach landings."

And you, oh king, like everyone else in Fremainn, are too prejudiced against those Cymric cousins of yours to even consider making peace with them. "Who else, then?"

"It will need be one of the rulers of the Sacsanach—Saxons, in their tongue."

"Offa of Mercia was certainly the strongest king in Britain," Fothad murmured, "possibly too strong for any safe alliance, but at any rate he died four years back."

Aedh snorted. "Too strong, indeed. He signed some manner of pact with none other than our ambitious Frankish Charlemagne. Yes, and if rumor's right, Offa died just as he was making his own plans against the Lochlannach. Well, with Ceolwulf on the Mercian throne, those plans are certainly lost! He's not half the ruler Offa was."

"Just as well, I would think," Ardagh murmured, and received a wry glance from the king.

"Beortric," Fothad said suddenly, looking up from his map.

"Beortric!" Aedh echoed in delight. "King Beortric of the West Saxons—yes, of course: powerful but not too powerful, ambitious but not obnoxiously so. He's said to be a singularly affable fellow; he's reigned rather peacefully for . . ."

"Sixteen years or so," Fothad supplied.

"Yes, and if I'm correct, he's married to one of Offa's daughters . . . Edburga, I think her name is."

"Yes."

Aedh nodded, clearly pleased. "That means an alliance with Wessex is indirectly an alliance with Mercia as well, with no awkward complications attached of who's stronger than whom. Perfect. And Wessex—Beortric's land," he added to Ardagh, who had already puzzled it out—"Wessex has even suffered a Lochlannach raid or two some few years ago."

"How unfortunate for them."

"And fortunate for us." Aedh beamed at the prince with blatantly overdone charm. "Prince Ardagh, I understand that Wessex can be quite a pleasant land."

"Can it, indeed?"

"Of course, it's already too late to travel so far this year; autumn is already past the best time for sailing, and winter is definitely not the time for an ambassador to set out. And before we can do anything else we shall have to go through the formality of a general meeting of my counselors first. The Sacsanach have not been exactly kind to our British kin. I suspect," the king said blandly, "that we're in for a good deal of shouting and bluster."

"Without a doubt." Ardagh's voice was equally bland. "And I suspect that those British kin are distant cousins."

"Very."

"Convenient. I will need some schooling in the ways and language of Wessex, naturally. I'm a swift learner, as my lord Fothad will, no doubt, attest, but there *are* limits."

"Of course," Aedh agreed. "So now, eventually matters will get themselves straightened out. Let's just say that I'm sure you'll enjoy your visit to Wessex."

"Oh yes," Ardagh agreed, "I think that I may."

But his smile was not at all charming or dutiful.

One of the safest places for two lovers to meet in Fremainn was out here in the bright daylight in the center of the grassy field, with no possible hiding places to let even the most suspicious soul find fault in their being together, nor any way for anyone to overhear what they said.

Which, Ardagh thought, was just as well. He and Sorcha had been strolling together, apparently innocently, but all the while he had been hunting for a way to say what he must say.

No way but the blunt truth. "Sorcha. King Aedh has decided to use me as an informal sort of ambassador."

She eyed him warily. "Where? Surely not to Leinster."

"No. The king wishes to send me to King Beortric of Wessex."

Sorcha froze, stricken. "Wessex!"

Startled by her shock, Ardagh soothed, "Ae, love, it's not the Land Beyond Beyond."

"It's far enough! Ardagh, do you have any idea of our human distances? You don't, do you? We're not talking about some magical blink-of-the-eye trip there and back again, but a journey of only the good Lord knows how long, first by boat, then over leagues of foreign soil. And there's so much that could happen, so much that could go wrong—why, even in the simple crossing from Eriu to—Ardagh, you can't, you mustn't—"

"No, no, Sorcha, you're missing the point. Listen to me, calmly. Calmly."

"Go ahead," she said grimly. "I'm listening."

Ardagh took a deep breath. "Last night I made one more attempt to open a Doorway. It failed. Yes, that's why I've been dragging myself about so wearily. You've seen me collapse from backlash before: you know something about how much strength the effort would have cost me. With this latest failure," he continued, fighting to keep his voice level, "I believe I have completely exhausted whatever little spells I've been able to find in Eriu."

"B-but you haven't—you can't—"

"Listen to me. Wessex is new soil; foreign soil. At the very least, I'll be able to keep myself healthy by drawing on its forests' natural Power, just as I do here. At the most—I am hoping against hope, as you humans would word it, that I'll find something more useful, more Powerful, there. I might even," he added with a sudden savage burst of longing, "find the spell to open the Doorway home."

"I see. You . . . wouldn't just go, would you?"

"What—"

"Ardagh, please: Sidhe honesty."

"I know no other sort. Go on."

"If you opened a Doorway in Wessex, one that would let you go home, you wouldn't leave me here alone . . . would you?"

"Ae, never. Sorcha, never."

Her laugh was shaky with relief. "There is something to be said for having a love who can't lie."

Ardagh cocked his head to one side, studying her. "But there's something more than worry in your eyes, I think."

"I don't doubt it. For one thing, I'm envying you."

"Envying!"

"Och, Ardagh, you know how things are for noble-born women in this land. I'm not a slave, but I'm not exactly free, either. I've never left the region, my love, let alone travelled to a foreign land. And," she added sharply, "I don't think much of this 'woman patiently waiting for her man to return' role."

"I never saw the point of it, either. In my Realm you could go where you pleased, with no one to say—" He brought himself up short. "But we aren't in my Realm."

Sorcha grinned, a little too sharply for true humor. "What say you? Think you could smuggle me along in your gear? Or maybe I could take a scene from a bard's tale and disguise myself. Think I'd make a convincing boy?"

He had to laugh at that. "Powers be praised, no!"

"Ah well." The not-quite humor faded from her eyes, leaving them bleak. "Then, hate it or not, wait I must. When do you leave?"

"Not till the spring, at least. It's already too late in the year for travel. Besides, as I told the king, I may be a swift learner, but even I need *some* time to study a new land." He paused, listening to a faint, distant clamor. "Yes," Ardagh continued, "and before we can commit to anything, the king's council must first finish their debate."

To his surprise, Sorcha threw back her head with a genuine burst of laughter. "And here I was worried! That could take years!"

I doubt it, Ardagh thought. But he, bemused anew at the human way of trying to avoid the unavoidable, said nothing. Of course the council would make its decision, and of course it would rule as Aedh wished; they did not often go against the High King's will. Like it or not, the prince knew that he would be leaving this land in the springtime. He must.

But he would, all the Powers grant, return.

A Small Murder
Chapter 6

Muffled in a hooded cloak, runes in a pouch at his waist, Osmod made his unchallenged way through the darkening, nearly empty streets of Uintacaester. Coins slipped to the guards had gotten him easily out of the royal compound (he'd heard their snickers: "Not the first noble to go hunting common fun."). The rune Eolh would protect him from unwanted attention and Ger would see him safely back again.

He glanced about, hunting. If he was to ensure that Worr truly never remembered what had happened back in the forest, this nuisance of a task must be done.

If only everyone's will was as easy to snare as that of Edburga. But then, Beortric's queen half *wanted* to be snared; an arrogant woman, that, who must always have someone over whom she, the daughter of the late, mighty Offa, could feel safely superior. Beortric, on the other hand . . .

Osmod shook his head. Soft Beortric might be, but he was discouragingly content with himself and his lot: such a will was, in its own complacent way, strong and smooth as stone. Stone could, of course, eventually be shaped, but only so very painfully slowly. Ah, those tales of the sorcerers of lore, able to work their wishes with nothing more than flicks of their will!

He gave a snort of disgust and hurried on. The air was still full of the scents of cooking fires and food, and there was a sudden burst of laughter from this house, a soft snatch of song from that. But the city was definitely settling down for the night; there would be no witnesses.

There, now. That rather ramshackle building in this decidedly less desirable corner of the city was definitely an inn of the common sort. And where there was such an inn, there was prey. First, of course, he had to go through the farce of actually *wanting* to be in such a place, sitting at a rickety table in the crowded, dark, smelly common room and pretending to be drinking a watery and probably outright unclean horn of ale. Yes, but there was his goal, that young woman: a scrawny, sad-eyed creature, her blond hair braided in what she probably thought a fashionable style, her tunic a worn but still gaudy yellow that branded her for what she was. A pity she didn't have more meat on her, but . . .

The whore forced what was definitely a false smile of welcome onto her lips as she saw him. Osmod beckoned to her.

"Never mind the games," he said shortly before she could start the tired old bantering of seller-and-client. "You see," he added, jingling his purse, "I have coins enough."

She blinked, clearly a little startled at his bluntness. "There's a room nearby, my . . . ah . . . my lord, and—"

"No. I would rather not risk vermin." Too brusque. A wise hunter didn't frighten off the prey. Osmod hastily softened his voice to a charming croon. "The night's warm, my dear. We can find us a more pleasant place. Won't you come walking with me?"

Of course she agreed; she needed those coins badly, judging from the skinny body pressing up against him in simulated passion as he wrapped his cloak about both of them. Ignoring the not-quite-clean smell of her, Osmod strolled with her out into the night and took what he hoped wasn't too obviously a relieved breath of clean air.

"Now, isn't this better, my dear . . . what *is* your name?"

Her voice was a surprisingly shy whisper. "Emma, my lord."

"Emma," he purred. "A pretty name. Have you no family, poor Emma?"

She shook her head.

"Tsk, poor Emma, all alone."

Osmod glanced about. No one in sight. He suddenly pushed the startled woman off her feet into a narrow, not-quite alley, blank wooden walls on both sides. She twisted about where she'd fallen, trying frantically to recover her false smile of welcome, but Osmod could scent the exhilarating smell of her fear. Yes, ah yes, the Power was stronger when the prey was afraid. He threw himself down on her, slapping her when she struggled, seeing her eyes widen as she stared up at him and realized the truth for the first time, seeing her terror rise. Before she could scream, he had a hand over her mouth, whispering, "No, ah no, no sound, fear me, yes, fear me but silently."

Now. Now her terror was at its peak. Osmod slipped out his knife and neatly slashed the jugular vein, ready for the spurt of blood, careful not to stain his clothing. He drank as she struggled, tasting the salty sweetness, *feeling* the intoxication of her life force feeding his, and the Power, the wild, wonderful Power rising within him. . . .

The prey went limp beneath him. Osmod got to his feet, shaking slightly, fastidiously wiping his mouth with a scrap of cloth. He was growing very weary of this, of having to slip down into the city at night like some young idiot on the prowl, pretending to be interested in this whore so sadly without family, or that lonely beggar no one would miss. He was most definitely growing weary of finding places to safely dispose of same. Life must have been far, far simpler back in the days of slavery. Then, no one kept track of a man's belongings, human or otherwise, save himself. No one would have noted or cared if a slave or two quietly disappeared.

Ah well.

He knelt again, tracing a quick circle about the corpse. Rummaging in his pouch, Osmod drew out the runes Thorn and Haegl, symbolic of Chaos and Destruction. He didn't really believe in the Dark Forces, not as personified beings, but it never hurt to be careful. "For you, Lords of the Underworld," he whispered, touching the runes to the late whore's head and heart, "blood and a life for you. I worship you, I worship you, I worship you."

There. That should be sufficient. He scuffed out the circle, leaving the corpse where it lay; there was blood enough still draining out of it to make a suitable sacrifice to Whatever. A quick glance to be sure he'd left nothing behind . . . no.

He shuddered suddenly. How many times now had he done this? Osmod could vaguely remember the first, slain with his father's help. At the time, Osmod had been little more than a boy awestruck at being allowed to join that so very secret cult, to take part in so drastic a ritual. But as he'd tasted that first victim's blood and life, he had felt the first wild rush of Power, felt his own not yet suspected magic stir and wake and knew in that moment just how different he was, how pleasingly superior. He'd been wise enough to keep his mouth shut about it, watching, learning. The others, even his father, had quickly proven themselves to be frauds, decadently cruel for decadence's sake. There had been no Power in them. But he . . .

Smiling slightly, the ealdorman headed back towards the royal compound. He was, as far as he knew, the cult's last surviving member. Charlemagne had exterminated the rest—and had been quite right to do it, not on any ridiculous moralistic grounds but simply because its members were too incompetent to live. If one must kill, there should be a point to it; any mindless beast could slay.

Power, now, Power was definitely worth it all. If only there was some way to *fix* the magic, hold it at this higher peak! But it would drain away all too soon, leaving him needing yet another hunt, another victim.

So be it. Right now, he had spells to work, traps to set.

I don't wish to be king; I don't need that pomp or peril. But if only I can find a way to catch and hold the Power, ah, then I become true ruler of the land.

If only. Bah.

Worr woke suddenly, as he often did, staring up into space. Beside him, Beortric was still asleep, his heavy, middle-aged face defenseless and relaxed as that of a boy, and for a moment Worr could not move, overwhelmed by an unexpected rush of tenderness. Ah, he was so lonely, this king, this man, so grateful for any sign of affection.

God knew he didn't get it from his wife. Edburga did her best to rule her husband, and Beortric . . . Worr sighed. Beortric was too gentle a man to fight her.

It isn't right, it isn't just.

But that was Beortric, like it or not. Gentle. Caring. The room was filling with the first grey light of morning. Reluctantly, Worr slipped from the bed, careful not to disturb the sleeping king, then stood for a moment looking down at him, not at all sure of his emotions. Without warning, he was stabbed by the all too familiar knife of guilt. This was sin, what he and the king did together, all the priests said it was sin—yet it hardly felt like anything at all evil. And besides, how could he resist? Beortric had always been so kind to him, and if this brought the king some comfort in return . . .

I don't love him . . . do I? This is purely out of service to my king—bah, what nonsense! Of course it's more than that. I—I don't know what I feel about him, but it's certainly more than cold duty.

But the guilt remained, a burden weighing down his soul. Hastily, Worr dressed before anyone chanced to find him here. He brushed a gentle hand across Beortric's brow, then sighed and slipped away. The two warriors watching the door had been carefully chosen to uphold the fiction that Worr was merely guarding his king; they let the ealdorman pass without so much as a glance, and Worr hurried on to his own quarters.

Ah, but now he was far too restless to abide. He should go to the royal chapel, pray for forgiveness.

For what?

I cannot see it as sin, I cannot!

Worr roused a sleepy servant and had the man fetch his horse. He wouldn't be needed in court this morning; maybe a brisk ride would ease his soul. Worr set his horse to a brisk trot down through the city. The streets were just beginning to fill, and the first merchants' cries met his ears:

"Fish! Fresh, fresh fish!"

"Vegetables fit for a royal table."

"Ribbons! Ribbons!"

The music of Uintacaester, Worr thought, and smiled in spite of himself.

But one thin, shrill thread of sound didn't belong to that music. The ealdorman reined in his horse, listening. A scream . . . someone wailing in horror . . . it wasn't his business, surely, and yet . . .

It was. He was an ealdorman, a noble of the ruling class. What happened in this city, even to the commonest of folk, could not be ignored. Worr sighed and turned his horse in the direction of the screams. He felt his nose wrinkle despite his best intentions; this was far from the best corner of the city, and it stank.

But there was the screaming woman, crouching at the mouth of what was far too narrow to be called an alley. She was of the commonest sort, judging from that too-brilliant tunic, but the horror in her eyes pulled him from his horse.

"What—"

But then he, too, saw the body. A woman, a dispassionate part of his mind noted, young, dead. No, not just dead: murdered. Whoever had killed her had done a rather alarmingly neat job; her throat had been cut as daintily and cold-bloodedly as though she'd been nothing but a rabbit—

A rabbit. The memory hit him with the force of a blow. How could he have forgotten, even for a moment? That rabbit, with its neatly cut throat pressed to a man's mouth. To ealdorman Osmod's mouth, yes, and him with the look of a sated demon.

A ritual killing. He'd thought that then, for the brief moment he'd thought clearly about it at all. A ritual killing—like this one. And that meant that the poor woman's blood had also been . . .

But Worr couldn't bear to finish that thought.

Beortric must know of this, he thought blindly, *Beortric must be told.*

Hopes and Dreams
Chapter 7

" . . . and the highest Wessex nobles," Ardagh recited in a fair imitation of Fothad's most teacherly voice, "are ealdormen, who make up the Witan, the law council, while a rank below them lie the thegns, and . . ."

He paused, glancing at Sorcha as she walked the chilly autumn rounds of Fremainn with him. "And you have not heard one of three words I've said."

"I have!" she protested. "I'm glad to hear how quickly and well you've been learning about Wessex and its ways."

"But?"

"But what do you think? I can hardly take joy in anything that keeps reminding me how soon you'll be leaving. And I—och, my love, I'm sorry, I don't mean to keep whining about something that's unavoidable. It's just . . . I've said this before but . . ." She shook her head impatiently. "What it is, is that I feel so—so damnably helpless! I *hate* having to wait here like a useless little nothing and I *hate* the idea of not going with you. But most of all," she added, a touch more gently, "I hate, och, I hate with all my heart knowing I'll not be knowing what's happening to you."

He grinned. "Now that, at least, is a problem I think I can solve. See this? With any luck at all, we should be able to speak to each other through it."

"That?" She eyed the little clay thing skeptically, "Isn't this the amulet you tried using that other night? Just after the battle against—"

"Leinster? Yes."

"You said it failed."

"It did. Only, I think, because it just isn't strong enough to work anything as Powerful as opening a Doorway. But it still does hold its own tiny magic—and that, if I'm correct, will be enough for something as relatively simple as linking us two—"

"Simple!"

"Hush. It would be simple, since we're already linked on a psychic level by our love. In fact, it shouldn't take more than a drop or two of mingled blood to seal the charm." He raised a wary eyebrow. "Are you willing?"

"I'm not sure exactly what you're proposing, but I—I suppose so—Ouch!"

He'd pricked her finger, letting a drop of blood fall onto the clay. Before she could protest, Ardagh pricked his own finger as well, murmuring the gentlest of persuasion spells, telling the clay that *yes*, it was porous, and *no*, what it was absorbing was not foreign to it, not foreign at all, but part of him, part of her, part of their being, part of their thoughts. . . .

The prince let out a great, shuddering breath. "That begins it."

"Are you all right?" Sorcha asked in alarm. "You've gone so pale!"

"Sunlight *truly* doesn't like Sidhe magic. Besides," he added in resignation, "I only said that the spell should work. I never said it would be easy." *Not in this magic-poor Realm, at any rate.* The prince glanced down at the amulet, which now showed not the slightest sign of bloodstains. "Fortunately, I won't have to do any more work on the thing until nightfall."

"And when it's done, we really will be able to—to talk from afar?"

"Yes."

"And distance won't weaken the contact?"

"Not as long as you continue to love me. And I, you."

That earned him a wary glance. "I assure you, I don't fall so easily out of love."

"Of course not. Nor shall I." Ardagh paused, considering. Ae yi, as well now as later. "There's something more I must tell you. King Aedh knows who and what I am. Don't look at me like that! I could hardly deny the truth, not after Aedh witnessed my battle with Gervinus."

"But he's never said—"

"No. The king has kept my secret."

Sorcha's smile was quick and wryly understanding. "Wise of him. He doesn't want to cause a riot—or to have everyone thinking him mad."

"Exactly. But I doubt he'd be surprised to learn that you, too, know about me."

"He would be spectacularly unobservant if he hadn't figured it out by now!"

"Ae, true. At any rate, I think the king would greatly appreciate your passing news along to him."

She took a deep breath. "'Messenger' isn't as romantic a role as 'ambassador,' but yes, of course I'll do it. Though any personal messages from you I intend to keep that way!"

He grinned. "I would certainly hope so!"

But Sorcha paused, frowning slightly as she studied him. "There's one thing you must, you really must, let me do before you leave. No, no, let me correct that: before another day passes."

"What?"

"Do you love me? Do you trust me?"

"Yes! Sorcha, what—"

"Then," she said firmly, "you are going to finally let me trim that wild mane of yours! And no," she added, "I have not accepted that you're leaving. No, I never will. But—cursed if I'm going to let you go off to a foreign land, let alone wander around Fremainn any longer, looking like a shaggy barbarian!"

Alone in his guest house that night, Ardagh sat studying the amulet, running a hand absently through his hair. Sorcha had been almost as elegant at her self-imposed barbering task as a Sidhe; though she'd left his hair fashionably long, he no longer felt like a wild pony with a burr-snagging, jagged mane.

Should have had it trimmed long ago. But the thought of trusting my throat anywhere near humans bearing iron . . . Ardagh shuddered.

He was wasting time. This wouldn't be a fraction as difficult as opening a Doorway, nor would there be the slightest likelihood of failure. Clenching the amulet in his fist, the prince shut his eyes. He drew his breath in sharply, visualizing the spell he was about to use. Yes . . . it shouldn't need more than his own will, and not too much of his strength.

Opening his eyes, Ardagh began his chant, seeing the amulet and only the amulet, shutting out all the rest of the world and quietly convincing the clay that it was no longer *it* alone, it was part of *him,* of *her,* of *them,* chanting . . .

. . . and chanting . . .

. . . and . . .

He came sharply awake, staring into blackness. What—Yes . . . he had finished the spell . . . ae yes, and it had worked. The amulet, split as neatly in half as though he'd cut it with an axe, was definitely charged with Power. Ardagh wrapped each half separately in a precious square of spidersilk cut (not without a pang) from his one and only Sidhe tunic, then paused to yawn and rub a hand over his tired eyes. Not surprising that he'd fallen asleep for a moment; he'd used a fair amount of magical energy. More than should have been necessary.

Every time I think I've adjusted to this cursed Realm . . .

The spell had also taken far longer than it should. The hour was now somewhere in the deepest part of the night, judging by the *feel* of it. Ah well, at least the work was done and he could hie himself to bed and a much more comfortable sleep than—

The sound of a hesitant knock on the door brought Ardagh starkly alert. Who would possibly be calling at this hour?

Cadwal. The *feel* of his aura was unmistakable—as was the unexpected cloud of misery shrouding the man. Ardagh brushed back his hair, straightened his rumpled clothing and, face composed into a mask of Sidhe calm (even though, he jibed at himself, the human probably couldn't see him in the darkness) called: "Enter."

The door swung open. Cadwal stood in the entrance, peering into what, to him, would have seemed total blackness. "Prince Ardagh?"

"Of course."

"I . . . ah . . . thought you might be still awake. Hoped you were, anyhow. I wouldn't dream of disturbing you, particularly not at this hour, but . . ."

"But you have some trouble weighing you down. And obviously it's nothing you can share with a priest—or with King Aedh—or you would already have done so. Come inside, man, and shut the door."

Since Cadwal couldn't very well see what Ardagh was doing, the prince didn't bother looking for flint and steel, but lit an oil lamp with a simple flick of will, blinking in momentary discomfort as the sudden small flare of light burned at his darkness-adjusted sight. The flame quickly settled down to a steady little yellow glow, and Ardagh gestured to the room's other chair. Cadwal sat as warily as though he expected the thing to suddenly sprout fangs, and Ardagh fought down a sigh and asked, "Why come to me?"

"Because . . . oh hell, this sounds ridiculous and I wouldn't blame you for throwing me out, but . . . do you have a spell or something that lets a man sleep without dreams?"

"A spell!" That, Ardagh thought, feigned astonishment

nicely. "What makes you think I would know such a thing?"

The mercenary shrugged, a little too casually. "Hell, I don't know. Just that . . . you being so foreign, the ways of your land being so strange . . ."

So foreign. *You know, don't you? You know on some deep inner level what I am, and don't want to accept that you know. Ae, humans.* "Dreams," Ardagh said without expression. "Foul ones, I assume."

"Very. I know," Cadwal added fiercely, "it's a weakness, but it's one I damn well can't afford. And before you ask, yes, I did try going to priests and all that, but I don't dare let everyone know I'm getting soft or—"

"Anyone," Ardagh cut in, "may suffer from disturbed sleep." *Particularly a human who has led such a harsh life.* "It's hardly a sign of failure."

"But—"

"But I certainly agree with you: The leader of the High King's mercenary band can't afford to be weakened by lack of rest."

His very matter-of-factness seemed to be more soothing to the human than any soft words might have been; Ardagh saw not a muscle twitch in Cadwal's weatherworn face, but the faintest spark of hope flickered in the mercenary's eyes. "Then . . . you can help?"

Ardagh hesitated, considering. "No one may be totally without dreams," he said at last, which was certainly the truth. "And I can promise nothing." *Which is undeniably true as well.* "But . . ." Ha, he'd found the memory he'd been hunting. "Yes, I do know a charm for sweet sleep. Something even a . . ." *human* " . . . a man not of Cathay can perform."

It was a very basic spell, a charm taught to every Sidhe child. Whether or not a magickless human could get it to work . . . who knew? But the charm required no special movements, no surge of Power, and Cadwal couldn't possibly do himself any harm.

Besides, even if the magic isn't sparked into life, the

thing still might work by the simple power of suggestion.

Cadwal was a quick study. It took only the shortest of time before the words were set in his mind. He started to stammer out thanks, but Ardagh, all at once embarrassed at the human's embarrassment, shook his head. Deliberately brusque, he said, "The hour is late. I wish to sleep."

That was true enough. But once he was alone again, the prince sat musing over what had just happened.

Ah well. Humans had such self-tormenting minds. Not surprising that some long-buried horror or sense of guilt might unexpectedly spring up to torment a dreamer.

Then why do I feel troubled? I'm certainly not worried that Cadwal's going to blurt out "The prince isn't human," or some such nonsense. No . . . this has nothing to do with him. . . .

Nothing, indeed. Something to do with the journey, then? The Wessex lands? Ardagh frowned, frustrated. He had never been talented in prescience, even in the Sidhe Realm. And yet there was something . . . something. . . .

Nothing. The danger, if danger there was, had no true form, or else was so distant even scrying would hardly detect it. Or maybe it—

Maybe it doesn't even exist. The hour, the prince repeated to himself, *is late. Go to bed, you idiot. Things in this Realm always do look brighter in the morning.*

Things, Beortric of Wessex mused, rarely did look brighter in the morning, no matter what folks believed. He stood in the doorway of his hall, to anyone watching merely a man enjoying the brisk bite of the clear air, but his thoughts were dark. Worr had come to him yesterday with so bizarre a tale that had it been anyone else reciting such nonsense, Beortric would have ordered him away. But Worr . . . Worr, the king thought, would never lie to him. Yet . . . that tale . . . to accuse an

ealdorman of such a thing as murder, no matter that the
slain had been no more than some common whore, to
accuse him of the darkest of sorceries . . .

What am I to do? What am I to do?

Edburga would know. Oh yes, Edburga never hesitated to pass judgment. She would rant and rave as she
always did, and in the end he would give in to her, as
he always did, just to keep the peace. Beortric snorted.
His wife would rule the land if he let her!

Yes, and he could just hear Edburga shriek that he
was dithering again, stalling when he should be acting.
Something must be done about Osmod. But what?

Beortric let out his breath in a shuddering sigh. And
now Edburga would accuse him even more shrilly of
stalling. Maybe he was. But you could hardly up and
indict an ealdorman of such fantastic charges. Not unless
they were true.

Enough of this. He would bring Osmod and Worr
both before him, and see how matters went from there.

Osmod just barely managed to keep the look of
bewildered innocence on his face as he listened to Worr's
horrified accusations. What wild things the youngster was
spouting—even if they were true. At least Beortric had
shown the good taste—or perhaps the cowardice—to
keep this a private matter between the three of them.
It would have been very awkward, indeed, if the king
had decided to bring the affair before the entire Witan.

He came back to full attention with a jolt. Worr was
in the middle of declaiming: " . . . the blood had been
deliberately drained from the poor woman's body and—"

"Deliberately," Beortric echoed, his eyes wary.

"I swear it. The—the slash that had slain her was as
neat as any made to dispatch a rabbit. And thinking of
that made me remember . . ." Worr shuddered. "I don't
know how I could have forgotten it, but recently, when
we were out on the hunt, I saw this man, Ealdorman
Osmod, holding a rabbit he had just slain."

"Is that such a crime?" Osmod asked, wide-eyed. "Granted, a rabbit is hardly mighty game, but the meat—"

"The rabbit's throat had been neatly slashed. Its body was . . . the ealdorman had . . ." Worr paused, plainly fighting with revulsion. "He had it pressed to his lips. And he was . . . drinking its blood."

A flood of possible reactions stormed through Osmod's mind. He quickly rejected outrage (too much chance for unbelievable melodrama) and mockery (a wise man didn't mock the king's . . . friend) and settled for astonishment. "W-what?" *Yes, let the words tumble out as though uncontrolled.* "That—how—that is the most . . ." He stopped as though overwhelmed, then gave the laugh of a totally amazed man. "My lord Worr! Is that really what you thought you saw?" *Charming smile, now, just a touch, charming twinkle to the eyes.* "I had just slain the rabbit, yes, but all I was doing was looking closely at the creature to see if its fur was worth saving."

Worr looked like a small boy who's been patted on the head by adults. "But—I saw—"

"Come now," Osmod soothed, "the forest was dappled with shadow; the light was already fading. If I had to stare so closely at the rabbit I was holding, it's not at all surprising that you, seeing me from a distance, could have been tricked by the twilight." *And you believe me, don't you, you can't help yourself, you do believe me, I will it.* "No shame in making an honest mistake." He could feel Worr's resistance, heard the young man manage a defiant, "But . . ."

You do believe me. I hold the runes in my will, I hold your mind in my will. You do believe me.

In another moment, he was going to pant aloud from weariness or simply fall over.

You do believe me. You do believe me.

Worr's shoulders sagged. "I'm sorry." It was bitterly said. "I had no right accusing you of such a terrible crime. If you wish to settle this by combat—"

Too winded by his effort for speech, Osmod waved

a casual hand. But he must speak, put in a final touch. Somehow he managed not to sway, somehow managed to keep his voice from shaking. "Nonsense. Though some might say that the death of a common whore is hardly a matter worthy of a nobleman's interest, I say it does you credit, my lord, that you show so much concern."

There. That was backhanded enough to silence Worr. And Beortric, being Beortric, was watching his favorite with gentle eyes: he had pretty much forgotten all about the original charge.

For now, Osmod thought, *for now. No matter what I do, the seeds of suspicion, as the saying goes, have already been planted. But if they start to grow,* he vowed, *I, not Beortric, shall cut them off.*

Revelations
Chapter 8

Osmod, alone in his bedchamber, crouched over the bits of rune-carved bone spread out on the clean white cloth, then let out the softest of frustrated sighs. His rank entitled him to this separate house, though of course it was barely an eighth the size of the royal hall, lacking elegant carvings or gilding, but it was still part of the royal compound. Which didn't give him much privacy, even when privacy was most vital. Such as now, with the runes showing him:

Nothing. Not the slightest trace of pending trouble. In fact, this reading was so very bland, as had been the two he'd already cast this night, as to seem almost a mockery. Granted, the days had been deepening into winter without his having sensed even the smallest hint of suspicion from the king—but Beortric was such an inoffensive fellow he wouldn't believe there was even an out-and-out rebellion till it struck him down.

As for Worr . . . Osmod tapped a thoughtful finger against his chin. Out of the many castings of the runes, there had been one —though, disconcertingly only one— revealing trouble from the youngster.

A hint. Possibly not even a true one. Typical of the Lords of Darkness—assuming that They exist. No, no, They must exist; who else would be so frustratingly vague?

But that was the way things went. He dare not ignore the Darkness now that Midwinter was fast approaching.

The darkest hour of the longest night of the year was, all the strictures claimed, the time when the Lords gave up the greatest Power to Their followers—but only in exchange for the greatest risk.

For one long moment, Osmod toyed with the idea of forgetting the whole thing. Plain, mundane political power was surely enough.

Of course. And he was a woad-blue barbarian.

A Midwinter offering could, by the rules, only be human. And for it to be of greatest risk, that could only mean performing the sacrifice right here within the royal compound.

Osmod swept up the runes and slipped them back into their soft leather pouch. So far, no one had missed the kitchen boy who'd been last year's offering, or the elderly servant of the prior year. But back then, there hadn't been the awkwardness of Worr planting doubts in the king's ear, either.

Ah well. He would simply have to be more cautious. Osmod scrambled to his feet, shivering a little; the hall's central fire had, of course, been banked for the night. He straightened, listening . . . yes. At this time of year, when the thin song of the wolves could be heard out there beyond the city's walls, it might not be considered too bizarre for someone to meet an unexpected end at the fangs of some starveling creature even within Uintacaester.

I hope You appreciate the dangers I'm facing, Osmod thought, only half-jesting. *Let's hope that the Power I receive in exchange is worth the trouble!*

Worr stirred restlessly, unable to sleep for all the bed's cozy warmth, and heard Beortric's drowsy protest. But now he couldn't get comfortable at all; the king had pulled most of the heavy furs to him and what was left wasn't keeping out the drafts.

It was more than mere physical chill, Worr thought in misery. Every time he did manage to close his eyes, he kept seeing the terror-stricken face of that poor little whore, even after so many days had passed. And sometimes he dreamed that Osmod loomed over her, smiling his charming, charming smile.

"Damn!"

It had been whispered just a touch too fiercely. Beside him, Beortric stirred, asking drowsily, "Worr? What's wrong?"

"I don't know. I don't. Maybe it's just the time of year."

"So close to Christ's Birth, you mean?"

"So close to the old pagan darkness," Worr corrected. "Maybe it's just that. But . . ." He turned earnestly to the king, staring into Beortric's sleepy eyes. "It's Osmod. Wait, wait, please let me finish, I don't know what— why—please, Beortric. We must see what he's doing this night."

The king's gaze sharpened. "You sound like some hysterical girl. If you've had a foul dream—"

Worr groaned. "It's not that. It's . . . I don't know what it is. I feel . . . I feel as though someone's been tampering with my mind: Osmod. Yes, yes, I know this really does sound like a girl's hysteria, and if I'm wrong, I-I'll accept all penalties for false witness. But—Beortric, believe this: I just don't think I'm wrong."

Osmod smiled thinly. It had been almost pathetically easy to lure the boy to him with gentle words and feigned kindness: the servant—what had he been, some young kitchen lad, perhaps?

No matter. He had been all too willing to believe that a fine, noble ealdorman should have taken a sudden interest in him. The boy had been pretty enough under the dirt for that to be credible, had Osmod's tastes run that way. Which, he thought with a touch of dark humor, they did not.

A pity I'm not Worr, he told the limp body. *You might still be alive. A pity, too, that you were such an*

*insignificant creature. No family, no friends, no one to
miss you. So it goes.*

He'd strangled the boy almost, but not quite, beyond
life. Now Osmod delicately cut his prey's throat, finishing
what he'd begun, enjoying the sharp taste of blood, the
wild thrill of Power renewed. The servant had been
better fed than the whore; his young life force was so
much stronger that it was a pure delight to drink.

But even as he luxuriated in this hot new strength,
Osmod kept one corner of his mind clear on what would
come next. When he was done, he would disguise the
body in a roll of worn cloth, see that it was burned like
so much trash. And if any should discover the contents
of that roll, why, all he need do was feign surprised
horror with everyone else.

Yes. And that burning would complete a symbolic
triple death: just the devious type of sacrifice the Lords
of the Underworld were said to like the most. And the
whole thing was being done right under the noses of the
royal court. The Lords should definitely like that as well.
Maybe this time the Power wouldn't fade; maybe this
time he would be as magically strong as he wished. And
then, and then . . .

Osmod shut his eyes in ecstasy.

"Oh *God!*"

His eyes flew open at that shout of horror. Beortric!
Beortric, and that damnably honorable Worr at his side
like a faithful hound. Osmod let the body fall, snatching up his pouch of runes. No time to hunt for the ones
he wanted: he thrust his fist about them all, praying that
would be enough. Before Beortric could do more than
draw in breath, Osmod cast all his hastily summoned will,
all the strength he had just gained from the sacrifice into
this one desperate cry:

*"You have seen nothing odd, nothing. You have seen
nothing. You have seen nothing. Nothing. Nothing!"*

Sobbing with the effort, Osmod fell limply forward
over the body, too drained to move, sure harsh hands

were about to seize him. But . . . there was nothing. Just as he had willed it: nothing. Blank-faced, Beortric and Worr both were walking away.

With a gasp of relief, Osmod let himself slide into exhausted darkness.

He woke aching and sore and frighteningly . . . empty. Terrified that the effort of controlling both Beortric and Worr had destroyed his magic, Osmod fumbled with numb fingers for the pouch of runes. Nothing, he felt nothing—

No. The touch of Thorn sent the faintest of tinglings through his mind. The magic was still within him, but sadly worn.

Not surprising, he thought with weary humor. *It takes a bit more Power to erase the memory of a human slain than of a rabbit!*

With a groan, Osmod rolled over onto his back, stretching out tired muscles, admitting reluctantly that the perilous memory hadn't truly been erased. Ah no, he'd merely placed a patch over a pit. Sooner or later that patch was going to give way, and then—

Ah well, Osmod told himself, deliberately forcing a light mood, *the time for change was long overdue. You knew that. And Egbert will make a fine ruler.*

But first Beortric and that awkward and damnably too-honorable Worr must die. Osmod had seen enough folks die by now, many by his own hand, not to be squeamish.

Yet those victims had been nobodies. These two, king and noble . . . how could he . . . ? Yes, and it must be done in such a manner as to attract not the smallest shred of suspicion to him.

How, indeed? A tool. A tool. Who could he use, who—

"Edburga!" The answer came to him so suddenly he nearly staggered, wondering for an uneasy instant if this had come directly from the Lords of Darkness.

Bah, of course not. It was such an obvious, logical

choice. Edburga had no friends at court, thanks to her bitter, savage nature. There would be no awkward political complications. She already, not surprisingly, loathed Worr; it was evident enough to be a common part of court gossip. And she was, Osmod thought, most conveniently under his control.

Ah yes. Edburga would make a splendid assassin.

What, Ardagh Lithanial wondered absently, testing the weight of the practice sword, was winter like in Wessex? It certainly couldn't be more disagreeable than winter here in Eriu, which had turned into its usual damp, dank, chilly self. Never a decent snowfall, never a nice, crisp, bright-skied day . . . *never anything even remotely like the clear, crystalline Sidhe winter—*

No. Let yourself sink too deeply into what Cadwal called *hiraeth,* the bittersweet longing for what couldn't be, and you lost all hope for what was.

Cadwal, yes. Ardagh watched the man's approach with a slight smile. At least that silly little charm for sweet sleep seemed to have helped him.

It *had* helped, hadn't it? Ardagh felt his smile fade at the sight of the weary, troubled eyes. But Cadwal didn't volunteer any information, asking only, "Ready to go a few rounds?"

Ardagh saluted him with the sword. "Of course." Very much aware of how survival in this land depended on weapons skill, the prince practiced his swordplay whenever he and Cadwal both had the time free. And preferably, Ardagh thought, whenever they could manage to avoid an audience.

Nothing like a cold, dank grey day for that.

A little more perilous to duel with even these blunted iron blades, but a touch of danger did make things more realistic. Besides, there wasn't enough of the cursed metal to sicken him.

They fought in silence for a time, working their way gradually up from the basic warm-up exercises to genuine swordwork. Ardagh could feel himself starting to smile, enjoying the elegant, quick dance, enjoying the fact that his Sidhe reactions hadn't been slowed at all by this human Realm. Of course, things might be different in Wessex.

Wessex. The thought hit him like a shock of icy water that very soon now he would be heading once more into the unknown, alone and friendless as before—

Ardagh gave a startled yelp as fire raced along his arm. Cadwal was instantly at his side, wild-eyed—presumably seeing his head on a pole for injuring a princely guest—and trying to see the wound even as Ardagh tried to keep it hidden, insisting to the mercenary, "My fault, not yours. I let my mind wander. It's all right, really—"

"It's not all right, dammit—"

"You don't have to—"

"I do!"

Cadwal had already grabbed his arm and pulled back the sleeve before the prince could stop him. Ardagh saw the worry in his eyes change to . . . what? Shock? Horror? The horror of a man seeing the solid world turn to mist? "There's no blood." It was almost a whisper.

"No," the prince agreed.

"There's a burn. The sword burned you. The *iron* burned you."

"Cadwal," Ardagh said softly, "I think you had best sit down." Swallowing dryly—iron burns, he was coming to learn, tended to hurt out of all proportion to their size—he added, "I think we had both best sit down."

"I think we must, indeed. I've got some salve in my chambers, stuff that's good for burns—that *is* the sort of burn that can be healed?"

Ardagh nodded. "Lead on. I really would like to sit down."

Cadwal's quarters were spotless as ever; the mercenary refused to give himself the slightest chance to slide into an exile's apathy. He busied himself with finding the pot of salve and a clean strip of cloth, then stood hesitating so long that Ardagh finally took the pot from him and treated the burn himself.

"It's not serious," he assured Cadwal. "A scorch. I've gotten worse." He glanced up. "Sit, man, before you fall."

Cadwal sat, staring.

"Go ahead," Ardagh said after an awkward moment of silence. "Say what you're thinking."

The mercenary gave a gusty sigh. "What I'm thinking is that you're something other than anyone would believe."

"And that is?"

Cadwal never flinched. "I'm not sure exactly what. Maybe . . . Tylwyth Teg."

"No." Ardagh's mind was racing through a hasty *Should I? Should I not?* But there was the evidence of the iron burn to explain. And . . . there had once been a lonely night and this human's comforting welcome to a fellow exile. The prince added frankly, "Not Tylwyth Teg. But they are distant cousins."

"You mean I'm *right?*"

It came out as such a squawk of astonishment that Ardagh couldn't hold back a burst of laughter. "Didn't you expect to be?"

"Well, yes, but . . ."

"Ae, I'm sorry." Ardagh forced himself back under control. "I have no business laughing at you. And before you collapse from the weight of curiosity, my race isn't Tylwyth Teg but Sidhe. I really am a prince, my brother really did exile me for what he falsely thought was treason, and I really do wish no harm to these folk who have given me sanctuary. Does that satisfy you?"

"'Satisfy' isn't quite the word." Cadwal was looking as dazed as if Ardagh had grown wings and flown away. "*Dewi Sant.* Sidhe." He shook himself like a dog shaking off water. "I knew it but didn't know it, if that makes sense."

"It does."

"*Damnio.* The world's stranger than I dreamed."

Aedh, Ardagh mused, had said almost exactly the same thing when *he'd* learned the truth.

But Cadwal was once more regarding him with that wild horror. "If you're real, the Sidhe I mean, that means all the Others are probably real, too."

There was a desperate edge to his voice, the sound of a man hunting frantically for solid ground, and Ardagh said, "Probably. But not necessarily in this human Realm. You don't have to worry that reality is falling to pieces about you."

"Glad to hear that." The tone was light, but genuine relief glinted in Cadwal's eyes. "Sidhe," he said again, this time with less shock in his voice. "No wonder you won't wear iron armor! Yes, and here you've been going into battle against iron blades. Your pardon, but that's a damnably foolish thing to do!"

"So Sorcha told me. Cadwal, stop staring at me. I have *some* resistance to the metal; I'm not going to fall to ash." *No. All I do is collapse if there's too much of the cursed stuff about, or now and then burn myself if I get overconfident: certain smeltings seem to be more treacherous than others, with no way to know which is which in advance. No problem. Hah.*

Cadwal, regardless, was still staring. "Sidhe," he repeated yet again. "And there I was the other night bothering you with my human problems. Asking if you knew a—a spell. *Iesu,* and wasn't *that* a stupid question?"

Ardagh frowned slightly. "A spell that isn't working for you any longer, I take it."

"I . . . no. Not for the past three days or so." The man shrugged. "It's nothing."

He plainly wasn't going to say any more without prodding. Cursing human stubbornness, Ardagh said, "You've been humanly kind to me—ae, don't look so embarrassed; you have. And the knife-fighting you taught me saved my life. I haven't forgotten. Be honest with me. Why did you come to me that night?"

Cadwal's eyes were all at once the eyes of a trapped

wild thing. "Because . . . I . . . because . . . *damnio*. Because of Gwen."

"Gwen!" Ardagh straightened in surprise. "But you told me she was dead."

"She is." Cadwal's voice was rigidly controlled. "But maybe you can tell me why she keeps coming back." The control slipped ever so slightly. "A-at least, I think it's she. The dreams or whatever they are stopped for a while after you'd taught me that spell, and I dared to think that was the end of it, but now . . . Look you, what's happening is that every night I've been hearing her voice calling to me in my sleep, all the way from Cymru, Gwen's voice pleading with me to free her, free her soul."

His eyes were suddenly painfully bright. "I'm no mystic, Prince Ardagh, I'm a mercenary. Give me a battle, sword to sword, and I know exactly what to do. This . . . if Gwen's soul really is trapped . . . I don't know how to help her! Prince Ardagh, you'd know more about such things than any of us. Is it true? Can my Gwen really be someone's prisoner? Or . . . am I just going mad?"

"You're not mad. I'd have *felt* the psychic chaos the moment you approached. As for anything else—I don't know."

"But—"

"I can hardly know very much about human souls or ghosts. And if she really is calling to you from Cymru, I certainly can't prove anything from this far away."

"Figured. That's why I decided I'm going to have to go with you."

Ardagh stared. "But there's a death sentence waiting for you if you're caught in Cymru!"

"There's insanity hanging over me if I stay here, and maybe the damnation of Gwen's soul. Look you, it's not as if I'm abandoning King Aedh. My men are loyal to him; you don't often get an employer who treats mercenaries like honorable folk, and they appreciate it. This won't be a long journey, God willing. Dyfrig can lead them well enough while I'm away." Dyfrig ap Gwilim was, Ardagh knew, Cadwal's second-in-command. "Not a scrap of humor to our Dyfrig, but he's honest as rock and a good, clever fighter; he'll keep the king safe."

"I won't be stopping in Cymru."

"Not on the way out, I know that. But you're not going to be in Wessex all that long, God willing. Figure I'll have my chance after you've met with King Beortric."

"You've worked it all out, haven't you?"

"Tried to. You're going to need some sort of escort other than pretty courtiers." Cadwal shrugged. "Might as well be me."

"In other words, you're going, with me or without."

"You got it."

"And it doesn't bother you that your travelling companion won't be human?"

Cadwal winced. "I can't swear to that. But I'm going, no matter who's my companion."

Ardagh sat back, studying the man. "I can't guarantee your safety. I can't even guarantee my own!"

"I don't understand. Why not just magic us there?"

"Think, man! Do you really think I would be languishing in this human Realm if I could wield that much Power?"

Cadwal blinked. "There is that."

The prince sighed, seeing stubbornness and honesty both in the man's eyes. "I can trust you." It was as much command as comment. "In my native Realm, yes, I could magic myself, as you put it, here or there with little more than the wish. Here . . ." He shrugged slightly. "Let's just say that in this Realm, my abilities are rather restricted."

"But you're not without magic?"

Ardagh laughed shortly. "You sound like a small boy hoping for wonders."

That roused a wary chuckle. "Och, I do, don't I? But you have to admit this sort of thing is far from my experiences."

"Mine, too," the prince drawled. "And yes," he added, relenting, "I do have some Power left to me, though it's nothing spectacular." Ardagh could see skepticism plain on Cadwal's face and gave a mental shrug. Humans would believe what they wished, regardless of facts. "Which," the prince continued, "is why we'll be making the journey to Wessex by perfectly mundane means."

"'We,' eh?"

"We. You already told me as much. So be it." Suddenly Ardagh smiled, and saw Cadwal's puzzled frown. "I was just thinking of that journey. And the human societies about which I still know so very little."

"I speak the Saxon tongue. Know your enemy and all that."

"Enemy?" Ardagh echoed uneasily.

"Och, not to you and not to Eriu." Cadwal's voice was wry. "Let us just say that Cymru has had more dealings with the Saxon folk than Eriu and leave it at that. I know a fair bit about how they live, too."

"And you won't let prejudices get in the way, I trust."

Cadwal snorted. "You know me better than that."

"I'm glad to hear it." Ardagh got to his feet, stretching warily. Under the soothing salve, the burn had almost stopped hurting, and he was all at once too restless for further conversation.

But he suddenly stopped at the doorway and turned back to the watching human. "Quite frankly, friend Cadwal," the prince said, "I was not looking forward to travelling alone—yes, yes, I know the king will send an escort with me. But there will be none among them with whom I can speak freely. Save for you. Cadwal, I admit it: I will be very glad of your company."

Renovations
Chapter 9

She couldn't remember. Something odd had happened just before, Edburga was vaguely sure of it. Something odd had been said to her, but she could not remember what it had been or who had said it. Or had the words come from her own mind? There had been something about a drink . . . someone had been urgently whispering about a drink . . . about Worr . . .

Worr. That was it. She would be rid of him. Yes. The potion she had mixed under the goad of that whispering voice was quick to act, quick to cut off any hope of breath. Worr would neatly drink and neatly die. And Beortric? Beortric would soon forget.

That was it, just as the whispers told her. Of course. She would poison Worr.

The world failed to come into focus, but it didn't matter. She had the drinking horns, one in each hand. (And for a moment Edburga wavered, wondering, had she poured the poisoned drink into one horn or both? But the voice was whispering to her; she must go on; she must believe this was right and Worr would die.) One horn for Beortric, the ritual first drink of the evening given to the king by his wife. (Though Edburga could not remember ever having followed this ritual before; but the whispers were telling her, yes, yes you have.) One horn for Worr, the last he would ever taste.

Moving through a dreamy haze, Edburga crossed the crowded, noisy, smoke-filled hall and saw and heard nothing but the whispers in her mind telling her what to do. She would give the drinking horns to Beortric and Worr and watch them drink.

She would be rid of Worr.

It was, Osmod thought, the finest acting he had ever performed, and the most difficult. Keeping up this facade of perfectly charming fellow, sitting here at the king's table as was his right as ealdorman, smiling as casually as though politely hiding boredom. And all the while he was hiding his desperate concentration behind that calm facade.

At least Bishop Cynbert was still not back from Rome; at least Osmod was spared that potential distraction. But that hardly made his work any easier as he drew Edburga from the women's side of the hall, a drinking horn in each hand.

Ah, Edburga. It had been so simple to plant the thought of murder in her head; one mention of Worr gone, and the red flames had shot up in her mind like so much wildfire. And the means—like any other noblewoman, she had a sizeable herb garden. She also, unlike most other noblewomen, had a sizeable knowledge of poisons. That she hadn't already poisoned Worr was a miracle. But getting her to slay both Worr and Beortric in one . . . not easy, not easy. Her angry will was, in its own frenzied way, unpredictable. If failed now, if his hold over her failed now—

No. He would not even think of failure. He would merely watch and wait, and try to ignore his ever more painfully pounding heart. Edburga was hardly the sort to exchange light words of courtesy; she clearly even begrudged the slight bow necessary to hand her husband and Worr the drinking horns. Now, if only . . .

It was done. Osmod sagged in his seat, fighting not to gasp but still not able to relax, retaining his hold on Edburga's will, worrying now that the poison might not be strong enough. What if it failed to kill outright? What if it merely sickened Beortric and he lived to learn the truth?

Lords of the Underworld, if you want your servant alive to do your work . . .

But he dare not show even the slightest hint of tension. It took every bit of his sorcerous control, but Osmod managed to keep himself sitting in apparent calm, mimicking with all his might a man who anticipated nothing more than dinner, a man who—

Beortric surged up from his chair, his eyes suddenly wild with the effort to breathe, a hand at his chest. A storm of wild cries tore through the hall: "The king! The king is ill!"

No! Not just ill, he can't be merely—

With a crash, Beortric fell across the table, thrashing desperately about for air, his face purpling. Just as suddenly, his struggles stopped, and he lay still amid the wreckage of dinner. A man's voice cried out in horror: "He is not ill! The king is dead! King Beortric is dead!

"Poison . . ."

It was the faintest of choked gasps. Worr, Osmod realized, and thought in heart-stopping terror, *The dosage wasn't enough.* Somehow, Worr had dragged himself to his feet, somehow he managed to stare for what seemed an eternity right into Osmod's eyes.

He knows, he knows, Dark Powers help me, he knows! He isn't going to die, but I will, I—

But all at once Worr lost his desperate struggle. Quietly, almost as though resigned, he fell lifeless beside the lifeless body of his king.

The hall erupted into a chaos of shouts and screams and panicked people rushing blindly about. Osmod sagged back in his seat, dizzy with relief and exhaustion, so drained that he could not have moved to save himself. His grip on Edburga's will fell away, and he saw horror flash across her face as she all at once knew what she had done, horror closely followed by sheer terror: No one realized yet who'd done the poisoning, but it wouldn't take long for everyone in the hall to guess the answer.

Osmod roused himself with a great effort. This one last link must be severed before he collapsed. "Flee," he told Edburga beneath the storm of noise, and only she heard. "Edburga, flee the land."

He saw her sob once, saw her hand cover her mouth. Then Edburga, no longer queen of Wessex, turned and fled. And in the crush of confusion, no one marked her passage. No one save Osmod.

Go, Edburga. Your usefulness is ended. And I—I am safe.

Egbert, once prospective prince of Kent, and possibly of all Wessex, now nothing more than a young man in exile, slept with a knife close to hand. It was his custom—particularly now that his captor-patron Charlemagne was far off in Rome and some of the Frankish court left behind here in Aachen just might fancy some deadly sport. Now he came surging up from sleep, knife drawn, seeing a shadowy figure there in the darkness, thinking, *This time it's real, someone's sent an assassin to—*

"No," a calm voice said. "I'm not a foe. Wait. Let me light a lamp so you can see me."

It had been said in the Saxon tongue of Wessex, the sound infinitely sweet to Egbert's ears. He waited tensely, ready to attack if he must. There was a small flare of light, a flickering as the lamp's wick caught. . . .

So now, who was this? A man stood alone in the yellowish glow, hands raised slightly to show he bore no weapon. The light was too uncertain to let Egbert guess the man's age, but he was definitely blond of hair, blue of eyes, and his pleasant face was vaguely familiar. . . . Egbert hunted for a name and after a moment said tentatively, "Osmod?"

"Ah, I'm flattered that you remember, Your Highness. It's been . . . what, sixteen years now?"

"Indeed," flatly. "You're the last person I would have expected to see here. Especially," his sweep of a hand took in the bedchamber, "here."

"I needed to speak with you rather urgently—and secretly."

"But how did you get into—"

"Please. We both know that nothing's impossible."

"With sufficient coin. Of course." Egbert didn't relax his grip on the knife's hilt. "Speak."

"I'll be blunt. King Beortric of Wessex is dead."

Egbert just barely hid the wild shock of hope that blazed through him; only his years of pretending to be a harmless nobody allowed him to say as calmly as though they were discussing the weather, "Is he, now? How? He wasn't that old a man. And from what I remember of him, I can't believe there was a battle."

"No battle. The talk at court is that his wife was his murderer."

"His wife!"

"You do remember her, don't you? The high-headed daughter of late King Offa? As to the truth of what she did or didn't do . . ." Osmod shrugged. "The fact is: she's fled. And the king is most undeniably dead. Ah . . . I see that my news interests you!"

Egbert could feel his heart racing so fiercely he nearly staggered. *Oh God, to be out of this place after all this time! The throne of Wessex vacant, and I—* In a voice suddenly choking with hope, he asked, "What of the Witan? Have they chosen a successor?"

"Oh, they're still debating back and forth and getting nowhere. Beortric left no heir of his body; I'm sure that information drifted to you here in Aachen. As for other candidates . . ." Osmod shrugged again. "I don't know how much you recall of how the Witan operates."

"I wasn't too young to recall them agreeing with Beortric to exile me."

"A boy, yes, then. A man, now. Oh, and before you

ask," Osmod added cheerfully, "yes, I did reach Aachen with astonishing speed: lucky winds and the like."

"Even so late in the year."

Osmod shrugged. "I didn't say the trip had been easy, just swift. Very swift. Believe me, Your Highness, the Witan is still meeting." Osmod took a small step forward, blue eyes earnest. "The Witan will choose you. They must."

"But you know nothing about me!"

"More than you think, I suspect. You aren't totally isolated here at Charlemagne's court, Your Highness. Not for the . . . ah . . . curious."

"The ambitious, you mean."

"Why, Your Highness, is there anything wrong with ambition?"

Egbert hesitated, wondering. "No," he said at last.

"So. You have the strongest claim to the throne, you are strong and handsome—don't wave that away, Your Highness, we both know that folk, contrary to all the priestly teachings, do judge by outer appearances. So," Osmod repeated, ticking off the points on his fingers, "you are tall, handsome, hale and young—but no longer too young."

"I blush," Egbert said dryly, and saw the man grin.

"More important, Your Highness, you look so much like your late father, Heaven rest him, that no one can deny your lineage. I . . . ah . . . don't suppose you have some token of his as further proof? Of—your pardon— legitimacy?"

"His seal ring." Egbert had held it safely hidden all these years.

"Ah, splendid. The Witan *will* choose you, Your Highness. Particularly," Osmod added with the slightest of dramatic pauses, "when you are there to remind them you still live."

"What—"

"Yes. I can get us away from here as easily as I got myself in."

"You can guarantee lucky winds back again, eh? Winter weather notwithstanding."

"Something like that." Osmod paused, grin fading. "I can do my part, Your Highness. I can and will get you safely back to Wessex. But before we go a step further, you must decide. Do you want the throne of Wessex?"

God, yes! "Words are all well and good," Egbert hedged warily. "But who stands behind them? I'm not naive: good looks aren't enough to win a throne. And I've been out of sight for sixteen years; the people aren't going to know who I am."

"The golden delight of the Witan, that's all they'll need to know. That will win you initial support. What happens after that . . . well now, Your Highness, once you're on the throne, that will be up to you."

"That still doesn't answer my question: If I leave my 'sanctuary' here and risk returning home, who will I find willing to back my claim?"

"Everyone."

It was said so flatly that Egbert wondered just how bad things had gotten in Wessex. Or just how influential Osmod had become. Yet, oddly enough for an ealdorman, there seemed to be no guile at all in the pleasant face or those clear blue eyes. *I've been an actor all these years,* Egbert reminded himself. *Why shouldn't he be acting as well?*

And yet . . . and yet . . . there was something honest about those eyes, something that told him, whispering in his mind, *this is a man you can trust.*

Could he? Egbert frowned slightly. "Why are you doing this? And please don't give me those tired old words, 'rightful ruler.'"

"Ah, but you are!" But Osmod was smiling again, eyes alight with wry humor. "Of course I want to see you on the throne of Wessex."

"And you beside me as advisor. Weren't you that for Beortric?"

"Of course. One of his several ealdormen, at any rate.

But he had lost most of his interest in the wider world. He listened only to his . . . favorite."

"Ah." Egbert hadn't missed the subtle emphasis on *favorite*. "A pity. And you expect me to have larger concerns?"

"Expect? I *know* it, Your Highness."

His grin was infectious. Even as a small part of his mind was wondering why, after sixteen years of perpetual caution, he was being so suddenly, so completely trusting of a virtual stranger (*almost as though Osmod had cast a spell—no, ridiculous*), Egbert felt himself grinning as well.

"We shall see, ealdorman. Get me out of this comfortable prison, get me the throne of Wessex, and we shall see."

"I can ask no more," Osmod said, and bowed.

Ambassador at Large
Chapter 10

Springtime, Ardagh thought, clinging to the rail of the merchant ship (*no, no,* boat *is more the word, and a wallowing, awkward one at that*). Or at least what might conceivably be passing for such a season if one were of a charitable mind. He would *not* care to try plunging into those chilly "springtime" waters.

Aedh, not really surprisingly, was rushing the season a bit, desperate to win those Wessex allies before the Lochlannach could set sail.

Optimist.

The king must have paid the ship's owner well to get him to travel this early in the year. But the journey so far hadn't been exciting or romantic or even particularly dangerous. What it had been, Ardagh decided, was out-and-out tedious.

He glanced sideways. Cadwal, looking definitely the worse for wear, was clinging to the rail as though he meant to leave the imprints of his fingers in the wood. "Feeling better?" the prince asked, and got a glare in response. "I take that for a no."

Cadwal stalked away, face desperately rigid. The prince shook his head, amused, and raised the tiny amulet to his lips once more. "Forgive the interruption," he said softly to the far-off Sorcha. "Let me see, where were we?"

"' . . . and so here we are,'" Sorcha said, mimicking his voice with, he thought, fair success, "'sailing across an obnoxiously rough sea on an obnoxiously smelly boat.'"

"Ah. Yes." The prince glanced up to make sure that no one was watching him talking earnestly into half an amulet. The little thing did work exactly as intended, but its weak Power meant that he had to hold it practically to his mouth and use a fair amount of will to make it work; they'd quickly discovered that Sorcha, having no magic of her own, could not spark the amulet into life at all.

No one was watching. Ardagh continued, "The captain keeps his craft clean enough, I'll grant him that. But smelly it most certainly is. I will never be able to get the stench of fish out of my nostrils."

Sorcha's voice sounded, not surprisingly, distant and faint but it also was disconcertingly amused. "My poor, put-upon darling. At least you didn't get seasick."

"There is that. Cadwal hasn't been so lucky."

"Och, poor man. He must be so embarrassed."

Ardagh snorted. "Not really. It takes a good deal to disconcert someone who's managed to survive whatever crises life throws his way."

Sorcha chuckled. "Such as you, my love, such as you."

"Ha." But the prince was still thinking about Cadwal. Ever since learning that Ardagh really was of the Sidhe, the mercenary hadn't said more than a dozen words to him. *He's nervous—no, no, he's out-and-out afraid of me,* Ardagh thought, *though the man would never admit it. Afraid, rather, of what I am, or what he thinks I've become. What a ridiculous nuisance!*

And how ridiculous to realize just how much he'd been depending on Cadwal's friendship. How much he'd been depending upon having someone he knew at his side.

How much he'd been dreading a return to the total aloneness of his first arrival in the human Realm—

No. Time enough to deal with that when they came ashore. At least there was this: Cadwal's eerie dreams had ceased since they'd come aboard this boat. Not surprising. Sendings, if such they were, would be blocked by running water. That, Ardagh thought wryly, must be worth a good deal of physical and mental discomfort to the man.

"Ardagh?"

He started in guilt. "Yes, love, I'm still here. We should be reaching shore soon enough, or so the captain assures me." Ardagh glanced up again. "And here the man comes now. Till later, love."

At first the prince had thought hopefully that this collection of buildings coming into view was royal Uintacaester. But no, he was assured that they had merely reached the trading port of Hamwic, which lay at the mouth of the River Itchen; there was still a journey inland to be made.

Ae, humans.

But it was hardly fair to blame them for not owning the Power to lightly enchant themselves *here* or *there*.

Bah.

They came ashore by the simple means of beaching the tough little ship on the wide strip of bare shore; apparently the tide rose high enough to neatly float the ship off again when its owner was ready to set sail. The sailors quickly put a gangplank down, then stood aside. "If you would, Your Highness."

Ardagh stepped gladly down onto dry land, followed by Cadwal (even more grateful than he, judging from the relief in the man's eyes, to be ashore) and their Eriu escort: five of those in all. Not a grand retinue, perhaps, but, the prince thought, more than sufficient. As he stood waiting for his body to adjust to land, his nostrils full of the scents of sea and fish—and, as the wind shifted about to blow from the north, massed humanity—Ardagh looked about in sharp Sidhe curiosity. Hamwic, rather surprisingly, had no defensive walls, only what looked like a boundary ditch.

They clearly haven't yet run afoul of the Lochlannach!

Within the ditch's circle lay some unexpectedly straight streets paved with what looked from here like gravel (no such thing as a city plan back in Fremainn, he thought, or, for that matter, paved streets) and a good many more houses than the prince had expected. Most, at least as far as he could see from out here, were single-storied, their walls of wood, their roofs of thatch.

Which, of course, makes the whole town highly flammable. But with all this water easily to hand, people probably don't worry very much. I wonder if the same is true of cities inland.

His nose wrinkled at the smell of garbage; that, alas, did seem to be a normal part of human places, with their lack of civilized or magical sanitation. But even so, Hamwic seemed clean enough; the midden heaps, or however else they disposed of waste, were out of sight.

Clean enough—fortunately. Etiquette and common sense both dictated that Ardagh and his escort wait here while a messenger hurried off to the king at Uintacaester with the news of this foreign—and royal—envoy's arrival.

There was an awkward time of mutual staring: these folk, like those Ardagh had left, tended to be fair of hair and skin, though their narrow faces could never have been mistaken for any from Eriu. Most of them were clad in leather-wrapped leggings and woolen tunics dyed every shade from dull brown to startling red; some wore cloaks as well, though nothing as practical as Eriu's all-encompassing and virtually weatherproof woolen *brats*.

Cadwal was practically radiating tension. The prince murmured to him, "Calmness. This is better than the boat."

Cadwal snorted at that. "Most things are. I won't embarrass you, don't worry. Just don't like being studied."

"One can hardly blame them. This may be a trading town, but it still can't be every day that they see a foreign envoy." Particularly, Ardagh added to himself, one led by a prince who, despite his human garb, made such an exotic figure.

Ae-yi, let them stare and chatter as they would. It gave him the chance to adjust his ear to the Saxon tongue as it was spoken by natives. Yes . . . his lessons had been good enough for a start; he would sharpen his knowledge of the language once he'd heard a suitably noble accent to copy by magic. As for what they were saying . . . he most heartily agreed: a prince could hardly be expected to lodge in some common inn. Hardly a difficulty, surely; so busy a town must have a nobleman or woman overseeing matters for the king.

There was. Soon enough, Ardagh and his escort found themselves welcomed into the residence of the local ealdorman, one Eadric. Ardagh glanced about as he waited for his host to appear, welcoming his first look at the inside of a Saxon home. Eadric's home was basically one large, rectangular hall that could easily have held two of the common houses, while the thatched roof, supported by sturdy beams and crossbeams, was far enough overhead to be dark with shadow.

Or is it just soot from that central fire? I suppose this lord has the same problems with ventilation as the folk of Eriu. And here I was hoping that someone *had discovered the joys of windows.*

"I bid you welcome," a sudden voice cried, "welcome, indeed!"

A plump, cheerful man clad in a brilliant red, elaborately embroidered tunic glinting with gold and jet was hurrying down the length of the hall, an equally plump, equally brightly clad woman scuttling beside him, a flock of servants scurrying in their wake. As the gaudy couple drew near, Ardagh dipped his head politely. This could only be Ealdorman Eadric with, presumably, his wife.

Eadric hadn't stopped chattering cheerful greetings all the while. "Of course you are welcome here," he went on, his eyes bright with excitement, "welcome for as long as you choose to stay."

Meanwhile, Eadric's wife was simpering at Ardagh like an awestruck girl. "It's not often our home is graced by someone of royal blood," she said, and all but giggled.

"Still," Eadric continued with just the slightest warning frown at his wife (which she ignored), "it shouldn't take very long to receive word back from court. King Egbert is—"

"Egbert!" Ardagh interrupted sharply. "I thought your king's name was Beortric!"

"It was, God rest him, it was. But he's gone on, as they say, dead for less than a year, and young Egbert rules now."

And isn't this splendid? A new king, a totally new personality about whom I know nothing—so much for a quick and easy mission.

The great royal hall Uintacaester was already half-full; there were always those courtiers so nervous about their status that they'd come to any such event far earlier than need be. Osmod, light blue tunic at just the right length, cloak at just the right angle, his only ornament a necklace of gleaming jet, strolled to his place, nodding at this man, smiling genially at another. Fools, many of them, ambitious fools, but not a one of them was ever going to suspect his true feelings.

Ah, here came Egbert—*King* Egbert, Osmod corrected silently. He did make a most thoroughly regal figure, as Beortric, soft and indecisive, never had. And it hardly hurt the royal image—even, Osmod thought smugly, as he had first pointed out to the then-exile— that Egbert's still-young face was so strongly, elegantly featured, that his hair was so golden, his bearing so proud.

Now, if only his will was just the smallest bit less firm . . .

In the sixteen years of the late king's reign and his own stagnation, he'd forgotten how difficult and overwhelming an intelligent mind could be. But: *Patience*, the ealdorman told himself. *Continue to be friendly and useful, and every day entangle yourself just the tiniest bit more in Egbert's mind, and if the work seems maddeningly slow, no one ever said sorcery was easy.*

At least Egbert was being most suitably grateful to the ealdorman who'd helped him to the throne. Of course. New king that he was, he needed to know there was at least one of the nobles he could trust—or at least not mistrust as strongly.

And of course, Osmod thought dryly, he, the so-loyal ealdorman, was always ready to lend a helping hand—though naturally never doing anything blatantly or firmly enough to make it look like coercion.

Friendly, Osmod thought, *that's me. And, come what may, there's this convenient thing: Egbert harbors deep ambitions for eventual conquest, even if he hasn't shared them openly. And so do I.*

The Witan, naturally, were another matter: all those disparate, not yet quite trusting minds with all those different levels of prejudices and cleverness. But Osmod had already managed to twist a few weaker wills to his own. Eventually the stronger ones would follow—as long as Egbert followed up on the fine beginning he'd made in his first few months as king. All would, with time, be well.

If only the cursed runes would cooperate, instead of giving him, each time he cast them, a disconcertingly vague *possible change* and *possible danger*.

Ridiculous.

But then Osmod heard what Egbert was saying, and came bolt upright:

"An emissary from King Aedh of Eriu is on his way to Uintacaester. What Eriu might want from us . . ."

But Osmod didn't bother listening to the rest of it. Eriu. Far-off, all but unknown Eriu. *Possible change*, he thought wearily. *Possible danger.*

The runes, it seemed, hadn't been lying after all.

Ardagh glanced about with quick Sidhe curiosity as he, his Eriu followers and his Saxon escort travelled along. A good, wide road, this, paved with large, worn cobblestones (old, his Sidhe senses told him, far older than these folk), though the occasional stretch of rough ground or holes told of fading maintenance. Small, neat farms lined the road to the left, interspaced with patches of forest not quite as dense as that of Eriu. A good deal of oak in that forest, wonderful, he'd learned, for the building of house or ship. And yes . . . even with all the human dwellings, there should be enough natural Power left to keep him healthy.

The Itchen rushed its way to their right. It ran, according to his guide, up from Hamwic all the way to Uintacaester but, alas for swift travel, was far too shallow at most times of the year to support decent river traffic. As the party crossed the Itchen over a small stone bridge, Ardagh felt the same prickle of (older than these folk) and wondered, *Relics of the . . . what did Aedh call them? The Romhanach—no, no, the Romans, that's what they called themselves. Long gone from these lands, but judging from what they left behind, they must have been master builders.*

Cadwal, riding beside him, was once again tense as a nervous cat. "Relax, man," Ardagh murmured. "These folk are only human."

"They are *Saesneg*." It was a fierce mutter. "I may have sunk as low in honor as a warrior may, but I have never yet borne sword for one of their race. This land," he added in a soft, savage voice, "was ours once. They came, and came in greater numbers than we could withstand, driving us back till the only land we hold is my own Cymru and the narrow realm of Cernyw."

"All that could hardly have happened in your lifetime."

"No, of course not!" But then, before Ardagh could find anything safely noncommittal to say, Cadwal shrugged. "Old hatreds," he said with a visible attempt at self-control, "die slowly."

The prince thought of Eirithan, the brother who had so gladly seen him cast into exile and who would hardly weep over his death. "If they die at all." It did not come out quite as emotionlessly as he would have liked. "But try not to let the past get in the way of the present."

That earned him a glare. "I would not dishonor King Aedh."

"Neither would I, Cadwal, neither would I." Ardagh added, with a sudden sly little sideways look, "At least the Saxons have done us some good." At Cadwal's startled glance, the prince added blandly, "They have you talking to me normally again, almost as though I hadn't turned into a demon."

To his satisfaction, he saw the hardened mercenary actually blush. But then they came out of a last clump of forest into cleared farmland on all sides, and Ardagh straightened in the saddle. On the horizon sat a grey ridge that was far too regular to be natural. "Well now," he said. "That can only be Uintacaester. At last."

"At last," Cadwal echoed, but so grimly that the prince winced.

Don't fight me, Cadwal. I have difficulties enough already. Please, my prickly human friend, if friend you truly are, don't add to them.

Encounters
Chapter 11

Ardagh glanced up at Uintacaester's sturdy stone walls and towers—the first true stonework that he'd seen in these lands—and frowned slightly. "Now those," he said to Cadwal without thinking, "were never built by these people, any more than was the road."

The mercenary glanced at him in alarm. "How would you know that?"

How, indeed? "The stones whisper of *age*," the prince said after a moment, "of other times and . . ." He saw the wary mask drop once more over Cadwal's face, and let the rest go unspoken. Human cautions, human fears . . . he was growing heartily weary of them. But of course saying anything like that would be further reminding the mercenary of who and what he was, so Ardagh contented himself with nothing more satisfying than a sigh.

Ae, but look at this. The stone walls had led him to expect something more within their circuit than—wood. Just as with Hamwic, he was faced with a sea of wooden houses, one or two stories, most with thatched roofs, some topped with neat wooden shingles, all of them crowded in together as though just inviting a flame. If the city hadn't yet suffered a fire—but it already had, if what his uneasy Sidhe senses were telling him was accurate.

Yes, and they rebuilt almost exactly as before. How very . . . human.

But they had at least some sense: a great, wide street,

paved with very worn but still serviceable cobblestones, ran arrow-straight east to west, bisecting the city. (Old, his Sidhe senses added once again, a Roman street, surely, old as the walls.) The current inhabitants might not have built it, but had at least been wise enough to keep the street in repair. It would act as a decent fire-break, as well as allowing traffic to travel through Uintacaester with relative ease.

Relative, Ardagh repeated to himself. As his party rode along the old Roman road—High Street, his Saxon guide informed them—their horses' hooves clicking against the cobblestones, they were almost instantly swarmed by a noisy, curious crowd.

Ardagh just barely kept his face from showing his sudden rush of panic, overwhelmed as he was by the smell of massed and not totally clean humanity, by the cold, burning *feel* of iron and the impact of a psychic storm of human emotions. Yes, and added to all this chaos were the mingled stinks of beast and smoke and garbage. Ardagh felt a shudder of sheer disgust shake him. Waste disposal would definitely be a problem in a close-packed city like this.

I couldn't tell this to my dear, human Sorcha, but that never-ending pressure of humanity in Hamwic drove me nearly to distraction. At least there I knew it was a finite ordeal. Here, it's going to be far worse—

No. Things were as they were. He was not a weak-minded human. He would adapt.

Of course. No problem at all. Hah.

All right. He'd already learned one way to adjust to the physical and psychic onslaught that was humanity, the never-ending waves of sound and sight and smell, and that was to analyze it as coolly as possible. Willing himself to calmness, Ardagh studied his audience as dispassionately as he could, forcing himself to see not a mass of noise and odor but a group of individual lives.

Interesting. In a way. Almost everyone here seemed to be fair of hair and skin, as had been the population of Hamwic, and the prince fought back a self-conscious urge to touch his own black hair, wondering if there were *any* brunettes in this human Realm. The style of clothing here was predominantly the woolen tunic, worn knee-length over the leather-wrapped leggings for the men, ankle-length for the women; the more prosperous the person, Ardagh guessed, the more brightly dyed—and thereby more expensive—the clothing. Solid colors; no one seemed to go in for the cheerfully loud plaids he'd seen in Eriu.

Phaugh, here was another problem with living packed in together with poor sanitation and no magic: the easy spread of disease. Ardagh noticed a fair number of folks suffering from eye or skin disorders, and felt his stomach try to rebel.

No. Stop that. Their misfortune, not yours.

But what if there were some illness omnivorous enough to attack a Sidhe? There had been none in Fremainn, but then the people of Fremainn had been, for the most part, a healthy lot. The prince saw one young man with eyes nearly crusted shut, and felt a new shudder shake him.

Idiot! he snapped at himself. *Even if by some wild mischance there is some such illness that can affect you, you won't be here long enough to contract it!*

Powers willing.

No. He was letting his self-control slip. Ardagh firmly turned his concentration back to studying the folk around him. The men were all clean-shaven, and . . .

And their narrow faces (narrower, at any rate, than those of Eriu) gave him an uneasy little twinge: closer to his people's general shape of face, yet *wrong*, so very disconcertingly *human*.

Or is it just that I've grown so used to the folk of Eriu that I accept them as the norm?

That wasn't such a comforting thought, either, and Ardagh deliberately thrust it from his mind. Being on horseback gave him the height to see over the sea of yellow hair; beyond, other streets branched off on either side of this one. A good deal of Uintacaester would appear to be divided into a grid. Another little touch of common sense: Fire would still be able to spread, but at least there would be some hope of keeping it from eating the entire city—barring destructive wind, of course—and some chance of safe evacuation.

Not that this chattering crowd seemed to be at all worried about anything. Most of the men were watching him with the mix of awe and suspicion he'd seen often enough on the faces of Eriu's men; very well aware of the effect of Sidhe beauty on humans, he thought wryly that he could pick out husbands and fathers with daughters by the heightened wariness in their eyes.

The women were more openly curious and—yes, no doubt about it in a good many of them—downright interested.

Sorry, he told them silently. *There will be no complications.*

But the people seemed to be demanding some sort of gesture. Ardagh waved a polite, regal hand and received a delighted cheer in return.

And they don't even know who I am. No, no, they do know: novelty, that's what I represent, yes, and spectacle. How . . . nice.

The breeze shifted slightly, bringing him a new wave of animalistic human odor. He was *not* looking forward to the close confines of a Saxon court!

Ah well, one did what one must. And who knew? Odors aside, the visit might not be unbearably unpleasant. Some of the architecture *was* rather attractive, always a good sign, surely, as far as civilization was concerned. To his left, a great structure two or three streets back from High Street loomed over the lesser buildings in the foreground. He couldn't see too much of it from here, but its high roof and tower were quite elegantly peaked, and its wooden shingles glinted in the sunlight with what looked like gold but was more probably gilt.

Without a doubt, a place of major importance in the city's life.

Sure enough, his party made a left turn towards it, their horses' hoofs now crunching on gravel. Ardagh saw that the building was a great wooden rectangle and square tower, both set with elegant arched windows. It sat almost haughtily back from the others, and the prince wondered aloud, "The royal palace?"

"The cathedral," he was told in a somewhat condescending tone. "*There* is the palace, just beyond it."

Ah. The royal residence would be, the prince assumed, equally imposing, like Fremainn a complex of buildings rather than one palace—he assumed it because the whole thing was hidden almost completely by a high wooden palisade; little could be seen but the gabled roofs. Those, like that of the cathedral, were covered with shingles that glinted almost dazzlingly bright in the sunlight, as though the entire roof was worked of gold.

They do like their gilding, don't they?

"Forgive my ignorance," Ardagh said to the human who'd spoken, so mildly that the man flinched. "We are to be lodged there?"

"Uh . . . yes, Your Highness."

"Then by all means take us there."

"At once, Your Highness."

Egbert, once a hopeless exile, now King of Wessex, sat his throne in the great council hall with casual ease (an ease still, he admitted, a bit feigned), elbow on armrest, chin on fisted hand, and pretended to be deeply engrossed in what the Witan was debating. But try though he would, this discussion of wheat and corn that hadn't yet sprouted, yet alone been harvested, just was not interesting enough to keep his mind from wandering.

This was what a good deal of a king's day entailed: coping with bureaucracy and the minutiae of a land's daily life. Growing up seeing a royal court firsthand as he had, Egbert had expected nothing more—but that didn't make the tedium any easier to endure. No, no, his mind insisted on making grand jumps into the future. It wasn't too early to set about finding himself some politically useful wife and start founding his dynasty. And as for what that dynasty would inherit . . .

Egbert smiled ever so slightly, indulging himself in a quick vision of himself at the head of a conquering army, expanding Wessex's borders, engulfing Mercia and all the other Saxon realms, even—why not?—the lands of those quarrelsome Cymraeg. A united Britain, he thought. United under one rule: mine.

Someday, he promised himself. *Someday.*

Ah yes. When he was not still so very new to the throne. When proposing anything as dramatic as conquest wouldn't be looked at askance. When people had learned to trust him. If the years in exile had taught him anything besides how to hide in plain sight it had been patience. Time enough to worry about expansion when he'd won Witan and commons both totally to his will.

A bright blue gaze caught his attention: Osmod, smiling almost conspiratorially, almost as though he'd caught the gist of his king's musings. Egbert found himself smiling back, then caught himself and fixed his face back into its severe royal lines. That was the way with Osmod: he could get almost anyone to like him. And there didn't seem to be anything but open approval on that pleasant face. There never was. Never the slightest reason to think the ealdorman was anything but thoroughly his.

Osmod the ever-smiling, Egbert thought. *Osmod the ever-friendly. Osmod,* the king added dryly, *the highly ambitious. You didn't help me onto the throne out of pure altruism, my noble friend, we both know that.*

Nothing wrong with that; the man would be unnaturally saintly were it otherwise. Osmod would welcome expansion, no doubt about it—with himself playing a vital role.

Oh, not on the battlefield. Our friendly ealdorman

would never make a good warrior. But as an adminis-trator, perhaps . . .

Egbert shook his head fractionally. Osmod really was a likeable fellow, and he just might be as honest as his smiles implied. But he was also as cunning as he was pleasant. You didn't let such a one out of your sight, not if you didn't want him slipping his pleasant way into your role and pushing you into oblivion. Far better, come what may, to keep Osmod at his side as a counselor. A valu-able man that way. Very valuable; Egbert admitted to himself how much he'd come to welcome the ealdor-man's counsel. Having him here kept Osmod safe. In every respect.

Don't, as the saying goes, disturb the sea till you're ready for the waves.

Ach, yes, but waves there were, and not of his mak-ing. Out of nowhere had come the complication of King Aedh of Eriu. Barbaric land, that, Egbert mused, with its many regal subdivisions: a High King ruling over lesser kings. A situation that was just asking for civil war—barbaric, yes. Even if, he added honestly to him-self, it had been Eriu's monks who'd spread the Faith to his own Saxon folk.

But that had happened ages back. For year after year there'd been almost no news out of Eriu; the country had kept quite deliberately to itself. What could be bringing it out of isolation now? What could Aedh be about? Egbert realized with a shock that he knew a disconcertingly small amount about the man, next to nothing about the way he thought or plotted.

I'll find out more, soon enough. It shouldn't be long before his ambassador arrives at court. And then . . . and then, I think, our Osmod shall earn his keep. If he can't charm the very heart and soul of that barbarian envoy, I shall be very surprised, indeed.

"Hopefully," Ardagh murmured into his little amulet-half, "this house, which is one of the many buildings

within the royal enclosure, is to be mine for the length
of my (short, Powers grant) stay."

"Amen," Sorcha murmured back. "What's it like?"

Ardagh glanced about. "It's a rather simple wooden
hall, with an equally simple separate sleeping chamber
to be reached by an outer ladder, but the place smells
of blessedly clean wood and herbs. It is, my love, far,
far better than the cramped quarters we all had to share
in Hamwic. However, I could do very nicely without the
obsequious swarm of servants who seem to come with
the hall and—here they come again. Till later, love!"

At least, Ardagh mused, the servants had had courtesy enough to let him rest for a bit—and, though they
didn't know it, speak with Sorcha—and remove the
worst of the dust of travel (though, ae, how he missed
the luxury of Fremainn's bathhouse!) before pouncing.
The Saxon tunic that he was offered was dyed a deep,
rich blue that, he had to admit, went very nicely with
his fair skin and black hair and was of such a fine, soft
woolen weave that it could only have come from the
royal chests.

A nice touch of courtesy, that.

The leggings, once they were properly wrapped, fit
no worse than those worn in Eriu. Ardagh, rather to the
dismay of the servants, determinedly wrapped his *brat*
about the whole thing (after, of course, those servants
had frantically shaken the dust out of it); he was, after
all, here as a representative of the High King of Eriu.

*Might as well look the part. As much as a Sidhe prince
masquerading as a prince of Cathay acting as an ambassador of Eriu can.*

The day was still reasonably early. "The king is in his
hall," a servant told Ardagh earnestly. "Will it please you
to follow me?"

And what would you do if I said no?

Cadwal must have been thinking the same thing,
because Ardagh heard the smallest of smothered laughs
from him. The prince shot a quick glance his way (seeing

the mercenary still, defiantly, totally, in his own non-Saxon garb) and received what was almost a grin.

"Lead on," Ardagh said to the servant.

Ardagh stopped in the doorway of the king's royal hall, not so sure of welcome in this foreign place that he didn't want to take a look about him first. He also, the prince admitted to himself, needed to give his system at least some chance to adapt to the presence of so many humans—and their iron—in a closed space. The first time he'd entered a hall back in Eriu, his stomach had rebelled; he had no intention of suffering a similar indignity here.

The hall here was as large as he'd expected, all of wood, of course, sleekly fitted planks forming the walls, heavy beams supporting the roof. But it was also so dimly lit that it took a moment for his vision to adjust.

Ha, no wonder it was dim. There were no windows, and sunlight slipping through the smokeholes far overhead could only do so much. A row of central fires, together with a candelabra hanging from a chain driven into a crossbeam, added some smoky, shadow-filled light.

A pity there wasn't better lighting, Ardagh decided, because the hall was rather impressive, in a gaudy, crowded, human way. No. Not quite true. Aedh of Eriu depended on simplicity of design and plain, whitewashed walls to deliberately throw the emphasis on himself, the High King of Eriu who had no equals. This king, this Egbert of Wessex, chose instead to surround himself on all sides with exotic trappings. There was a barbaric splendor to the row of colorful round shields and equally bright woven hangings all along the walls, the intricate carvings ornamenting every wooden surface. The ubiquitous gilding was everywhere as well, glinting in the firelight. The high roof was held up by great square beams. With its many curved rafters, Ardagh mused, it looked like nothing so much as the overturned hull of a ship.

The cold burning of iron—from blades, from tools, from just about everywhere—was as coldly unpleasant as he'd expected, but still within bearable limits. The overall *feel* of emotion from the humans . . . it wasn't the casual contentment of those in Fremainn; these folk were comfortable enough but, Ardagh guessed, not quite yet at ease with their new king.

The smell, unfortunately, was every bit as heavy as he'd feared: a mix of human, smoke, grease and hound—he started as one of the latter determinedly pushed its cold, wet muzzle into his hand, presumably intrigued by his nonhuman scent.

At least the creature isn't trying to attack me. That would be embarrassing.

Ardagh gave the dog a stern pat to send it on its way, succeeding only in getting it to stop nosing him and stand at his side. So be it. He glanced down the length of the hall, seeing row after row of what could only be noble councilors and courtiers perched on padded benches. There, centered nicely in a bright red canopied chair, sat King Egbert of Wessex.

And isn't he a splendidly barbaric sight?

Barbaric in appearance, at any rate; Ardagh knew better than to judge by outer seeming, particulary where humans were concerned.

Ae, but these folk did seem to like their bright colors! Egbert was clad in a scarlet tunic edged with glittering golden embroidery, the color just barely missing conflicting with the red of his chair and complementing the brightness of his golden hair; his leggings were deep blue, and gold and amber gleamed warmly from about his neck. He was nicely regal in bearing and handsome in what Ardagh was beginning to recognize as the sharp-boned Saxon norm. Only the faintest hint of shadow in the blue eyes revealed that this man, former exile and new king that he was, had already endured harsh lessons and learned much from them.

Ambitious, Ardagh realized with a sudden shock of

insight, *very much so,* and felt just the barest prickle of unease. *But is he ambitious enough to be a perilous ally for Aedh?*

Nothing was going to be simple about this mission, was it?

A bustling, anxious-looking Saxon who presumably was a royal herald, cleared his throat and proclaimed in a voice loud enough to echo off the high rafters:

"His Royal Highness, Prince Ardagh, envoy from High King Aedh of Eriu!"

King Egbert, looking up as casually as if he hadn't already noticed Ardagh in the doorway, met the prince's gaze across the hall, and gave a gracious if slightly condescending wave of a hand.

"Enter, underling," is it? *Watch, human.*

Well aware of the demands of drama, the prince stalked forward with full Sidhe grace, Sidhe elegance, saying without words, *Envy though you may, you can never be my equal,* the folds of his *brat* swirling about him almost as dramatically as a spidersilk cloak. He heard the startled murmurs start up on either side; they most certainly had not expected such exoticism in an ambassador from Eriu.

Good. Let them stay off balance.

The king was not so easily impressed, nor had Ardagh, remembering Aedh's unflappable manner, expected him to be. One did not come to rule without first ruling one's self. But the prince did surprise a reluctant hint of something that might have been uneasy approval in the keen blue eyes.

I win this round, do I? Human, they played such games at my brother's court, too. Games I always won.

Save, his mind reminded him with brutal honesty, for the last.

He had never yet bowed to a human; he was not about to start now. Ardagh gave the smallest, most polite and politic dip of his head, royalty greeting royalty, and received the same from Egbert in return.

"Prince Ardagh."

"Prince Ardagh Lithanial, whom some" *though never me* "have named Prince of Cathay."

A golden eyebrow shot up. "So-o! You are far-travelled, indeed!"

You've heard of Cathay, then. Hopefully "heard" is all.

"Indeed," Ardagh agreed with perfect truth.

Egbert settled back in his chair, fingers steepled. "A prince makes an unusual envoy."

Ardagh smiled his most urbane smile. "Who better to understand the game of politics?"

"Than one who must always play it. Granted."

"Besides," the prince added, still the essence of charm, "King Aedh has shown me much kindness. How better to repay his hospitality than by serving as his envoy?"

Egbert's smile was wary. "How, indeed? It's the 'why' of it I wish to learn. No, not just now, Prince Ardagh. You and your men must be weary and hungry from your travels."

"It *has* been a tiring journey."

But then Ardagh forgot all about politics and delicate duels with words. He saw, and *felt* before he saw, and in that moment the world seemed to freeze about him.

There at Egbert's side, standing a bit behind the royal chair, was a richly clad ealdorman whose face was pleasant and warm as the springtime sun—and whose blue eyes held the same stunned disbelief Ardagh knew was in his own:

The ealdorman who bore the strongest innate Power Ardagh had ever sensed in a human.

The ealdorman who was, without the slightest of doubts, the most cold-blooded of sorcerers.

Storm Warnings
Chapter 12

It took every bit of his Sidhe will, but Ardagh managed to force his attention away from the staring, equally stunned sorcerer-back to King Egbert. Luckily, since the moment of magical recognition had been on the psychic level and taken almost no time at all, neither king nor court had been aware of it.

Egbert, Ardagh realized, was making some polite conversation about, fortunately, nothing much. The prince answered with similar trivialities, all the while *feeling* the sorcerer's Power still tingling against his own and wondering. It was true that Queen Eithne bore a touch of innate magic, but only a touch. Here . . . granted, this was still relatively weak Power, weaker by far than anything to be found in the Sidhe Realm—but that it should be found at all in one of the human kind—

Ae, he was letting his mind wander again. King Egbert was inviting him to dinner. Ardagh once again forced his concentration full back to the king and dipped his head in courteous acceptance.

A dinner that includes the sorcerer? That shall be . . . interesting. Who is he? Someone of importance, judging from his proximity to the throne. Egbert's pet advisor? And how does his presence alter matters?

Who could tell? And time enough to mull things over later. First he must be sociable, and use the opportunity to learn more about Egbert.

Ambitious Egbert.

With an ambitious sorcerer as well?

And here I thought matters were already complicated beyond untangling. Nothing's ever simple in this Realm, nothing!

Lords of Darkness, Lords of Darkness . . .

Osmod, alone in his hall, the servants having been summarily banished, clenched his teeth to keep the half-hysterical litany from escaping. But, Lords, Lords, who would have expected that? Who *could* have expected that? The envoy, the so very exotic envoy from Eriu, the prince from far-off Cathay—who would have expected that he would also be someone who fairly radiated Power? Osmod shuddered convulsively, remembering. Almost, almost, he'd screamed out his shock.

And wouldn't that have been stupid? Stupid and fatal.

But somehow, he thought, marvelling at his own self-control, he'd managed, somehow he hadn't cried out, "Sorcerer!" there before them all, but had stood as calmly as anyone else.

Oh yes. Calmly. Until at last my nerve broke and I scurried off like some idiot of a terrified boy, almost before Egbert gave me leave.

No real damage done. He'd managed to make it look like some frantic call of nature, embarrassing but thoroughly understandable. Besides, the prince had already left. And had he sensed Osmod's Power even as Osmod had sensed his?

How could he not?

Yes, yes, but what would that recognition mean? There had been nothing to sense but the bare fact of Power present. Just how much had the prince been able to learn from him?

"Lords of Darkness," Osmod whispered, then stopped short. The Lords, assuming that They existed, did *not* like Their worshipers to show such weakness. And yet, how could he stay calm? Possible change, the runes had promised, possible danger, they had warned, and oh, this once they had been very honest!

Does Egbert know what he's welcomed into his court? No, no, of course not. To him, this newcomer can be nothing more than the ambassador he claims to be, a little more unusual than most, perhaps, but no one to alarm a king.

Yes, and what of Aedh of Eriu? Did he know? Bah, who could tell how those barbaric Celtic minds worked? But how could Aedh not be aware that the man he sent here as his envoy fairly blazed with Power?

The envoy who called himself Prince of Cathay. Remembering those cool, slanted, alien green eyes, Osmod felt a shudder half of alarm, half of wonder race through him. Cathay? It was, he supposed, possible. After all, who knew what went on in a land so far away it seemed almost mythical? Maybe Prince Ardagh really *was* from Cathay. Maybe *all* the members of his royal house were magicians. Maybe they'd sent him first to Eriu and now to Wessex because they were plotting to—

To what? Invade? Overwhelm the world? You sound like an overwrought idiot!

Of course there wasn't any dark international plot. He certainly would have sensed any deception so very overwhelming. No, for whatever reason, the prince was just what he claimed: the envoy not of his exotic homeland but of Eriu.

Really? What would a Prince of Cathay be doing so far from home? Unlikely that he was wandering so far by choice; royalty didn't have that option.

And slowly, Osmod began to smile. Well now, wasn't this interesting? The only other option was that the man was, prince or no, an exile, one taking shelter where he could find it. The smile sharpened into a grin.

Exile. How perfect. This meant that the oh-so-mysterious prince of Cathay dared not do anything to upset what could only be an already precarious position.

Reveal an ealdorman's sorceries? Ah no, Prince Ardagh would dare say nothing of the sort!

Of course that means I can't say anything about him, either, not without raising some interesting questions as to how I come to know about sorcery.

Ah well. There were other ways than the most obvious to deal with problems. First he would wait and see what Aedh's ambassador actually wanted of Egbert. Who knew? It just might be something of use to the king—

And to me as well.

Indeed? Then why can't I believe it?

Osmod let out his breath in a long sigh. The runes hadn't been particularly helpful so far, but perhaps this time . . .

He wasn't at all surprised when they told him just what they'd been saying all along: *Possible danger.* One more casting, Osmod thought. For . . . luck.

But this time what he got was an unqualified: *Danger.*

Wearily, Osmod scooped the runes back into their pouch and got to his feet. Lovely choice. Possible danger or outright danger. As though the runes were teasing him. Well, he'd not really been expecting much else.

Dinner should be interesting, to say the least.

Ardagh looked about with sharp curiosity. Well now, if the king's meeting hall had been grand in its gaudy human way, the royal banqueting hall was even more so. It was almost fully twice the size of the first, though with the same arched roof like the upturned hull of a boat. The far end of the hall was mysterious with shadows despite a multitude of candles, and the whole place was certainly twice as splendid as the meeting hall, rich with intricate carvings, bright with gilding, hung round with a glittery rainbow of weavings heavy with gold thread.

Twice as splendid, yes—but twice as smoky, Ardagh reflected, *thanks to that row of central fires. Phaugh, and one could cut the smell with the proverbial knife: men, grease, food and who knows what else.*

No. He was letting Sidhe prejudices overwhelm him. This hall was, when he stopped to analyze it all, no worse than what he knew from Fremainn. In fact, there was a definitely sophisticated aspect, what with the rows of trestle tables covered with nicely bleached linen and gleaming with that elegant Saxon glassware, jars and goblets in various shades of blue or green or glowing gold. No tableware, of course; he hadn't expected any after living at Fremainn.

There was the royal table. No mistaking the canopied chair, as red as Egbert's council chair, set midway down its length. No other chairs; everyone else, it seemed, sat on communal benches that looked comfortably cushioned.

No one was seated yet, but a crowd of nobles milled about, chatting together: he was, judging from the looks he was intercepting, almost certainly the main topic of conversation. Ardagh noted a separate little group of women, and smiled to himself to see their shy—or not so shy—glances his way.

Some things do reach across cultures. Or races.

The blast of a horn cut into his thoughts, evidently the formal call to dinner. Nobles bowed like so many reeds in the wind as King Egbert, splendid in a gold-brocaded tunic so deep a red it was almost purple, entered and took his place. A deferential servant guided Ardagh to a seat beside the king; the prince had expected no less. The rest of his entourage was shown to lesser places, but Cadwal, refusing to be shaken off, grimly took up a position behind him.

"Are you planning to stand guarding my back all night?" Ardagh whispered over one shoulder.

Cadwal's mutter sounded suspiciously like, "Damned right."

He just cannot bring himself to trust these folk!

Not, Ardagh admitted to himself, that he was so trusting, either, not in a strange court in a strange land. Most certainly not since the sorcerer was being seated on his other side.

Not the dining companion I would have chosen.

The king glanced from one to the other, presumably wondering at their sudden edgy tension, and said, "Prince Ardagh, I don't believe I've introduced Ealdorman Osmod to you."

Ardagh exchanged a polite nod with the ealdorman, very much aware that Osmod was as uneasy as he. Egbert, of course, could hardly sense anything on the magical level, but he must have felt at least a trace of the wary hostility between the two, because he gave a grin that might almost have been genuine and added, "Our Osmod is a very valuable fellow, one of my most trusted advisors."

"How . . . pleasant."

That slight, quite deliberate hesitation thinned the too-cheerful grin a bit; Ardagh, glancing sideways, caught a hint of annoyance in Osmod's eyes as well, and smiled demurely.

"Osmod," Egbert continued to the prince, now almost as though in warning, "shall be included in our council meeting tomorrow. I'm sure we will all benefit from his wisdom."

"Wisdom is always welcome. And, alas," Ardagh added, glancing again at Osmod, "is so rarely found."

There was that so very satisfying glint of not-quite anger in the ealdorman's eyes, but Osmod dipped his head as though accepting a compliment. "I shall do my best."

"Which, I'm sure, will be most intriguing." Ardagh added smoothly to Egbert, who was showing clear signs of annoyance himself by this point, "And I agree, tomorrow will be a fine time to discuss why I am here."

While tonight will be a fine time to puzzle out the truth about your sorcerer.

Ah, but enough delicate dueling. Customs here were going to be difficult enough without adding the edge of subtle combat.

There did seem to be some quirks to dining. For one,

Ardagh had hardly expected to find the women segregated from the men, seated at the far ends of the hall, but there it was.

I can hear Sorcha's comments about that!

As for the men, they were clearly placed according to rank: the closer to the king, the higher in status. Not surprising; Aedh practiced something of the same arrangement. Before any food was served, servants came around with basins of water.

"For washing one's hands," Osmod said to the prince with exaggerated kindness, as though speaking to a child—or a barbarian.

But Ardagh didn't deign to reply. *Not subtle enough to score a point in our duel, human, and you know it.* He turned from the table as Egbert had done to let a servant pour water over his outstretched hands, then let another servant cautiously pat them dry with a linen towel. This handwashing custom was sensible enough—assuming that the water was clean.

"Now we say a prayer in thanksgiving," Osmod told him. "Ah . . . your people *do* pray?" It was said as though with nothing but innocent interest, but the intent was obvious.

Egbert, overhearing, tensed slightly, but Ardagh merely smiled. "Ealdorman Osmod, you might not know this," he said, his voice bearing exactly the same amount of seemingly innocent interest, "but the folk of Eriu *are* Christian."

"I never doubted it!" The dismay sounded almost genuine.

Maybe now you'll stop trying to push me into something small and manageable? And do you realize that, perforce, you've dropped the subject of what my *people do?*

That these people should deem it necessary to say a prayer before eating was hardly unusual; so did the folk of Eriu. As he did at Fremainn, Ardagh politely lowered his head and waited till the brief ritual was completed.

As he'd expected, not even Osmod dared to interject one of his veiled insults during it.

So now, here came a touch of the exotic. It was apparently the norm for the queen to serve the first drink of the evening—and for all Ardagh knew, every subsequent drink—to king and guest.

I can hear Sorcha about this, too!

Since Egbert was as yet unwed, the task of cupbearer fell to the highest-ranking noblewoman, a stalwart, strong-faced young woman who apparently was cousin to the king. Ardagh gave her his most charming smile but received only the most remote of smiles in return. In fact, there did seem to be an odd little touch of tension in the hall.

"You may have heard about the lamentable death of my predecessor," Egbert murmured in response to Ardagh's raised brow.

"I was told he was poisoned," the prince said warily. "Possibly by his wife."

"This was how the deed was done. Poison in his drink." A glint of humor in his eyes, Egbert raised his cup to Ardagh but did not drink. Ardagh heard Cadwal's ever-so-soft intake of breath and nearly laughed aloud.

I don't frighten that easily. And Egbert is hardly about to poison a foreign envoy without having heard his message.

With a cool smile at the king, Ardagh took a sip—ale? Yes, and of fine quality. Egbert chuckled, saluted him with raised cup, and drank as well.

Odd. Glancing slyly sideways, Ardagh noted that during this little byplay, Osmod had flinched ever so slightly. Why? Painful memories of having witnessed the king's death? Or could there be something more to it?

Not a trace of anything to be read on the magical level; for all his weak Power, the sorcerer still knew better than to leave a trail of emotions to be found.

Bah, he was probably merely hoping that I choked.

Unlikely that Osmod had the Power to alter the

contents in the prince's food or drink, and the ever-watchful Cadwal would note any physical alterations. But even so, very well aware of how close this potential enemy sat to him, Ardagh kept his magical senses fully alert.

But nothing untoward seemed to be happening, and after a time the prince let himself relax ever so slightly. The food at this court was agreeable enough for human cuisine and, despite the occasional difference in season-ings and cooking styles, not outlandishly unlike that which he usually saw at Aedh's table: course after course of stewed, boiled or roasted pork, beef or poultry and quite a variety of breads. There was also, he noted, more to drink than any sensible man would care to imbibe.

Midway through the meal, a man appeared before the royal table, a rectangular stringed instrument—a lyre of some sort, Ardagh guessed—under his arm.

"A scop," Osmod murmured to the prince in his falsely informative, slyly patronizing way.

"You refer to the man, I assume," Ardagh said with-out expression, "not the instrument. Though of course either may be tightly wound or high-strung. Or out of tune."

That earned him a chuckle from Egbert and a grudg-ing little quirk of a smile from Osmod. "Witty, Your Highness. Quite witty to make such cunning wordplay in what for you is a foreign tongue."

"Oh, I think we both hold a language in common," Ardagh said, looking full into the sorcerer's eyes to make it clear that he referred to the language of magic. Now was the test: If Osmod was innocent of sorcery, he would merely be puzzled.

The human gaze faltered first. No proof there; few humans could hold a determined Sidhe's stare. "Do we?" Osmod murmured, so softly that it would have been impossible for anyone but Ardagh to hear. "We must experiment someday to see if that is, indeed, the case."

"We must, yes."

As casually as though they'd been discussing the weather, Osmod turned back to where the scop was tuning his lyre. "A scop," he continued, as lightly as though there hadn't been an interruption, "is what I think you might call a 'bard' in the tongue of Eriu."

It was. At a signal from Egbert, the scop began a chant in a firm, dramatic voice, using chords from the lyre to underscore the action.

And action there was, even though Ardagh at first was totally lost. Apparently the story was so well known to most of the audience that they didn't mind that what they were hearing was clearly cut from a longer tale. He frowned slightly, determined not to ask Egbert—and certainly not Osmod—trying to puzzle out the meaning from the intricate, alliterative words.

The story seemed to be about a monster of some sort—a demon?—who was terrorizing a king's hall, and doing a properly bloody job of it, until a foreign hero came to fight the creature, tearing the arm from it and killing it.

The scop lowered his lyre. There was the proper moment of respectful silence, then the equally predictable roar of enthusiasm from the audience. To the accompaniment of still more cheering, Egbert rewarded the grinning scop with a ring from his hand (Ardagh cynically supposed the king had previously chosen that ring as one he wouldn't miss), then turned to the prince.

"To forestall your questions, what you've just heard was a portion of the tale of the great hero, Beowulf. What, if I may ask, did you think of it?"

Ardagh paused, wondering if this was an honest question or some devious human test, wondering just how blunt to be. "I have no quarrel at all with the scop," he said after a moment. "He has a fine voice and a grandly expressive style. And while I don't pretend to understand all the poetic wordplay, 'swan's riding' for sea and the like, the language and rhythm of the tale were most beautifully shaped. However . . ."

Egbert lifted a brow. "However?"

"However, King Egbert, if *I* were Hrothgar and a monster was coming every night to eat *my* men, I doubt I'd be doing little but passively waiting for more and more of my men to be killed like so many sheep. I'd be out there setting a trap for Grendel."

The king burst into laughter and raised his cup in ironic salute. "Bravely said! And I imagine you'd catch that demon, too, and leave poor Beowulf with nothing to do."

I would, indeed. But I doubt you'd believe the methods I'd use. Then again, the prince added, glancing sideways once more at the suspicious Osmod, *maybe you would.*

There was the faintest of snorts from Cadwal and the mutter of, "Finn mac Cumhail."

Ah yes. Finn mac Cumhail of Eriu. Ardagh was not about to tell the king of that earlier, similar tale of Finn, the long-ago hero who had saved the king's hall at royal Tara not from a monster but from Aillen, a dark and deadly being out of the Hollow Hills. Cadwal, the prince thought dryly, was not going to allow the *Saesneg* so much as a bit of poetic originality.

So now, still more drink was being brought forward. Apparently these folk—or rather, these men, since the women seemed to have silently retired—found nothing improper about drunkenness. Ardagh had no intention of losing even the slightest edge of his will to ale, but the others seemed to have no qualms about it at all.

Including, much to Ardagh's surprise, Osmod. Granted, the ealdorman wasn't drinking overly heavily; he wasn't such a fool as to risk revealing the secret of his Power. But still, the prince thought, watching as Osmod joked loudly with his king across Ardagh as though the prince didn't even exist, for a wielder of any Power at all to surrender even the smallest bit of his self-control . . .

He's so used to being the only one with Power that he dares be careless. Ha, yes, he is an amateur, isn't he?

No. That, he was not. Osmod's guard slipped for only an instant. But it was long enough to reveal the shape of his sorcery to Ardagh.

Ae, no, Powers, no . . .

This trusted ealdorman, this royal advisor, was more terrible than fictional Grendel could ever be.

This ealdorman was nothing less than a human monster.

The Storm Brews
Chapter 13

Somehow, he couldn't quite remember how, Ardagh had gotten out of the royal hall. Somehow he'd made it back here to his own quarters and banished all the servants with a fierce wave of his hand, leaving only Cadwal at his side.

Cadwal, who was all but blazing with worry and confused anger. "Pardon me if I'm not showing the proper respect, but—what in the name of all the saints was *that* about?"

Of all times for him to drop his self-imposed shyness towards the Sidhe. Ardagh sank to the bed, burying his face in his hands, feeling his dinner as a heavy weight in his stomach. "I had no choice."

"And what does *that* mean? One moment we're all nice and politic, all smiles and charm so thick you could cut it with a blade, the next you're stammering out apologies about being overcome—with what, I haven't the faintest idea—and rushing from the hall. *Iesu,* I thought you'd been poisoned! More to the point, Egbert is probably going to think the same thing."

Ardagh glanced sharply up at that. "I didn't have time to consider it."

"Should have. I had to stop and spin them all a pretty tale of suddenly hitting fatigue; I'm not sure the king believes it."

"Don't lecture me. I appreciate what you've done. But

I repeat: I didn't have a choice. If I'd stayed, I would surely have killed someone."

"What—who—what in—"

"Is it the custom here for a king to keep a sorcerer at his side?"

"What!"

"Is it?"

"No, of course not! This is a Christian kingdom, much as I hate to be admitting anything civilized about the *Saesneg*. No Christian king would stoop to sorcery. Not," Cadwal added darkly, "in public, at any rate. Why do you ask?"

"Because," the prince said slowly, "one of the ealdormen at Egbert's court is undeniably working some very dark form of sorcery, indeed."

Cadwal stared at him, caught openmouthed, closed his mouth, opened it, tried a stammering, "Och. Well. I . . ." Clearly realizing that wasn't going anywhere, the mercenary cut himself off, shaking his head. "I keep forgetting who—what—who you are. You'd know things no one else would. About . . . uh . . . I mean . . ."

"Magic," the prince said flatly. "The word you're hunting so fearfully is 'magic.'"

"Magic, yes." Cadwal rushed that out as though glad to be rid of it, then added hopefully, "You . . . couldn't be mistaken, could you? This once? I mean, this can't be a common sort of thing among humans . . . ?"

Unspoken behind the words was a desperate, *Please God, no*. Cadwal had already had his rational world shaken enough, and Ardagh granted him a curt, "It's not, not at all," and saw a flicker of relief in the man's eyes. "As to being mistaken," the prince continued, "could you be mistaken about the shape of a sword? Or rather, if someone showed you a sword that was fair to see but was made of some base metal, could you be fooled?"

Cadwal let out his breath in a hiss. "No. Of course not. That certain, then."

"That certain."

"*Och fi.*" It was, Ardagh knew by now, the all-purpose Cymric exclamation. "Who . . . uh . . . is he? The sorcerer, I mean."

"Osmod. Ealdorman Osmod."

"The man who was sitting beside you! I thought there was something more than just nasty little 'my land's better than yours' word duels going on between you two. Osmod. A sorcerer. *Iesu.*"

"Your 'Jesus' has nothing to do with this one, I assure you."

Cadwal gave a sharp little bark of a laugh. "True enough. All right, so Egbert's got himself a pet sorcerer." The mercenary stopped short, shaking his head. "Never thought I'd find myself saying something like that. And meaning it. Ah well, he's here, he's real, and I'd guess that the king's got him at court to guard against anyone trying assassination. Ha, or merely trying to cheat him in political deals."

"Perhaps."

"That's got to be it," the mercenary rushed on. "Maybe it's not exactly ethical and all that, but I guess you really can't blame a man who's had such a perilous childhood for wanting to protect himself in any way he can."

"There are no excuses for this."

"Maybe, maybe not." Cadwal brought himself up short again, as though suddenly realizing how he was chattering. "All right. Never mind that. This is all getting so thoroughly weird I admit that given a chance I'd just up and run away like some panicky fool of a boy—but that's my problem, not yours. I'll go out there and be sure that everyone accepts that you weren't poisoned. Got to warn you: You may still get a swarm of royal physicians wanting to study you."

"If they must. They'll find nothing wrong. And thank you."

"Och, well, if you really want to thank me, you'll give me more of an explanation."

"Such as?"

"Look you, the only way I can put this is bluntly, and if you take insult, I'm sorry. But you . . . aren't human, and so I hardly expected human scruples from . . . you."

"From one of the Sidhe, you mean. Saying the name won't damn you." The prince took a deep breath, struggling to calm himself, brushing back his hair with a not quite steady hand. "Go on. Finish what you would say."

Cadwal shrugged. "Not much else *to* say. I just never would have thought you of all people would get so worked up over a human—"

"He's a murderer! Worse than that, he—he—Cadwal, I *felt* this, back in the hall when his guard was weakened a bit by drink, I *felt* it, I *know* it: the man has . . ." Ardagh shook his head, overwhelmed with renewed horror. "The man," he began again, barely able to form the words, "has slain children."

"Ah. That *is* bad. But still—"

"Children," Ardagh repeated, choking. "Precious young lives—don't you understand? He's slain *children* for Power as casually as you might kill a rabbit. Cadwal, I can't do this! I can't deal with these folk, not with—with—ae, my language doesn't even have a word for it!—not with child-killers—"

"Is that what you're going to tell King Aedh?"

The words hit like icy water. Stiffening, the prince snapped, "Clever. Very clever. Go on."

Cadwal couldn't have missed the menace behind the simple words, but he continued steadily, "What *are* you going to tell the king? That you're going to let a whole alliance go to hell because you've gotten finicky?"

Ardagh shot to his feet, so choked with his sudden rush of rage he could barely gasp out, *"Finicky!"*

Cadwal never flinched. "Got a better word for it? Yes, I know you're horrified; never saw you lose control like this. Yes, I have some idea by now of what a child's death means to one of your kind; I've heard the tales."

"Tales! Oh yes, tales told by humans! We're not talking about some soft, pretty human piety, some . . . yes, some *finicky* reluctance to hurt someone who's too small and weak to fight back. Ae-yi, you humans breed so easily you probably can't even see the point. But if you kill children, you not only end their lives without giving them a chance *to* live, *you kill the future!*"

"Didn't mean to insult you, I already said that. And you needn't shout. I saw what happened back when we were fighting off the Lochlannach. I saw you nearly get yourself killed trying to save their chieftain's boy, and I saw the despair in you when he died anyhow." Cadwal sighed. "I'll admit it, humans don't always feel as strongly about youngsters as we might; that's a fault in us, I guess, but that's the way we are. But you did swear something to King Aedh, didn't you? And—"

"And," Ardagh cut in, biting off each word sharply, "an alliance to protect Eriu against those Lochlannach is far more important than Sidhe or human morality."

"I didn't mean it quite that—"

"I repeat: very clever. You know I swore to do my best for Aedh's cause; you know I cannot lie."

Cadwal wisely said nothing, and after a tense moment, Ardagh turned away. "So be it. I will be civilized, never fear. If an alliance can be safely won, I shall win it.

"But I shall not, I cannot, so much as speak to the sorcerer. If such a thing happens, if he forces the issue, I cannot promise to keep the peace."

"Understood. Hopefully you won't need to even give him another nod. And for what it's worth," Cadwal added in so suddenly somber a voice that Ardagh turned back to him in surprise, "I don't blame you. I've seen and done a good many things I'm not proud about. A mercenary can't be delicate-minded. But I've never yet made war on children. Never will."

"I knew that. You would never be standing beside me were it otherwise. But . . . thank you."

"Well, then! Glad that's all settled."

"Unfortunately, it's not. For one thing, we will surely be expected to dine at the royal table again."

"Och. I see the problem. The ealdorman's certainly going to be there, too."

"Exactly. I will not share salt with a child-killer."

What Cadwal thought of Sidhe codes of honor couldn't be told from his face, but all the mercenary said was a casual, "Not a problem, not yet anyhow. I wasn't looking forward to sharing food with the *Saesneg,* either. I'll give out the story that you're too worn out from the journey for any such formalities as another royal dinner."

Ardagh laughed without humor. "That should sound convincing enough after my flight from the hall. As long as they don't think I've brought some exotic illness into the city!"

Cadwal shrugged. "The worst that happens is, as you said, a swarm of royal physicians looks you over and finds nothing wrong. It buys us a day's peace, at any rate. After that, well, I've seen you at work, smooth words and all that. If you can't win over King Egbert within a day—"

But Ardagh held up a thoughtful hand. "I have an uneasy little suspicion that it's not going to be quite so simple."

The mercenary groaned. "Why doesn't that surprise me?"

"Cadwal, do me this favor, if you would. When you go out there to reassure Egbert as to the state of my health, look around a bit. Talk with them. You can wander more freely among the ordinary folk than"—his wave of a hand took in his exotic appearance—"could I."

"Right," Cadwal muttered. "I could. Even if they are *Saesneg.* All right, man—Prince Ardagh, I mean—don't look at me like that. I'll behave myself."

"I'm delighted. Go out there, if you would. See if you can't find out for us just who it was who actually put the king on his throne."

He saw alarm spark in Cadwal's eyes. "You think it's our sorcerer."

The prince nodded. "See if I'm not right."

He waited, wondering if he should contact Sorcha. *Ae, Powers, Sorcha . . . I miss you, my love, I miss you more than I ever would have believed I could miss another.*

But what could he say to her? Tell her about Osmod? In the Sidhe Realm, there wouldn't be a question—but then, in the Sidhe Realm no one would be bothered by the thought of magic. Ae, Powers, what would a human do? Never tell her the whole truth, not if what he'd seen of folk in Fremainn was accurate: They protected their loved ones from needless worries.

Exactly that. She was human; he would try human ways. And at any rate, why should he burden her with new worries? That would be nothing but selfishness.

That made the prince sit back in surprise. Concern about others, worry about others—he *had* come far and far again from his homeland! And just now yet another reminder of that fact was not exactly soothing. Ardagh determinedly set about banishing such thoughts, calming his mind with Sidhe disciplines . . . calming . . . till at last time meant nothing. . . .

He came back to himself with a start at Cadwal's wary cough. Stretching, the prince asked, "Well?"

"First of all, Egbert finally did accept my story and sends his sympathies: you are still to meet with him tomorrow, but are excused from all festivities till you feel rested."

"Good enough. And the second point?"

"Och, well, you were right. There's not a soul not willing to tell the heroic tale of how Ealdorman Osmod braved the terrible winter seas to bring the king safe to his throne, and how the seas most miraculously turned calm."

"Miraculously." Ardagh put a world of sarcasm behind the word. "A hero. Possibly one claiming heavenly aid. And well placed at court."

"Wonderful, isn't it?" Cadwal asked dryly. "Means Egbert's going to trust him, too, or as near to trust as a king's going to come."

"Wait. There's yet another problem."

"*Iesu*. Now what?"

Searching for an easy way to describe a magical concept in an awkwardly unmagical human language, Ardagh asked, "Have you ever seen how the *drualas*, the . . . I think they call it mistletoe here—"

"Yes."

"Have you ever seen how delicately it insinuates itself into the host tree, till it's virtually unremovable?"

"Save by a blade," flatly. "But we can hardly use a blade on an ealdorman." Cadwal paused, eyes widening slightly. "Is that what you think Osmod's done with the king's mind? Woven his sly way into Egbert's will? Is that *possible?*"

There was a hint of panic behind that cry. "In my Realm, yes," Ardagh told him. "In this one, it's just barely less rare than a man taking wing and flying off. You needn't worry that Osmod can seize your mind from you. Besides," the prince added thoughtfully, "even if such things *had* been possible here, I would certainly have sensed any major tampering with the king's will. No. Osmod could never get a firm enough grip to truly affect Egbert's judgment."

"How frustrating for him."

"Ah, but what he can do, even with this Realm's limited Power, is heighten those opinions Egbert may already possess."

"*Damnio*."

"Well put. This means that convincing him of anything he and Osmod don't like is going to be twice as difficult."

"Osmod can sense your . . . uh . . . your magic, too?"

"Definitely."

"Things keep getting better and better. That means he's going to see you as a rival? Maybe even an enemy?"

"Probably. Why, Cadwal," Ardagh added with a sardonic little smile, "don't look so stricken! Think of the challenge!"

The mercenary snorted. "I'd rather think of us safely back in Eriu, if it's all the same to you."

Ardagh, about to give some offhanded quip, sighed. "So would I," he admitted softly. "Believe me, so would I."

Osmod sat amid the storm of confusion that had followed in the foreign envoy's sudden leaving and struggled with his mind and will. Damnation! Why in the name of all the Darkness had he drunk so much? Had he been that stupidly confident of his dominance over the foreign magician? How much could Prince Ardagh have learned from him?

Never mind. What was done, was done. And hopefully no harm to it.

But, damn and damn again, if only he had the time and solitude to use the runes to clear his head—

"Osmod."

The ealdorman glanced up, then shot to his feet. "King Egbert. Ah, how is the foreign envoy?"

Egbert sank into his chair amid the wreckage of dinner, brusquely waving away would-be helpful servants. "Leave us, all of you! *Not* you, Osmod." His fingers steepled, his blue eyes thoughtful, the king said, "Prince Ardagh was, or so his rough-hewn Cymreig bodyguard assures me, merely overcome by fatigue. Do you believe that?"

"It *is* a long journey from Eriu to here. Even with pauses along the way."

Egbert snorted. "In other words, you don't. What were you saying to him, Osmod? What was going on between you two?"

"Why, my liege! Surely you could hear us?"

"Surely you can pretend I could not. What were you discussing?"

Osmod forced an innocent little smile onto his face.

"Nothing outlandish! There really wasn't much at all. Oh yes, I admit, I did play with words a bit, testing his wit a little. He is quite a clever man, King Egbert."

"And I am not a fool. Were you deliberately baiting him?"

How would Egbert want this answered? Osmod hesitated over it only a moment, then said honestly, "Yes."

"Yes!"

"But only as a precaution. A royal envoy, particularly one who actually *is* royal, is going to be so well schooled in smooth, politic words that the truth behind that diplomatic wall will be difficult to learn."

"And so you decided to see if he could be shaken. For the good of the realm, of course."

"My liege, please don't forget that the good fortune of the realm is my good fortune as well."

"Cleverly put. And," Egbert added, holding up a warning hand, "possibly just a little too glib."

"My liege!" Osmod put just the smallest amount of will into the words, stressing, *I am loyal to you, loyal, always loyal.*

Did it work? "I'm not accusing you," Egbert said after a pause that was disconcertingly long. "I know you are loyal to me, always loyal. As long as it suits you. And no, don't argue. I know exactly how much I owe to you. And you must admit I haven't been ungrateful."

"You've been most generous, my liege."

"Stop being so unctuous, Osmod. I'm not angry at you. In fact, I rather approve of what you've done, if not quite when you chose to do it. As for that 'when' . . . tomorrow, see what you can do during our meeting with Eriu's emissary. See if he can, indeed, be shaken."

"It will be," Osmod said with utter sincerity, "a pleasure."

He bowed almost to the floor to hide his smile.

Dreams and Nightmares
Chapter 14

The hour was late, late enough, Ardagh hoped, for most of the humans in the royal enclosure to be asleep.

Cadwal definitely was, lying there on his pallet, hand near sword hilt even in sleep; Ardagh suspected that the mercenary could spring into full wakefulness as quickly as a predator. The prince stepped soundlessly and carefully over the gently snoring man, then paused for an instant, bemused all over again by the phenomenon of snoring: yet another difference between his people and humanity.

I wonder, does Sorcha—

No, no, dangerous subject, Sorcha asleep close enough to him for him to learn—no! Blocking that chain of thought from his mind, the prince slipped carefully down the ladder, avoiding creaking wood as best he could, to the ground floor and past the rest of his slumbering—and yes, he thought with a touch of humor, snoring—entourage out into the night.

Ae, chilly out here.

He stopped to get his bearings, hearing faint sounds of humanity at rest, the occasional quickly stifled laugh or brief snatch of conversation, smelling hints of wood smoke and earth and less pleasant aromas. The royal enclosure was almost totally without light. All cooking fires would be banked by now, but the occasional flicker of a torch indicated a guard on duty. Ardagh glanced up. The moon was the smallest silver sliver up there in a slightly overcast sky, but Sidhe night-vision hardly needed much light.

The quiet was wonderfully welcome. As Cadwal had predicted, that sudden flight from the royal hall had brought about a visit from the royal physicians, a busy, chattering lot, but Ardagh had finally managed to shoo them away. They'd left convinced, as far as he could tell, that the foreign envoy was nothing worse than weary.

Weary of humanity, that's for certain.

But he was not likely to be disturbed again, certainly not at this late hour. The night was his.

The prince turned sharply, suddenly alert. Yes. *There* was the *feel* of sorcery that could only mean Osmod. Ardagh grinned as sharply as a wolf and moved silently out into the night, warily keeping to the darkest corners just in case some guard should decide to patrol. Memories of stalking another sorcerer, the false Bishop Gervinus, stirred, and the prince's grin thinned. He had spent all too many sleepless nights tracking that one, trying to prove to himself as well as to others that Gervinus's wall of piety was a sham, that behind it lurked Darkness.

But Gervinus was dead, sent—if the Christians were right—shrieking to Hell and the devils with which he'd toyed. And Gervinus, after all, had borne not one scrap of innate magic, which had made proving his sorcery so ridiculously difficult since there was no way to sense what wasn't there. Osmod . . . Osmod was another matter. Ardagh wasn't sure exactly what he'd be able to learn without alerting the sorcerer to his presence. But, as the Sidhe saying went, all knowledge was, eventually, useful.

Even if not always in the fashion that one expected.

Osmod sat cross-legged on the floor of his bed-chamber before a clean white cloth, alone in flickering candlelight, the room Warded against eavesdroppers, sat holding a handful of runes and with eyes shut, calming his mind. Or, he corrected wryly, opening his eyes again, *trying* to calm it. None of the disciplines seemed to be working tonight; no matter what he did, his thoughts insisted on returning to the foreign envoy, to Prince Ardagh of the eerie eyes and quick wit. And the alarming sense of Power.

With a sudden convulsive jerk of his hand, Osmod let the runes fall, then snatched up a rune at random, hunting an omen.

Oh, an omen, indeed. By the flickering light, he saw that what he held was Thorn, the most perilous rune of the lot. Osmod closed his hand about it, wondering. There was great Power in this sigil, battle-Power to strike down an enemy. But it, being a singularly treacherous thing, could just as easily strike down the wielder as well.

Still, he thought with a little stab of anger, it might be worth the risk—

Bah, nonsense. Why should I endanger myself over that . . . foreigner? There are safer ways to destroy him if it comes to that.

And why bother destroying him at all? Why feel this burning need to do so? Osmod frowned, puzzled at himself, then gathered up the runes. Enough of this nonsense. He'd try a formal divination, as formal as could be worked indoors, and see what he could learn—or at least what the tricky runes would deign to tell him— about the prince. Maybe that, Osmod thought with a touch of wry self-humor, would set his mind at ease.

Maybe.

And then again, maybe not. The runes specifically dealing with Prince Ardagh were telling him plainly Eoh, Yew, meaning that the prince was amazingly strong and long of life.

Not exactly what I wanted to see.

Ac and Asc, Oak and Ash, honor and perserverance. Yew, Oak and Ash—bah. Yes, and the prince's past was, at least as far as the runes were insisting, full of an eerie, exotic strangeness— Osmod hissed in disgust. This wasn't the reading for a human, it was something more suited to one of the elf-folk out of the old pagan days!

No. No more of this foolishness. All it probably meant was simply that Prince Ardagh, being from far Cathay, was just too strange for the runes to read with any accuracy.

Egbert, now . . . ah, there was another matter. Osmod settled himself amid the scattered runes, hunting the ones he sought, turning them as he wished them, Rad, yes, upright and Oss, inverted . . . self-control and dominance brought together. Ah yes, this was far more practical than wasting time and emotion trying to read that foreigner.

With the most delicate care, Osmod tied the two runesticks round with a small strand of stolen golden hair, Egbert's hair, in a symbolic binding—the part representing the whole—and willed, *I, the ruler, he the vassal, I the master, he the slave,* just as he'd been doing every night for what seemed an eternity. It was agonizingly slow work, reminding him of the old tale of the sparrow wearing away the stone by each day dropping one drop of water on it. But it was working, surely it was. Egbert's will was far, far stronger than ever that of the late Beortric had been, but even he could not resist magic's force forever. And lately there had been definite signs of his softening to Osmod's wishes, signs that had to be more than merely a king agreeing with a reasonably trusted subject who—

Osmod straightened with a startled hiss, clutching the runes convulsively. What—who—someone had been spying on him!

Impossible! The room is Warded!

He scrambled to his feet, hunting witnesses. . . .

No one. The Wards still held. The servants were all asleep downstairs, and it was impossible for anyone else to have stolen in here.

No one? With a curse, Osmod rushed to the chamber's one window, cast open the shutters.

There in the night, barely visible, stood a tall figure, green eyes glowing in the darkness like those of some uncanny cat.

"Prince Ardagh," Osmod heard himself hiss.

As though he'd heard, the prince turned smoothly and vanished into the night.

What has he seen?

No, ridiculous. No one could see into a shuttered room, not even with the one candle casting its little glow, no one . . . human.

"Oh, you idiot!" Osmod snarled at himself. Of course the prince was human; no matter what the runes had hinted, what else could he be? And there was no possible way for a man, even one with those uncanny eyes, to have seen anything.

But the worry continued unabated: *What does he know? What, oh, what does he plan to do?*

"And what," Osmod wondered aloud, "shall I do to block him?"

What, Ardagh wondered, had Osmod been about? Some manner of magic, no doubt about that. He'd sensed Power being used—but what type of magic had it been?

Nothing I've ever felt before, that much is clear.

Not very comforting. It was nigh impossible to fight a magic without knowing its shape and name.

Ah well, with any chance at all it wouldn't come to a fight. Much as he'd love to see the child-killer sent shrieking to whatever Place of Punishment received Saxon Christian murderers, Cadwal had been right: an alliance against the Lochlannach was more important than individual justice just now.

At least whatever spell Osmod was casting wasn't either very Powerful or particularly successful.

And for now, Ardagh told himself, since he could hardly go back there now that Osmod was aware of him, that was all the comfort he could take from this night's work.

His entourage, as the prince picked his delicate way through them, were all still peacefully asleep.

Not so Cadwal. He moaned and muttered in his sleep, plainly caught fast in the throes of nightmare. Ardagh heard him murmur "Gwen," the name of the man's dead love, and wondered in sudden alarm if this really was only a dream.

Ae, no, not this, not here. I thought he was free of this.

Hastily kneeling at Cadwal's side, he hunted with Sidhe alertness for magic, wondering if Osmod could have something to do with—no, not Osmod. Something . . . he almost *felt* it, something vague there at the very limit of his senses . . . magic? Or . . . could it, Ardagh wondered uneasily, possibly be the wavering edge of human sanity? He still knew so little about human minds—

In sudden frustration and renewed alarm, the prince snapped, "Cadwal, wake! *Cadwal!*"

The mercenary sat bolt upright, hand snapping shut on Ardagh's arm with a warrior's powerful grip. The prince's first reaction was pure Sidhe outrage that a human should dare—

But this human could hardly realize what he was doing. Even though Cadwal's eyes were open, he was still very much asleep.

Yes, and clinging to me as though his sleeping life depends on crushing my arm to the bone. At least he didn't draw his sword on me!

Putting more than a little Sidhe will behind the words, Ardagh commanded, "Leave that realm. You are alive, awake. You are awake. Awake!"

To his relief, he saw life flood back into the blank eyes. Cadwal stared at the prince for an uncomprehending moment, then suddenly shuddered, releasing his grip, sagging with despair.

"The dream, then," Ardagh murmured, resisting the urge to rub his arm.

"The dream. Och now, what are you doing?"

"Be still. You know I'm not going to hurt you." *Even if you've left finger-shaped bruises on my arm.*

Cadwal froze, determinedly rigid as Ardagh stared into his face, into his eyes, into as much of his essence as was possible in this Realm, hunting for any sign at all of intrusive magic. At last the prince sat back on his heels with an angry little sigh.

"Well?" the mercenary asked warily. "Find what you were hunting?"

"No, curse this human Realm for its resistance. Or maybe yes. I can't be sure."

Once again there had been, just for the quickest of instants, that faintest, most tantalizing trace of *something*, like a fading wisp of mist, but when he'd tried to pursue it—nothing. It wasn't Osmod's doing, that was all Ardagh knew with certainty. Ae, and now that he had time to consider it, he wasn't even sure that anything odd had ever been there at all!

"I'm sorry, Cadwal," the prince said and, seeing the trouble shadowing the mercenary's eyes, truly meant it. "I can't tell you anything useful. The alien magic—or *non*magic—of this Realm is confusing my own."

"Now that's truly comforting." Cadwal wiped a hand over his face. "Can you at least tell me this much: *Was* it my Gwen?"

"Ae, Cadwal. I wish I could—or could not."

The mercenary shuddered again. "I thought I was free of the dream. That it wasn't anything other than . . . well . . . longing. *Hiraeth.*" That meant, Ardagh knew, that bittersweet ache for something that could never be again; in the days since his exile, he'd come to know that word all too well. "I mean," Cadwal continued, "I've heard of men having recurring dreams, and nothing supernatural about it."

"You *are* in a land full of your people's ancient foe," Ardagh reminded him, fighting his frustrated rage at being reduced to platitudes, "as you've told me often enough."

"Yes, yes, and having to be polite to them, too. That's certainly strain enough to trouble anyone's sleep, but—

"If only the damned thing wasn't so *real*." Cadwal rubbed his hand across his face again, then glanced wryly at the prince. "This would be a good time for some mead, wouldn't it?"

"The way it was that lonely night when we drank together? It would, indeed!" Ardagh got to his feet, stretching cramped muscles. "But I doubt these folk would appreciate our raiding their larder, particularly not at this hour."

That forced a little bark of a laugh from Cadwal. "Now there's an image! A Sidhe prince and a Cymro mercenary caught in the act of robbing the King of Wessex."

"Ridiculous, yes. This whole journey is ridiculous. Here, now, this should help for the moment." Reaching out a hand, Ardagh murmured a tranquil incantation. The words didn't take much concentration, Powers be praised, and while they wouldn't mean anything to Cadwal, hopefully the circle of calm would include him.

Yes. Ardagh saw some of the trouble leave the human's eyes. "I don't know what you did," Cadwal said, "but— thank you."

"Mm. Right now there's nothing else to be done but try to settle down for what's left of the night."

Cadwal snorted. "*I'm* not going back to sleep."

"Good." All at once very weary, Ardagh unpinned his *brat*, letting the length of wool unfold itself from about him, then threw himself down on the bed, glad of its softness, not bothering to undress any further. "Then *you* can stand guard."

"Anything in particular I'm guarding against?" the mercenary asked with something of his usual self-control.

"The Powers know. I don't."

"Didn't learn anything useful out there, then?"

Ardagh, just at the point of relaxing, sat up again in surprise. "You know I went outside? I thought you were asleep."

"I was. But I'd never have reached this age, being what I am, I mean, if I slept heavily."

Except when the dream has you in thrall. "Cadwal, I do tend to underestimate you. And no, I didn't learn anything other than what I already suspected: Osmod is, indeed, working magic, but his Saxon magic is not anything like that of the Sidhe."

"Not a good thing, I take it?"

"Neither good nor bad in itself. You need to know the—the shape of a magic before you can counter it." A yawn slipped in before he could stop it. "Right now, since Osmod knows no more about my Sidhe magic than I do about his Saxon spells, neither of us can use Power against the other."

"Ah."

"At least I've unnerved him a little. Which may or may not prove useful. Hopefully, it will keep magic out of my negotiations with Egbert. Though somehow I doubt it." He yawned again, and let himself fall back on the bed. "Ae, enough. At least you had a chance to get some sleep. I haven't been there yet." Closing his eyes, Ardagh added, "A lack I plan to remedy right now. Tomorrow—no, by now it's probably today, is going to be quite . . . interesting."

"And why," he heard Cadwal mutter, "doesn't that surprise me?"

Diplomacy
Chapter 15

The hour, Ardagh mused, blinking in the sunlight just creeping over the edge of the royal palisade, was still disgustingly early. Egbert seemed to share that concept with Aedh: Keep the rest of the world off balance by acting before everyone but he was quite awake.

Sure enough, there Egbert sat in his great audience hall, his tall, well-built figure brilliant in scarlet and gold, his hair gleaming like a heavenly halo in an early ray of sunlight filtering in through a smokehole (a deliberate positioning of the royal chair to get that effect, the prince thought cynically), and looking as coolly alert as an experienced warrior. Which, in a way, of course, a king was.

A successful king, at any rate. Which is to say a still living one.

As Ardagh had expected, Osmod was there at the king's side, definitely not as awake as Egbert (the result, no doubt, of too much late-night spellworking) but looking even now so charmingly urbane and downright likeable, Ardagh thought, that one could almost forget what he truly was.

Hah.

Not exactly to the prince's surprise, only a few members of the royal council, the Witan, occupied the rows of padded benches: These would be the most important—and the most trustworthy—of the nobles. News spread quickly enough in a royal court as it was; in

Egbert's place, Ardagh knew he would have wanted at least a brief respite before the envoy's message became common knowledge.

Egbert met Ardagh's gaze as though just noticing his arrival and dipped his head to the prince with a nicely calculated smile, not too thin, not too warm. The regal blue eyes remained coolly speculative, however, as the king bade him enter with a gracious wave of a hand.

No more of this casual 'Enter, servant,' eh? Learned our lesson about that, have we?

Two servants scurried forward with a cushioned chair, which they placed facing Egbert's own. Ardagh stalked forward and sank to it with full Sidhe grace, wishing again for a spidersilk cloak to fall into elegant folds about him; the stiffer woolen *brat* just didn't allow the same grand gesture.

"God give you a good morning, Prince Ardagh."

"And to you, King Egbert."

"You are quite recovered from your sudden fatigue?"

Ardagh smiled. "I doubt I'll need to make so dramatic a rush from your hall again."

They went on for a time saying nothing much, playing the political game of polite, meaningless pleasantries that seemed to be the same, Ardagh thought, in every court, human or Sidhe. He waited with inhuman patience; sooner or later, it would be the human, not he, who surrendered.

Sure enough: "And how fares my brother king of Eriu?" King Egbert said without warning.

Ah, at last. "Quite well. He sends you, as I'm sure you know, the warmest of greetings." *He sent them to the king of Wessex, at any rate. Whoever that turned out to be.*

"As do I to him." The king paused. "It's rare to hear any word at all out of Eriu. How are matters there these days?"

"Quite prosperous," Ardagh said pleasantly. "King Aedh is a wise ruler, strong in arms, strong in his people's welfare. And Eriu thrives under his rule." *All of which is true. Hyperbole aside.*

"A rich land, I hear, fertile and green."

"Frequently." *When sorcerous storms don't destroy it.* "Of course . . ." the prince added, almost casually, "there are the occasional nuisances. Any rich land is certain to have thieves hungering after it."

"Thieves?" Egbert asked, so very carefully without expression that it sounded an alarm trumpet in Ardagh's mind.

So-o! Are we that ambitious, oh King of Wessex? "Why, King Egbert," Ardagh purred, "surely you couldn't have thought I referred to *you* when I mentioned thieves. I would never be so insulting!" *Not in so crass a fashion, at any rate.* "No, no, of course I was speaking of others."

He saw by the faintest of starts on the parts both of Egbert and Osmod that this last little not-quite insult had struck home. *Ambitious, indeed, the two of you.* And that raised an intriguing new question. *I wonder, King Egbert, just how much power is behind you.* He hardly meant Osmod. *Are you secure enough on your throne to be backed by nobility and military in any potential . . . expansions?*

That was something he really needed to learn before he could strike any alliances. But right now he could hardly not deliver *some* message from Aedh. "Surely," Ardagh continued smoothly, hiding with every bit of Sidhe charm the fact that he was now feeling his way along, "you have heard of the Lochlannach?"

"Not by that name—" Egbert began, but stopped as Osmod whispered in his ear. "Ah. The Northmen from the Land of Robbers. What of them?"

"Perhaps you've had no personal experience with them." *Yet.* "But of course you know of the Lochlannach raid here in Wessex during the . . . ah . . . late king's reign."

Something flickered in Egbert's eyes: Annoyance?

Impatience? "That was nothing more than a brief attempt at plunder. It came to nothing."

"Really? I had heard that a Saxon reeve lost his life in the encounter."

Again he saw that odd little warning flicker in Egbert's eyes. "He made a mistake. And paid for it. And you most certainly did not come all the way from Eriu to tell me what I already know."

How much of this is you, Egbert, I wonder, and how much Osmod's prodding? "Oh, I would not waste my time and yours. But I wonder if you also know that there have been other unwanted visits from, as you so nicely put it, the Land of Robbers, both in Eriu and on Charlemagne's own coast."

"My sympathies to the rulers, but again, those are matters that hardly affect this land."

In other words, Ardagh thought, *if those lands are weakened, so much the better for me.* "Your land has a coastline. And yes, forgive me for reminding you of what you already know. But I saw how nicely your prosperous town of Hamwic lies there on the sea's edge, openly waiting for visitors. How, if I may ask, could it be defended with no walls at all?"

"There are far closer landfalls for the sea thieves than Hamwic."

"Granted. But I've seen their ships, beautiful and swift in the water as so many dragons. And I don't have to tell you how quickly information flies. Nothing as minor as mere distance is going to stop them should the Northmen choose Hamwic as a target."

"Prince Ardagh, exactly what are you trying to say?"

"Perhaps," Osmod murmured, "that he knows a little too much about these thieves."

"Perhaps," Ardagh returned, just as gently, "because I have fought them at King Aedh's side."

That caused quite a stir among the nobles. Egbert held up a hand for silence, one golden brow raised. "I've yet to hear of anyone battling the Northmen."

"It can be done. And yes," the prince continued before anyone could speak, "the battle can be won. Without," he added as a sly stab at Osmod, "magic."

And thank you, Osmod. You've given me a nice chance to put in a casual word of warning about Aedh's military might.

Egbert frowned slightly. "If Aedh can fight off the Northmen so easily, why come to me? Surely this is more than a social visit and warning."

"Your pardon, King Egbert, but I hardly said the battle was an easy one. We won, yes, but what we held off were only two ships. There are certainly going to be larger forces sailing from those harsh northern lands."

"We can't know that."

"Can't we?" Osmod wondered. As Egbert glanced at him, the ealdorman said, "I may be doing our guest a grave injustice, and if so I crave his pardon, but . . . Prince Ardagh, you are very much a foreigner, as foreign to Eriu as you are to these lands. We've already had evidence of your clever wit."

"What are you saying?" Ardagh asked, very softly.

"We have only your word that you are who you claim. Oh, I'm not saying you have not come as King Aedh's envoy. And I don't doubt that the High King of Eriu is a shrewd and clever man indeed. But even the shrewdest of men can be tricked by—"

"What's this, ealdorman? Do you think me in league with the Lochlannach? Do you call me a liar, ealdorman?"

It was said with such quiet menace that Ardagh saw Osmod flinch. "No, of course not! But how would you know whether or not there will be larger raids—or even if there will be raids at all?"

The human's eyes were guileless, his face open and innocent. *Oh, nicely acted!* Ardagh thought, but could not say. "There will be more raids, King Egbert, because simple common sense dictates it. Look you, if you were a land-poor warrior with a swift ship to your name and

heard of rich loot to be taken with minimal fighting—
and as you, yourself, have said, no one, save King Aedh,
has battled the Lochlannach—what would you do?"

Egbert smiled thinly. "Point taken. But why should you
think there will ever be more than the occasional . . .
nuisance?"

"Ae, King Egbert, think." His voice slid into smooth
Sidhe charm, his will put smooth Sidhe persuasion
behind the words. And not a man so much as stirred
as he continued, "The lands to the north are harsh and
chill, the winters long and dark and empty of sun. The
ground is rough and rocky, the harvests few." *See those
lands,* he told them under the words, *see their cold bitterness.* "The Lochlannach sail out from that desolation,
sail south to these fertile, warmer lands. Do you think
they have no eyes, oh king? Do you think they have no
memories?

"The Lochlannach see these lands, these warm, lovely,
green lands." *As do you, see them with a Northman's
wonder.* "Returning to their cold northern wastes, they
remember. They hunger. And they envy.

"And so it is, oh king, so it is that someday they will
return with an eye not just for loot. Ah no, they will
return in wave after invading wave to make the warm,
green lands their own. To stay. To rule."

"Now, easy to say, 'That's another land's problem.' But
how can you be sure it will be another land they pick?
Ah, but now picture this:

"See the Lochlannach sailing south, sure of their luck.
Their guard is down, their minds are easy. After all, have
they not been looting these lands without the slightest
bit of trouble? Such shock, such horror to find the warm
green lands barred to them, to find not one but many
kings confronting them! Let it be so, oh king. Let the
land-thieves find no safe harbor, no easy landfall. Let
them leave enough of their dead in the south to abandon all hope of ever ruling here. Let them flee forever!"

There was a long silence when he had finished—a

silence all at once broken by the sound of one man's ironic applause. The nobles came back to themselves with a collective start, stirring and murmuring restlessly. Ardagh, ignoring them, turned to meet a cold blue stare. Osmod. Of course. He would have had just enough Power not to be held so easily.

"Well spoken, Prince Ardagh," the ealdorman drawled, "well spoken indeed."

And you don't believe a word of it. More, you're going to try insuring that Egbert doesn't, either. Not if I have any say about it, sorcerer! "King Egbert—"

But: "We will think on this," Egbert said, scrambling to his feet with the air of a man waking from a dream, causing a storm of activity among the nobles, who'd been caught off guard by his sudden move, and effectively declaring the meeting at an end.

Yes, we shall, Ardagh told him silently, watching the king leave. *We shall, indeed.*

Now what, Osmod wondered, following his king, had that been about? Oh, the prince had just given a beautiful performance, no doubt about that; with that elegant voice and delivery, Prince Ardagh had almost had *him* believing. But what had been behind it? Just how ambitious was this foreign prince and, for that matter, the High King of Eriu behind him?

"Well?" That was King Egbert, turning suddenly on him. "Come, walk with me. Alone. What did you make of all that?"

Osmod feigned a cheerful smile. "The prince would make a wonderful scop."

"Indeed. He had me fairly held in that web of words he spun. But what about their message?"

What, indeed? "Oh, a pretty tale, my liege," Osmod hazarded, "well calculated to make us believe that the danger is real."

Egbert looked sideways at him. "You don't believe it, then."

"Ah well, it *is* a bit difficult to accept that thieves could band together like something out of a scop's song, let alone that they could actually gather in such great numbers as to form a unified army."

The royal glance was skeptical. "Stranger things have happened, Osmod. Such as a queen murdering her husband. Such as a man returning from sixteen years of exile to successfully claim a throne. Do you really think it so very impossible that the Northmen could ever become a threat?"

Osmod sighed. "I won't say yea or nay to that; no *Christian* can hope to see truly into the minds and hearts of pagan thieves."

Egbert's narrow smile showed he'd caught the emphasis on *Christian*. "Implying that our foreign prince is not of the Church? That, I should think, is more a matter for Bishop Cynbert—assuming he returns from Rome in time to meet Prince Ardagh—than either of us."

"Ah well, true enough. And yet . . ."

Egbert stopped short. "You seem very sure the prince is in league with the Northmen, Osmod. Have you any proof?"

"Not a word, alas. Nothing but my instincts. Which," the ealdorman added steadily, "have yet to play us false."

"Instincts."

"They brought me to Aachen, my liege."

"And of course ambition had nothing to do with it. No, don't answer that; we've been over that ground often enough since you brought me back to Wessex. I'm not challenging you, Osmod. On the contrary, I must admit that I'm more than a little uneasy about our visitor myself."

You should be; I've been willing it into your brain strongly enough! But Osmod waited silently until Egbert said suddenly, "I'm not about to send him rudely away, if that's what's bothering you. We've had almost no dealings with Eriu, but I don't need sudden discord with King Aedh. However, I'm not about to rush into an alliance with a stranger, either. At least," he added, "I *assume* that's what our smooth-tongued visitor was implying. An alliance with a foreign land, an unknown land, against the Northmen." Egbert shook his head. "It seemed so likely, so logical while Prince Ardagh had us snared in that pretty web. Now . . . *are* the Northmen a threat? I don't have time for that to be," the king continued dryly. "There are too many other matters to attend."

"Matters closer to home."

"Exactly."

Osmod took a deep breath, organizing his words with care. "My liege, we both know that the sea thieves have never raided in any number larger than two ship-worths of men. Yes, it's true that they are said to raid efficiently—but to be quite blunt, how much efficiency can it take to sack an undefended, isolated monastery?" He saw Egbert brusquely cross himself at that, and hastily followed suit, continuing, "The Northmen are barbarians, and I say that not as an easy insult but as fact. Barbarians fight among themselves, loyal to one petty chieftain, one clan. There's never been the slightest sign that such as they can ever cooperate, long enough to form an army, let alone an invasion force."

"Nicely spoken. Logical, in fact."

But doubt lingered in Egbert's eyes. He didn't really *want* to believe in a Northern threat, Osmod knew; he didn't want anything to distract him from his plans for expansion.

Our plans, Osmod corrected silently, and said, as casually as he could, "You need not be concerned, King Egbert. There are ways, I need not tell you, of quietly being rid of the prince without any shadow being cast on—"

"No," Egbert snapped. "I am not finished with this matter."

Damnation! Osmod felt his hand clench as though he still held the runesticks Raido and Oss, and began a hurried, "But is it wise—"

"I will speak with him again, Osmod, even as I told him. Later."

In his voice was the tension of a man who could not be pushed any further. Half the point of diplomacy, Osmod thought, was knowing when to yield. The essence of resignation, the ealdorman bowed, putting into it all a courtier's practiced grace. "As you will it, my liege."

He straightened to see the king already halfway to the royal stables, but made no move to follow.

Ah well. This wasn't exactly a loss. "Later," after all, gave one a good many opportunities to deal with "now."

"That," Cadwal murmured as he fell in beside the prince as they left the royal hall, "was beautiful. You actually had *me* believing it."

Ardagh glared at him. "Did you think I was lying?"

"Och, no, of course not, I know better than that. What I meant was just that . . ." Cadwal shook his head. "Well now, I'll believe every tale I hear about Sidhe word-magics after this."

"Bah. That was a farce, nothing more. I should have been able to woo and win the king to us with just a few words. Instead . . . you saw what happened."

"The sorcerer, you mean?"

"Exactly. My words had no hold over him at all." Ardagh strode on, fuming. "That, I should have expected. But the king's reaction—" He stopped so sharply that Cadwal had to swerve like a cat to keep from colliding with him, and turned to glare at the human. "It would have been natural enough for Egbert to feel some uneasiness about an alliance being so suddenly proposed. But you saw what happened, Cadwal: instead of debating the matter, he fled from the very thought of such a concept."

"Hey now, don't glower at me like that! It's not my fault."

"No. Of course not." The prince turned away impatiently, striding forward again, Cadwal in his wake.

"That's what you meant last night," the mercenary said, "what happened just now, about the influence the sorcerer has on his mind."

"Yes. Osmod doesn't have enough control to rule Egbert's thoughts, but he *can* heighten the king's emotions just enough to interfere and sharpen his opinions just enough to make our stay here more difficult."

He heard Cadwal mutter something brusque in his native tongue. "Now isn't that wonderful?" the mercenary asked. "Every time you propose something Osmod and he both don't quite like, the king's going to up and run."

Ardagh chuckled in spite of himself at the image of tall, handsome Egbert, bright red tunic, gold ornaments and all, scurrying off like a frightened hare. "I assure you, things aren't quite as bad as that. And if it ever does come to a battle of magical wills between Osmod and myself, let me assure you that mine is . . . ah . . . not exactly weak."

He caught a sly glint of humor in Cadwal's eyes. "More tactful, that, than saying outright 'stronger than any mere human's.'"

"Ah." The prince stopped again, this time not quite as sharply. "The whole of it right now is that I actually wasn't trying to snare Egbert. Not yet."

"Could have fooled me."

"Ae, Cadwal, you've never experienced the full force of Sidhe persuasion! But, no, before I do anything as drastic as binding Eriu and King Aedh to anything, there's some missing information to be gathered."

"Such as?"

"Such as Egbert's true feelings about conquest versus alliance. You don't see what I mean? Yes, of course he's ambitious—but there's more to a man than one emotion! I couldn't accurately read him, not in the tangle of emotions from everyone else in the hall."

"In other words, if you want to figure out what makes

Egbert work, you're going to have to get the king alone. How do you figure to do *that?*"

Ardagh shrugged. "Right now, I have no idea. But there's something else we need to learn: namely, how far the Witan would be willing to support royal ambitions."

"Mm. Military support, you mean."

"Clever man."

"Hell, military's my profession. And you think Egbert's too new on the throne for them to fully trust him."

"Indeed. And before you ask, no, Osmod almost certainly doesn't have the Power to control them as well." Ardagh paused. "You were the best choice to deal with the common folk. This time," he added with a sharp little grin, "the mission is mine."

The mercenary made a nice little parody of a courtly bow. "With my blessings, Prince Ardagh." He straightened suddenly. "What about Osmod?"

"What about him? He won't attack us. He can't."

"Not by day, maybe. But what about during the night? Magic's stronger then, isn't it?"

Ardagh paused, considering how best to word what he wanted to say in human terms. "In a way," he said finally. "In this human Realm, at any rate. There are fewer minds awake to serve as distractions." In the Sidhe Realm, where everyone could see as clearly by night as by day, folk woke or slept whenever the fancy took them.

"Distractions," Cadwal said. "Tell you what: I'll stay awake—"

"You won't. Humans, I've learned, need their sleep more than do my kind, and neither of us can afford having you weakened from lack of rest. I'll set Wards tonight, just to be on the wary side." Ardagh paused, studying the human, then added quietly, "You need not look so alarmed. I mean to ensure a dreamless sleep for you."

Cadwal's face was far too well schooled to betray emotion. But relief was very plain in his eyes. "For that,

Prince Ardagh," he began formally, "and for the help you gave me last night—"

"Hush. I did what I could. Frustratingly, it wasn't very much."

"It helped. It did help. And now—"

"And now," Ardagh said, "enough talk. When we are finished with this whole ridiculous mission, we shall see about learning the truth behind your dream. And no," he added sharply, "before you say something foolish, I am not showing your human 'pity' or sentimentality; I don't truly understand those emotions. I simply do not like leaving a magical puzzle unsolved—and I do not wish to see someone who has aided me be harmed."

"Ah. Right. Well, whatever, I do thank you."

"Good. Now, go and do . . . whatever. I have work to do."

Walking the Night
Chapter 16

Ardagh straightened sharply, there in his night-darkened bedchamber. Now, what . . . ? Had that been a sound? He glanced about the room yet again, then shook his head at his folly.

This was getting ridiculous. Osmod could not possibly be spying on him, any more than he in turn had been able to read Osmod's magics the night before. And of course no one was physically up here besides himself but Cadwal, and Cadwal was snoring peacefully, his bizarre dream blocked by the Sidhe spell for sweet slumber; the charm's slight Power had been strengthened, or so the prince hoped, by its having been spoken this time by a Sidhe.

But . . . there *was* something. It wasn't his fancy. Not in the room, not even too close to the hall, but . . . something.

"Ardagh?" That was the faint, distant sound of Sorcha's voice. "What is it? What's wrong?"

Ae, he'd almost forgotten about the amulet! The prince looked quickly down at it. "I'm not sure, love. I *think* that someone's watching. I also think that I'd best go out there and do a bit of investigating."

"Be careful!"

"Sorcha-my-heart, it's night. There's nothing out there but humans. I can *see*; they can't."

"And you, my love," she said, "are being most infuriatingly overconfident. Humor me. Be careful."

He chuckled. "Don't worry."

"Hah."

"I'll be as careful as possible. And I'll do my best to return shortly."

"Again, hah."

"Till later, love."

Ardagh carefully put the amulet away. As he'd expected, Cadwal, who'd already proven himself a light sleeper, stirred as the prince passed him. "Wrong?" the human muttered groggily, but there was nothing groggy about the way his hand snapped shut about the hilt of his sword.

"Nothing's wrong," Ardagh said hastily. "Go back to sleep, Cadwal."

He put just the barest touch of will behind the words. With a grunt, the mercenary turned over on his pallet and, after a moment, resumed snoring. Ardagh nodded and moved silently out into the night.

Ah, yes: Osmod. Of course, Osmod. There he was, standing in deep shadow, invisible to human eyes but quite clearly revealed to Sidhe sight. More than simple sight: Ardagh's Sidhe senses also showed him the faintest glimmer of Power surrounding the human.

Well now, look at this. He's used magic to give himself night-vision. Clever of him.

Stealing up on a man who could see him and, for that matter, probably sense his approach through Power was no easy thing. Ardagh held back a grin—teeth tended to glint revealingly in the darkness—and slid forward, careful as predator or prey, delighted at a challenge such as he hadn't faced since the Sidhe Realm.

But, rather to his disappointment, it didn't turn out to be a true challenge. A Sidhe would always be more at home in the night than any human could ever be, and Osmod's Power was a very finite thing. "Good evening, my lord ealdorman," Ardagh purred from just behind him, and had the satisfaction of seeing the human start badly and just barely bite back a yelp.

Osmod, though, recovered disconcertingly quickly. "Prince Ardagh. You couldn't sleep, either, I see."

"Oh, the night's so fine and fair it seems a shame to waste it in sleep." *True enough. And I'd rather be spending it talking with my dear Sorcha. But sometimes one takes what one is given.*

"King Egbert and I missed seeing you at dinner."

"My people," Ardagh said blandly, "have many rituals." He had long since learned that humans tended to accept the most amazing nonsense if it was said with enough authority, filling in the gaps in logic themselves.

"Rituals that interfere with such mundane matters as dining," Osmod said with mock sympathy. "Such a nuisance."

"One is as one is." *There's another nice, vague statement!* "And the king was gracious enough to have food sent to me." *Which, of course, I tested for suspicious additions.* "Come, my lord. Will you not walk with me?" *I'd rather cut you down for the child-killer you are, but again, sometimes one takes what one is given.*

Osmod's sideways glance told Ardagh *he* would rather see the prince in the humans' Hell, but the ealdorman smiled—that betraying white glint of teeth in the darkness—and said, "If it pleases you."

It doesn't. Being near *you doesn't please me.* "After you, my lord. You know these ways better than I."

They strolled together for a time within the royal enclosure, startling the occasional guard. Osmod pointed out this landmark and that; Ardagh said little but thought a great deal. None of it friendly.

Civilized, he reminded himself. *We must be civilized.* "My lord Osmod," the prince said suddenly. "Shall we be blunt with each other?"

"Shall we? About what?"

"You seem to have taken a strong dislike to me. Might I ask why?"

Osmod stopped, eyes widening in very nicely feigned astonishment. "Prince Ardagh, you misunderstand me!

It's not my place to like or dislike. And surely you've given neither my king nor me any reason for hostility."

Oh, smoothly turned! "My lord Osmod, we both know each of us bears a secret we would not wish others to learn. Ah, and don't give me that pretty start of surprise; you know perfectly well what I mean."

"Do I?" The human's eyes glinted coldly.

"And let me state this here and now," Ardagh continued quietly. "Were we other than we are, yes, you would indeed be my enemy. Possibly even to the death. I do not *like* those who harm children."

"Prince Ardagh! How could you—"

"*However,*" the prince continued over Osmod's indignant protestation. "However, I am not here as some wild-eyed avenger, but, even as I've said, as an emissary from the High King of Eriu. How I feel about you, my lord, or how you feel about me really has no part in that."

"You offer me wild insults, you make bizarre accusations—Come now, Prince Ardagh! Do you really think I would ever do anything that might endanger the realm?"

In a moment, if you thought it would be to your advantage. "King Egbert trusts you," Ardagh said. "I would not question his judgment. I ask only this, my lord: Let me finish my mission in peace and depart the same way."

"What," Osmod asked flatly, "makes you believe I would do anything else?"

Ardagh sighed. "What," he retorted, "makes you think I don't know you've already tried that 'anything else'? My lord, by now you must surely have realized that ours are two very different styles of Power. We cannot, like it or not, successfully attack each other. Leave it at that."

Osmod's smile was as thin and cold as the edge of a blade. "I had no intention of doing aught else."

And that, Ardagh thought, *is as blatant a lie as ever I've heard from a human.* But there wasn't much else he could do but say curtly, "Wise of you. The night has

become quite cool. Go home, my lord Osmod, before
you take a chill."

Ardagh sat once more in his bedchamber, listening to
Cadwal snore. The mercenary had awakened again when
the prince had returned, then slid right back into sleep.

Lucky you.

That little encounter with Osmod had not gone as
smoothly as he would have liked. But then, it hadn't
turned into a battle, either. There was that. It had been
a near thing, though, Ardagh thought, what with having the child-killer so close yet being forced to be civil
to him.

Darkness slay him since I cannot.

Worse than forced civility to know that, for the sake
of politics, he could tell no one of Osmod's true nature,
worse still to know that he must let the man live.

A shudder of sheer disgust shook the prince. Powers,
to be free of this place!

Ae, but Sorcha! The hour was late, but . . . "Sorcha?"
Ardagh asked softly, testing.

"Ardagh!" She answered so quickly that he knew she,
too, had been sleepless. "That was no 'I'll return in a
short while!' What happened?"

"Nothing much, love. An encounter with one of the
ealdormen. Not a particularly friendly fellow," he added
in wry understatement, "but I think we've come to a tentative understanding."

"Am I right in taking that to mean he won't interfere?
When you speak with the king?"

"I hope he won't. If he does—" Ardagh brought himself up short, realizing that there really wasn't much he
could do in retaliation. "Ae, never mind. I'm just letting
this foreign place get the better of me. Being overly cautious."

"Is there such a thing as overly cautious in diplomacy?"

He chuckled. "Good point. And 'cautious' is certainly
how I've been spending my time these days."

"So you keep telling me." Sudden impatience tinged Sorcha's voice. "What you haven't told me yet, my secretive love, is anything solid. Ardagh, I don't know why you're doing this, but—stop trying to shelter me."

"I . . ."

"Hah, that stopped you! You can't push me aside with a lie like a human; you *have* been hiding something. Yes, you've given me very nice images of what everyone and everything looks like, but there must be something more than surface details! Come, love, you've told me that you spent most of the day learning—but learning *what*?"

"Less than I'd like."

"Ardagh!"

"Yes, yes, I was only teasing. Did it ever strike you how very ludicrous this all is?"

"A Sidhe prince serving as ambassador for a human king, and all because of a pack of sea thieves? Now what could possibly be ludicrous about that?"

"Why, Sorcha, such charming skepticism! All right then: I spent a fair amount of time today learning how the Witan feels about their new king. Truly feels, that is, under the smooth, politic surface. And what I've learned is predictable enough. Egbert, even though he's been on the throne so short a time, is the court's delight."

Sorcha snorted. "Hardly startling. After sixteen years of a passive, unglamorous king, well now, people being what they are, it's no wonder that they see Egbert as a bright new beginning—particularly if he's as young and handsome and vital as you say."

Ardagh smiled. "Ah, my clever lady."

"And don't patronize me, either! As the daughter of Aedh's Chief Minister, I'd be singularly unobservant if I didn't know *something* about how the court mind thinks."

"Ae, true." Ardagh let out his breath in a silent sigh. "Forgive me. After a full day of this, it's not easy to stop playing the political game."

"Of saying nothing and hiding everything. Believe me, I know that one. I've seen Aedh and my father play it with the court often enough. But please, what else about Egbert? It's not just me: The king will want to know."

"Indeed. Yes, Egbert is the golden young hero, at least for now. And yes, apparently a good deal of resentment had been smoldering at the Wessex court during the last years of Beortric's reign. These are, after all," *bloodthirsty idiots* "folk of warrior stock," he improvised hastily, "and they're weary—with the eagerness of those who've never had to fight—of peace."

"That might not be such a bad thing," Sorcha said slowly. "It could mean that they'd be happy to work off all that pent-up aggression on the Lochlannach."

"It's possible. But before anything else can be done, I of course need to win over Egbert. And that," Ardagh added with wry honesty, "is not going to be easy."

"He must be an incredibly stubborn man, even for a king, if he can resist Sidhe wiles." Sorcha gave a sudden delicious little chuckle. "*I* certainly couldn't!"

Ardagh grinned into the darkness. "Humans have their wiles, too, my human love." He paused thoughtfully. "I do have to wonder if winning Egbert over is such a wise idea. Even if we gain him as an ally for Aedh, is such a land-hungry ruler going to be a safe one?"

"Och, who can say? I told you, Aedh sends word that he trusts your judgment completely."

"I suppose," the prince said dryly, "that that's a compliment, and that I should be glad of it." *Instead of being angry that he's neatly put his burden on my shoulders.* Ah well, he *had* given his word to Aedh to do something about safeguarding Eriu against the Lochlannach. *Serves me right; I should know after all this time not to give my word so freely.* "Right now, I frankly can't think of any other choice. Egbert it must be, unless I learn something truly and totally impossible about him. With any luck at all, I'll know more about the man tomorrow.

"But it's still tonight, my love," he added, voice softening to velvet. "And I am weary of politics. Let us discuss more . . . pleasant things."

"How do you *do* that? Shift subjects and moods so suddenly? So thoroughly!"

"I am what I am, Sorcha. I can't be human."

There was a long pause. Then he heard her resigned little sigh. "A pity. It would make things so much—tidier."

"It would. Or, for that matter, if you were Sidhe. But there's no use wanting to change the immutable. Come, my love. We have this small, precious time to share. Let's not waste it in Might Have Beens."

"No," Sorcha murmured, her voice almost as velvety as his own, and Ardagh smiled into the night. "No, my love," he heard her purr, "waste it we shall not."

Osmod paced the length and breadth of his bedchamber, far too restless to sleep. The prince . . . that encounter . . . that strange, alarming, infuriating encounter . . .

If ever, the ealdorman thought with a flash of dark humor, he'd had any doubts about Prince Ardagh's pedigree, they'd just been resolved. No one but a prince could ever have shown such complete, absolute, self-assured *arrogance!*

The lines of battle had most definitely been drawn. *Oh yes, for what good that does!* Prince Ardagh, curse his haughty soul, had been quite right. Their two forms of magic were totally alien to each other. Although . . . did that really mean he couldn't work harm on the prince? Just because he couldn't puzzle out how the other's magic worked, did that mean Prince Ardagh would be quite immune to the effects of battle-runes? Maybe, Osmod mused, he'd been letting the prince's smooth words trick him, too.

But again, why did there need to be a battle? Facing an enemy was one thing, fighting him another. Why

not just take the prince at his word? Let him negoti-
ate as he would. Let him make his pacts. And then,
Osmod told himself, simply watch him leave and know
that that's the end of the matter.

No. If Prince Ardagh left with an alliance between
Wessex and Eriu, that would hardly be the end of the
matter. Ever. And when he came right down to the hard
and sharp of it, Osmod mused, did he really want to see
such an alliance?

No, again. He stopped short, leaning on the window-
sill, not really seeing anything—save for the images in
his own thoughts.

Northmen, now . . . or rather, the prince's emphasis
on them. Osmod shook his head impatiently. This nonsense about their being a threat was just too unlikely.
That pack of seafaring barbarians could never amount
to more than the occasional thieving nuisance. Forming an alliance with Eriu against a threat that didn't exist
would be the height of uselessness. Worse than useless.
Therefore, there had to be some secret meaning behind
the obvious surface of the words—but what?

Osmod turned sharply from the window, resuming his
restless pacing. All right, then. All right. Say that, bizarre
though such an idea might be, the Northern threat was
real. Who would they be more likely to attack? Wessex,
so far to the south, with the rocky coasts of the Cymru
kingdoms between it and the northern sea? Or Eriu,
sitting out in the open, right in the path of any south-
bound ships?

And so it's Eriu that benefits from any alliance, not us.

No, no, wait, it wasn't so simple. An alliance between
Wessex and Eriu would mean sending men and arms to
defend the island. That was fine as far as it went, because
once one had troops on foreign soil, one had opened
a nice door towards future occupation. But although
Egbert could field quite an impressive army, given the
Witan's approval, sending any of it as far away as Eriu
would mean spreading his forces dangerously thin.

And is that *Aedh's real goal? Weaken us so that he can invade? Or, more realistically, take our trade routes?*

No and no again. That didn't make sense, either. Eriu was positioned too far from the mainland to make practical use of those routes.

Of course, Osmod admitted, stopping thoughtfully by the window again, Aedh *might* have intended nothing at all sinister. There was a certain logic to the image of forts lining both coastlines, particularly when added to the natural fortifications of Cymru's harsh coast. Such an alliance would be quite formidable, able to catch any marauding Northmen between them and . . .

No! That still meant taking valuable warriors away from Wessex. It meant weakening Egbert's chances just when he stood at the edge of doing what no Saxon king yet had done: conquering and uniting all of Britain.

This is ridiculous! First and foremost, there is no Northern threat!

Enough. The disadvantages of an alliance far outweighed any possible advantages. And there was another factor, one he'd been delicately avoiding:

Magic.

Ah, yes. Were an alliance to be made, Prince Ardagh would be using his powers to shape whatever followed. He would be forever the enemy. *There* was why he could not be allowed to go in peace. *There* was why he must be stopped.

Were an alliance to be made. He would, Osmod vowed, staring grimly out into the night, allow no interference, not from Eriu, not from meddling Cathayan princes. No matter what must be done, he would see to it that Egbert triumphed. And so he would—*Egbert would*—rule.

There would be no alliance.

The Wild Hunt
Chapter 17

Egbert sighed and rolled over in bed, reaching out to pull the bed curtain aside a fraction. Ach, morning, or nearly so, judging from the pale grey light pouring in. Morning, and he could have sworn he hadn't slept more than a few turns of the hourglass.

The woman beside him squirmed in her sleep, whimpering like a puppy, trying to avoid the light, and Egbert let the curtain fall back into place, watching her without like or dislike. Leofrun her name was, and she was no one particular, chosen not so much for her beauty or abilities in or out of bed as for her simple devotion to him; it would not let her betray him, nor would she ever have the wit to ask anything of him but the occasional trinket.

Egbert turned away. This was a fine thing for a king, reduced to taking only the safest and more innocent-minded of bedmates! But those years of exile, he admitted, could not have left him anything but a very wary man.

A man who would survive, God willing, come what may. A king who would rule.

He groaned. This chain of thought brought up the subject of that alliance yet again. That damnable alliance. He'd been *dreaming* about the cursed thing, in the brief snatches when he'd actually slept, mostly seeing Osmod solemnly warning him, *no, don't do this thing.*

The smallest chill slid down Egbert's back. *Had* those

been dreams? Only dreams? Everyone knew that saints and demons both could send visions while men slept.

Hah. Osmod would make a rather poor saint. And, ambitious or no, he's hardly a demon!

And yet, the dreams had been so insistent, so unnervingly real. There, Egbert thought, was the true reason he'd not slept. *I must be a king,* he told himself wryly, *if my sleep has grown so troubled!*

Ach, but that alliance . . . so easy to say no to it, to be rid of the whole stupid situation by simply sending Prince Ardagh back to Eriu with some polite, politically noncommittal message.

Or maybe not so polite? Osmod's tentative suggestion teased his mind: *"There are ways, I need not tell you, of quietly being rid of the prince . . ."*

No! Even if it could be done without obvious blame being attached, a king could hardly go about ridding himself of all inconveniences. Particularly not royal inconveniences. Besides, Prince Ardagh, for all his haughty elegance, had hardly done anything to warrant murder!

Egbert yawned, then sat up, brusquely pulling the curtains aside. "Leofrun. Up, woman. Out with you."

She gazed blearily up at him, for a moment no more wit in her eyes than in those of a cow. *Is this what I've come to?* Egbert thought with a flash of disgust.

But it wasn't Leofrun's fault. She was as God had made her. *Aren't we all?* the king thought, then answered himself, *No. We only begin as God makes us. What we make of ourselves after engendering and birth is something else entirely. We are, in a way, our own creations.*

And this was a ridiculous time for philosophy. Or near-blasphemy. "Leofrun! Morning's here. Up with you."

He shoved, not ungently, to get her on her feet. Leofrun, still blinking sleepily, her hair a wild yellow mane, threw on her tunic and padded uncomplainingly away. The guards, Egbert knew, would let her pass

without question or comment. And now that they knew
he was awake, servants would be in here shortly to tend
to him.

Morning, and he still didn't know what to do about
that alliance.

Save take refuge in a king's usual tactic. *Stall,* Egbert
thought. *Stall and see what happens on its own.*

It was starting to be a fair, bright day out there. The
air was nicely cool and sharp. No urgent business waited
this morning.

Perfect hunting weather. Yes, the king decided. A
good, fierce hunt would be just the thing to banish
shadows.

Osmod rubbed a hand over his eyes, then yawned
again, so powerfully he felt his jawbones creak. Morning already, and he'd surely had no more than a few
moments of sleep. Morning, and he'd spent all the long
hours of the night sending dreams to Egbert, willing
about the alliance, *no, don't do this thing.* Had all that
effort worked? Had any of it? Surely Egbert had
received some of the repeated messages, some of the
emotion behind them: a combination, nicely designed,
Osmod thought with a moment's self-congratulation, of
alarm and worry and concern-for-the-land.

He yawned again, stretching wearily. It would have
been most satisfying if he could have, at the same time,
sent distrust of Prince Ardagh into the royal mind, or
at least planted the seeds of such distrust. But there were
limits to what he could do.

*Let Egbert be hostile to the thought of an alliance.
That will be enough. And meanwhile I, oh, I will deal
with our magical prince.*

The day, early though it was, was already promising
to be fair, early enough in the season to not be too warm.
A perfect day for a hunt, Osmod thought.

Of many things.

The morning was still barely more than a band of grey lightening the sky and the ground was still chill and damp with dew, but Ardagh and Cadwal, grinning at each other, were already exercising their swordplay together. Both of them, the prince knew, were glad of the chance to let off frustration and pent-up energy in at least this illusion of action—although Ardagh was still cherishing the memory of the night before and pleased as well with the small bit of magic he'd worked just before sleeping. Whether or not that magic had any effect . . . he would learn, soon enough. And then, maybe . . .

Ae, stop this mental wandering! That's how you got burned the last time!

The rest of their small entourage loafed nearby, watching, making amiable wagers and jests. Ardagh suspected that Cadwal, somewhere at the back of his mind, must have been worried about giving him another iron-burn, particularly since they'd had no choice but to use real swords, but that wasn't stopping the mercenary from providing him with quite an enthusiastic challenge and—

"Hold," the prince said suddenly, lowering his sword. He brushed back damp strands of hair from his eyes with his free hand. "We seem to be disturbing the neighbors."

It was one of the royal servants, glancing nervously from prince to mercenary and back again, bowing hastily to Ardagh. "Don't look so worried," the prince drawled. "We won't behead you. What would you?"

"The—the king—King Egbert—"

"So I gathered he was named," Ardagh said solemnly, and heard a choked-off snicker from Cadwal. "No, no, go on," the prince told the flustered servant. "I won't interrupt again."

"Ah. Uh. King Egbert offers his greetings for the new day. He will partake of a royal hunt—"

"Ah!"

"—and—and invites you to join him."

"Does he, now?" Ardagh smiled. "Tell King Egbert that I will be happy to accept."

As the prince watched the relieved servant scurry off, Cadwal hissed at him, "You can't go!"

"'Can't?'"

"Och, you know what I mean. Look you, I'm not trying to insult you, but—hell, don't you see? Forest, the confusion of a hunt, nobody really sure where anybody else is—you couldn't ask for a more perfect time or place for a 'stray' arrow, a 'misthrown' spear. This has got to be a plot, something the sorcerer's planned to get at you!"

"More likely, to get me alone."

"Same thing!"

"No. Hush. It could also be something that *Egbert* has planned to 'get at me' so we may speak in relative privacy. It could," Ardagh added slyly, "even be something else entirely. We can't know what without accepting the invitation."

"But—you—" Cadwal threw up his arms in disgust. "How can you sound so calm about it?"

"Come, Cadwal, walk with me a bit before our muscles cramp up. Now then," the prince continued once they were out of anyone's hearing, "do you think me a fool?"

"No, of course not. But—"

"I have already refused to join the royal dinner. I can hardly refuse to join the hunt as well. Especially since," he added casually, "I had something to do with it. Stop staring, Cadwal, or at least blink. You look like an owl."

"How did you . . . ?"

"I sent a little touch of persuasion to Egbert last night." Ardagh gave a short, humorless laugh. "It wasn't easy. Osmod had set up enough . . . ah . . ." He shook his head. "This language doesn't have the term for it. Let's just say that sending that little magic was about as easy as sailing a tiny craft through endless fog."

He saw a flicker of nervousness in Cadwal's eyes. "Osmod's really been a busy fellow, then," the mercenary said in a voice that was carefully neutral.

"Oh, he has. A frustrated one, too, since—no insult meant, Cadwal—no human has the will or the sheer magical stamina he needs."

Cadwal looked at him in something like admiration. "You *are* good. No," he added dryly, "insult meant. Got us so neatly off the subject of the hunt I didn't even realize where we were going. But I'm putting us right back on the road. Osmod won't need magic to—"

"Come now, don't you think I calculated in the chance of an 'accidental' assassination? I'll be wary, no fear of that, wary on *all* levels." He saw from Cadwal's slight flinch that the man understood. "Besides," the prince added cheerfully, "if anyone tries to attack me while my attention is elsewhere—well, now that's why you'll be coming with me."

"Hadn't planned on anything else. Beats sitting here doing nothing."

"Your enthusiasm," Ardagh drawled, grinning, "overwhelms me. First let's get into dry clothing. And then—off to the hunt."

Ardagh drew in a deep lungful of air spicy-sharp with the scents of wild growth. Ae, Powers, but this was wonderful! Not true, deep forest, of course, not so close to a human city. There were signs of humanity all around him, felling of trees, clearing of underbrush—the wide dirt trail itself. But as the hunt rode further out from Uintacaester, the prince saw that there was still some wildness left. He took a second deep breath of air almost as free as that in true forest, sensing at least a trace of the wild earth-Power all around him, and suddenly laughed aloud.

Egbert, riding beside Ardagh on a stocky bay stallion, small as all the Saxon horses seemed to be, quirked an eyebrow upward. "You are in good spirits this morning, Prince Ardagh."

"How should I not be on so fine a day?" *Particularly since there's just enough Power to pleasantly feed my*

*own. Enough, at any rate for one small spell. And you
are so conveniently riding a stallion.* "And don't you
agree that it's good to be away from the city for even
this short while?"

"Oh yes." That was a heartfelt exclamation. "I don't
have to tell you, surely, how welcome—and rare—I find
any time away from court." But then Egbert shrugged.
"A king's life."

"Indeed." Ardagh winced at an unexpected stab of
memory: The last time he'd hunted like this, a spear
in his hand, had been back in his brother's Realm. Then,
enemy wills had forced Ardagh to cast his spear not at
the hunted wyvern but at his brother, and only by the
fiercest of struggles had Ardagh managed not to kill
Eirithan. There had been no trial, no chance for him
to prove his innocence. There had been only banishment.

Not this time. I will not be used this time.

Osmod, as though aware of Ardagh's determination,
rode up on the king's other side just then, looking, the
prince thought, like any normal, innocent man enjoying
a day outside. But Ardagh caught the hint of weary
shadow in the apparently cheerful eyes.

You were *up late, weren't you?* Ardagh thought. *Tsk.*

He heard Cadwal, who had been guarding the prince's
flank, urge his horse forward a touch as though by
chance, balancing Osmod's move, keeping a closer watch
on the man.

*Appreciated. But Osmod isn't going to try any
oddnesses, not with so many others as witnesses.*

All around them was the cheerful turmoil of the hunt,
men shouting and laughing, horses snorting, bright red
banners snapping in the wind. The hounds coursed up
ahead, a mass of wagging tails; they might not have
found any game yet, but they were enjoying the outing,
too. Ardagh waited with a little less than full patience.
This was the one element he couldn't control. If the
hounds didn't start up a quarry—

Ha, but the amiable sniffings and yappings suddenly sharpened into baying. Horns blared. A stag! They'd started up a fine, spring-fat stag. As the hunt charged forward, Ardagh grinned, bent over his horse's tossing mane, riding as though as eagerly blood-hungry as the others but actually hunting something else entirely.

Ah yes, here was a narrowing of the road, with trails branching off in all directions. Easy for a hunting party to become accidentally separated. Ardagh reached out his will, not even trying to snare a human mind, no, no, touching an equine mind instead, the king's stallion, telling it, *Mares! Mares running this way!*

And—now! Ardagh turned his own horse aside and sent it racing off at a tangent, crashing through the underbrush along what was probably a deer trail, ducking and dodging branches. He could hear Egbert, having no choice in the matter, following closely after him, hissing curses when he didn't dodge quite in time, swearing creatively at his eager stallion.

Cadwal's going to be furious, left behind like this. No help for it.

At last Ardagh slowed his horse to a trot, listening. Behind them, the clamor of the hunt had faded into silence, and he reined in the animal altogether, glancing over his shoulder. The king's stallion had stopped of its own accord, snorting and curvetting in very clear equine confusion at the lack of mares.

"King Egbert," the prince said. "It *was* you following." *As though I didn't know it!*

The king, fighting his prancing, puzzled mount, said something hot and decidedly unregal under his breath. "We've lost the stag. And the hunt. And," he added, looking around at what, to his human senses, must have looked like trackless forest, "ourselves."

"Annoying, I agree. But we're not in any danger, and as soon as the rest of the party realizes we're missing, they'll be looking for us. They'll find us soon enough. Or perhaps," the prince added, as Egbert angrily kneed

his horse forward, ignoring Ardagh, "we shall find them."
And you're not getting away from me that easily.

Ardagh urged his own horse after the stallion, riding
beside the king, leaves brushing at his legs and twigs
crackling beneath the horse's hoofs, and smiled to himself. Egbert hadn't the slightest idea that his stallion had
been lured aside. More to the point, the spell had been
so small that Osmod wouldn't have sensed it, either. "Ah
well," the prince said, with the air of a man making light
conversation, "at least we've been given a rare chance."

"Eh?"

"Why, to talk, King Egbert, to talk. Yes, and in relative privacy."

The king glared. "About what? The alliance?"

"Now, did I ever mention anything about an alliance?"

Egbert snorted. "Not in so many words. But why else
are you here?"

The prince raised a languid hand. "King Aedh might
have heard about your coming to the throne." *Then
again, he might not.*

"And sent a courtesy message? Using a prince as
messenger?"

Ardagh grinned. "That does sound unlikely, I admit."
He glanced around, deliberately theatrical. "We're quite
alone. Come now, tell me, just between us, what *would*
you think of such an alliance?"

It hardly mattered what Egbert thought of so seemingly naive a question. The prince knew that it was
impossible for humans *not* to think, no matter how
briefly, of a suggested subject, and for an instant to
radiate their true emotions about it. At least for those
with the skill to read such things.

Arrogance, Ardagh sensed. *Pride. Power-lust. Worse,
ruthless land-lust. And this isn't Osmod's influence. This
is the true Egbert.*

Ah well, he'd hardly expected any less. Aedh wasn't
such a sweet and tender fellow, either, though lacking
in that absolute arrogance: No king could be soft. And

such total ambition as burned in Egbert didn't mean complete defeat.

But it's certainly going to make things more difficult.

How *did* one form a safe alliance with someone who'd just as soon conquer his allies?

"King Egbert—"

"I hear them," the king cut in. "The hunt's just ahead." With the eagerness of a prisoner escaping, he prodded his stallion into a canter, crashing through the underbrush, leaves and bits of twig flying. After a moment, Ardagh sighed and followed.

But then he reined his horse in so sharply the animal nearly reared, every Sidhe sense all at once screaming *Danger!*

There, thinking himself hidden in the underbrush, was Osmod, magic gathering around him.

"I wouldn't," the prince said. "And you might as well come out of hiding. I see you quite plainly." *And was wondering when you'd show up.*

"What were you doing with the king?"

"Nothing that concerns you, ealdorman."

"What were you doing?" Osmod insisted, kneeing his horse forward to block Ardagh's way, his eyes blazing. "What plot were you working?"

"No plot. The very opposite of one, actually. Move aside, Osmod."

"Not till I learn what I wish. And don't think to escape me. The king's too far away by now to hear us. The hunt's moved on. There's no one to help you."

"I need no help," Ardagh said flatly. "And I don't like false theatrics. Come, I'll even give you a warning: I'm at my strongest here in the forest. But I don't wish to fight you." *What I wish is to see you dead. But Egbert would never forgive me for your death.*

"Don't you? A pity, because I do!" Deliberately, Osmod raised a small, limp form—a rabbit, Ardagh saw—deliberately pressed it to his lips, drinking.

"Is that supposed to horrify me?" the prince asked.

"Believe me, I've seen far worse than a bit of blood-drinking."

Osmod grinned, red staining his mouth. "I wasn't trying to frighten you. You have your Power," the sorcerer purred, "I have mine."

Fugitives
Chapter 18

Ardagh *felt* the forest's Power stirring all around him, pulling at him, reacting to the two intruders who bore their own Power. Fighting against its seductive lure, he snapped, "Osmod, this is insane. I told you once already, our magics are too different; we cannot use them against each other."

"I have only your word for that. And I'll never have a better chance to be rid of you." The human tossed the dead rabbit casually aside and sprang from his terrified horse, flinging the reins around a branch, never taking his gaze from Ardagh. "No prince, no alliance, no encumbrance. An accident, don't you see? Hunting accidents happen all the time."

Oh, you idiot. "Sometimes," Ardagh said in grim resignation, "the hunted wins," and subtly closed his hand about the hilt of his dagger. Somewhere along the way, he'd lost his hunting spear, but a knife was good enough. He'd learned knife fighting from Cadwal, and he could certainly move more swiftly than any human. One swift thrust—

No! Impossible to explain a dead Osmod to Egbert if it's my knife in the child-killer's throat. It must be magic, then, Darkness take him, and we'll see what happens.

The prince leaped down from his own nervous horse, letting it go as it would, not wanting it in his way, and gathering his magic to him. If only this cursed Realm had enough Power in it for one quick, efficient killing spell!

As well wish for a dragon to come zooming down from the skies. The only thing to do right now was simply Ward and hope he could swiftly find the key to dealing with Saxon magic—

Magic that Osmod was unleashing right now! Hands clenched about what seemed to be bits of bone, he shouted out savage Words. They meant not a thing to Ardagh; they sounded only like distortions of the Saxon tongue. But definite Power glowered behind them, and the prince cast up a quick wall of will, blocking—

Nothing! Magic there was, but alien, eerie, its shape, its *feel* once again like nothing he knew, magic whirling uselessly about him in a fierce wind. And his own, ae, his own Power could do nothing, either! Of course he hadn't been lying to Osmod, they really could do no magical damage to each other—but the two waves of disparate, discordant Power had to go *somewhere.* Tangling and recoiling off each other, they spiralled up in a sudden, vicious gale. Pelted by a stinging storm of leaves and twigs, Ardagh heard trees begin to sway, creaking ominously, heard branches snap and crash to the forest floor, *felt* more than the gale, *felt* a wrongness growing, growing—

We could . . . we could tear a hole in Reality like this, he thought breathlessly. *Alien magics clashing . . . should have realized this might happen . . . can't stop, though . . . not till he does . . . if one wave's gone, if the Power's out of balance . . . it'll kill us both. I'm not dying for his stupidity.*

"Stop," the prince gasped out, less firmly than he would have liked. "Stop, you idiot, now, or we both die."

"Coward," Osmod gasped back, staggering as he said it. "Coward . . ."

But of course a human, even one with some Power, had less magical stamina than a Sidhe. Osmod gave way without warning, falling helplessly to his knees. The tangled mass of Power, now perilously unbalanced, tore free, and Ardagh desperately caught at it before it could blaze totally out of control. He drew as much Power, his own and the forest's addition, as he could absorb into himself, dizzy with the sudden unexpected feast, cast the excess, the alien, Saxon side of it, into the earth, the air, the very heart of the forest. Some of it returned to its Saxon host, restoring Osmod. Ardagh sensed that much and couldn't do anything about it. Stumbling back against a rock, dazed and shocked with this strange, strange magical-backlash-that-wasn't and struggling to catch his breath, he *felt* the wild wind—

Vanish as though it had never been.

I did it. Whatever it was I just did. Just in time, too, I think.

Far too narrow an escape. He stood panting helplessly, shaking, watching the still equally helpless Osmod. Ae, he'd been right the first time! A plain knife was going to be far more useful than magic in settling this, and to the Dark with political complications.

Oh, yes. If only he had the breath to do anything. Ardagh took an unsteady step forward, not quite sure what was going to happen.

The forest exploded into a new storm of sound and color. Something large, solid and gasping crashed into the prince, nearly knocking him over—a stag! The hunted stag, reeking of fear and despair, the baying hounds close behind. The hunt had turned this way, by chance or maybe even pulled here by the wild magic-storm.

Just what I didn't need!

As Ardagh scrambled frantically out of the way, the hounds leaped at the stag, dragging it down almost on top of him, making the kill so close to him that blood nearly spattered his clothing. The prince lost his footing, twisted, trying not to land in the midst of the snapping, snarling hounds, catching a dizzying montage of faces, hunters, courtiers, King Egbert, faces savage with predatory joy. As Ardagh struggled to his feet, his hand closed reflexively about a smooth, solid object, and he came up clutching—ha, the hunting spear he'd thought lost.

Not wise! Osmod was going to—

He was, indeed. Before Ardagh could get out a word, Osmod, seizing his chance, hurled himself against the king as though defending him, shouting, "No! Assassin, there—see—his spear—he was set to cast it against you!"

"Liar!" Ardagh protested savagely, raging at seeing his history repeating itself. "I would never stoop to—"

But Osmod drowned him out, screaming at the king like a man at the edge of righteous hysteria or sheer nervous exhaustion, "He's an assassin, foreign assassin! There was never any plan of an alliance. No, no, he's been sent to slay you, to slay you during the hunt!"

Ardagh would have thrown the spear just then, and thrown it straight at Osmod, but harsh hands caught his arms before he could fight them off, tearing the weapon from him, trying to pin him against a tree. The prince drove his elbow back fiercely as he'd learned from Cadwal and heard a man grunt and lose his grip. But there were others, damn them, too many others; he couldn't fight them all!

And then he heard a familiar voice shouting war cries in Cymreig. A horse crashed into the men holding him, bowling them over, and Ardagh caught a quick glimpse of the mercenary, drawn sword flashing in one hand— yes, and with his own horse's reins clutched in the other hand as well!

Oh, brave man! Clever man!

The prince leaped up as quickly as ever a Sidhe moved, landing astride his horse, grabbing up the reins Cadwal threw at him. As though they'd rehearsed the move, they charged straight at the hunting party, men scrambling desperately out of the way, and raced on, whipped by branches, pelted with leaves, their horses scrabbling their way along the winding trail.

"Road's this way!" Cadwal yelled.

"Good!" Ardagh gasped back. "The more of a lead we get, the better. They'll be after us."

"Really? Never could have guessed. Don't want to know what you did back there, but let's get the hell out of here!"

"Agreed!"

Ardagh, bent as low as he could over his straining horse's neck, mane practically whipping at his face, felt wild shudders still racing through him, the shivering of roused magic that hadn't quite relaxed. Amazing that he hadn't already collapsed from backlash—but then, it hadn't really been a failed spell, had it, and—no, no, he was dithering, and ae, but he was going to enjoy a good, peaceful collapse when it finally did hit. If ever he had the time to allow it.

The prince glanced sideways. Cadwal rode with no grace at all, but he stuck to his mount like the proverbial burr. No problem there.

Yes, but horses weren't magical beasts; they couldn't run full out for long. It would take some time for the hunting party to get themselves sorted out, remounted and go after the fugitives, but his mount's breathing was already harsh in his ears, and if it collapsed now . . . Ardagh looked fiercely about for sanctuary, seeing nothing but forest, field, forest, field, field, no cover, no place to hide. They weren't going to get much farther, and he and Cadwal wouldn't have a chance of fighting off a whole royal hunt—

No, wait! Something that way, something seen not with the eyes but *felt* with his already overactive magical senses—yes!

"Follow me!" he shouted to Cadwal, and pulled his mount sharply to the left.

The mercenary must have been puzzled, but he followed without question. They urged their rapidly tiring horses across a plowed field, jumped them over a low hedge, then raced as fast as the weary animals could manage over a grassy plain into a wilderness of scrubland.

"No cover here!" Cadwal protested.

"It doesn't matter," Ardagh said, hunting. "Ha, yes, there! That's what we want."

"Nothing there."

"Trust me! There isn't time to explain—here!"

He pulled up his panting, wild-eyed horse, leaped from the saddle, sent the tired animal staggering on its way. Cadwal, muttering something that sounded suspiciously like, "Save me from suicidal Sidhe," followed his lead, slapping his horse on the rump to get it moving. "Now what? What the hell?"

"Nothing to do with the Christian hell." Ardagh shuddered, certain with every Sidhe nerve that *danger,* that *sorcery,* was imminent. "Nothing to do with Christians at all. See? There, there, and there." Ae, he was chattering! Have to control himself, control the Power—

"What?" Cadwal asked. "Some darker spots in the earth? Forming a . . ." His voice trailed into silence.

"A circle," Ardagh finished for him. "That we're standing within. Indeed."

"Old. It has to be, if there's this little left of it."

"It is." Ardagh flung his arms about himself, pacing back and forth restlessly. "Old at least as the stone circles I've seen in Eriu."

"We have them in Cymru, too," Cadwal began, then stopped, staring. "You can tell?"

"The age? Not exactly. However . . ." Ardagh shook his head, unable to explain the *feeling* of past and present in one. "They, whoever those ancient 'they' were, used wood this time rather than stone, for whatever reason. That's why there's nothing left to see." *With human sight, at any rate.*

"Yes, but—"

"It doesn't matter what they used," Ardagh cut in impatiently. "Someone died here, someone of great importance. Yes, and died willingly, I'd guess, probably in an effort to eternally guard the land or some such *'human'* foolishness. Someone of Power. A stupid waste of magic in my opinion, but he's buried right under where we stand."

"*Here?*" Cadwal glanced down as though expecting spectral hands to reach up and drag him under.

Ardagh brought himself up short at the circle's edge, came back to Cadwal's side, far too nervous with uneasy Power to be still. "He's long gone. But a shadow of his protection, his magic, really does remain, seeped into the soil as it were. Enough to draw me here. Enough," the prince added grimly, "to help us. I hope."

Cadwal straightened. "Against *spears?* There's that much magic?"

"No. Against—"

He broke off with a hiss as the attack he'd been expecting suddenly struck. Osmod couldn't have loosed too much sorcery, not while surrounded by the king and his men—but whatever it was he had sent was riding the winds swiftly, and if it wasn't anywhere nearly as foul as a demon, it was still unpleasantly of the Dark, and viciously unhappy about being forced out in daylight.

Unhappy enough to tear out our hearts.

"You of the Past," Ardagh said swiftly in his native tongue, feeling Power blazing up within him all over again, "you of the land, you of the earth and wind and water, come to me. Come now, come face the Darkness, come!"

As he chanted his hastily improvised conjuration, the prince called on the Power he'd gleaned from the forest as well: the Power of circle and long-dead magician, of earth and forest and self—yes, yes, by all the Powers, of self, and yes, it was working! All the forces were responding as one, the circle was blazing into magical life, blue-white fire to Sidhe eyes. Yes, ae, yes, and the joined Power was surging through and through him!

Overwhelmed, Ardagh threw back his head with a wild shout, almost drunk with the fierce joy of it, the joy of at last—after how long, how long?—feeling true magic blazing within and without. He cried out defiance in the

Sidhe tongue, defiance and magic and pure, inhuman mockery, and hurled a savage flame of Power at the Sending.

And hit the mark. Whatever Osmod had sent flinched away as though seared by white-hot flame, screamed like the wind and, like the wind, was gone.

Dazed, nearly bewildered by the threefold Power still surging in the circle, Ardagh staggered and almost fell. Cadwal, wild-eyed, reached out a tentative hand, but the prince shook his head, gasping, "I'm all right."

"You sure? Good." The mercenary whirled at a distant shout. "Because," he added laconically, "we've got real trouble now. They've caught up with us."

"So that's why the Sending was so weak!"

"Weak! What—"

"Osmod knew he couldn't slay us. No, no, delay us was his plan, delay us just long enough—damn him!"

Neither the king nor Osmod were with this group; Osmod would have been too weary, and Egbert . . . it was all too plain why Egbert had sent the hunters on without him.

Cadwal saw it, too. "They mean to kill us. Without staining royal hands with inconvenient blood."

And they weren't going to waste time or energy about it. Ardagh saw spears raised, knew there wasn't a chance of escape.

But I will not die, he thought, still half-maddened by the magic crackling all around him, *I will not die, no, not with all this Power still alive, even if the humans, stupid, stupid things, can't sense a thing, all this Power and this will to live—*

And Cadwal saying something about Cymru and coming all this way just to die—

—and Osmod to be repaid—

And Cadwal saying something else about at least he'd see his Gwen again—

—and we aren't going to die, not like this! We will not die!

Even as the spears cut the air, Power surged up in a blaze of intolerable wildfire. Ardagh heard himself scream in shock and rage and pure, fierce determination to survive, even as he felt reality tearing itself to shreds about him. He snatched blindly, convulsively at Cadwal—

And then there wasn't anything at all.

"That's impossssible!" King Egbert shouted. "Men do *not* simply—*disappear!* Don't tell me these ridiculous stories not even a child would believe. If you lost them, be honest enough to admit it!"

Miserably, the men repeated their story. Yes, they had found Prince Ardagh and his man trapped on foot in the middle of nowhere. Yes, they had cast spears at the two. And yes, somehow, no one could say exactly how, the prince and the warrior had disappeared in one great, fierce rush of wind.

"Sorcery," someone murmured, and hands moved in furtive signs against evil. "Demons."

"Idiots!" Egbert roared. "Come, we shall see this oh-so-miraculous site for ourselves!"

He urged his horse into a swift, ground-eating trot, and the others hurried after. As they rode off, Osmod moved beside Egbert, doing his best to keep up the facade of outraged defender-of-the-king. Not so easy, since he was fighting an inner battle with wave after wave of horror. The truth was so plain, if you had the knowledge to understand it. Of course the prince and his man had disappeared. It really had been sorcery, though he doubted anything as drastic as demons had been involved. Sorcery, yes—but sorcery more powerful and alien than anything he'd ever wielded.

"There it is, King Egbert," one of the men was saying nervously. "That's the very spot. See? Those are our spears still sticking in the ground."

Egbert, much to Osmod's dismay and ignoring the storm of terrified protest from the others, dismounted and stalked the area on foot. "Nothing," the king said at last. "No place they could have hidden, no way they could have escaped . . . nothing."

"Men," Osmod reminded him delicately, "do not simply disappear. But we don't need anything as dramatic as sorcery, either."

"No?" Egbert crooked up a wry eyebrow, a world of skepticism in his eyes.

So, now, Osmod thought. *The king doesn't want to believe in anything as indifferent to royal power as Power. Good, Egbert, very good. You make my work so much easier.*

"No," the ealdorman echoed. "Remember that Prince Ardagh claims to be from Cathay. We have no reason to doubt him. About that, at any rate."

"Meaning?" Egbert asked.

"Meaning, my liege, that of course it wasn't sorcery! The prince must have had some small Cathayan charm for—for bewildering the eye."

"But . . . we saw . . ." one of the men began hesitantly.

"What you saw, all of you," Osmod said with a carefully casual smile, "was nothing more than a trick, a clever trick. We've all heard stories of the false wonders Eastern conjurers can work."

"A trick," Egbert said flatly, showing not the slightest sign of belief or disbelief. "So be it. As for what the man intended . . ." He studied Osmod thoughtfully. "We shall discuss that matter. Later."

So be it, Osmod repeated silently. And wasn't this a ridiculous thing, having to defend Prince Ardagh from charges of sorcery?

But he didn't dare let that perilous subject be considered even briefly.

Ah no. Lords of Darkness, no. Worse, far worse, than alien magics was this sudden realization: Now Prince Ardagh had nothing to lose. Now he had no need to keep secret either his own Power—or that of Osmod.

Maybe he won't care. He's escaped, after all.

No. With all that princely pride and arrogance, the man was not going to be the sort to forget an enemy, or the wrongs done to his honor by that enemy.

I must find him. No matter how I do it or what it requires, I must find him. And silence him, theatrical thought or no, forever.

A Game of Fox and Hounds
Chapter 19

Ardagh groaned. Powers . . . he ached in every bit of him, mind and body together. And this bed was ridiculously cold and hard, and there didn't seem to be . . .

A bed at all. Frowning slightly as consciousness began to slide back into him, the prince opened his eyes a crack to find himself lying facedown on bare ground, his fingers dug into the soil as though he'd been trying to take root. Astonished, he pushed himself halfway up, only to sink back down with a second groan. Moving swiftly was *not* a wise idea.

"You all right?"

That was a familiar voice . . . ah yes. Cadwal. Ardagh turned over onto one side very, very carefully, realizing only now that he was wrapped not only in his own *brat* but in that of the mercenary as well. Kind of Cadwal, keeping him warm.

Warm? From what? It had been full day—it was still full day. The prince managed to roll all the way over onto his back, staring up at green: leaves far overhead, dappled with sunlight. Trees? Forest? Where . . . ?

"Are you all right?" Cadwal asked again, worry and urgency in his voice.

"I . . ." Ardagh swallowed dryly, tried again. "I think so." He sat up warily. The air smelled and *felt* different, more richly green-scented than before, less civilized. "How long was I . . . ah . . ." *in trance? asleep?* Ardagh gave up trying to find the right word and finished awkwardly, "Not conscious?"

"You were asleep—at least I think it was sleep—for pretty much a day. Didn't so much as stir for the whole time, and I have to admit I kept checking to make sure you really were still breathing. You *sure* you're all right?"

"Give me a moment." He had, then, had that long-overdue collapse, close to a genuine magical backlash in intensity. But apparently, judging from the restored way he felt, he'd spent the time unconscious instinctively drawing Power from the earth back into his exhausted self. *Clever me. A pity I don't remember any of it.*

But all of him finally seemed to agree on being awake and aware. "Yes," Ardagh said belatedly. "I'm all right."

"Good! Then—what the hell happened? And *where the hell are we?*"

Ardagh took another deep breath of the foresty air, looking about at ancient trees growing thick together, a wilderness that plainly hadn't been touched by humans for a long while. Yes, and he and Cadwal were inside an even more ancient circle—

A circle made not of long-rotted wood but of badly weathered stones like so many worn grey fangs. Ardagh stared at them in wild wonder.

"Good questions, Cadwal," he murmured. "I wish I had an answer."

"But you put us here!"

"I . . . did, didn't I? A shame that I don't know how."

"What do you mean?"

"All that Power . . . the spears coming at us . . . I was past the point of clear thought by then."

"*Iešu,* yes. If I hadn't known better, I'd have thought you were drunk."

"I was. In a way." Ardagh brushed tangled hair back out of his eyes with a hand. "I really *don't* know what I did, not specifically. There was Power from the circle, from the forest, from me. . . ." He paused, considering.

"The only possibility is that, in all that confusion, I somehow opened a primitive form of Gateway."

A Gateway! For an instant Ardagh froze: Powers, the implication of what he'd just said so casually—

No. He knew with sudden bleak Sidhe honesty that whatever he'd done had never been strong enough to cross Realms.

"A Gateway," he continued, his voice not quite steady, "that threw us from one circle to another. Yes, before you ask, both circles are very firmly in the same human Realm."

Relief flashed across Cadwal's face, but he said only, "Thought so. Hoped so, anyhow. In fact, I could almost have sworn at first, from the . . . the feel of things, that we had landed in . . ."

His voice trailed off. "Go on," Ardagh prodded.

"Nothing."

He clearly wasn't going to continue. After an awkward moment of silence, the prince said, "At any rate, both circles, wood and stone, were presumably built by the same or at least by closely related peoples. Otherwise, we would never have been transferred so neatly."

The human blinked. "How casually you say that!"

"Ae, Cadwal, believe me, there was nothing casual about it! Working with so many different strands of Power, improvising so wildly—by rights I should have torn my mind—or us—apart."

"*Dewi sant!* I'm glad I didn't know that at the time."

Ardagh shrugged, deliberately casual. "Obviously I didn't damage me or us. But as to where, or even when we landed—I'm afraid that I haven't the vaguest idea."

Cadwal shook his head wryly. "Just when I start forgetting who you are—really are, I mean—I get this sort of reminder."

"Eh?"

"No human could ever be so—so damned *calm* about magic."

Ardagh looked at him blankly. "What good would panic do?"

"See what I mean?"

"Cadwal, we're alive and unharmed and safely away from our foes. . . ." *Osmod.* "For the moment," the prince added darkly.

Cadwal caught that change in tone. "You mean to go back."

"Indeed. Once was foul enough; I will not let my name be blackened a second time. Most certainly not by a lying, treacherous . . ." He censored himself just in time.

"Human," the mercenary finished without expression. "Before you start planning any revenges, let's see about surviving here and now, shall we?"

Ardagh gave a sharp little laugh. "Excellent idea." He got warily to his feet, testing. Yes, his head was clear, his body under his control, though he was all at once hungry enough to eat wood. "The ones I don't envy right now are our men."

"The ones stuck back in Wessex." Cadwal paused an instant, then shook his head. "Och, well, we can't help them. Hopefully, they'll find their own way out of trouble."

"Indeed." Unwrapping the mercenary's *brat* from about himself, the prince tossed it back to him. "Thank you for the loan."

Cadwal caught the length of wool deftly in midair. "Think I wanted to see you freeze in the night? And be left alone in the middle of nowhere?"

Ardagh hesitated, puzzled, trying to imagine a human's point of view. "It couldn't have been easy for you," he hazarded, "not knowing what had happened to me, not knowing where we were."

Cadwal only shrugged. "Couldn't help it. Can't be as calm as one of your folk, but I try not to worry about what I can't help."

"Wise man." Ardagh glanced about at forest and forest, and felt a sudden wild shudder shake him. "I seem to

be repeating myself. Being falsely accused of a crime,
I mean, then thrown all unprepared into a strange land.
Ae-yi, at least this time I'm not alone."

"And the season's spring. Shouldn't be difficult to live
off the land for . . . however long it takes."

Ardagh raised a brow at this complete self-confidence.
"It was spring back then, too, when I first arrived. *I*
didn't find living off the land so easy!"

He'd obviously sparked some unpleasant memory.
Cadwal glared. "Of course not! You're a prince."

"Yes, but—"

"You think a mercenary's life's all nice and comfortable and under a roof? Hell no, there were long stretches
back before we was lucky enough to get into Aedh's
employ when my men and I were hardly living any better than a pack of wolves. Believe me, I know the value
of everything down to the smallest grub."

"I . . . see." It was delicately noncommittal.

"Ah well," Cadwal muttered, almost in apology, "you
are a prince, aren't you? Can't expect royalty to have any
wilderness training."

"Very true." Chastened, the prince asked, "I . . . don't
suppose there's anything to eat?"

"Here. Figured you'd be hungry after sleeping so long."
Cadwal unwrapped a packet of leaves—*not grubs,* the
prince thought wildly, *oh, surely not grubs*—and handed
Ardagh a good-sized, thoroughly well-cooked lump of
meat. As the prince took it gingerly, the mercenary
explained, "A rabbit blundered on us last night. I'm still
pretty good with a sling."

Ah, rabbit! Relieved, Ardagh bit into the meat. It was
tough and decidedly chewy and could have used season-
ing, but it was *food*. "You didn't *have* a sling," he managed between mouthfuls.

"Want to bet?" Cadwal grinned. "Easy enough to make
one out of any handy strip of leather."

"And the fire? Of course. You made it by rubbing
sticks together."

"Hell, no! I'm not *that* primitive. Always carry flint and all that in my belt-pouch. Look you, we're not as unprepared as you seem to think. We're both dressed in good, solid hunting clothing, and neither of us is afraid of a bit of walking."

There was an unvoiced question at the end of that. "No," Ardagh agreed.

"Good. We've got two swords and knives between us, several useful bits of cloth and leather, the means for making fire and finding shelter, plenty of food if you're not too fussy about what's edible—we'll survive."

The bare edge taken off his hunger, Ardagh rubbed his hands together to clean them as best he could. "Right now, I don't think I'd be fussy at all about what's edible."

"Not a problem. We'll forage as we go along."

"Assuming we can figure out where we are and where we want to be." The prince glanced about. "That oak looks like a good, sturdy tree, and it's taller than its neighbors. Let me see if there's anything out there worth finding."

"Right. You may be the taller of us, but with that lean build of yours, I suspect you're the lighter."

Glad to be doing something useful, Ardagh caught a convenient branch and scrambled up and up, peering through leaves.

Mm. Forest and more forest all the way to the mountains looming on the horizon, though he suspected that rough ground hid beneath the canopy of leaves. Wait, though . . . a hint of smoke, there to the west . . . too narrow and regular to be wildfire. He came hurrying back to the ground. "That way. There's an estate of some sort, maybe . . . two days of walking away."

Cadwal snorted. "Make that two days to a week."

"Two days."

"Och, well, whatever. The time's not going to get shorter for the waiting."

"And now who's being calm about the whole thing? Who's so beautifully under self-control?"

"You think so?" Cadwal glanced back over his shoulder with a grin. "Unlike some I could name, I *am* human, and we humans do have our fears of the unknown. Particularly after we've been dumped from one place to another without so much as a warning."

"Ah."

"Let's just say it was one long and lonely night, and leave it at that."

The tiny garden was barely more than a small, quiet pool surrounded by grass. It was a private little place, set almost by chance up against a windowless wall of Lord Morfren's own manor house, blocked off on two of the other three sides by equally windowless outbuildings.

Right now, it was also a crowded place. Three plain men in plain white robes ringed the pool, staring as intently into the still water as if they were hunting their own salvation.

Which, in a way, they were. They called themselves simply Tywi, Tegan and Tegid, all three no longer young, all three clean-shaven save for drooping, greying mustaches and so ordinary of face and form that not one of them would have been noticed in a crowd.

All three styled themselves mages.

By contrast with their blandness, the fourth man, much younger than they and pacing restlessly behind them, stood out like a blazing beacon. Clad in a rich woolen tunic and hose dyed a spectacular red-violet and blue, gold glinting from the torque about his neck and the thick bracelets on his wrists, he was lean, sharp-faced and aristocratic, bright gold of hair, dramatically dark of eye, and stubbornly narrow of mouth.

He was also fairly radiating a very dangerous impatience.

"Well?" His voice was sharp as a whiplash. "You've been staring long enough. What do the omens say?"

The three plain men glanced nervously at each other.

Dyfyr ap Meilyr had been a hard master, fierce and cruel and totally without patience. Morfren his son had, in these ten years since Dyfyr's death, all too often proved his father a master of self-control by contrast.

"Well?" the young lord insisted again. "You told me that you had the man. Where is he?"

"We . . . did have him," Tegan began, very warily.

Morfren, of course, fastened on the slight hesitation with the fierceness of a hound. "*Did?* What do you mean by *did?* Has he somehow managed to escape you?" He was, the three mages knew from long experience, warming himself up to a goodly rage. "Are all your vaunted powers nothing but so much mist? Have you been lying to me all this while?"

"No, my lord," Tywi assured him hastily.

"Of course not, my lord," Tegid added, quick on Tywi's heels.

"It's just that—"

"The distances involved—"

"And he's moved so rapidly over—"

"—water—we can't track anyone over water, you know that, my lord and—".

"I will not hear any excuses." It was said in so suddenly cold and hard a voice that all three mages looked up in alarm. "Cadwal ap Dyfri murdered my father. After even so long a time, there must be—there *will* be justice."

"Uh . . . yes, my lord."

"Of course, my lord."

"We will find him for you, my lord."

"'Find' isn't enough! You are to *bring him to me!* Do you hear that? You will bring Cadwal ap Dyfri to me— or I shall see you burned as sorcerers!"

He stalked fiercely away, leaving the three men drained and terrified in his wake.

Morfren ap Dyfyr, Lord of Tirsyth, kept up his determined pace all the way to the women's quarters. Waving the servants brusquely away, he stood in the doorway, heart racing. The two of them, his wife and his mother, sat sedately over their needlework, the sunlight striking the multicolored piles of wool, sparking their colors to jewel-brightness. His mother, by contrast, was a stern, somber figure in her eternal dark robes. Lady Gwarwen's face was set into rigid lines, lean as the face of a warrior. Her needle stabbed into the cloth, Morfren thought, like a blade into enemy flesh. She made his Elin, pale of hair and face and gown, look even less substantial than ever.

Morfren swallowed convulsively. "Mother."

She glanced up. "Well? Don't hang back like a child, Morfren. Enter."

Morfren took the seat she indicated, furious at himself. He was a man, curse it, the lord of his estate! Yet all his mother had to do was say *do this,* and he jumped to her bidding.

You should have been a warrior, he told her. *You should have lived in the ancient days and killed your foes and taken their heads.*

"Well?" his mother snapped again. "What is it? Have those useless creatures of yours actually managed a spell? Don't flinch, Elin!" she added. "You know very well what we're about."

Elin nodded shyly, head down, and Lady Gwarwen gave an impatient little hiss and turned back to her son. "What you saw in her, besides good bloodlines—"

"Mother . . ."

"It's not as though she's actually given you an heir save for that one scrawny little—"

"Mother!"

"All right, then." Her eyes were hard as grey ice. "What have you done about justice? What have you done about avenging your father's death?"

Morfren winced. Ten years of this, ten years of keeping the past alive and fresh in his mind. As though he needed reminding of his father, so tall and fierce and splendid—the very image of the perfect noble lord.

As though he needed reminding of how totally he failed by comparison.

"They . . . almost had him," Morfren said reluctantly. "But next time—"

"Almost!" Gwarwen shrilled. "They're lying to you."

"Och, Mother, what other choice is there? The assassins I sent into Eriu never came back—for all I know Cadwal thought they were nothing but petty bandits. I can't send warriors there! If King Aedh didn't destroy us, our own king would! There *is* no other way but this." He paused, unnerved by her silence. "They really *did* have him once, you know that."

"What, in Eriu? He shook them off easily enough!"

"It wasn't their fault. He crossed running water. You know how that throws off a spell."

"I know the excuse those liars gave you."

"But they found him again in the Saxon lands—"

"And lost him again! You should have those frauds burned at the stake and be done with it!"

"No. Not yet. Don't you see, Mother? Cadwal ap Dyfri is moving towards us, slowly but definitely—"

But she'd already shut him out, turning back to her needlework as though he wasn't even in the room. Morfren opened his mouth, shut it, got to his feet in frustration, bowed, and turned away.

"Bring him to me," his mother said without looking up. "Bring your father's murderer to me. Avenge my husband's death. That is all I ask."

Fighting back the urge to shout, to say a hundred things he'd definitely regret, Morfren choked out, "It will be done."

But just as he was leaving the women's quarters, he heard his mother's parting thrust: "Prove to me that after all these years you aren't a failure."

Before he could even hope to retort, the door was shut gently and firmly in his face.

Blessedly alone in the secrecy of their cramped little closet of a room after the debacle at the scrying pool, Tywi, Tegan and Tegin sagged wearily in their chairs.

"Be nice if we really *were* sorcerers," Tywi said, and the others snorted.

"While we're at it," Tegid drawled, "it would be nice if we could fly to the stars."

What they were, at least what they tried to be, wasn't sorcerers but *derwyddon*, druids; cousins, all three were descended from members of that late, honorable rank. But so much had been lost over the years, so much destroyed by Rome in more than one way, that they could only guess at the proper rituals.

Those rituals, that was, that could actually be safely performed within a Christian holding. This was not a good time for pagans, particularly not pagans with even the smallest claim to magical gifts.

"Small, indeed," Tegan muttered. "Better for us if we had no gifts at all."

Tegid gave a harsh little bark of a laugh. "Or had kept our stupid mouths shut about them instead of being so damnably greedy."

Tywi frowned at his cousins. "Lord Dyfyr was generous enough."

"Oh, indeed. When he deigned to remember us. Or wasn't raging or raping." Tegid straightened. "Don't glare at me like that. We both know exactly what sort of a man he was. I never really could blame that Cadwal fellow for killing him, not after . . . what happened to that unfortunate woman Cadwal loved."

"What's past," Tywi cut in, "is past. Lord Dyfyr has been dead for over ten years. Lord Morfren is our lord and master, has been all that time, and what he orders, we do."

He got to his feet, glancing at the other two. "Come, my colleagues-in-disaster. We're not total frauds: We did find Cadwal not once but twice. We even managed to send dreams to him—"

Tegan snorted. "And paid for those Sendings with headaches so vicious I thought my mind would break."

"Yes, yes, but the point is that we did do it. And if we don't find him again and lure him here . . . well, we all know that our dear young lord won't hesitate to carry out his threat. And his sweet lady mother would probably help pile up the firewood. "So now, cousins, enough talk. To work! I don't know about you two, but I, for one, have no wish to burn."

Lost and Found
Chapter 20

Ardagh glanced about at a peaceful forest night, seeing nothing more alarming than the occasional quick, nervous blue or green glint of small animals' eyes, hearing nothing more alarming than the hundred natural little chirps and rustlings that seemed normal to a forest in this Realm.

"And so, my love," he continued to the distant Sorcha, "here we are. Wherever 'here' may be."

"Och, Ardagh—"

"Sorcha, my heart, I know this may not sound very helpful, but please don't worry."

"Don't worry! You're lost in the middle of—of—I don't even know where, and you tell me not to—"

"Sorcha. Sorcha, love—"

"And don't 'Sorcha, love' me as though I were a child! What are you going to do? How are you going to survive?"

"That last apparently isn't a true problem, at least not according to Cadwal. He's quite wise in the ways of living off the land. And the weather's been nicely cooperative as well, dry and pleasantly warm."

"Fine, wonderful, I'm so glad you're enjoying the holiday—but how are you going to get back?"

"I'm afraid that I *can't* get back, not yet. I gave my word to Aedh, remember, to find aid for Eriu, and so, find it I must."

"But you surely can't return to Wessex!"

"No?"

"Ardagh!"

"Listen to me. Listen. My honor has been stained, my name darkened. Once was bad enough; right now there's not much that I can do to avenge myself on my brother and his court. But I *will not* let myself be dishonored by—" he changed the sentence in midbreath from the slur he'd been about to issue against humans to a safer "—by these folk as well."

"Honor," she said. "That *is* what worries men the most, isn't it? Keeping their oh-so-precious honor intact."

"Oh? And women don't worry about honor at all?"

Sorcha sighed. "Of course we do. It's just that—och, Ardagh. Just bring yourself back to me, that's all I ask. Just bring yourself back."

She broke the contact, and Ardagh sat for a time in total stillness, thinking of her, thinking of them, wondering with a bittersweet longing and hopelessness that must surely be Cadwal's Cymric *hiraeth*, what could ever be between them.

No. He didn't have the luxury of worrying about Perhaps and Maybe. First: Osmod. That the sorcerer would be frantically hunting him was obvious, nor was the man likely to give up without good cause; Osmod would be terrified by now that the prince would unmask him.

I will. Eventually.

He doubted that the men he and Cadwal had been forced to leave behind were in any real danger—nor were they a danger to him. It was unlikely that Egbert would risk complications from Eriu by harming them, and they certainly would have nothing harmful to say against Ardagh.

Osmod, the prince thought again. *All this trouble is your doing. Wait, Osmod. Worry and wait.*

His sudden smile had nothing at all of humor or humanity about it.

As Osmod entered the council hall, he saw Egbert glance sharply up, a thin ray of morning light glinting dramatically off the king's golden hair. "Well?"

The other Witan members were already there, Osmod noted, all of them watching him wide-eyed, perched on their benches like so many wary birds ready to take flight. He fought down the ridiculous urge to shout *Run for your lives!* at them just to see what would happen, and bowed low before the king.

"Nothing, my liege," he told Egbert. "Just as before, nothing." *Nothing, indeed. For two days now the runes haven't given me the faintest clue as to where our wandering prince has gone.* But of course he wasn't about to tell that frustrating, perilous fact to the king. "The prince's men," Osmod said instead, "have by now been questioned every way up to the edge of actual torture— which last we both agreed would not be wise to inflict on another king's subjects—"

"Indeed."

"—and all I've heard from them is that Prince Ardagh is," he imitated their barbaric Eriu accent as best he could, "a strange sort of fellow, not someone we can figure out all that easily but what do you expect from a prince, and a foreigner at that?" Osmod stopped to take a breath. "In short, my liege, they haven't said the slightest word that might be taken as suspicious."

"Are they that skilled at lying?"

"No . . . I think not. In fact, after two days of listening to their ramblings, I haven't a doubt that these are nothing more than innocent dupes. Left behind," Osmod added delicately, "as sacrifices."

Egbert leaned back in his chair, watching him through half-lidded eyes. "For us to slay like the Saxon barbarians we are, eh? And in doing so, cause a ripple of trouble between Wessex and Eriu?"

Osmod took a step forward in earnest, feigned, outrage. "Do you see just how clever our treacherous prince is? He wasted not not the slightest chance to cause discord!"

"Perhaps," Egbert murmured, "perhaps not. One part of this matter fails to make sense. There is no possible reason, either political or economic, for Aedh to have sent an assassin."

"Oh, I wondered at that myself. But there's another way to look at this. Prince Ardagh probably *was* sent from Aedh of Eriu as an envoy."

"In other words, he tricked Aedh as well?"

"Is that really so impossible? You heard how smoothly Prince Ardagh spins a web of words, how convincingly he speaks. Just because he was playing the role of an envoy from Eriu doesn't mean that he couldn't have been in someone else's pay at the same time." Osmod shrugged. "He's a foreigner, after all—more than that, an exile. He can hardly be constrained by any civilized code of honor."

Egbert raised a skeptical eyebrow. "In someone else's pay? Whose?"

"Ah yes, that is the question, isn't it?" Osmod paused as though genuinely puzzled. "I wondered about that, as well. Who, we must ask ourselves, would stand the most to gain from your—God and his saints prevent it—death?"

"An intriguing point," Egbert said dryly.

Isn't it? Osmod agreed silently. *And with any luck at all, one of these dolts will pick it up and play with it as I wish—ah, yes, here we go. I see several mouths opening.*

After an initial murmuring of confusion, one voice cried out, "Mercia," as Osmod knew someone certainly would. It was, after all, the most blatant choice. "King Cenwulf of Mercia."

"No, no," someone else protested. "Too obvious!"

Of course it is, you idiot. That's the very point! Obvious is just what I want. Now shut up!

But he didn't need to say a word. The others were

already shouting down the naysayer: who else could it have been, after all? No one else here in Britain had the might, neither Saxon nor those wild men of the Cymric kingdoms. Surely not Charlemagne, off in Rome being crowned Emperor! Charlemagne certainly had the might for open attack, should he wish it, and no need at all for subversive actions, but he had never expressed even the slightest interest of leaving the mainland to conquer the British kingdoms.

There it was. Certainly no one else in Britain *but* Mercia was of sufficient might and strategic placement to make so daring a move!

As the debate continued, Osmod kept his face carefully blank. But he was thinking, *Mercia, yes,* and letting himself picture Wessex victorious over so goodly a stretch of land, the two kingdoms combined into one twice as mighty. Yes, ah yes, what a lovely image!

But was the time right? Was this too soon a move—

Nonsense! There was no such thing as "too soon," and only cowards worried about the time being propitious. All he must do was keep tempers and patriotic feelings roused like this, and the Witan would grant whatever he—whatever Egbert wished.

Glancing at the king, Osmod caught the same glint of cynical amusement and clear ambition in Egbert's eyes that he knew must be in his own. For a moment, king and ealdorman looked at each other in perfect accord.

And this is all due to you, Prince Ardagh, however indirectly. Curse you wherever you've run, I still will need your death. But for the moment at least, you are so very much more useful to me alive!

"Two days," Cadwal said blandly.

Ardagh, tired and travel-worn, glared at him. "I was wrong. I admit it."

"Don't worry." The mercenary, looking disgustingly healthy aside from the dust of travel, was clearly being magnanimous in victory. "Misjudging distance is a common mistake of . . . well . . ."

"Of idiots new to the woodland. Yes, yes, I admit that point, too. But you must admit I haven't held you back."

"No, indeed. Don't know how you do it, but I've never seen anyone go through underbrush so smoothly. Or scoop fish so easily out of streams with a bare hand. You move like a . . . well, like one of your people."

"You never will get used to saying 'Sidhe,' will you?"

"Probably not." Cadwal grinned. "You do seem to be getting used to the wilderness, though."

"Probably not," Ardagh mimicked. "At least by now I know something about what's safe to eat, thanks to you. 'No plants with that milky sap, unless you know 'em, no fruit that's got five segments, no older bracken, no mushrooms unless you really recognize them—'"

Cadwal grunted. "Make me sound like a nagging father."

"Hardly that. Just like a wise man. For a . . ."

"Human. You never will get used to saying that, will you?"

"Once again: Probably not. Cadwal, do you still have no idea where we are?"

"I'm . . . not sure," the mercenary said so evasively that Ardagh glanced at him.

"Meaning?"

"Meaning that the plants, the trees, everything around here is just so very familiar. But I haven't seen anything specific, any special landmark that can actually make me stop short and say, yes, this is where I am."

"You . . . don't think we're in Cymru, do you?"

"Och, I told you, I don't know. There hasn't been anything that couldn't be found on the other side of the border, either. And no, humans don't have any weird homing instincts to— What? What's wrong?"

Ardagh had come sharply alert, listening with every Sidhe sense. Ignoring Cadwal, he took a wary step to one side, listening, listening. . . .

"I am of the Sidhe," he called out tentatively in his native language. "I am of the Sidhe. What clan, what people are you?"

Nothing.

Very suspiciously nothing. Not the mere silence that meant the absence of any watcher, but the total suppression of sound, as though that watcher was trying very hard indeed not to be found. Ardagh's ears caught the softest, softest rustle of underbrush—

"Gone," he said in disgust in the human tongue.

"What? *Iesu*, man, what?"

"For an instant I could have sworn that I *felt* the touch of . . . not Sidhe, no, but . . . kin. I could have sworn . . ." He straightened. "No. Whatever, whomever, might have been out there is definitely gone now. Ha, if I wasn't merely picking up some odd echo of my own Power reflected from the forest."

"Is that possible?"

"To quote you, I don't *know*. All I can tell you for certain is that I'm positive we're not in any immediate danger. Other than from the mundane world, that is."

"Reassuring."

"Ae, come," the prince added, suddenly uncomfortably restless, "let's move on. The sooner we sleep under a safe roof, yes and in a genuine bed, the happier I'll be."

He took the lead, very much aware that this time the eyes watching him warily belonged only to Cadwal.

The boy, thought Osmod, had been quite carefully selected. He was a nobody, one of the small, scrawny, unmemorable multitude of underservants at King Egbert's court, and very young. That last fact was, Osmod knew, the only way to be even remotely sure of his innocence. Innocence was, after all, out-and-out essential for this final, desperate attempt at scrying.

The boy was also very clearly nervous about being here in the ealdorman's chambers, particularly this late in the evening, particularly with no one else around.

"Don't be afraid," Osmod said to him, keeping his voice as gentle as possible given his impatience. "You won't be harmed if only you do what you're told. And," he added with sudden sharpness, "one thing I told you was not to watch me!"

No. Snapping at the boy was only going to make him so terrified that he would be useless. "I didn't mean to frighten you," Osmod crooned, and saw the faintest hint of relief. "And I won't hurt you. You want to help me, don't you?"

Half-hypnotized, the boy nodded, and Osmod smiled and continued his soft purr. "Of course you do. And all you have to do to help me is look into the bowl. That's right. Look into the bowl. Good boy. Look into the bowl, only into the bowl. See only the water. Very good. Empty your mind—don't flinch!" he added as he put his hands on the boy's narrow shoulders and felt the slight body tense. Biting back his annoyance, Osmod continued more gently, "Don't flinch. You won't be hurt. Just keep looking at the water, the clear pool, the mirror . . . look into the mirror . . . that's right. . . .

"Now, see him . . . see the prince . . . see Prince Ardagh . . ."

He gradually threw more and more of his will into the effort, overwhelming the boy's mind, joining that innocent young strength to his far-from-innocent own, feeling the doubled energy clearing his senses, letting him see more than what the boy saw . . . letting him see . . .

Ach, nothing.

No. Not quite nothing. There was the faintest tingling, the faintest misting of the water . . . far away, he realized suddenly. No wonder this was all so vague, so difficult to trace. The prince was astonishingly far away, and Osmod felt a chill run up his back at the thought of how much Power that transition must have taken. More Power than he even wanted to consider.

He really did *disappear, he and his man as well.*

Far away, yes . . . but there was something else

troubling the image. Frowning, Osmod deepened his
hold on the boy's mind, drawing more and more strength
from it. And all at once, with so sharp a shock that he
nearly lost the image altogether, he realized the truth.
Someone else—no, some*ones* else was involved. No, no,
more than merely involved: They were hunting the
prince—no, Osmod corrected, for whatever reason, the
one they sought was the prince's companion. Right now,
though, that amounted to the same thing.

And these mysterious, nervous hunters, he could have
sworn, also bore the faintest touch of Power. . . .

"Yes," Osmod murmured, bemused. "Yes." Quickly, he
withdrew his will from the boy's mind. What an interesting situation. Making use of such a thing wouldn't be
easy, not at all. But if he could manage it, the results
should prove most valuable, indeed.

First, though: With a quick clench of his hands, he
snapped the boy's thin neck. Cutting the narrow throat
deftly, he drank the young life and blood together,
delicately, careful not to stain himself or his belongings,
delighting in the fresh new strength rushing into his
mind and heart. Yes, ah yes, splendid! And the boy had
been so small; it would be so simple to be rid of his
body.

Three hunters. *Three nervous, near to panic hunters.
They'll be so very glad of aid,* Osmod thought, smiling.
They'll be glad of aid—no matter what the source.

And as for Prince Ardagh, well now, anything that
blocked his path was fine. Especially the loss of his one
ally, that far too loyal Cymric mercenary. Farewell, then,
to him—and farewell, soon after, the Lords of Darkness
only grant this, to Prince Ardagh!

Hiraeth

Chapter 21

Tywi, self-proclaimed mage and would-be druid, woke with a start, blinking confusedly in the darkness. Strange, so very strange! The dream had been odd enough in itself, a wild swirling of mist and shadow, leaf and tree. But there had been more to it than mere visual bewilderment. Tywi could almost have sworn that someone had actually spoken to him as well, not as part of the dream, but somehow *through* it, like a man shouting through a fog from far away, saying words sounding so faint and distant he almost hadn't heard the sense of them.

Tywi paused, considering. Dreams could be strange things, yes, without any need to add Otherliness to them. And yet, no, the message hadn't been merely part of his own mind's fancyings; the more he thought about it, the more certain he became.

Cadwal. There was something in the message about Cadwal ap Dyfri. Something about him being here in Cymru—yes! Something about him coming this way!

Was it possible? Tywi knew better than to disregard *all* dreams. Oh no, while some were downright useless, idle fancies of an overwrought brain, many were so much more. Some, indeed, were nothing less than out-and-out messages from the Powers Themselves.

But had this really been one such? The old stories all made it perfectly clear that when a god chose to reveal holy words to a follower in a dream, that follower knew it, yes, here, now, no doubt about it.

The old stories. No such being told nowadays. And yet, here he was—och, no, he'd talk with the others before making any sweeping decisions. Shaking his head in confusion, Tywi got out of bed and padded barefoot through the darkness to the sleeping alcove usually occupied by Tegid—

Who met him halfway there, blinking sleepily, a dim figure in the darkness saying, "I had the oddest dream just now, almost as though—"

"Someone was sending you a warning?" Tywi gasped.

"All about Cadwal ap Dyfri, yes. How did you—"

"I just heard a similar warning, myself! And—"

"Tywi, Tegid!" It was Tegan, looking tousled, sleepy, and, despite the fog of darkness hiding most of his face, thoroughly alarmed. "What are you two doing here?"

"Did you have a dream?" Tegid asked sharply.

"Yes! It was—"

"Containing a message about Cadwal ap Dyfri?"

"What—you, too?"

"That's right," Tywi said, fumbling with a candle till he'd gotten it burning. He glanced at the other two over the small, flickering light. "The same dream for all three of us."

"A god . . . ?" Tegid asked warily.

"Or a demon. Or another mage with a grudge against Cadwal. Who can say?" Tywi shrugged, a little too casually. "The days when the gods identified themselves to their worshipers seem to be long gone. But whomever—or whatever—our mysterious informant may be, there seems to be no doubt about his, her, or, for all we know, its message:

"Cadwal ap Dyfri has, indeed, returned to Cymru. He is, all the Powers be thanked, coming straight to us. We will at last be able to put an end to the whole messy business."

Ardagh bit back an impatient sigh. He had to admit that by now, their third day of wilderness travel, he was managing well enough, far better than he'd ever dreamed of coping back during his first dazed wandering in Eriu's forests. But that, the prince thought, didn't mean he was actually enjoying this—this—barbarism!

Powers, what I'd give for a bed that's something more than broken boughs, a roof that doesn't shed leaves— no, no, for nothing more than a simple hot bath!

He had been aching to scry out Osmod, aware of the sorcerer like the most distant but menacing of storms. But Ardagh reluctantly had to admit that it was too great a risk. A magical backlash, here in the middle of wilderness, might well prove fatal.

Onward. That's all there is right now: onward.

They had been climbing a rough, rocky slope for some time, weaving their way up through the tangled underbrush, stepping carefully over the treacherous footing. Cadwal, in the lead this time, reached the crest of the hill—

And froze, outlined starkly against the sky as though turned in a moment's sorcery to stone.

"Cadwal?" Ardagh hurried up to join him, alert in every nerve. "What is it?"

"Look."

The prince obligingly glanced about. Scenic. Greypurplish mountains, deep green forest. Yes, and there, perched dramatically on a rugged hill, a ringed fortress reminding him vaguely of those in Eriu: a main house of stone surrounded by several thatched outbuildings, the whole estate or king's holding or whatever it was lying safe within its wooden palisade. Peaceful as an artist's rendering, the entire scene, with nothing alarming about it, nothing to put a man into such a total state of shock—

Ah. Suddenly knowing exactly what the reply was going to be, Ardagh asked, "You finally know where we are, don't you?"

"Cymru." Cadwal's voice was so choked with emotion it was barely understandable. "More than that. The kingdom of Gwynedd. The land of my birth. I have," he added, all at once shaking uncontrollably, "come home."

Memory sharp as a blade stabbed through Ardagh. *The glimpse of my own homeland, shown to me, shown to the exile, in that one agonizing instant by my treacherous brother, then shut off from me in the next—*

He could sympathize with Cadwal, ae, he could. But: Cymru? Gwynedd? How could this be . . . ? The prince hastily traced back in his mind to the chaotic moments when they'd transferred from circle to circle, trying to recall what each of them had said, trying to reconstruct what Cadwal might have been thinking. Wait now . . . yes, Cadwal had, indeed, been concentrating on Cymru just at the crucial instant, no doubt concentrating specifically on Gwynedd—

And as a result interfered with Ardagh's wildly improvised magic to transfer them specifically *to* Gwynedd.

But Cadwal—Gwynedd— "You can't stay here!" the prince cried. "Powers, man, you're in grave danger!"

No reply.

"Cadwal! Look you, I know ten years have gone by and that's a long time for humans—"

"Not long enough."

"Exactly! Surely you can't have changed *that* much. If anyone here recognizes you as the exile who slew his liege lord—yes, yes, I know you were perfectly justified in your action, but I doubt these folk will accept that."

"If they catch me," Cadwal said dully, "my life's forfeit."

"Don't say it as though you no longer care! You wouldn't have survived this long if you didn't want to live or—"

"Didn't think a Sidhe would care about what happened to a human." He shrugged, ignoring Ardagh's gasp of sheer, furious frustration. "I'm not going suicidal, if that's what's worrying you. And I'd just as soon not die just yet."

"Well, then!"

"You can't get us magically out of here, can you?"

"No."

"So. Like it or not, here I am. At least now," Cadwal added, his eyes bleak and hard as stone, "no matter what else happens, I can finally learn the truth about my Gwen."

Ardagh felt a little shiver steal up his spine. Warning? A hint of prescience? "Powers willing," he said uneasily.

"Amen to that."

And, the prince added silently, *can matters possibly get any more complicated than—no. I'm not even going to try finishing that thought!*

Osmod sat staring blindly into the fire, alone in his bedchamber, clenching his teeth against the blaze that seemed to be racing through his brain, fiercer than the physical flames. Lords of Darkness, what had he done? He could barely think, barely sit upright, he could feel his heart pounding so savagely it seemed about to burst, and suddenly the last of his strength was gone and he could no longer stay upright. Osmod sagged sideways onto the floor, welcoming the coolness of the planks, thanking all the Lords of Darkness that he'd had the sense to dispose of the boy's body before trying any sorceries, groaning with the never-ending pain in his head, the fierce surging of blood in his ears.

But I did it. I reached them. All the way to Cymru. I reached them, sent the message. Now if only they act . . . the three so-called mages, if only they act. But it doesn't matter, not now, not yet. I did what no other sorcerer has done. I reached them all the way across the land to Cymru with my will alone.

And killed himself in the process?

No, no, that wasn't possible.

"I did it," Osmod moaned in desperate, defiant triumph, then slid helplessly into a well of darkness.

Ardagh stared across the little campfire at Cadwal. The prince had been wary of building any fire at all, anything that might reveal their position, but the mercenary had given him neither argument nor agreement, and at last Ardagh had decided that the benefits of warmth and, for Cadwal's sake, light outweighed the risk. Remembering the mercenary's lecture on such things, he'd gone to a great deal of care to gather only the driest, least likely to smoke, wood. But Cadwal—ae, Cadwal sat as he had sat for all this night, staring wordlessly into the flames without really being there at all, his face showing no more life than the side of a boulder.

"Gwynedd," the prince said at last, tired of the silence. "This kingdom is, obviously, new to me. Can you tell me something about the way of things here?"

A shrug.

"Look you, Cadwal, I'm not exactly thrilled by the idea of wandering in unknown territory. I know you'd rather brood, but I really would like to learn *something!*"

Cadwal glanced up at that. "Not much I can tell you, not after so long away. Hell, I don't even know for sure which king's on the throne, whether it's still Hywel or someone new."

"Yes, but what *is* Gwynedd? A kingdom like Eriu?"

"Something like. One king, a good many underlings of various nobility and power. Land's broken up into various steads, *maenorau*, estates, I'd guess you'd call them. One of those *maenorau* belongs—belonged to Dyfyr ap Meilyr. The late Dyfyr ap Meilyr, may he burn in Hell."

"The murderer."

"The *bastart* I slew, yes. The place would belong to his son now, Morfren, and I wish him never joy of it, the weak son of a hard, cruel father and an iron-cold, joyless mother."

"You make it all sound as charming as the complications at my brother's court. And to think we both actually *want* to go home to such things."

"Ironic, that's us." But then Cadwal's quick little wry grin faded. "I just want to be sure my Gwen's safe, that's all. The rest doesn't matter. Just as long as she's safe up in Heaven."

"Add a little prayer while you're at it, would you, that we stay safe here in mortal realms as well?"

Ardagh meant that only half in jest. All at once chilled as though a cold wind was blowing, he pulled his *brat* more closely about himself.

And do I want to go back to dealing with my brother and his court? Powers, no. But that doesn't mean I don't ache with every bit of me to be back in my own Realm! No more dealing with humans and their never-ending problems, no more—

Sorcha?

Why? Ardagh asked whatever Powers might be listening. *For that matter, why me?*

But of course there was no answer, and the prince shrugged slightly, watching Cadwal from across the fire. The human shrugged as well, the two of them exchanging a wordless, resigned message of: What is, is.

Whether they liked it or not.

"Cymru!" Sorcha exclaimed.

"The Kingdom of Gwynedd, to be precise." Ardagh glanced down at the amulet, picturing Sorcha's astonished face, wishing with all his heart that he was there to soothe away her shock. "My love, don't ask me to explain any hows or whys in detail, because quite frankly, I can't. Remember that I was working with three different sources of Power, I was so dazed by the mix that I wasn't sure *what* I was doing, Cadwal and I both were desperately thinking of escape, and he . . ."

"And he, being only human, had in his mind the first place of refuge he'd ever known. His homeland."

"Exactly."

"Poor man. The shock of it . . . suddenly being home yet knowing you're still an exile—"

"I've been there."

"Och, love, I know. I also know what it's done to you. Cadwal . . . isn't trying to find his death, is he?"

Ardagh winced, glancing at the mercenary. Cadwal had spent a restless night, but now, with the dawn nearly here, he had finally sunk into an uneasy sleep, curled up by their banked campfire. "I'm not sure," the prince said after a moment. "Not if I have any say in the matter, at any rate. I firmly intend to get both of us out of this alive. And no, alas, before you ask, I can't just magic the two of us away, because—"

"Because you don't know what you did the first time." He heard Sorcha sigh, the softest of whispers. "Yes, love, I understand that much of magic's workings by now. But forget magic for the moment. Why can't you just—turn around? Walk away? Go west or south or somewhere safer than Gwynedd?"

"We could. The problem is that now that we're here, Cadwal is determined to learn the truth about his lost love."

"But she's dead!"

"That . . . ah . . . seems to be a subject open to some debate. Cadwal has, it seems, heard her and possibly even seen her, or her ghost, or—or the Powers know what. No, before you ask, he's not gone mad, at least as far as I can tell, and I don't *think* he's suicidal."

"But . . . a ghost? Is that . . . possible?"

"Ae, who can say? I'm hardly an expert on this Realm and its supernatural! What he's seen and heard could be real, could be a trick, could be anything!" Ardagh took a deep breath. "I only wish I did know more about this land in particular: the customs, the politics, the whole ridiculous situation."

"Hasn't Cadwal told you anything at all?"

"Oh, I've gathered some small bits of information from him, but it's been like plucking feathers from a *litheren*— that's a stony-hided, vicious-minded, nearly plumeless bird—much hard work and little to show for it."

"I wish I could help you. But I'm afraid that all I know for sure is what I gleaned from Father's maps. Cymru is the overall name for a full tangle of kingdoms, Gwynedd, Powys, Dyfed, Gwent, I don't even remember the rest of them."

"A pity," Ardagh said sardonically. "A pity that I can't combine this unplanned visit with some practical politicking; get at least some good out of the whole affair."

"No."

"No, indeed. From what I've been able to pry out of Cadwal, it's no use trying to forge an alliance with King Hywel or whoever's wearing the crown right now."

"Cadwal's right. There's not one of the kingdoms strong enough to be worth the effort of an alliance."

Or, Ardagh added, *that of fighting human prejudices.*

"Look you, my love," the prince said suddenly, "no matter what you think about Cymru, I'm in no danger in this land; the people here don't know me, they have no reason to be my foes."

"Yes, but Cadwal—"

"I'll do my best to keep them from harming him— and do my best to find out what or who is behind . . . behind whatever it is that's tormenting him. Ae-yi, who knows? Maybe we really *will* learn the truth about his lady and—"

"Gwen!" Cadwal shouted, sitting bolt upright, so suddenly that Ardagh nearly dropped the amulet. Hastily breaking contact and slipping the amulet back into its pouch, the prince saw Cadwal scramble to his feet and sprang up as well, staring in astonishment at:

At . . . Gwen? Was this really that long-lost woman? Her figure glowed faintly, eerily, in the dim light, but it looked almost real, almost solid, as it slowly retreated, a woman of middle height, brown hair, strong, lovely, worried face. . . .

"Gwen," Cadwal whispered, a world of pain and longing in his voice, and took a shaky step forward. "Och, Gwen." What else he said was in his native Cymreig and unintelligible to Ardagh, but the meaning was clear enough.

Ae, Cadwal . . .

In that moment, the prince knew he was as close to understanding that human emotion, pity, as ever he'd come. For Sidhe sight saw far more clearly. And Sidhe senses reacted to *lives, human lives, there beyond the bushes! Human lives, and the smallest brush of Power with them as well!* This, Ardagh knew with a shock almost of sorrow, was no ghost, no almost-living revenant at all: nothing but illusion. A trick—

Yes, and one meant to lure Cadwal to his death! Ardagh hastily grabbed the man's arm, struggling to hold on as Cadwal fought to free himself. "No! Cadwal, no, listen to me, she's not there, she never was there, it's just a trick!"

"I see her, dammit, I hear her!"

"It's illusion!"

"No! I failed Gwen once; I'm not going to fail her again!"

He tore free, shoving Ardagh savagely aside, and raced off in desperate, terrified pursuit. The prince hurried after him, thinking, *At least he's drawn his sword, at least he's not unarmed,* then stopped so sharply he nearly fell, melting hastily back into the shadows.

An ambush!

Of course it was—his senses had been all but screaming the fact—an ambush, and the magic-dazed, anguished Cadwal was running right into it. A ring of warriors sprang out of hiding, swords drawn, torches blazing, and the mercenary stopped short, his face grim and bleak with sudden acceptance, and raised his own blade.

Curse them all, now he does *want to die!*

But rushing blindly after Cadwal wasn't going to help either of them, particularly since his darkness-adjusted sight was being dazzled by the light. Ardagh waited, blinking frantically, sure that the noble Morfren ap Dyfyr had to be nearby. Surely the man wouldn't let his father's slayer die so easily—ha, there he was. No doubt about that rich clothing, that proud bearing. A youngish man, not particularly strong of feature, and not a scrap of kindness to him.

I can't understand what the two of you are snarling at each other, but the gist is clear enough: taunting on Morfren's side, defiance on Cadwal's. He really doesn't care about living; if he can take Morfren with him, that will be enough.

Not for me, it won't!

Wait, now, wait . . . little by little, the ring of warriors were being drawn into the byplay, little by little they were growing fascinated by this small, deadly drama and lowering their guards. Yes, ah, yes— Yes!

Whipping out his sword, Ardagh leaped to the attack, lunging at this man, slashing at this other, dodging blades and torches, feeling his sword hitting armor, cutting flesh, not interested so much in killing as in causing as much confusion as he could. Not much room to maneuver, but—

"Ae!"

A torch slammed against his wrist, hard enough to send his blade flying from a suddenly numbed hand. All at once Ardagh found himself unarmed in the midst of angry, iron-wielding humans who had no idea who he was—

And who had not the slightest reason in the world not to kill him.

A Small Revenge
Chapter 22

Trapped, about to die at the hands of human warriors, Ardagh, too stunned by the sudden turn of events to think about anything but survival, found himself falling into the graceful moves of *Tarien'taklal*, the unarmed form of Sidhe combat he'd once (so long ago it seemed!) taught the sickly young Breasal.

Weird, weird, I've never used it before, not in combat, I don't know why I'm using it now, but—Powers, look at this!

It was working, it was actually doing what it should, he was sending this man flying aside with a twist of the arm, hurling that one to the ground—ha, no, he wasn't going to die just yet! Despite the raging Morfren's shouts, the warriors were so confused by this strange attack they were falling back. Cadwal's sword flashed and flashed again, bloodred in the torchlight, as he cut a way free of the warriors, and Ardagh, catching a glimpse of the mercenary's face, saw in his eyes the madness of pure despair driving him, telling Cadwal to kill and mindlessly kill till he, too, was slain—

Have to shock him out of this, and quickly! Tarien-'taklal was all well and good, but you couldn't go on being successful with something you'd never before used as a weapon, and—yes!

"Cadwal!" Ardagh shouted in sudden inspiration. "Cadwal, help me! Help!" And he hurled no little will behind that.

It struck. No matter how Cadwal felt about it, reflexes honed by years of determined survival weren't going to let him desert a comrade—or die, either. Sanity blazed in his eyes, and Ardagh gasped at him, "Run!"

"Damned right!"

They raced together out through the forest, sheer desperation and Ardagh's keen night-sight giving them the edge over the jumble of bewildered, furious warriors they'd left behind them.

"There," Ardagh gasped. "Down there."

The earth fell away in a sharp bank. An ancient oak had crashed partway down the slope, some of its roots still clinging to the top. Ardagh and Cadwal scrambled down the bank and wriggled into the cramped little space beneath the roof of matted roots. They froze there like hunted wild things, trying not to pant or make any other sounds, Cadwal with his hand still clenched on his sword hilt, both of them waiting tensely. They heard the warriors crash past overhead, torches probably more hindrance than help in all that tangled underbrush, heard Morfren's shouts, heard the wild turmoil gradually fade and fade. . . .

And finally vanish altogether.

"They're gone," Cadwal said. He struggled out of the earthy cave and let himself slide down the bank to the mossy ground below. Ardagh followed, brushing himself off as best he could. Phaugh, this new coating of leaf mold and dirt on already stained and dirty clothing was the last indignity—no, no, safer to say probably only the *latest* indignity—of the journey!

"You're not hurt, are you?" he asked the bedraggled Cadwal, keeping his voice warily down.

"Not more than scratched, thanks to you. And thanks, I guess, for getting me out of that."

"'I guess'? Were you going to let Morfren have the triumph of seeing you die?"

"No, damn him! I only wish—I wish—och, I don't know what I wish. Yes, I do. I want to get drunk. So roaring drunk I can't stand or see or . . . think."

"Excellent idea," Ardagh agreed with delicate sarcasm. "What a pity that we can't do anything about it. We'll just have to wait."

"Heh. And you—what in the name of all the saints was that weird thing you were doing?"

"Tarien'taklal."

"Ah . . . right. Whatever. Just tell me this: If you already knew such a good style of hand-to-hand fighting, why did you insist that I train you? For that matter, why in hell haven't you been using it all along?"

Why, indeed? "I don't know," Ardagh admitted awkwardly, feeling his face growing hot. "I never really even thought about it. *Tarien'taklal* is just . . . something everyone learns. Everyone of noble birth. For the training in grace, muscle control—I don't know. None of us would ever actually think of *using* it, not in combat."

"Heavens no," Cadwal said, mimicking Ardagh's fastidious tone with ruthless accuracy, "not for something as brutish as actually *hitting* someone. *Iesu.* Really are different, you and me."

"Sidhe and human?"

"Noble and commoner."

"Ah. Not totally."

"Guess not. Didn't know the Sidhe could blush."

"Life is full of surprises." Ardagh glanced speculatively back up the slope, then sighed and started the climb.

"Here, now," the mercenary called after him in alarm and a fierce, wary whisper, "where are you going?"

"I left my sword back there." Hopefully one of the humans hadn't found it, because that would mean the complication of hunting the hunters. *The way everything has gone so far, I wouldn't be surprised if that happened as well!* "Besides," the prince added, pausing in midclimb, listening with more than physical hearing, "there's something I've left unfinished. Wait there—no, on consideration, I think you may want to be a part of this. Come on."

Ardagh paused long enough to be sure Cadwal was following, then scrambled all the way up and started surefootedly back to the site of the ambush, the mercenary right behind him, moving almost as silently and swiftly.

Good. It's going to be morning fairly soon, and I want to get this done before I lose the advantage of darkness.

Messy. No dead bodies or wounded left behind, but the ground was torn and definitely the worse for wear. Ha, but at least something had gone right: There was his sword, lying unharmed where it had fallen. The prince gladly snatched it up, quickly wiping it clean with a handful of grass and slipping it back into its scabbard. He straightened, listening anew . . . yes. The three of them were still where they'd been; he hadn't expected them to be the sort who'd run off on the hunt with the others.

"How softly can you stalk?" he whispered in Cadwal's ear.

"Soft enough. Who're we hunting?"

"You'll see. Come."

Ardagh stalked forward, quiet and intent as any predator, Cadwal following with reasonable—for a human— silence, stealing about behind the prey.

Three of them, yes, just as the prince had sensed, sitting where they'd fallen in sagged-shoulder weariness: three men of no particular distinction. No distinction, that was, save for the faint hint of Power about them.

Ardagh smiled with Sidhe contempt. Power? It would surely have taken all three of them working themselves into complete exhaustion to have ever created the illusion of Cadwal's Gwen and transferred the image into his sleeping mind.

Fortunate humans, not to have burned out your brains in the process. Still, you did do a credible job. And how, I wonder, did you know where to find Cadwal? How did you know that he'd returned to Gwynedd?

The prince expanded his senses carefully, probing very, very delicately. . . .

Osmod! Ae, no, that wasn't possible. Ardagh probed again to be sure: No doubt about it. It had, indeed, been Osmod who'd sent them the warning. *All the way from Wessex—Powers, that's amazing!* And alarming. *Unfortunately, I can't do anything about him just yet. But in the meantime, I don't want you three trying anything like this again, so . . .*

"Beware," he hissed in the Sidhe tongue, and bit back the laugh that would have spoiled the effect as the three yelped and turned as one, nearly falling flat in their hurry. He saw their faces actually blanch at the sight of him: there was still enough darkness to give his eyes their normal—and eerie to humans—nighttime glow.

But he hadn't expected them to gasp, "Tylwyth Teg!" And it was said with such absolute certainty, such absolute recognition that a little thrill of excitement shot through him.

The sense I had of being watched by—by kinfolk— it really was *some of the Tylwyth Teg! There really* are *folk out of Faerie in this land.*

He stored that fascinating fact away for the moment. Far more important to put the fear of Faerie into *these* folk.

How? He didn't speak their tongue; they certainly didn't speak his! But to have Cadwal translate for him— no. That would definitely spoil the effect.

"Stand beside me," he murmured to the mercenary. "Where they can see you clearly. But say nothing."

Putting on his most regal, most haughty pose, guessing that they could see enough of him in the ever-brightening light to appreciate the effect, Ardagh began in the Sidhe language, using gestures to help the meaning along, "You are not to harm the man Cadwal ap Dyfri!"

Cadwal, with a perfect sense of drama, moved to Ardagh's side as suddenly as though conjured, his face absolutely blank of expression. All three men started, all three made furtive signs against evil.

"You are not to harm Cadwal ap Dyfri, not by weapons"—that was easy to pantomime—"nor by Sendings!"

That was not quite as simple, but from the way they flinched, wide-eyed, when he imitated a man concentrating on spellcasting, they got the point of it.

"I have taken Cadwal ap Dyfri under my protection!" Ardagh told them fiercely, and placed a possessive hand on the mercenary's shoulder; Cadwal obligingly didn't stir a muscle, and the prince bit back a smile. *You'd make a fine performer, my mercenary friend.* "Do you understand what I'm saying, you ignorant, pathetic would-be fools of magicians? *I have taken Cadwal ap Dyfri under my protection!*"

Oh yes, they understood! They were nodding and bowing to Ardagh and Cadwal both and edging nervously away, radiating fear. In their eyes was the worried, almost studious look of three men who have suddenly decided to change their land and occupation.

Ardagh stifled the urge to shout, "Boo!" after them to speed them along, and stood in aristocratic stillness, smiling thinly, watching them go.

There, now. He relaxed, removing his hand from Cadwal's shoulder. "I told you I meant to get back my sword. More to the point, there will be no more tormenting dreams for you."

"You mean *those* were the sorcerers? Those three pathetic little *nothings* were the ones who almost drove me mad? *Damnio!* You should have let me kill them."

There was a brittle edge to Cadwal's voice; this was, for all his strength, a man at the end of endurance. "Those are not worth the staining of your sword or honor," Ardagh told him quietly.

"Yes, but—"

"They weren't sorcerers; nothing so grandiose as that. Only three more or less ordinary men with a touch of Power and a terror of disobeying their master."

"Yes, but still, all those terrible nights, them daring to touch my memories of—of Gwen . . ."

"Tsk, Cadwal, did you think I would let them escape unpunished? Do you grant me Avenger's Right?"

"What—"

"Do you grant me Avenger's Right?"

"Uh, yes, I guess—"

"Good!" Ardagh grinned sharply—and judging from Cadwal's shocked start, it wasn't at all a human grin. "Wait. I should be able to do this properly, even in this Power-weak Realm." The prince shut his eyes, seeing the three bland faces, holding them in his mind, firm in his mind . . . yes. He gathered his will, his inner strength, gathered it, gathered it . . . yes! Ardagh hurled *fear* to their minds and *fear* to their hearts and *fear* to all their being, *fear*—

The prince broke off, staggering with such sudden heavy weariness that he nearly fell. Cadwal instinctively reached out a steadying hand, then snatched it hastily back. "*Dewi Sant* preserve us, what did you do to them? Fairly had *me* . . . ah . . . wetting myself, and I wasn't on the receiving end!"

Ardagh managed a somewhat predatory grin. "Avenger's Right: the right to serve as surrogate avenger. You gave me the freedom to act: I sent a goodly shock of fear into their minds. Something to haunt their nights and shock them anew if ever they think of attacking you again." *Something so basic shouldn't have drained me like this—but that's this cursed Realm for you.*

Cadwal was studying him with unreadable eyes. "What?" the prince asked breathlessly. "Didn't like that?"

"I did, I'll admit it. Devious sort of revenge, but hell, after all those foul, sleepless nights, it's grand to think of them getting something good and nasty in payback. Just wouldn't want you as an enemy, that's all."

"You're not. You won't be."

"I won't be, right. Wouldn't be that stupid! I get the

feeling Sidhe revenges aren't ever anything as simple or quick as death."

"They're not," Ardagh said flatly. He took a deep breath, another, feeling his racing heartbeat beginning to slow back to normal, then frowned at the mercenary. "*Now* what's troubling you?"

"Now I'm wondering: You couldn't do something like that to Osmod?"

"Powers, no! Not without killing myself!" Ardagh started back towards cover, legs still shaky, Cadwal at his side. "It's one thing to send fear into three nearby minds," the prince continued, "minds touched with just enough Power to hear me but lacking true evil's strength. Osmod, on the other hand . . ." He shrugged expressively.

"Is neither soft nor untouched by evil. Got it."

Ardagh glanced sideways, not liking the shadow he saw in Cadwal's eyes. "She could never have returned," he said very gently. "Even if your lady's soul really had been snared, freeing her would have meant sending her on to . . . to wherever."

"I know that," Cadwal snapped, then shuddered. "Didn't mean to attack you. And at least now I know Gwen really is safe. It's just . . . *damnio*. I almost wish Morfren *had* killed—"

"While we're on the subject of killing," the prince said hastily, "why did you let Morfren live?"

What was left of animation drained from Cadwal's face. "I could have killed him; *Iesu*, but I wanted to. It's not so much what he did as the way he did it! Honest revenge is one thing; even a feud, one clan against another, still has something of honor about it. But that . . . using Gwen to get at me, fouling her memory—I wanted to tear the life from him with my hands.

"But it wouldn't have ended there. Morfren has an heir. A son. Told me so during his taunts, and he'd no reason to lie. It wouldn't have ended there, no. Before I could end my exile, I would have had to go and slay his son as well. End the line. Murder a baby. I—I—no. Not even to end my exile. I won't stain my soul like that."

Cadwal cut the air sharply with a hand. "Enough. More than enough. Let him live out his miserable life tormented by his bitter bitch of a mother, may her curses stay within their fortress walls. And *God*, let's get out of this place!"

"And quickly. Just because we dodged the hunt once doesn't mean the hunters aren't still after us." They weren't deep enough into the forest's shelter yet; Ardagh glanced uneasily up at the ever-brightening sky, the streaks of light staining the east. "Particularly since now the warriors can see where they're going—"

"Damn them," Cadwal snarled, "they certainly can. Here they come—and this time they've brought hounds!"

Cousins

Chapter 23

Osmod groaned. How long had he been wandering, hunting, fleeing? All about him was flame, nothing but ugly, alien grey and black and yellow flame, a forest of fire, a wilderness, a world of it—Hell? He had never really believed in the formalized Place of Punishment preached by the priests. But now he had to wonder. Had he died? Was this really Hell after all and was he damned?

Ha, but if he was, then his enemy was dead and damned as well, for Prince Ardagh was here. Osmod raced through the world of flame, hunting the prince— even as the prince hunted him in a never-ending circle of frustration and fear and rage. And all the while, the flames burned and burned unchecked.

Royal Physician Octa, a solid, balding man well into middle years, straightened with a sigh of weary frustration. Behind him in the ealdorman's bedchamber, two servants, one belonging to Osmod, one to the king, crowded together in the doorway, and Octa admitted reluctantly over his shoulder, "Before you ask, no, I don't know what to say. In all my years of practice, I've never seen anything quite like this."

"A brain-fever . . . ?" one of them asked doubtfully.

"Ach, yes, of course it's a brain-fever—but one of no natural sort."

Out of the corner of his eye, Octa saw both servants nervously sign themselves, and turned to glare at them. "I didn't mean that. I don't think there's anything

demonic about this." He paused. "And yet . . ." Octa
glanced at his noble patient again, watching the
ealdorman twisting in restless sleep, almost as though
pursued by something terrifying—demons?—and shook
his head. "And yet . . ."

"Will he live?" That was Osmod's man.

"That's what King Egbert wants to know." That was
the royal servant. "Will Ealdorman Osmod live?"

"What do you want me to say? I'm not God!" He
wasn't about to tell these underlings that he'd already
done all he knew: bled the ealdorman (the moon being
in the right quarter for that), plied him with potions,
even tried reciting some of the more potent healing
charms, all without much success. "If the fever breaks,
and quickly," the physician continued, "yes, there's every
chance for a swift, complete recovery. If not . . . ah well,
we're all in God's hands, now, aren't we?"

But Octa felt the smallest of superstitious chills steal
through him. Some of the things the ealdorman had
murmured in his feverish sleep had been alarmingly
dark, no, no, almost terrifyingly dark. *A delirious man
may say many horrid things,* the physician reminded
himself sternly, *and mean none of them.*

That was surely the truth here. Of course it was!
Nothing but fever dreams, mindless delirium. Ealdorman
Osmod was such a charming, pleasant man, after all. He
never would even think of such evil deeds—he'd be out-
and-out horrified to learn Octa was even considering it.
And that was the truth of it.

Wasn't it?

Live, Octa told his patient silently. *Live and prove the
lie to what you've said here.*

Live.

Ardagh flung his head up, listening. "Curse them.
They've caught our scent again."

Cadwal groaned from where he'd flung himself down.
"Can't you do something? Cast a spell or some such?"

"What would you have me do? Turn them all into pretty blue butterflies?"

"Just make them not see us, that's all."

"The humans, yes, not a problem, even with this Realm's weaknesses. The hounds—can't fool an animal for long, not one who tracks by scent. And no, I can*not* change our scents! But can't *you* do something?"

"What? You see any army with me? And I sure can't set a snare big enough to catch that whole swarm of hunters." He got to his feet, stretching what were obviously weary muscles. "Come on, time to flee. Again."

This, Ardagh thought breathlessly, racing wildly through the forest with the equally breathless Cadwal panting at his side, was rapidly growing beyond all bearing. He hadn't yet had a respite long enough to let him regain his magical strength and Cadwal and he were coming straight from a battle, which meant the brief snatches of rest hadn't let them regain their physical strength, either—and here they were being chased by hounds and humans like two hunted stags!

How long have we been hiding, running, running, hiding? He caught a quick glimpse of the sky through leaves, not really surprised to see the light already fading. *All the day, curse them!*

Chased all the day, yes, with barely time to snatch those few precious moments of rest, to eat or drink or, worst of all for a Sidhe, to restore his Power while there was all this wild forest Power so tantalizingly around him.

Morfren, Darkness take his vengeful little soul, is showing a downright obscene determination!

Useless attempt at wit. Humor wasn't helping. He was just too tired. His throat was burning for lack of water, his head was aching—his whole body, legs, lungs, all, was aching. And the hounds—the hounds, Ardagh realized, *liked* his scent, just like that fool of a dog back in Egbert's court, they found his alien Sidhe scent so intriguing that they didn't want to lose him even though the forest's shadows were rapidly deepening.

Darkness take them! Ardagh didn't mean the earthly night. *Darkness take them all!*

He risked a quick glance at the mercenary. Cadwal wasn't going to last much longer; in addition to that same sheer exhaustion plaguing Ardagh, Cadwal was still on the edge of shock from having found and lost his love a second time.

And I . . . I'm not going to last much longer . . . either. Have to stop. Rest. Restore my Power.

Not a hope of that. Yes, yes, and what made it more maddening yet was knowing that this hunt, in fact this whole chaotic mess, was caused, when one came down to it, by Osmod—ae, yes, it always did come back to Osmod, didn't it?

Your death, Ardagh promised him. *Your death.*

Oh, of course. Simple. He merely had to find a way to fight an unknown Power, a magic of which he'd never even heard! No trouble at all. And before he could do that, he first merely had to find a way to escape these stupid, vindictive, preposterous *humans!*

How dare they? he thought in a sudden blaze of fury. *How dare these mere nothings chase a prince of the Sidhe?*

And all at once it was past the point of any enduring. "Enough!" the prince cried, skidding to a halt, dragging the startled, alarmed Cadwal back with him.

"What the hell—"

Ardagh ignored him. "Tylwyth Teg! Hear me, Tylwyth Teg!" It was shouted in the Sidhe tongue, which was, he hoped, close enough to their own for them to understand him. "I know you hear me, sense me, see me! I am Ardagh Lithanial, Prince of the Sidhe"—he was hardly going to mention his exile, not here, not now—"and I place the Bonds of Sanctuary on you!"

That was an archaic ritual, but the only one his tired

brain could find. Unfortunately, it was a ritual more often
ignored by the various branches of the Folk than hon-
ored—and it was ignored now.

Damnation.

"Tylwyth Teg!"

He could hear the baying of the hounds, alarmingly
close, he could hear the crashing of bodies tearing
through underbrush, and Cadwal murmured uneasily,
"Hope you know what you're doing."

So do I! "Tylwyth Teg! Listen to me, cousins!" *Most
distant cousins.* "Would you let even so distant a kinsman die like this? Would you let one of the Folk die
at the hands of *humans?*"

"Thee be of bringing them all down about our heads,
that shouting of thine," a woman's voice said quietly. Her
accent was strange to Ardagh's ear, her syntax more so,
but it was still understandable enough.

"Yes it is and a human with you, you've brought,"
murmured another woman. "Fine, sturdy fellow, this,"
she added, a touch of forthright admiration coloring her
soft voice, "but human be he still."

The prince straightened, frowning, his Sidhe vision
seeing through the growing darkness without difficulty.
Ah yes, there they were, standing in the twilight shadows as though merely part of the forest, a few slender,
graceful shapes, men and women both. They were somewhat smaller than the Sidhe, but just as slanted of eye;
their pale skin glowed faintly in the darkness. A shimmer of magic surrounded them, a fog of glamour, Ardagh
realized, to make them invisible to human eyes, inau-
dible to human ears, though of course they were con-
spicuous enough to one of his race.

Not, naturally, to Cadwal, who, being human, was
blind and deaf to their presence. "Don't know what
you're doing," he muttered, "and I hope it's not just
talking to empty air, but whatever it is, you'd better hurry
up at it. I hear the damned hunters again."

So did Ardagh; no mistaking the shouts of men

hurrying after their hounds—and the sound of hounds who had just sighted their prey.

But I can't hurry, curse it! If I'm to claim sanctuary, the proper rules must be followed—ridiculous though it seems right now!

Heart racing, desperately keeping his face a mask, the prince bowed slightly in the Courtesy of Regal Blood to Those of Unknown Status, wondering if the Tylwyth Teg would even recognize the gesture. "This man is with me as a friend. The humans want both our lives, and I ask shelter in both our names."

A sigh, soft as the twilight breeze. "Pity, it is," someone murmured.

"For aiding does he beg, far-flung cousin of ours?"

"Do they insult me, far-flung cousins of mine?" Ardagh retorted coldly. "Surely they are wise enough to know the Sidhe never beg."

"Dammit, man," Cadwal muttered, staring at the hunters, "they've got spears. Swords aren't going to help us. We've got to get out of here *now!*"

Don't I know it! But the prince forced his voice to stay as cool as though merely discussing the weather, his face a still, regal mask. "Are my cousins afraid, perhaps?" he asked sardonically. "Afraid of the human folk?" Ardagh let just the barest edge of sharpness into his voice. "Have you come to that, my cousins? Would you turn aside a kinsman out of fear of humans? Let him be slain like some common thief because you fear their vengeance?"

Powers, the hunters were leashing their hounds, pulling the dogs back out of the way of the spears.

And here we are, perfect targets! No time for more: he either won or lost, as Cadwal might say, on this one last throw of the dice. "Are you mere *servants*, then?" he snapped at the Tylwyth Teg. "Are you humans' *slaves?* Bah, I am ashamed to call you kin!"

"Softness, quietness," a man purred. "Jesting we did, only that."

"Come," said a woman sweetly. "Shelter, yes, we grant you this."

A spear cut through the air, stabbing into a tree just by Ardagh's ear, but he stood his ground, grimly refusing to flinch. "Shelter for *both* of us."

A sigh, heavy with resignation. "For both. The human, if so it must be. Come."

No, he thought in sudden wariness, knowing just how devious the minds of the Faerie Folk could be. "Shelter" wasn't a strong enough word; "shelter" held the uneasy implication that they could still be thrown out again to face the hunters, maybe after only the briefest moments of safety, without making liars of the Tylwyth Teg. Ardagh insisted, "Do you grant us sanctuary?" And he used a very ancient, very Powerful word, *seilnathal,* which meant a vow of provided safety.

Did the Tylwyth Teg know the word? Yes. He saw a startled glint in their eyes. Would they swear by it? For one long, unnerving moment no one spoke.

And then: "Yes. Granted it is."

The masking glamour expanded to include Ardagh and Cadwal, falling over them like a shimmering veil. *Oh yes,* the prince thought indignantly, sensing the Tylwyth Teg conceit, their feeling of superiority over the mere Sidhe, that went with it, *easy enough to cast such a thing when you haven't already lost Power defending yourself and have several of you pooling the magic to work it!*

But that wasn't going to stop him from being glad of the shielding. Ah, listen to the humans' confusion! The poor, terrified little hunters, they'd just seen their prey vanish in plain sight, hadn't they?

Yes, but wait, this was no time for complacency! Something was wrong, very wrong, and Ardagh glanced about, glanced up, *feeling* the truth of it, knowing in sharp alarm, "This spell of yours isn't going to last! You've stretched it too far, you've overreached your Power!"

Did they understand? Yes, yes, they could hardly fail to *feel* the growing flaw in the spell. But were they going to waste time in arguing? Ardagh braced himself for a renewed flight, but—

"True," the Tylwyth Teg snapped, just as the masking fog began to shimmer and fade. "Yes, come!"

The fog was fading—the fog was gone! Ardagh heard a great shout of pure superstitious terror from the hunters.

Right. Their prey suddenly reappears, and with Others as well—they probably think we're demons cast back up from their Hell.

And in their utter terror, their sudden panic-stricken religious fervor, they wouldn't hesitate to attack those "demons." Ardagh took a firm grip on Cadwal's arm. "Don't trust your eyes. Trust me. I'll explain when we're safe."

"Hurry, Sidhe, hurry!" the Tylwyth Teg hissed from the side of a huge oak, its roots curving out over the earth like great, gnarled arches. "In here, Sidhe, hurry!"

But Ardagh brought himself suddenly up short, just in time for a spear to flash by his cheek and slam into the tree, showering him with splinters. "Close!" Cadwal gasped.

"Too close!"

Another spear smacked into the ground by the prince's feet. He raced forward again, pulling Cadwal with him, dove into the sanctuary the Tylwyth Teg were offering.

"Wait!" the mercenary cried in alarm. "Stop! There's nothing here but a—a gap under that tree's roots—we can't all fit in there!"

"We can. What you're seeing is illusion. Close your eyes and trust me."

"Easy for you to say! What I'm seeing is us about to dash our brains out against a tree!"

But Cadwal squeezed his eyes shut, and Ardagh pulled them both inside in a frantic scurry, spears thudding into the tree and ground behind them. There was sudden silence, and the sense of no longer being quite in the same reality as before.

And, Ardagh thought with a fierce grin, as far as the hunters were concerned, their prey had once again simply . . . vanished.

Back to Hell, humans, that's surely what you believe. Very well, think of that, humans, and be afraid. For what goes into Hell, your teachings tell you, may yet return.

And so shall we.

Powers, of course, willing.

Seductions
Chapter 24

If all this doesn't put the fear of their deity into the humans, Ardagh thought as he and Cadwal followed their Tylwyth Teg guides out of human reality, *nothing will!*

The cavelike gap under the roots turned without warning, as he'd more or less expected, into a narrow earthen tunnel, which in turn quickly became a stone stairway leading down past stone walls. This in turn became a wide, high tunnel of smooth, seamless limestone that apparently stretched off in a straight line for some distance—or at least so Ardagh guessed, since even the Sidhe needed a *little* light by which to see.

One of the Tylwyth Teg, probably just as handicapped by the total darkness ahead as the prince, gave an annoyed little "Tchah!" In the next instant, a row of torches lining the walls burst into light, sparked, Ardagh *felt,* by a flash of magical will. The flames were a clear, pale blue, totally without smoke or heat.

A pretty device, thought Ardagh, who recognized it, *if not particularly Powerful. In fact . . . now that I think about it, I don't sense all that much Power anywhere. Mm, yes, and the fact that the torches weren't lit and waiting for us means these folk are fallible.*

Comforting to know, in a way. "Wait a moment, Cadwal," the prince said hastily in the human tongue. "Don't open your eyes just yet." Right now, he suspected, the human would have seen nothing but the terrifying illusion that he was buried alive in bare earth.

"Uh, sure," Cadwal agreed, probably suspecting the same thing. "Look," he added in a quick, nervous undertone, "I appreciate the sanctuary, or whatever this is, but wandering around blind in God knows what isn't my idea of fun, and I really would like to know what the hell's going on."

"I called to the Tylwyth Teg. They answered. You're in no danger just now."

"Just now? And isn't *that* reassuring!"

"I didn't mean it that way. Wait a moment more." Switching back to the Sidhe tongue, Ardagh told the Tylwyth Teg, who were watching them with great fascination, "Drop the glamour about him, if you would, so my friend can see where we're going."

A very put-upon sigh whispered through the tunnel. The Tylwyth Teg plainly had been enjoying the game of Bait the Human.

"Do it," the prince said flatly, royalty brooking no argument.

Another sigh, this time in resignation. "If it must be, it must," someone murmured. "Agreed. There. It has been done. Now, come."

The prince heard Cadwal's soft gasp as he suddenly could see the Tylwyth Teg. But to Ardagh's delight all the mercenary said after that first startled moment of glancing from them to the prince and back again was a laconic, "Cousins, I take it? Definite family resemblance."

There were admiring little chuckles from those of the Tylwyth Teg who understood the human tongue. Ardagh looked at them, now that he thought about it a bit insulted by the easy comparison, noting their small stature, their golden hair and foxy-sharp faces, and corrected dryly, "Distant cousins. Very distant."

"Brave of being, this the human is," a woman murmured, and there was genuine admiration in her voice.

"So suddenly into our place-world snatched, yet nothing of fear is within him."

Well now, interesting! This was surely the same woman who had made that rather flattering comment about Cadwal's appearance back in the forest. She moved quietly to the mercenary's side as innocently as though she meant merely to guide him.

Oh, indeed, the bemused Ardagh thought. *Guide him where is, of course, another matter.*

Trying not to grin, he watched as the woman, young—at least as the Folk reckoned age—slim, pretty and seemingly guileless, put a shy hand on Cadwal's arm, looking up at him as though he was an unexpected wonder. "Fear have none," Ardagh heard her murmur to the mercenary (who, by all the Powers, was actually reddening). "Nothing of harm here is there for you. Gwenalarch I am of the naming, and so vow I this." Seeing his blank face, she switched easily to Cymreig, presumably repeating her reassurance.

"Nothing of harm is there for you," the prince repeated with an inner laugh. *True enough, Cadwal, true enough.*

Well now, the human was an adult and hardly naive; he could speak and choose for himself. Gwenalarch was using no Power other than the normal magic of a woman finding a man intriguing, and since she had given her word to do him no harm . . . Ardagh shrugged, grinning to himself, thinking that Cadwal was a lucky fellow—and about time, too—and went on.

But as they moved forward down the tunnel, a sudden blaze of golden light burst upon them, and the prince heard Cadwal gasp in renewed shock, and nearly gasped as well.

Ahead lay a great hall, high of ceiling and dazzlingly bright, glinting with gold, silver, fire-bright copper, gleaming with tapestries rich with a hundred hues. A few of the Tylwyth Teg sat at a long table of polished, amber-red wood; others stood in small groups of two or three, their clothing richly hued as the tapestries.

To Ardagh's surprise, a few laughing, excited children raced among the adults, their cheerful noise an incongruous touch amid the tranquillity: human, most of them. Not surprising, given the Folk's tendency towards infertility and with the human world so near to hand. Changelings? Unwanted babies given freely? Whatever, they looked happy and healthy; none of the Folk, no matter what their race, harmed children.

They must be frequently taken up out of the caverns for light and air; they'd have to be. Humans cannot thrive without the sun.

He took a wary step forward, and every one of the Tylwyth Teg in the hall froze, staring in undisguised curiosity. Even the children, puzzled by the adults' behavior, stopped to stare.

Don't see strangers very often, do you? Particularly not a stranger who is one of the Sidhe, I take it.

Unfortunately, his Sidhe eyes could, like it or not, see through illusion—and after the first dazzled moment, he realized with a touch of regret that nearly all the splendor was just that—illusion. The rich clothing was nicely dyed, yes, but the fabrics were merely wool or linen. And the hall itself . . . Ardagh looked right through the glory of it to the plain grey cavern, the mundane reality, behind it, and felt a twinge of genuine disappointment.

Illusion. Nothing much more.

And why should I be disappointed? They never were known as the greatest mages, not even in the Faerie Realms.

No wonder, then, that they chose to live here in the human Realm, where any Power was a great marvel and they could be all but worshiped by those they deigned to let see them.

Did I really think that such as these could help me? That they'd somehow, miraculously, reveal a Power unknown to the Sidhe, a strength I lack? The strength

*to actually open a Doorway home? How could I be such
a fool?* Ardagh blinked fiercely, furious to find his vision
suddenly blurring, and snapped at himself not to be
more foolish yet.

Cadwal, of course, even with the Otherly glamour
removed from him, was still human; he could only see
all the splendid illusion before him as solid truth.

And the shock of it all must have been truly overwhelming. Cadwal topped short in the entrance to the
great cavern with a muttered, "No." Ardagh and Gwenalarch both turned to him in alarm, and he gave them
both a wild-eyed glance before turning to stare again at
what to him must have been a glorious, impossibly alien
hall.

"No. I'm sorry." In his voice was the unnaturally calm
desperation of a man who has finally gone beyond the
last of his endurance. "No. I . . . I could take the rest,
but this . . . this is just too much. Sorry. This is as far
as I go today."

Not surprising, Ardagh mused. It was amazing that the
human had lasted as long as he had, what with all his
world turned aslant again and again in the past day.
Gwenalarch gave a low, worried cry, having evidently
puzzled out enough of what Cadwal had said. She caught
him by the shoulders so that she could look directly up
at him, her face a study in genuine concern, and told
him gentle words in Cymreig.

Ae, clever! Ardagh thought. *No open seduction, nothing
alarming. No, no, she's being downright maternal—for
now. And, no doubt about it, she really does mean to help.*

Cadwal, being no fool, had to know exactly what he
was being offered—in addition, that was, to a peaceful
night away from everything. The mercenary glanced
uncertainly at Ardagh, a wild mix of confusion and longing on his face. The prince nodded ever so subtly—*yes,
it's safe, it's permitted*—and saw relief flash in Cadwal's
eyes. His hand in Gwenalarch's, the mercenary let her
lead him away.

"He shall of no harming come," a woman murmured, and Ardagh just barely kept from laughing aloud.

"I know," he said with great restraint. *On the contrary, this may prove the best medicine any could give him!* The prince turned to see who'd spoken:

So-o! This could only be the ruler of this clan, a woman lovely and ageless in the foxy-sharp Tylwyth Teg way—lovely enough to send a little prickle of pleasure through him. It had been long and long again, after all, since he'd seen any woman of the Folk.

Control, he warned himself, well aware of the casual awareness of authority surrounding her. Tall for her people, she came almost to his shoulder, her eyes as green as his, her hair a long fall of reddish-gold held back from her face by a thin silver coronet worked to resemble the graceful curl of waves. The Otherly silkiness of her gown was no illusion, nor was its color, a smooth bluish-green, the exact shade of ocean touched by moonlight; the fabric was patterned to shimmer like the waves with even the slightest movement. Not a gown or a coronet, the prince thought, for a cavern-dweller to wear. But then, the Tylwyth Teg were said to love the sea.

No sea, no bodies of water of any size, anywhere nearby. Odd.

Nothing odd at all about the way she was studying him, and unlike he, making no attempt to hide her pleasure.

Flattering, Powers, yes. And Powers be thanked that I am not a human, to let animal instinct reveal itself. One way or another. "Lady," Ardagh said smoothly, and bowed, royal to royal.

She returned the bow just as graciously. "Sidhe lord. Seldom-rare is it that the race of yours visits ours." A pause. "Tywthylodd am I, Princess Tywthylodd Gwythion of the Tylwyth Teg. Your name is for my knowing?"

She obviously hadn't been out there scrambling away from the human attack. "I am—ah, Ardagh Lithanial am I, Prince of the Sidhe."

"Ah. Pleased will you be to with us dine?"

Hunger, fiercely suppressed all during the long chase, woke with a roar. "Pleased, indeed, Princess Tywthylodd, and my gratitude to you. But first . . ." His rueful gesture took in his soiled, tired clothing and self. The princess smiled with a touch more amusement than his dignity would have liked.

"Of course," was all she said.

The bath had been wonderfully, magically hot, and Ardagh had nearly fallen into exhausted sleep in the middle of it. Only the sharp impression that he was being secretly watched kept him at all alert.

Tywthylodd? Possibly. Or perhaps it was some of the pretty little servants he'd shooed away (thinking that it lacked all courtesy to his hostess to, as it were, welcome the servants before the ruler). The Sidhe lacked the humans' ridiculous prudery about their bodies, and he knew he had nothing of which to be ashamed, so Ardagh had ignored the watcher or watchers, knowing they'd meant him no harm. Now he let other servants—male, this time—dry him with towels of human weave, though nicely soft, and bring him blessedly clean clothing, sky-blue tunic and sea-blue leggings, of human weave, again, but of exotic Tylwyth Teg design.

"This way, if pleasing you this is," one servant said politely, and led the prince back to the splendid-seeming hall. Princess Tywthylodd was already there, seated at the precise midpoint of the great table. If it had, indeed, been she watching him, she gave not the faintest sign of it.

"Come, Prince Ardagh, seated here be, by my side."

The food was not as elegant as he'd expected; earthly plain, but it was nicely seasoned and plentiful. All around him, the Tylwyth Teg chattered and laughed as they ate, surrounding him with a cheerful babble of noise, though none, not even the princess, tried to engage him in conversation.

Which was fine with Ardagh. This was the first true meal he'd had in . . . Powers, just how long had it been since he'd eaten a genuine, cooked-and-served meal? Unlikely that his hosts would try to poison or ensorcel him; the various races of the Folk generally saw betrayal during a meal as impossible falsehood. Besides, the prince thought cynically, even if these Folk had been . . . influenced by human behavior, his Sidhe senses would still warn him of any problems—

As they were warning him of one right now: Ardagh, seated to the right of the princess, who kept giving him sly little glances of approval, was growing very much aware of the man who sat to her left. He was as elegant as she, in robes of the same sea-blue richness. His hair was a shimmering mass of gold, his eyes a glowing dark green—and full of a light that was definitely not approving.

"If I may ask," Ardagh said with delicate care, "who is this?"

"This?" Tywthylodd gave the man a quick glance of casual affection. "Lord Cymyriod is this. My *cydwedd*."

Husband? Mate? For all he knew, brother? Though that was hardly a brotherly resentment in the brooding eyes. "My lord," Ardagh said with a polite dip of his head.

The Lord Cymyriod nodded curtly but said nothing.

Just what I needed: more complications.

Ah well, he couldn't worry about that right now. Hunger was finally gone, but heavy weariness was creeping back into its place. "Princess Tywthylodd—"

She stood, and of course everyone stood with her. "Pleased are you to with me walk, Prince Ardagh? Alone? It is to my thought matters have we to speak."

It is to my thought that sleep is what I want. But of course he couldn't be so unpolitic as to refuse his host. "It is to my thinking, too." *I just didn't want to worry about anything just yet.* "Please, lead the way."

But then Ardagh stopped at the sight of Lord Cymyriod staring with outright hostility. "If I may ask, Princess Tywthylodd," the prince said, "what, exactly *is* a . . . a *cydwedd*?"

"*Cydwedd?*" Tywthylodd shrugged casually. "That has a meaning . . . mm . . . consort. It has the meaning, consort."

"Ah." *A jealous consort. How splendid.* "Should he not join us?"

"It has no need of being so."

Of course not. I'll merely have to keep watching my back while I'm here.

They walked on together, her hand resting, feather-light, on his arm, echoing so strongly the very civilized ways of the Sidhe nobility that Ardagh nearly pulled away, remembering his brother's court, his brother's treacherous wife, Karanila.

But Tywthylodd was the ruler here, not her consort. And even though the small of his back was prickling, expecting an attack, Ardagh let her bring them both down a quiet corridor and out without warning into what seemed almost like a moonlit grove beside a tranquil lake, there under a sky rich with stars—

No, by all the Powers, there was no "seeming" about it! This wasn't illusion but reality, yes, and the lake mirroring the stars was real as well. Stunned, Ardagh told himself that maybe the Tylwyth Teg weren't quite as weak in Power as he'd imagined. Or rather, that their Power wasn't quite in the same shaping as that wielded by the Sidhe.

This wasn't a Doorway spell, no, nothing I could truly use to go home. A transfer spell of some sort, then, and so smoothly worked that I never even sensed it.

"Princess Tywthylodd . . ."

"No. Not yet. Here sitting shall we be."

It was a pleasant little space by the water's edge. There beneath the overhanging arch of a willow's branches was a divan so cleverly worked as to seem part of the tree and piled comfortably with cushions. It was, Ardagh noted, easily wide enough to hold someone lying at his ease.

Or rather, he reconsidered, *two* someones. *Oh, and*

isn't this perfect. There's a lovely lady of a race near to my own, a jealous consort to consider, and Sorcha to remember—though I'd guess she'd be understanding of the circumstances (wouldn't she?)—and—and I'm just too cursed weary to . . . do anything about it all. "First, Princess Tywthylodd, shall we not talk a bit?"

She smiled, but it was a very politic smile that failed to include her eyes; no matter what her motives in bringing him to this pretty seclusion, Tywthylodd, ruler that she was, plainly had no intention of letting down her guard quite yet.

"The Sidhe," she murmured, sinking to the divan and looking up at him with regal dignity, "common visitors to this land are not. Why is it you are here? And why," the princess added with the faintest frown of distaste, "is it that you be here with a human?"

He wasn't even about to attempt the different syntax of the Tylwyth Teg dialect. He also wasn't about to tell her the entire truth. "I am," Ardagh said slowly and carefully so that she could make no mistakes of comprehension, "with the human because the human and I have saved each other's lives so often that I've forgotten who's in debt to whom."

Ah, he was just too tired to stand any longer. Hoping he wasn't making some Tylwyth Teg declaration of more than he could deliver just now, Ardagh sat down beside her, then rather wished he hadn't; the cushions were so wondrously, tantalizingly, soft. . . .

No! He had to stay alert, at least for now. "As to why I am in this land at all: Ae, that is not quite so simple a story. Let us just say that Cadwal and I fell afoul of an enemy, a human foe—"

"Who?" she cut in.

"Not one who could ever threaten you or your folk."

"Yes, but naming him be."

Puzzled, Ardagh told her, "Morfren ap Dyfyr."

"Ah, that! Yes. A noisiness and nuisance he be, too late hunting, too early." Seeing the prince's blankness,

Tywthylodd continued with a touch of clear impatience, "See it not? *Our* time he spoils!"

Ah, of course. He'd forgotten, immune to sunlight as he was (presumably thanks to some vague, far-back taint of human blood—or so the court rumors had claimed—that also gave him his dark hair), that other Folk were not. The Tylwyth Teg, being among those unable to endure mortal sunlight, would not have appreciated Morfren's hunt cutting too close to dawn or twilight, the edges of night. Their time of freedom on mortal soil.

Tywthylodd's smile thinned ever so slightly. "He shall, thinking am I, with interesting incidents be meeting whenever our chosen land invades he."

"Ah . . . thank you in Cadwal's name."

"No, no, thanking not me! Fun shall be this!"

"Fun," Ardagh agreed wryly, seeing Morfren's life made miserable by Tylwyth Teg pranks every time he left his home, at least till the Folk grew bored with the game. *Even so, it will certainly stop him from bothering Cadwal again. What human wants anything to do with someone with Powerful friends?*

"But," the princess continued, "why be you in this land at all?"

Ardagh gave a weary ghost of a grin. "That," he told her, "is a question I've been asking myself often enough. Let us just say that I found myself enmeshed in human politics."

"So-o! Odd."

"Very." A dangerous subject; best to change it as quickly as possible. He did *not* want to let her know of his exile, and most certainly not of the fact that he was in the human Realm alone, with no Sidhe aid at his back. "Princess Tywthylodd, I understand your concern. But there is no peril to you or yours from that, or from either Cadwal or myself. This I freely swear to you."

She smiled again, and this time it was with genuine warmth. "So. Sidhe are no more of the lacking-of-truth than are my Tylwyth Teg."

Neither dialect had, of course, a word for "falsehood."
"'Lacking-of-truth,'" Ardagh murmured, "I like that."

"I have a liking of other things as well," the princess
purred, her glance running slowly over him, and now
her smile was very definitely warm. "I have, truly, yes.
And you? What think you, mm?"

To his horror, Ardagh realized he was about to yawn,
and just barely managed to turn it into a sigh. *I don't
believe this! A beautiful, willing woman of the Folk is
here beside me—and I really am too weary to do much
about it!* "Believe me, Tywthylodd," he said with rueful honesty, "it has been long and long again since I've
been so near a—a kinswoman, and oh, I do like what
I see, very much indeed. But it has been a long day, a
very long day, most of it spent running, and little enough
sleep before that."

"Ah. I see."

It was said without any inflection; her face was quite
unreadable. "Forgive me," Ardagh said again, and meant
it on every level, "but right now I'm just too cursedly
tired to give either of us much joy."

To his great relief, she merely gave a small, regretful
shrug, almost-amusement glinting in her eyes; if there
was anything all the long-lived Folk possessed, it was
patience. "Need for rush is there none," Tywthylodd
purred. "Stronger is joy for the waiting. Tonight . . .
the night is warm and clear, and no humans can come
nearby. Sleep here if this place has the pleasing for
you."

Oh Powers, how he longed to do just that, to just slide
sideways onto the cushions and worry about everything
tomorrow. But there had been something in that sly little
smile of hers, something uneasily reminiscent of a cat
that knows it will, eventually, snare its prey. Ardagh
hesitated, wondering if maybe she'd guessed more about
his status than he'd revealed.

A little security never hurt anyone, he decided. Since
none of the races of the Folk could lie, it was generally

considered a great breach of manners to ask a question that could not be evaded. *So be it*.

"Forgive me," Ardagh said carefully, "but I must ask for truth from you. I mean no insult by it."

"No insult is of the taking. Ask. Answer will I what I will."

"Am I safe here? Safe from harm of any sort?"

"You are."

There were many definitions of harm, and she had been just a touch too quick with that reply. Racking his exhausted brain for some more clearly defined reassurance, sure that he was missing some subtle detail, the prince asked, "May I sleep knowing I will wake without change to mind or will or body?"

"You may. The humans are, as I have the saying made, not of this place, and no one of mine—not even," she added with a sly little smile, "my so-jealous Lord Cymyriod—will be a disturbance."

She moved smoothly to her feet. Before Ardagh could see how she'd done it, Princess Tywthylodd was simply gone. Leaving him . . . wherever this was, and with not the faintest clue how to get back.

I should have worked a guarantee of freedom somewhere into all that. Should have. Bah.

He sat blinking groggily for a while, knowing he should be feeling more alarmed than he did, trying to focus on this sudden problem.

Impossible. *Just as Cadwal said, this is as far as I go today. Tywthylodd told me I was safe, she can't lie, I'll take her at her word—and . . . enough.*

Enough . . .

Almost gratefully, Ardagh surrendered to exhaustion, and dove into a wonderfully deep ocean of sleep.

Strange Alliances
Chapter 25

Sorcha ni Fothad, daughter of the High King of Eriu's Chief Poet and Minister, stood there in the royal fortress of Fremainn in the first faint grey light of morning, stood looking out over the dark mass of forest slowly growing into vibrant green—

Stood wishing with all her heart that she was far from here. *Ardagh* . . .

The softest of warning coughs made her turn, then bow politely. "King Aedh."

"You couldn't sleep, either, I see."

"Och, no. I . . . no." She wasn't about to tell the king that her dreams had been so dark, so full of worryings about Ardagh, that she'd decided it was far better to be awake. But Aedh smiled slightly; he'd guessed the truth.

"Of course you're worried about him," he said softly. "You wouldn't be human else." As Ardagh was not. Aedh hurried over that point. "My Eithne told me once—and then denied she'd ever said it—just how lonely it is for a woman waiting for her man to return."

"Life," Sorcha said shortly, "goes on. As it would whether or not women spent all their time in waiting and wailing. Your pardon if I'm speaking out of turn here, King Aedh, but you don't understand. We women are stronger—we've had to be—than you men would like to believe." *Oh, clever,* she snapped at herself, *insult both the king and his gender in the one saying.*

But Aedh only laughed. "Prince Ardagh is right. You're

wasted as your father's clerk. If the laws were other than they were, Sorcha, I'd make you one of my councilors, and you and the prince both could put the fear of the Lord—or whatever it is Prince Ardagh worships—into the others." He paused almost imperceptibly. "Where is he, Sorcha? Where is our wandering prince of the Sidhe?"

"I'm not sure. Where he was at last greeting, or—or at least so I hope."

"In Cymru," Aedh said in disgust. "I suppose I should be astonished that a mission to Wessex could ever end up so very twisted-about, but somehow I'm not. Not where the Sidhe are involved." He shook his head. "Who knows? The next time you hear from Prince Ardagh, he might even be aboard one of those elegant Lochlannach dragon-ships—yes, and terrorizing the whole shipload of those pirates into doing his bidding! Whatever," the king added darkly, "that might be."

"King Aedh! Ardagh is not a traitor!"

"Softly, lass. Of course he isn't. And I never meant to imply that he was. Principles of honor aside, our prince simply cannot lie, which means that he couldn't betray us even if he wished it."

"He doesn't."

"I know, I know. I only wish I knew what he was about!"

Sorcha shivered as a sudden damp breeze swept in over the forest. *Rain on its way. I hope you're dry, my love.* "Believe me, King Aedh, so do I. I haven't heard from him for—for far too long." *He wouldn't betray me, I know that. But what if Ardagh's hurt, or—or—or worse—no! I won't believe that!* "Right now," Sorcha said with fierce restraint, "I'd settle for just knowing where he is, and that he's whole and healthy and safe!"

"Och, well, I do, too." Aedh suddenly patted her hand in awkward comfort. "He'll be back. If the man's survived his brother's court and exiling, nothing in this silly little human world is going to be strong enough to stop him."

"He'll be back," Sorcha agreed. "He will be back."
God grant that it be so.

*He was in Eriu, Ardagh's sleeping mind knew that at
once. Yes, he was in Eriu, in Fremainn, though the distances seemed altered as only they could be in a dream,
the spaces between houses stretching out impossibly far
while he stalked his foe, the false Bishop Gervinus.
Gervinus was in the midst of some dark sorcery . . . yes,
the prince knew it now: the bishop was conjuring a
demon, and only Ardagh could stop him.*

Only Ardagh could stop him.

Only—

The prince awoke all at once, eyes snapping open. For
a moment he was wildly disoriented, expecting Fremainn, finding only a misty haze and the soft lapping
of water against land. The boughs of a willow arched
gracefully over him, and with a sudden shock of recognition, Ardagh knew exactly where he was: the Realm
of the Tylwyth Teg. This was the lakeside that brushed
up against the human Realm.

All around him was the peacefulness of early morning,
the first faint chirps of birds and rustling of leaves in the
soft breeze, though the mist kept out any trace of sun.
The air was cool and damp, heavy with the scent of wet
vegetation. Sometime during his sleep, he had slid from
the divan to the ground, taking some of the cushions with
him, and both they and the ground itself were wet with
dew. The prince sat up with a shudder of purely physical chill, realizing that otherwise he felt perfectly restored.
Once again his sleeping mind had managed to draw
Power from his involuntary direct contact with the earth.

But his mind had also conjured up Gervinus. Of all
the people of whom he could have dreamed, why him?

The answer wasn't difficult. His sleeping mind had
plainly been sending him a warning, not of the late,
unmourned Gervinus, but of his closest living parallel—
the very much alive Osmod. Ae-yi, yes, like it or not,

the matter between him and the ealdorman had gone far beyond being merely a personal feud.

A matter of dangerous ambition, that's what it is.

Gervinus, as his dream had so carefully reminded him, had plotted to control Eriu. King Egbert's ambitions clearly reached out for all of Britain. No peril to Eriu there, not really.

But Osmod's dreams were another case. Osmod's dreams barely stopped at Britain's shores. Ardagh frowned, wondering uneasily why he hadn't seen the threat right from the start. Was he still so much Eirithan's brother that his mind ignored a peril to mere humans?

The prince hissed in disgust. Hardly that!

What, then? Was it that I didn't want to see the threat? Was I in such haste to be done so I might return to Sorcha? Have I, then, grown so very . . .

But the only way to finish that thought was with the impossible: "human." And only humans worried over what had already happened.

So, now. Consider Osmod. Consider him and Egbert both: strong, determined, ambitious—with the sorcerer able to give his king a strength far beyond human military might. Without magic, it would surely take Egbert most of his merely human life to conquer all of his neighbors, yes, and to hold fast to his conquests. With magic, the combination of royal and sorcerous powers would tear right through any merely mundane defenses in a frighteningly short span.

Yes, and what then? Once Osmod and Egbert had finished with Britain, would they be content? Hardly. They would soon enough be reaching out across the narrow water from Britain to the nearest obvious challenge. Not to the Frankish lands, not when it meant facing the Emperor Charlemagne and his ties to Rome. But Eriu stood alone.

And I was the one who reminded Osmod and Egbert both that Eriu was there for the attacking. How very good of me.

This double menace to Eriu, military and sorcerous force united, would be far stronger than anything the lone Gervinus could ever have posed, even with the worst spells from his grimoire.

Darkness rend them both.

But again, only humans wasted time in futile curses. Ardagh got to his feet, restlessly pacing by the lakeside. He was not going to let his sanctuary or his human allies—most certainly not his human love—be imperiled, but he certainly couldn't fight the entire might of Wessex single-handedly.

Which meant that he'd been right all along: He couldn't just up and return to Eriu. Ae, no, he had to stop the sorcerer now, before any there were any military complications.

He must destroy Osmod.

But how? I can hardly go back to Wessex and challenge the man to a—a mundane duel! Even if I did, I couldn't fight Osmod's foreign style of magic.

Then he'd just have to learn how Osmod's magic worked, wouldn't he?

As easily as that. Hah.

And then Ardagh stopped short, struck by so strong a sense of *yes, this is what to do, this is where to go from here: the Cymric coast.* There, he knew it as surely as though someone had shouted it, he would find an ally. What or who that ally might be—ae, no, that was as far as the flash of foresight went.

So be it. I never was much of a seer even in the Sidhe Realm.

Well now, all this was promising a fascinating time ahead. But before he could do anything else, Ardagh reminded himself sharply, he first had to figure out how to get out of this pretty snare. Foolish to have gotten into the situation at all! But the prince accepted with Sidhe honesty that he'd just been too weary, mind and body both, to have avoided even so obvious a trap.

*They took away my sword and dagger, I see. Not
surprising. I wouldn't have left me armed, either.*

The lack of weapons didn't matter, not just yet. Ardagh
froze, concentrating, then shook his head in surprise.
Odd! No one was watching him, magically or mundanely,
he was almost certain of that.

*Tywthylodd must be very sure that I can't escape. Or
that I am hopelessly ensnared for . . . ah . . . lust of her.
Either way, it's a definite mistake on her part. Though
how I can make use of it . . .*

The prince stood with eyes closed and senses alert,
hunting this time for any trace of disturbance, any shimmering of reality.

He opened his eyes again in disgust. Nothing! Or else
the Tylwyth Teg transfer spell was simply too *ordinary*,
too much a part of this place after much usage, to stand
out.

*Of course. Everything else in this cursed journey's been
complicated. Why should this be any different?*

Ardagh got to his feet and prowled along the edge of
the lake, listening, scenting the air, hunting anything that
didn't belong in such a peaceful scene.

Still no trace of any Doorway. But there was a *feeling* of Power set and holding . . . yes. The mist grew
thicker as he went, finally turning almost solid.

Ardagh stopped, considering. A barrier. Not so much
to keep anyone in, he'd hazard, as to keep the outside
world out. No doubt any human wandering along the
lakeside would see nothing unusual, possibly not even
more than a hint of the mist itself, yet feel a definite
sense of *nothing here, turn back, go away.*

"Clever," the prince said aloud.

He tested. Sure enough, a short stroll away from the
lake into the vegetation brought him up against the wall
of mist once more. He walked back along the lake the
other way, following the curve of the shore. Ha, yes, here
was the ever-thickening magical mist again, at the other
end of this half-circle of lake. One firmly set loop of mist

encircled greenery and water. Ardagh knelt at the water's edge, watching carefully.

Yes. There were swarms of small fish, fingerlings he thought they were called, swimming towards the mist, then turning aside like a flock of birds hitting an invisible barrier. The ring of force extended below the surface, then, as well; no simple escape, then, by swimming under it.

No doubt there are more fingerlings on the other side of this thing, equally cut off from these their fellows. Clever Tylwyth Teg, indeed. They've made themselves a private garden out of this bit of mortal wilderness.

And in the process, trapped him in it. Why? Ardagh thought of Princess Tywthylodd's sly, subtle smile and gave a sharp little laugh. The "why" of it was obvious enough: she'd decided she liked this exotic Sidhe, this all-by-himself Sidhe, and planned to keep him here awhile. By not calling this an imprisonment, but merely a . . . what word would she use? Dalliance, perhaps? Yes, there was a fine euphemism. By calling this a pleasant dalliance with not the slightest hint of danger to it for her "guest," she could easily evade her vow not to offer him harm.

No harm—except from sheer frustration. I wonder if it's even morning out there in the human Realm. If, for that matter, it's even the same day.

Time sometimes ran strangely between the Faerie and mortal Realms. Fighting the sudden panicky thought that it might not even be the same *decade* it had been in Eriu, Ardagh whipped out the magicked amulet-half. "Sorcha? Can you hear me, love? Sorcha?"

Powers, maybe she couldn't hear him. Maybe it really wasn't the same time or—

"Ardagh!" It was an impassioned whisper, and Ardagh's heart skipped a beat with relief. "There are folks about! Wait . . ." After a time, he heard her continue, "I'm alone near your guest house. But it's morning! You've never contacted me in the morning! What's wrong? And *where are you?*"

Ardagh glanced wryly about the misty garden. "That, my love, is not going to be too easy to explain. But it *is* morning there?"

"Yes, of course. Ardagh, what—"

Ah, thank you, whatever Powers are listening, thank you!

Clearly no outlandish amount of time had passed. In fact, the odds were probably good that it really was the same day both here and there. "Thank you, love. I'm truly glad to hear that. As to where we are . . . Cadwal and I are still in Cymru. More or less."

"More or less?" she echoed incredulously. "Now what am I not going to want to hear?"

"Ah well, it's not that bad. You see, we've been given sanctuary by distant kinfolk: the Tylwyth Teg."

"That—that's the Cymraic Fair Folk? They're *real*?"

He chuckled. "Real as the Sidhe." Ardagh glanced quickly about. Maybe they weren't actually watching him, but sooner or later—doubtlessly sooner—someone was going to be checking on the "guest's" well-being. "Sorcha, I fear I must be brief. Cadwal and I are both safe and unharmed." *If trapped.* "I will contact you again as quickly as I may. Please, love, I know this sounds impossibly glib, but try not to worry."

"Hah!"

"Sorcha—"

"I know, I know. You have no choice in the matter."

Ardagh thought of Osmod and bit his lip. "That, love, is more true than ever. I'm sorry, I can't say more right now."

He heard her angry hiss of a sigh. "I'm getting truly weary of saying this, Ardagh, but: Come home. Finish up whatever weirdness it is you're doing and come home to me."

"As soon as I can, of honor. On that, my dearest one, you have my vow."

"I'd rather have *you*," she snapped, "and never mind the talk of honor. But things are as they are, you are as you are, and I'll try to take what comfort from that fact I can."

She broke off contact sharply, and Ardagh stood staring blindly at the amulet, aching for Sorcha with a ferocity that astonished him. Powers, ae Powers, just how strong was the force that was love?

How strong was *human* love? For the first time, Ardagh imagined this journey as it might seem to Sorcha: an endlessness of waiting, of worrying, of never knowing whether he'd return, or even if he was still alive. What if she grew too weary from the burden? What if she could no longer bear the strain of loving him?

I cannot lose her, not her, not this as well as all else. I cannot.

Ae, ridiculous. He'd might as well *be* a human for all the logic in this—this maundering chain of thought. He was not going to so suddenly fall out of love, and neither, from everything he'd ever seen and known and adored about her, was Sorcha.

Heh, Eithne doesn't fall out of love with Aedh every time he goes off to battle.

And while this separation was an unhappy thing for both of them, he wasn't going to end it by standing here and pining. Ardagh put the amulet safely away, and turned the current problem over and over in his mind, hunting weaknesses.

First: What disadvantages did he have? No physical weapons. Given. No way of using Sidhe Power against a Tylwyth Teg spell. Given.

Now: What advantages did he have? Rested, yes. Power restored, yes. What else? What else? There must be something less obvious. . . .

Ha, yes, less obvious, indeed! Princess Tywthylodd might have decided to keep this lone Sidhe here as her pet, but pets eventually had to be fed, and—

Pet? Not exactly. He was a prince of the Sidhe, which made him a rare, valuable being to the Tylwyth Teg, and Ardagh doubted that Tywthylodd was shallow enough to

want him only as a plaything. What else, then? Not as
a political bargaining counter; the two races had little
to do with each other.

"Darkness take it," Ardagh said in sudden comprehension.

Of course. What else could it be? Tywthylodd intended
him, and not her consort, to be the sire of her heir. No
choice about it on his part, of course; no matter how
he might feel about it, there were drugs, spells, to ensure
his constant fidelity. Granted, neither race was very
fertile, but given the situation, he and she just might
engender a child.

*One who would combine the Powers of both the Sidhe
and the Tylwyth Teg—now there's an intriguing idea. And
if we were both in my Realm . . . well, who can say what
might have happened? Here and now, though—no. Like
the wyvern, I do not breed in captivity. And I am most
certainly not going to risk creating an heir of mine who
would never even see the Sidhe Realm.*

Yes, but pet or surrogate consort, he still needed to
be fed. And that meant . . . yes, indeed, here was his
main advantage. The princess and her people knew very
little about him, other than that he was of the Sidhe.
And what did the Tylwyth Teg know of the Sidhe? That
they were an arrogant race? Aloof and oh-so refined?
Yes, that was the usual image of his race held by the
other Folk; he'd heard it often enough at his brother's
court. And he, of course, was no less than a prince of
the Sidhe. How else could these people see him but as
someone so regal and elegant he would never even
consider soiling his hands with anything as unpleasant
as physical violence?

My, but they are in for a surprise!

Ha, someone was coming. He could *feel* the shimmering in the air . . . there. Ardagh hastily threw himself
down on the divan, forcing himself into a stillness so
complete that it was almost trance. Just in case anyone
was overly curious, he meant to seem genuinely asleep.

But one part of his mind stayed alert and aware. Here came the mysterious someone . . . not Tywthylodd, no. A servant, almost certainly from the slightly subservient *feel* to him. Good enough. Ardagh waited, hearing the hesitant footsteps grow nearer . . . nearer—

He sprang from the divan with a roar, catching the servant by the shoulders, flinging him roughly down, pinning him against the ground. The scrawny little mouse of a man stared up at him, wide-eyed, not so much in fright as in sheer, stunned disbelief. *This could not be,* his expression all but screamed, *a Sidhe prince could not be acting like this, he just could not!* "Wh-what—"

"Shut up! I'll do the talking." *Bah, I sound like a villain from a children's tale.* Effective enough, though, judging from the way his captive winced. "I want you to get me out of here, *now.*"

"I—I can't."

Ardagh brought up a fist in fierce imitation of humans he'd once seen brawling. "I said, *I'll* do the talking! You got in here, didn't you? Get me out!"

"P-please, not possible, n-not me, enough of Power I—I—I have not!"

So much for that plan. "Then who does?"

"I—I can't—"

"You can, and will!" Grabbing the servant by the collar, the prince scrambled to his feet, pulling the man up roughly with him. *Good thing the fellow's small and light!* "You'll tell me right now, won't you?" He shook the servant slightly. "*Won't you?* Who has the Power to come and go from here?"

"Having that Power, the—the princess, of course, and Lord Cymyriod—"

"Lord Cymyriod! But Tywthylodd told me he couldn't. . . ."

No. Ardagh recalled suddenly that Tywthylodd had never actually said that the consort couldn't find his way in here, only that Cymyriod wouldn't disturb him. *I really was weary if I hadn't caught that.* Then, barring distractions, presumably from his princess, Cymyriod and his jealousy could have walked right in here while Ardagh was helpless in his sleep. *Thank you, Tywthylodd!*

"Fine!" the prince snapped. "Get me the . . ." Curse it, what was the word? "The *cydwedd*. That's who I want. Bring Lord Cymyriod to me."

"T-try, yes, I—"

"Don't try, *do!* Swear it to me: You will bring Lord Cymyriod to me, here, now. Swear it!"

"I—I—swear it I do."

"Good! Then obey me!"

He shoved the servant roughly away and watched the man scurry off in frantic terror into nothingness. Only then did Ardagh relax, sitting back down with a hiss of disgust, brushing his hands together as though barbarism could be rubbed off like so much dirt. Ae, but he was glad no one else had seen that!

How in the name of all the Powers can humans stand to act with such—such boorishness?

No. Time enough to be finicky when he was free. Now, if only he hadn't overacted too badly . . . yes, and if only he did get Cymyriod and not Tywthylodd as well! Ardagh rather doubted that she'd be sympathetic to his cause, or care what happened to human lands. Neither would Cymyriod, of course—but what Cymyriod thought hardly mattered so long as he came here.

He would. He must. Remembering the bitterness in those dark green eyes, the painful jealousy, the prince nodded grimly. Surely the consort hated his "rival" enough to want to know what that rival wanted. Surely Cymyriod would be too curious to resist?

Ah, yes. Ardagh sat back, smiling to himself. Here came Lord Cymyriod now, stepping lightly out of empty air, wary as a cat but pretending for all he was worth that it was a mere whim that had brought him this way.

A whim. With his hand resting ever so casually on the hilt of his sword, and Power shimmering about him. "My Lord Cymyriod. How nice of you to visit."

The dark green eyes glittered coldly. "I do no playing of games."

"Neither," Ardagh said, sitting up, "do I. Lord Cymyriod, we share something in common. Ae, don't glare at me like that! We do. We both want me gone from here."

He saw the faintest of starts; Cymyriod hadn't expected that. *And why not, I wonder?* "Not for my doing is that," the lord said. "Princess Tywthylodd—"

"Is not here. You are."

"No! Not for my doing is that."

"Afraid of her, are you?" Ardagh purred. "Afraid of your princess?"

"No! The finest of women is she, Princess Tywthylodd. Nothing is there of fear for her from me!"

Well, now. It was hardly fear in Cymyriod's eyes—or rather, Ardagh mused, it was, but hardly of Tywthylodd or even of losing his rank. No, no, this was a very real fear Cymyriod held of losing *her*.

"So-o," the prince murmured in sudden understanding, "no wonder you hate me! And here I thought it was something as shallow as jealousy. You love her, don't you?"

The lord stared, looked away, stared again, his fair skin redddening. "How . . . would you have the knowing of such?"

"How? Because I'm in love with my own sweet lady. I certainly recognize the signs by now." Ardagh hesitated, studying Cymyriod, considering. *You're still young, aren't you?* Age, of course, was difficult to tell with the long-lived Folk. *Young and just a touch naive.* "My lord, I admit I was planning to trick you and force you to let me out of here. Now, I don't think that's necessary."

"What say you?"

"Lord Cymyriod, your princess is a fine, lovely woman, and if things were different, well now, who knows what might have happened? Ae, don't bristle! Hear me out. I see that you love her—but as for me, my lord, I love my freedom and my own dear lady more."

No answer. Cymyriod was so blatantly concentrating on keeping his face impassive that Ardagh thought, *Young, indeed.* "Lord Cymyriod, do you *want* me here? Do you *want* to share Tywthylodd's affections? Maybe even lose them altogether?"

Ha, that struck home. "Not possible is that!"

"Then let me go."

"I . . . no," the lord muttered. "Let you go, I would have the liking of such a thing with a fullness of heart. Good it would be to never be seeing you again. But," he added reluctantly, "letting you go is not for my doing."

"Of course not. Everyone—" the prince meant Tywthylodd— "would blame you. But they won't blame you for this."

He lunged at Cymyriod, spinning him about, one arm going about the young lord's throat, the other twisting Cymyriod's swordarm behind his back. He felt his captive stiffen in outrage and stunned shock, and grinned. *Score another mark for brute force!* "There, now, my lord. I trust I'm not hurting you?" *Save for denting your youthful dignity a bit.*

Cymyriod, rigid with shock, said nothing, and Ardagh shook his head. "Inflexible, aren't you?" *Young.* "Just as well. This should look properly dramatic—and leave you quite guilt-free."

When the lord still didn't move, Ardagh prodded him, ever so gently. "Come now, you want your princess back with you and you alone, don't you? Yes? Then *move.*"

Compromises
Chapter 26

And here they were, transferred between one step and the next. Ardagh nearly staggered, just barely managing to cling to his hostage. It was no small shock to come so suddenly from the misty grey tranquility of the lake to the noisy crowd and brilliant golden light of the Tylwyth Teg's great illusion-hall. If Cymyriod had thought to struggle just then, he would have been free.

But no, something as crass as struggling would damage his dignity. Idiot.

Holding fast to the rigidly indignant Cymyriod, the prince glared as ferociously as he could at the astonished gathering of Tylwyth Teg, trying his best to project the aura of a truly desperate, dangerous man. It seemed, judging from their horrified faces, to be working.

Ah, look. No need to call for Tywthylodd. Here the princess came in a rush, silken blue-green robes swirling about her like the billows of the sea, the worried crowd hastily parting to let her through. Her face was regally impassive, but there was a look of not-quite-finished to her, as though, Ardagh noted with a touch of satisfaction, she'd come straight from a sharply interrupted sleep.

You caught me when I was too weary to think clearly; I catch you in almost the same condition. What a charming balance of ironies.

There was no appreciation of irony or anything else in Tywthylodd's eyes, blazing as they were with outrage.

"How dare you be coming here?" Her voice was sharp enough to cut stone. "How dare you my *cydwedd* be clutching?"

"How?" Ardagh retorted coolly. "The same way, Princess Tywthylodd, that you dared offer me sanctuary that quickly turned into a trap."

For a moment he was sure she was going to try some properly convoluted web of words denying it. But Tywthylodd must truly have still been dazed by sleep, because after that brief, tense silence, she merely shook her head and gave Ardagh so charmingly resigned and appreciative a smile that he could almost accept it as genuine.

"Done has been done," she said simply. "Release him."

"Not yet. First release my human friend."

So much for attempts at charm: her smile vanished, her eyes flashing with renewed rage. "No prisoner is he!"

"I'm delighted to hear it. And will be more delighted yet when you bring him here. Oh yes, and bring my sword and dagger, too, if you please. We," he added, giving Cymyriod the slightest of shakes, "can wait."

Tywthylodd paused only the briefest of moments, then snapped out commands, speaking so swiftly that Ardagh could hardly decipher her dialect. He waited with carefully feigned patience, hiding behind a mask of Sidhe calm, doing nothing but occasionally tightening his grip whenever Cymyriod tried to break free.

I wonder. Is Tywthylodd going to be vindictive enough to drag things out interminably? No. She wouldn't risk Cymyriod's life. Would she?

No. Apparently she really was worried about her consort—or, Ardagh thought cynically, about her own prestige should she let Cymyriod come to harm. Here came Cadwal now, dressed in an interesting hybrid of his own and Tylwyth Teg fashion and looking remarkably rested and . . . sleek.

He'd be purring if he could.

But the man's smugness vanished at the sight of Ardagh and his hostage. "*Dewi Sant, now* what?"

"Now," Ardagh said in Eriu's Gaeilge, "we have come to the end of our hosts' hospitality. You can, I think, take your hand from your sword's hilt. I doubt we'll be facing that type of combat." Of course the human was wearing his own sword and dagger; none of the Tylwyth Teg could have handled iron blades.

"All we need," the prince continued lightly, "is—ah, yes, here are my sword and dagger. Cadwal, if you'd hold them for me? My hands are . . . ah . . . rather occupied for the moment."

"Your requests have had their meeting," Tywthylodd cut in sharply in her people's tongue. "Release."

"I'm afraid not," Ardagh countered. "Not quite yet. We haven't yet settled one issue. You promised me safety, Princess Tywthylodd, yet gave me treachery."

"I? No!"

"Please. No word-tricks. We both know exactly what you wanted of me. It would have been an interesting experiment, princess, but I don't wish to participate."

"The human friend that is yours has already done so."

Was that the slightest hint of a sneer? "My human friend is his own free man. As I wish to be."

"Then go!"

"Oh no, Tywthylodd. That hallway to which you're so graciously pointing leads right back to Morfren's lands." Ardagh smiled urbanely. "My people's sense of direction is every bit as sharp as yours."

Her eyes said clearly where she wished his sense of direction to send him. "What, then, want you of me?"

"I want your folk to guide me and my friend *not* back the way we came—but to the Cymric coast."

"No. Too far a distance is that."

"Not for you, Tywthylodd. I've seen how easily you walk from cave to distant lake. A few small steps, one small transfer spell, and there you are. So, now. Walk us both from this cavern to the sea, and call this awkward situation closed. You can do that, can't you? The Tylwyth Teg have that much Power, don't they?"

"Arrogant are the Sidhe!"

"Arrogant is this Sidhe, perhaps—but he *does not break his word!*"

There was a horrified gasp from the Tylwyth Teg at that worst of Faerie crimes—and at his implying the guilt of their princess. "Oathbreaker am I not!" Tywthylodd said, words choked in rage. "Accuse me of such, shall you not!"

"What else could I call one whose idea of 'no harm' included my captivity?"

"It was not—"

"Tsk. I can play with words as prettily as you. We both know full well what you meant for me. We both know that freedom had no part in it. We both know that willfully depriving one of freedom *is* harm in any tongue! If you would cleanse your honor, Princess Tywthylodd, you will guide me and my friend to the Cymric coast, *now!*"

For one tense, endless moment, he was sure she was going to refuse. Ardagh was even going over a hasty new verbal attack in his mind when Tywthylodd said without warning, "Yes." Her hand stabbed out, pointing at two of her people. "You and you, guiding be."

"Guiding," Ardagh clarified, "to the Cymric coast and nowhere else, in the same time frame as now. You will guide us to dry land, safe land." Otherwise, they might end up on the wrong side of the coast, in—or under—the sea itself. "You will guide both of us, Cadwal and I, and we shall be unharmed *in any way.*" He paused. "Do you so swear?"

Tywthylodd's sigh was almost a hiss. "Yes. Yes! These two guides, I swear it, too, for them as ruler. Now, go. And be sure," she added darkly, "remembering shall I be."

"Remembering shall I be, too," Ardagh said sweetly. He released Cymyriod, who stalked away with rigid, patently artificial dignity, then bowed to Tywthylodd, equal to equal.

"Remembering, Princess Tywthylodd, shall I definitely be."

They had not gone down the tunnel for very long before Ardagh saw the difference and heard Cadwal draw in his breath in surprise. "That's daylight up ahead," the human said, "I'd swear it."

"It is," Ardagh agreed. "And I think I hear the sea." He sniffed. "Yes, and smell the ocean air. That's definitely the coast ahead."

The two Tylwyth Teg guides stopped short, shielding their eyes. "Truly, yes," said one, blinking like a dazed owl, "daylight is it out there."

"Sunlight," said the other, definitely uneasy.

"So it is." And they, unlike he, could not endure it. Ardagh dipped his head to them curtly. "You have fulfilled your vow. Be free to leave."

The two Tylwyth Teg bowed as one, and as one, scurried gladly back down the tunnel to their sunless realm. Ardagh moved warily to the lip of the tunnel, looking out. "Ah, yes," he said in satisfaction. "This is, indeed, the human Realm again."

The sun was almost directly overhead. Spread out below him lay a stretch of sandy beach framed by a crescent of sheer rock. Beyond, the sea rushed and rushed onto the shore, sparkling in the sunlight, and overhead the inevitable gulls shrieked and soared beneath a blue sky dotted with blazingly white clouds.

"Like an artist's imagining," the prince mused. "Almost too perfect."

"Good enough for me," Cadwal said shortly. "Good to be back."

Ardagh glanced back over his shoulder with a sudden frown, *feeling* . . . ah, yes. "This tunnel isn't stable. In fact, I think it's going to disappear the moment one or both of us steps out of it."

"Meaning?"

"Meaning that unless you wish to stay with your Gwenalarch forever, move outside when I do."

Cadwal gave a sharp bark of a laugh. "She's a lovely thing and we had a good time together, but she's hardly 'my' Gwenalarch. Disappeared right after we—well, you know. And after seeing the princess glare at you like that, I sure don't want to stay there."

"So. Shall we?"

They stepped together out onto a narrow, rocky ledge. Behind them, as Ardagh had expected, the tunnel shimmered out of the human reality, staggering them with a gust of wind that was air adjusting to what was no longer there.

"Well," Cadwal said after a moment. "Well. Here we are. Wherever." He shook his head. "Weird way to travel. But it's damned good to be back in . . . ah . . . we *are* still in Cymru? Same time and all that?"

"Yes. You won't turn to ash or anything so dramatic."

Wild relief flashed in the human's eyes, but all he said was a laconic, "Good. Then maybe you can tell me what the hell's going on?"

Ardagh let out his breath in a gusty sigh. "It's not an easy thing to summarize. You gathered that we had been given sanctuary? And promised that no harm would come to us? Yes? Let us just say that Princess Tywthylodd has a very vague idea of what 'sanctuary' means, and her concept of doing someone no harm is complex, indeed."

Cadwal frowned. "I thought that none of the—the Faerie Folk could lie."

"They can't. They can, however, be very devious about the truth."

"Like courtiers. Here now," the mercenary added in sudden alarm, "you didn't mean—you aren't hurt, are you? She didn't—"

"No, of course not. It wasn't that type of harm. Tywthylodd merely tried to hold me captive. It's not important, not—"

"Tried to hold you captive? But why?"

"I said it wasn't important."

"And I say you're hiding something. What? Did the princess want a ransom for you? Sure, from what you've told me about him, your royal brother probably wouldn't help out—"

"He would not."

"—but King Aedh certainly would, and if the princess sent word that—" Cadwal broke off abruptly, staring at Ardagh. "But that's not it, is it? No . . . you're embarrassed, aren't you?" The man grinned, and went right on grinning. "Och, and is *that* the way of it? *That* type of captive, eh?"

"Of course I'm embarrassed!" Ardagh snapped. "To get out of there, to get us both out of there, I had to act like a—a human lout, use brute force—and why are you laughing?"

"I'm sorry. Honest, I am. It's just . . . just the picture of you, a prince and all, having to . . . well . . . defend your honor against a pretty woman like that. 'Use brute force,' indeed!"

"The pretty woman, as you call her so lightly, is a ruler of her race. And she wasn't out to do anything as humanly bizarre as merely 'stealing my honor,' as you so quaintly call it. She meant to use me as the sire of her heir!"

That didn't help. Ardagh paused, fuming, watching Cadwal, red-faced, struggling helplessly for self-control. "I fail to see," the prince said coldly, "why something so serious as creating an heir should be so funny to you. Particularly when you've done the same thing."

Ah. That stopped Cadwal as suddenly as though he'd been slapped. "What?" the man gasped. "Wh-what are you saying? Gwenalarch—you saying what she wanted was a baby?"

"And very probably started one with you, yes. Tywthylodd hinted at that rather clearly."

"*Iesu.* They can know something like that so soon?"

"Apparently they could." Ardagh hesitated, then shrugged. "Women's magic."

"Gwenalarch. A baby. Oh, I didn't think she wanted me for my looks or youthful charm or any nonsense like that, I thought she just wanted some good old-fashioned fun, but—you sure? Really?"

Ardagh nodded. "The odds are good, with a human male and Tylwyth Teg female, that it will be a boy."

"*Iesu.* A boy. A son." To the prince's surprise, he saw Cadwal suddenly burst into a smile of almost dazed delight. "You know," the mercenary murmured, "I always wondered. I mean, for all I knew, not being a saint and all that, I might have sired a few youngsters along the way. Never could find out for sure. Now . . . a son."

"You probably will never see him," Ardagh warned him, very gently.

"Figured that. Just as well, I guess. What could I do for him, anyhow? A landless, aging mercenary—what could I possibly do for him?"

"Don't belittle yourself. I wouldn't be alive now if it hadn't been for your aid several times over. And remember that you did help give your son his life."

"Right. Sure." Cadwal took a deep breath, then asked, "He'll be well treated? Even if he's half-human?"

"Of course. None of the races of the Folk would ever harm a child."

"And happy, he's got to be happy—hell, listen to me blathering like an idiot! But yes, I saw all those cheerful youngsters; he'll have a good chance at being happy."

"A very good chance."

"Better than being a mercenary. Or an exile." Cadwal blinked, as though hit by a sudden new thought. "What about magic . . . ? Will he . . . ?"

"Wield Power? Very probably."

"*Iesu.* My son a magician. My son . . ."

"Are you all right?"

But Cadwal was still beaming as he glanced at Ardagh. "You don't understand. I'm not too thrilled with never getting to know the boy—or, hell, even getting a chance to see him—but that's the way things are. But now, no matter what happens to me, there'll still be part of me here in Cymru. Part of me that can never be exiled. And . . . you really don't understand a bit of this, do you?"

"Not all, not entirely. Most surely not as a human would. Still, I'm delighted that you're delighted."

Suddenly as that, the *feeling* of *an ally, here,* struck, so strongly that Ardagh whirled, staring wildly out over the sea, heart racing.

"What now?" There wasn't a hint of vagueness to Cadwal's voice. "You just came alert like a hunting hound, no insult meant."

Ardagh shook his head, never taking his stare from the horizon. "Now we must return to our work."

"Here? What are we going to do here?"

"Find an ally. My . . . call it a sense that's all but screaming it at me."

"An ally against Osmod."

"Yes, of course. But who or what that ally may be— of that, I haven't the faintest of hints."

"Right. Can't have things too easy, now, can we? And here we are, standing on this exposed ledge like a couple of . . . You do see something now, don't you? What?"

Hand shading his eyes against the sun, Ardagh stared with all his will. Ae, whatever it was out there was almost too far away to see at all. "I'm not sure," he said after a moment, "not yet. You're right; this is no safe place to wait. Let's get down from this ledge and under cover."

The cliff was sheer above them, but from the point of the ledge on down to the beach, rockslides had created a shallower slope, covered with treacherous bits of rock but passable. Ardagh and Cadwal slid and scrambled their way down to level ground, then picked their way across the rocky beach to a hiding place behind two great, weathered boulders.

Cadwal glanced back over his shoulder, then turned

fully, glaring up at the semicircle of cliffs. "I hope your feelings haven't led us astray."

"What do you mean?"

"I don't know about you, but I can't see myself making it all the way up those sheer things to the top. And there's nowhere else to go."

"Save," Ardagh said thoughtfully, "out to sea."

Cadwal whirled, staring. "A ship," he exclaimed. "I see it now, though I can't make out details. Wind's coming in towards land so strongly though, that it'll be close soon enough."

"So it will," Ardagh murmured absently, more intrigued by the force of his own premonition. *Why now? Why here? The only other time I felt a warning this strong was when Gervinus arrived in Eriu. But this isn't the same. This isn't a warning . . . not exactly.*

Neither he nor Cadwal said another word, tensely watching the ship smoothly sail towards land.

"There it is." Cadwal's voice was sharp with alarm. "Red-striped sail, dragon-prow—*damnio!* You know who those are? Those are Lochlannach!

"Your so-called allies are Eriu's worst foes—and here we are, trapped and just waiting for them!"

Old Acquaintances
Chapter 27

Lochlannach! Ardagh stared at the beautiful, deadly ship in a wild storm of confusion. "I don't understand . . . I know who and what they are, of course I do; I fought them. And yet . . . they are to be allies just now, I *feel* it."

He felt Cadwal's skeptical glance. "Can't your feelings be mistaken?"

"No! That is one of the few Sidhe talents left untouched by your human Realm."

"Allies. Those thieves. Allies. *Dewi Sant*, what else can possibly get twisted up in this journey?" The mercenary frowned, peering. "Haven't taken any loot yet, or at least not very much; the ship's riding too high in the water for that. Why do you suppose they've chosen right here to come ashore? No one about this place to raid, as far as I can see. Nothing but empty beach."

"I know why *I'd* come ashore," Ardagh said speculatively. "After a long sea journey aboard a wooden ship— a no doubt highly flammable wooden ship—I'd look forward to the first chance of getting ashore to light a fire and cook a hot meal, particularly in a place where I didn't have to keep a heavy guard while eating."

"Ha, I bet you're right! They're letting their bellies rule them."

"I know the feeling."

"You're not the only one. At least that means we don't have to take on any charging, loot-hungry warriors. Just

275

yet, anyhow." Cadwal glanced at Ardagh with one eyebrow crooked wryly up. "You really want to do this."

"I must. You can stay here if you'd rather."

"Och, right. Well, if we're to go down and be pals with
that lot, let's see if we can't find ourselves something to
eat before they get here. Should at least be some edible
plants. Don't want to die on an empty stomach, and
damned if I'll beg them for food!"

But for a time, Ardagh stood where he was. *I don't
understand this, I don't. Drawn to—to these. I can't be
losing my Sidhe abilities, Powers, no, that would be
like—like losing sight or hearing or—or . . .*

Or he was just going to let the matter rest for now.
It would take some time for the Lochlannach to safely
beach their ship and hunt for wood for their cooking
fires, assuming that really was all they intended. Cadwal
was right. Best to find something to eat while they still
could. The brain, after all, the prince decided wryly, did
tend to work better when it was fed.

And maybe then he would be able to puzzle out this
weirdness. About himself, about his Sidhe awareness,
about whatever else was going to go askew.

Maybe.

He fought his way up through layer upon layer of
darkness. For an instant he was awake . . . asleep . . .
awake. "Where . . . ?" Osmod, ealdorman and secret
sorcerer, croaked dryly.

A hand pressed the rim of a goblet to his lips. Osmod
drank thankfully, feeling the coolness of water soothing
what felt like a fire-seared throat. He glanced up to see
his personal servant, Bosa, holding the goblet and looking
surprisingly concerned. *Beat them enough and they fawn
on you,* Osmod thought, then tried again, "Where?"

A stocky, grey-haired man was shouldering his way past
Bosa to the bedside. The ealdorman blinked, trying to
place him, and finally said in triumph, "Octa. Physician
Octa."

"Ah, good. You know me. You are in your own hall, Ealdorman Osmod, in your own bed."

"What . . . happened?"

"You don't recall?" Octa frowned ever so slightly. "You were ill, ealdorman, feverishly ill for quite some time. You don't remember any of it?"

Osmod struggled with a mind that felt dull as so much lead. "I'm not . . . not sure."

But he was. All at once he knew perfectly well what had happened. He'd thrown that spell, that message from his brain to those of the three Cymru mages—and very nearly slain himself in the process.

Something of the horror he felt must have shown on Osmod's face because Octa, clearly misunderstanding the reason for it, said soothingly, "It's not important."

"I . . . did I say anything . . . strange?"

To his dismay, Osmod saw a flicker of uneasiness cross the physician's face. But then Octa said firmly, "Nothing but the strangeness of a man lost in delirium," and smiled. "You need not fear you revealed any royal secrets."

"Yes, but . . ."

"A moment, my lord, please." The physician placed a cool, competent hand on Osmod's forehead, then withdrew it with a satisfied nod. "The fever is gone and, God willing, will not return. You show every sign of making a complete recovery. And if you will excuse me, I will now so advise King Egbert."

"Yes. Of course."

"You might like to know that the king has been quite worried for you."

Osmod waved that away. Of course Egbert had been worried; the king would hardly want to lose one of his most more-or-less trusted advisors. But that didn't mean that Egbert would have shed more than the most perfunctory of tears over his loss. "Go," the ealdorman said. "All of you. Go. I wish to rest."

He lay rigidly still, listening intently. Ah yes. They'd all obeyed, even that ridiculously loyal hound of a Bosa.

Osmod forced unresponsive legs over the side of the
bed, then lay for a moment, gasping. After a slow, painful
struggle, he sat up, feeling the blood surging dizzily in
his head, wondering if he was going to faint.

No. He would not allow that. At last, body protest-
ing feebly, Osmod managed to stand, swaying, furious
and frightened at his weakness.

The runes, where are the runes? If anyone had
searched the room, truly searched it—no, no, if they'd
found the runes or anything else so very incriminating,
Octa would never have been so calm.

Unless the physician had been ordered not to reveal
anything? Ordered by Egbert—

No, again. This illness was making him stupidly, need-
lessly apprehensive. There were no dark suspicions, no
secret plots. Other than, Osmod told himself with weary
humor, his own.

Ah, Lords of Darkness be thanked, there was the
rune-pouch, lying where he'd dropped it, half-hidden
against one wall. Osmod knelt—angry that it was actually
more of a controlled fall—and scooped up the pouch,
pulling it open, tumbling a handful of runes out onto
his palm. . . .

And felt nothing. Not the slightest stirring of Power.
Nothing.

*Impossible! I couldn't have lost—the fever couldn't
have—there must be something else wrong.*

He dropped the runes back into the pouch, hands
shaking so badly they nearly spilled them all onto the
floor. All right. He'd try again, properly this time. Osmod
sat emptying his mind, emptying his mind. . . . Almost
calm, he poured the runes back out onto his palm.

Nothing.

He sat back in stunned dismay. The runes were no
more than lifeless bits of bone and wood.

Queen Eithne of Eriu frowned slightly, watching her
husband watching . . . nothing as he stood by Fremainn's

wooden palisade. She hesitated a moment, reluctant to disturb him just in case he was deep in political thoughts or other matters concerning the realm.

No. There was a certain vagueness to the look of him that told her he wasn't really paying much attention to anything, at least not to anything here. Eithne moved to his side and put a gentle hand on his arm. "Aedh? Where are you? What are you seeing?"

He started slightly at the touch, then put a hand over hers, giving it a gentle squeeze. "Prince Ardagh, if you must know."

"What—"

"In my mind, love, only in my mind." Still holding her hand, Aedh turned to face her. "Och, Eithne, I have to wonder if I did the right thing, sending him off like that. What is the man doing now?"

"Surviving, I trust."

Aedh snorted. "That, I don't doubt. If ever there was a survivor, it's our exotic, so-difficult-to-predict prince. But what *is* he doing? And, in the name of all the saints, why is he doing it?"

Eithne frowned, wishing she could tell her husband that she knew yes, Prince Ardagh was of the Sidhe and yes, he and Sorcha were communicating by magic, and yes, the prince was no longer even in Wessex. But of course Eithne couldn't reveal any of that without revealing her own magic—so perilous a talent for an ordained High King's wife—and so she contented herself with a vague, "You don't think he's finding you allies?"

"Oh, trying such a thing, at any rate, no doubt about that. But whether he'll succeed, and if he does, who those allies will be—or even, God help us, what—of that, love, I have no idea."

"Our daughter misses him fiercely."

Aedh grinned. Fainche was all of five-going-on-six, and definitely in the grip of her first baby romance. "I'm sure she does. So, I'm equally sure, do most of the women here. Particularly," he added more gently, "Sorcha ni Fothad, poor lass."

Eithne shivered slightly. "Och, Aedh," she murmured in sudden sharp pity, "what's to become of her? Of them both?"

He chuckled, putting his arm about her. "My romantic Eithne!"

"Aedh, please."

"I don't know, love. Right now, all I can do is hope that Prince Ardagh brings himself back soon and safely. Yes, and without dragging along a war as well!"

"He wouldn't!"

"No. Of course not. Still, one never knows with him. At least," Aedh added with a grin that wasn't quite amused, "there haven't been any new Lochlannach raids. I'd rather like to think that our unpredictable prince, in one of his incredibly complicated maneuverings, has had something to do with that."

Eithne laughed. "Come now, love, the man's not . . . not supernatural!" *Not exactly.* "For all his exotic ways, Prince Ardagh is just a man." *Not a human one, granted, but a man nonetheless.*

"As the women here would definitely assure you."

"Aedh!" She slapped him lightly on the arm. "Aren't you supposed to be in a council meeting right now?"

He smiled a deceptively lazy smile. "It will do them no harm to wait on me a little." Holding out his arm to her, Aedh added, "Come, my dear, let us stroll about Fremainn a bit."

But Eithne, still laughing, pushed him away. "You have work to do, husband."

"Look at this. A mere slip of a woman pushes about the High King of Eriu."

"She does, indeed. Now, go."

Chuckling, he went. Eithne turned to see, as she'd suddenly suspected, Sorcha ni Fothad watching her. "It's all right, dear," the queen said. "You don't have to look so embarrassed. I knew you were there."

"Forgive me. I didn't mean to spy. It was only that . . ." Sorcha impatiently brushed one of her thick red braids back over a shoulder. "If you must know, Queen Eithne, I was envying you. You and your husband."

"Oh, my poor Sorcha." Eithne impulsively caught the young woman's hands in her own. "He still loves you. Prince Ardagh will come back to you."

"I don't doubt it. It's what comes after the return that's worrying me. He's what he is, I'm what I am, the laws are what they are—if we could just up and run off to his land, I would in a moment. But we can't." Sorcha pulled away from the queen, blinking fiercely. "I love him. I'll never stop that. But . . . I don't know. I just don't know how much longer I can wait. How much longer I can hope."

"You will," Eithne said. "I know. I've had to spend too many lonely nights myself, wondering, praying, not sure if I'll ever see my husband alive again."

"Och, I'm sorry, I didn't mean—"

"Hush. Prince Ardagh will be back and all will look much brighter." She broke off, studying Sorcha. "When I first learned I was to wed Aedh, I admit that I was reluctant. Ha, no, I was terrified! I didn't want to be the wife of someone laying claim to the throne of High King. But I wed him, and I love him, and he is off fighting to hold that throne as often as he is here.

"And even so, even with the lonely nights and the terror, I regret nothing."

She could almost hear the thoughts screaming in Sorcha's mind, *But your love is human, your love isn't an exiled prince of the Sidhe, your love doesn't have the laws of two lands against the two of you.* "Och, Sorcha," she murmured, "I'm sorry. But don't be hasty. Don't."

"I won't," Sorcha agreed. But her steady eyes were unreadable.

Ardagh crouched behind a rock, Cadwal beside him, watching warily. Ah yes, the Lochlannach really were beaching their ship, bringing that elegant vessel carefully up onto the sand with the wariness of men who knew they might have to make a sudden retreat.

The raiders were as he remembered them: tall, weather-beaten, powerfully built men, mostly fair of hair and beards, men who moved with the unthinking grace of true warriors even while—yes, Ardagh saw he'd been right about this—scavenging for firewood. Their clothing was as he'd remembered as well, woolen tunics and leggings of good, sturdy, weather-impervious weave. Although they'd left their mail shirts on board in these relatively safe surroundings, of course they went armed even while gathering wood; a raider in a foreign land could never quite abandon caution. Ardagh thought wryly that he certainly did remember their weapons, those beautifully wrought swords and axes.

A good many of which were raised against me in that battle!

Listening intently to the Lochlannach talking and laughing with each other, cheerful even though they were pitching their voices warily low, Ardagh frowned slightly. Their language sounded vaguely related to the Saxon tongue, but it contained so many strange words, so many unfamiliar idioms, that the prince groaned. "Just what I didn't need," he murmured to Cadwal, "another language to learn."

"Eh?"

"Magically." The Language Spell wasn't a difficult one, nor, fortunately, did it demand much Power. Since it was fueled primarily from the magician's own energies, it could even be cast successfully in this Realm; he'd already learned that when he had first acquired Eriu's language.

Unfortunately, I also learned that while this Realm may allow the spell, it's not exactly friendly about such foreign things.

Ah well, the task wasn't going to get easier for the waiting. Bracing himself, Ardagh silently spoke the Words, willing his magic into sharp focus—

And was suddenly deprived of air, sound, light, thought—

Then just as suddenly was back in reality, finding himself lying crumpled on the ground, panting, drained, sickeningly dizzy. Cadwal was hovering anxiously nearby, but just then all that Ardagh could do was keep his head down and try not to be ill. At last he could blink up at the mercenary and gasp, "Done."

Cadwal was eying him as cautiously as though he'd turned into something alien. *More alien than the Sidhe, at any rate.* "*You* look done," the man muttered. "You all right?"

"Yes." His head was finally starting to clear, his stomach to settle. "Yes," Ardagh repeated more firmly, and struggled back to his feet, listening. "Ah yes, I can understand them now."

"They saying anything useful?"

Cautiously testing his new acquisition, Ardagh said after a few seconds, "They're hungry."

"*They're* hungry? Those bits of greenery didn't go very far."

"With any luck, we'll be sharing their meal."

"As long as we're not part of it."

"Hush, Cadwal. They're no cannibals."

"Only bloodthirsty pagan raiders. Your pardon about that 'pagan.'"

Ardagh waved him to silence. It wasn't going to be long before the Lochlannach, ranging more and more widely in their search for driftwood for the cooking fire, discovered them. "Enough delay," the prince said. "Ready?"

"Hell, no. But let's get it over with."

"Indeed."

Ardagh straightened with regal pride and stepped out of hiding. Not at all surprisingly, every one of the Lochlannach, sitting or standing, came fully alert, hands on weapons. But before they could draw blades, one man called out a commanding, "No! Wait."

So, now! This is clearly their leader, even if he doesn't look very different from the others. He fairly radiates authority, that's the thing, and—

"Powers," Ardagh said in complete disbelief. "I know this man."

"So do I," Cadwal hissed. "That's the one who led the raiders we fought off back in Eriu. The one whose boy died in your arms."

How could I forget? How could I ever forget?

He and the Lochlannach chieftain locked stares, just as they had then, but this time it was in mutual recognition; the chieftain was clearly just as astonished to find himself facing the foe who'd shown such compassion towards his dying son.

Now, though, the human wasn't dazed by grief. Now he could actually *see* Ardagh—and, the prince realized with a little shock, see him, being without a doubt a pagan, without any Christian prejudice or blindness.

The man believes in magic, he believes in Others!

His eyes wide with sudden awe, the Lochlannach chieftain made a gesture that could only be one of ritual respect. "Ljos Alfar!" he gasped.

The Elf
Chapter 28

Ljos Alfar? That, Ardagh thought after a bewildered moment, could only be the name, twisted into the Lochlannach tongue of course, of another very distant cousin-race: the Light Elves.

That fair, golden-haired Folk—humans must think them wonderfully pure. With my black hair, I'm just lucky the man doesn't take me for a Dokk Alfar, a Dark Elf, instead!

This was hardly the time or place to enlighten the man as to the great differences between the elves and the Sidhe. Ardagh stood with regal stillness, waiting. The human hesitated, a strong warrior suddenly thrown into a very foreign, restrained role, then asked warily, "Do you . . . speak our tongue?"

Ardagh dipped his head an aristocratic fraction, bemused at how easy it was to slip back into Sidhe aloofness.

The Lochlannach chieftain glanced briefly at his men, then, apparently getting no help from them, asked Ardagh in a sudden burst, "Will it please you to—to dine with us?"

Whatever they were cooking—fish and chunks of dried meat, the prince guessed, held over the fire on driftwood branches or daggers—smelled surprisingly good.

Hunger is, as the humans say, the finest sauce.

Ardagh dipped his head in gracious consent and sat, signalling to Cadwal to join him. What the Lochlannach

285

thought of his human companion, the prince wasn't sure. What Cadwal thought of them, Ardagh knew very well. But the man's face was a mask of cold dignity, revealing nothing.

The food didn't, after the first few bites, taste as good as it had smelled; some of the meat was smoked, which gave it an interesting flavor, but most of the fish was heavily salted, and some of it had definitely been carried about too long. Proof, as though the lightly riding ship hadn't been proof enough, that the Lochlannach hadn't had a chance to pillage the land for fresh supplies.

Ardagh nibbled elegantly, noting out of the corner of an eye that Cadwal was having no problems with his share. Presumably the mercenary had made do with far worse in the course of his career.

They were, of course, being watched by every one of the Lochlannach, awe in every eye. Ardagh looked down at the branch in his hands, fighting down the impulse to lunge at the men just to see them jump—suicidal with this perilous bunch—then glanced coolly up.

They all made a great pretense of *no, I wasn't staring, really I wasn't*, and the prince nearly laughed. Ruthless, deadly warriors, these, reduced to so many overawed boys by a touch of the Unknown.

Ae, he'd eaten as much of this so-called food as he could stomach. Ardagh put down the branch and looked straight at the Lochlannach chieftain. "I would speak with you. Alone."

The chieftain scrambled to his feet with a haste that spoke volumes, waving back those of his men who tried to follow. Ardagh briefly locked glances with Cadwal; the mercenary nodded ever so slightly: *yes, I can take care of myself.*

"Come," the prince said shortly, and led the chieftain down the shore away from prying ears.

They walked in silence for a time, just out of reach of the surging waves, sand and bits of shell crunching beneath their feet. The air, Ardagh thought, was wonderfully clean, if tainted a bit by the inevitable sea-reek common, it would seem, to every ocean—and by the animalistic scent of his companion.

Still, the human wasn't truly dirty, just a bit less washed than would be preferable. The prince acknowledged to himself that it would, after all, be difficult to bathe regularly while on board a ship in the middle of a salty ocean.

The Lochlannach chieftain wasn't exactly a savage, either, for all the aura of casual ferocity surrounding him; his tunic was a nicely dyed russet that complemented his yellow hair, and someone had cared enough to edge that tunic with intricate embroidery. The hilt of his sword was ornamented as well, inlaid with thin bands of gold and bronze. He and the prince were almost of a height, though the human was broader in the shoulders, with the strongly muscled build of a true warrior. There was, rather to Ardagh's surprise, a fair amount of clever wit in the blue-grey eyes.

Easier for me were he duller. Ah well.

A gull had been circling overhead for some time, crying almost as though giving demands. Now it suddenly darted down in a swoop so low the tip of one wing brushed Ardagh's face. He sternly refused to let himself flinch as the bird soared up again, and he heard the Lochlannach's awed gasp. There wasn't anything supernatural here; the Tylwyth Teg, when they came out to play here in the moonlight, probably threw tidbits to the seabirds. But if the chieftain wanted to believe it something more, he wasn't about to argue.

So. They'd walked far enough. Ardagh stopped and turned to face the human. He'd already decided not to mention his royal title; these Lochlannach were unpredictably dangerous enough as it was and he didn't want this particular example to try something foolish. Such as attempting to hold him for ransom. "You may call me Ardagh Lithanial," the prince said in his most regal tone. *You may call me that, since that's my name!* "That is all that I shall reveal to you, save that, yes, I am never of humankind." That, he thought, was vague enough. "I need a name by which to call you."

"Ah. I am the Jarl Thorkell Sveinsson, also known as Thorkell the Bold."

The word he used for that epithet could, Ardagh mused, just as easily have been translated as "Foolhardy." "A fitting enough title," the prince said, voice sharp as a blade, "for a man who was reckless enough to take a child into battle."

He saw the human wince at that. "Erik was nearly of warrior age," Thorkell said defensively. "And there wasn't to have been a battle, or I never would have—" He cut himself off sharply. "My boy died a good death, in combat, as befits a true warrior. And even if he—even if he was still so young . . ." The jarl broke off again, rigid with the effort at self-control. "Ah well, who can say what the Norns have woven for us?"

"Who, indeed?" Ardagh agreed in perfect truth, having no idea who these Norns might be. One thing he did already know was how humans often chattered or blustered to try disguising true emotion.

As Thorkell was doing. "'Fate none escape,' and all that. Erik's safe up there in Valhalla, and Uncle Ragnar will look after him." He shrugged, a little too lightly. "Meanwhile, I have two other boys growing at home."

And a wife who is, no doubt, still grieving. "Fortunate."

It was said so flatly that Thorkell frowned. "I don't mean to be taking anything away from you. Hardly that! What you tried to do for my boy, I mean. I saw you try to save his life, even at the risk of your own, and I . . ." Suddenly all the nervous bluster was gone. "Ask what you will of me," the jarl said quietly, "and if it's within what a human can do, it will be done."

Ardagh dipped his head in courtesy. "A truly noble offer." *I only wish I knew enough about your folk to know if you keep your vows!* "At the moment, though, all that I require is passage for myself and my human

companion off this charming but rather limited little
beach."

Thorkell stared. "Your pardon, but . . . well . . . can't
you just magic yourself away?"

*Careful, now. He can't possibly know how limited
Power is in this Realm.* "There are reasons," the prince
said severely, and let Thorkell make of that cryptic statement what he would.

Which, as Ardagh had expected of a human, was
something dark and mysterious and Not For Man to
Know. "Of course," Thorkell said, just barely keeping
from glancing nervously about. "You are welcome aboard
my ship. More than welcome, in fact."

A warning bell sounded in Ardagh's mind. "What does
that mean?"

The human didn't answer at once, and the warning
bell grew louder. "It's about luck," Thorkell said at last.

"Luck."

From the surprise in the jarl's eyes, this was something every self-respecting Alfar, Ljos or Dokk, would
have understood without explanation. But Thorkell continued without more than a momentary pause, "With
luck, everything to which a man turns his hand is golden.
Without it . . ."

"No one remembers his name and he goes down to
dust unsung," Ardagh completed, guessing.

"Exactly."

"Let me see if I can deduce the gist of this: Since the
disaster of your last raid, the murmur has gone about
your people that your luck has failed you. Now, you
think, with my presence, your luck has turned again."

The jarl smiled widely. "And has it not?"

"That," Ardagh said, absolutely without expression,
"remains to be seen. Shall we return to the others?"

Cadwal was waiting, the image of apparently total calm
for all that he was surrounded by warriors. But tension
was sharp in his voice as he asked, "Well?"

"I've won us passage from this pretty prison," Ardagh

murmured, voice warily low since he wasn't certain that none of the Lochlannach understood Gaeilge. "What else I may have won in the process, I'm not yet sure. But at least we'll be away from here."

Cadwal stared. "Sail with *them?* You're going to *trust* these barbarians?"

For answer, Ardagh looked about at the warriors, merely looked, putting no menace into it at all. The Lochlannach busily looked away, some of them making furtive signs against evil that reminded him of those made by equally uneasy Christians. "You see?" he said to Cadwal.

"Right. They're cowed. Till something happens that their friendly 'Alfar' can't solve."

"Tsk, Cadwal," Ardagh purred. "I'm not all *that* Powerless. And let us take one crisis at a time, shall we?"

"Right." This time it was said without any sarcasm. "And the first crisis I see," the mercenary added with a groan, "is that I'm going to have to set foot in yet another ship."

The prince gave an involuntary little chuckle. "Ae, I'm sorry, I don't mean to mock you. At least these are much more elegant than the . . . thing we rode from Eriu."

Elegant, indeed. The Lochlannach ship was built of smoothly overlapping planks—oak, the prince guessed, since that seemed to be the most durable wood in this Realm—and was long and sleek as the dragon whose intricately carved head crowned its prow. As Ardagh looked down the sleek lines that spoke of deadly speed, he found his hand itching to stroke the ship as though it were a living beast.

Hearing Thorkell come up beside him, he turned to see the jarl beaming with pride. "Like it, do you?"

"It is truly beautiful."

"It is that. This is the *Sea Raven,* and a finer ship you'd be hard-put to find. In the world of men," the human added hastily.

Ardagh bit back the decidedly perilous urge to say,

I know, I've seen it in retreat. One did not insult a host's prize possession. And, courtesy aside, if Thorkell didn't want to mention that he'd last seen Ardagh fighting against him, this was hardly the time to remind him!

Cadwal's right. What do I do when something happens that I can't magic away? No. I was right as well: one crisis at a time.

It hadn't surprised Ardagh to see how quickly the beached ship could be returned to deep water; after all, he'd seen it happen during the battle back in Eriu. What he hadn't seen was how efficiently a Lochlannach dragon ship was arranged. Standing aboard the *Sea Raven*, he saw that it was almost as long and narrow as a racing craft. Craning his head back, the prince saw that the great square sail was lashed to a long cross-pole that could be turned by ropes to catch the wind. The tall mast could be lowered—convenient, Ardagh guessed, for storage during the bitter Northern winters, in addition to providing less resistance for rowers; these sat on the two-man benches lining the sides of the *Sea Raven*, dropped down from the central deck.

And efficient rowers these men were, even with the mast raised, quickly bringing the ship back to open water. Ardagh caught his balance easily, a little unnerved by the reminder of how swiftly the Lochlannach could strike and be away again.

I'd be happier, too, if there wasn't that great mass of an iron anchor there on the aft deck as well.

The wind rose. Rigging creaked, then, with a sudden boom, the great sail caught the wind and billowed full.

"Pretty as the belly of a woman with child," Thorkell murmured, then called, "Up oars!"

All thirty oars snapped up in unison and were quickly shipped, impressing Ardagh anew.

Bad enough to fight these folk on land. I would hate to have to fight a sea battle against them.

The wind blew steadily from the north. "See?" Thorkell crowed. "Thor is kind to us. Or is it," he added
warily, "that it's you who've brought us the wind?"

Thor? Presumably that was some Lochlannach deity,
possibly Thorkell's own patron. As for the wind:
Ardagh . . . smiled, no more, no less. *Oh yes, by all
means let us build up the mystique of the Ljos Alfar,* he
told himself dryly. *At least until the time when he wants
some great and wondrous magic from you.*

Magic he really would have to work, somehow, if he
and Cadwal were to remain safe. A dangerous game, this,
Ardagh mused. *Like playing with barely leashed ice-
wolves.*

Not much that he could do about it right now. Save
pose like the arrogant Faerie being Thorkell expected
and ignore the human, staring out to sea as though aware
of far-distant wonders.

As the *Sea Raven* sailed on, Thorkell went astern to
speak with Olaf, the steersman. Ardagh hesitated, then
decided that a little more image-making never hurt
anyone. It was, he knew, ridiculous to stand in the prow
of a sailing ship, regardless of all those romantic visions
in various tales of the hero looking bravely ahead; since
the wind pushed the sail—and boat—forward, any foul
odors on board were pushed forward as well.

And yet, and yet . . . *For the sake of drama,* Ardagh
thought, and posed.

Drama, he quickly realized, didn't have long hair to
whip it in the face. Drama also didn't get chilly.

*This Tylwyth Teg clothing may be pretty, but it cer-
tainly isn't warm. I should have held on to my* brat *like
Cadwal.*

Who was, unfortunately, busy trying not to "feed the
fish," as that charming human phrase put it. *Poor Cadwal!
I only wish I knew some charm against seasickness!*

Ah well. Hopefully the man's stomach would soon
settle by itself. Ardagh returned to playing the noble Ljos
Alfar, trying not to shiver.

"Would this help?" asked an eager voice, and the prince turned to see a woolen cloak being proffered by one of the Lochlannach, tall, slender and fresh-faced, his cheeks and chin covered with the downy growth that young human males seemed to sprout as their first beards, his eyes full of delighted awe.

"Thank you." Ardagh swirled the cloak dramatically about himself (why not go for the grand gesture, after all?) and pinned it quickly in place, deft after all this time in Eriu in fastening iron brooches without touching them. "You are . . . ?"

"Einar Sigurdsson, Einar th-the Scald."

Of course, Ardagh thought with a touch of humor. He knew that a scald was the Lochlannach equivalent of a Celtic bard or a Saxon scop: a man of high talent and status. Logic told him that it was unlikely for a scald of any such status to be part of a raiding party. *A scaldling, then, a poet-in-the-making.* But, seeing the open wonder in Einar's eyes, the prince hadn't the heart to say other than, "I hope to hear some of your poetry someday."

"I can sing something now!" the boy said eagerly.

Ae. "Here?" the prince countered. "Won't the sea air hurt your voice?"

"Oh, no! Not at all. Wh-what would you like to hear, my . . . ah . . . my lord? I know most of the old chants and tales and even some of the runic spells, and I also have some of my own—"

"The runic spells," Ardagh cut in sharply. "What are these? Something known only to your people?"

"Why, no," Einar said in surprise. "Runes are also used by other folk: the Angles, the Saxons, I guess some others, too. They're used for inscriptions and other things like that, but there's great magic behind them, too; you'd know, of course, how," his voice dropped dramatically, "how the great god Odhinn hung himself from Yggdrasill the World Tree to gain knowledge of the Power behind them."

Odhinn. This was evidently another Lochlannach deity, and one, judging from Einar's expression, of vast but perilous power.

But the youngster was waving that away. "That's all ancient lore. Never mind that now. Let me sing you *my* poems."

"Not just now, Einar, if you please. Wait till we can do them proper justice. And don't worry," Ardagh added. "We will definitely talk of these things again."

We shall, indeed.

Sorcha's first words to Ardagh as he initiated contact not long after were a flat, "Where are you this time?"

"Ah, this is a little bizarre—"

"More bizarre than finding you in a—a Tylwyth Teg lair?"

"In a way. Sorcha, love, Cadwal and I are sailing in a Lochlannach dragon ship. The *Sea Raven,* to be precise."

To his utter amazement, she burst into laughter.

"Sorcha? What—"

"We—we were right, King Aedh and I, we were joking that the next place you'd turn up would be on a Lochlannach ship, and—and here you are! This is all just too—too ridiculous, and—

"Och, but Ardagh, should you be talking with me? I mean, is it safe?"

Ardagh glanced up to find Olaf the steersman staring at him.

The prince stared right back, and Olaf hastily turned away. "Safe?" Ardagh said with a laugh. "Love, right now, the more magic I show, the safer I am! You see, these folk all believe with all their barbaric enthusiasm that I am none other than a Ljos Alfar. That, Sorcha, is their name for a Light Elf, a very distant cousin-race. The Lochlannach may have my race wrong, but at least they've recognized me as a magical being. I'll come to no harm, believe me. And ae, but it feels wonderful not to have to deny what I am!"

"That's all well and good and I'm happy for you—but what in the name of all the saints are you doing there? Ardagh, I don't have to remind you—"

"That these are the enemy? Of course they are, and no, I do not, I don't have to remind *you*, turn traitor." Quickly, he summarized the escape first from the Tylwyth Teg—omitting only the reason why Princess Tywthylodd had wanted to keep him her captive—then from the pretty prison of the cliff-lined beach.

"I don't understand," Sorcha complained. "You're not some magickless human. How could you let yourself be trapped there at all?"

"Not trapped, driven, and not by the Tylwyth Teg. Sorcha, I have had, and am still having, the strongest of *feelings* that these people, enemies or no, will prove to be our allies."

"What! How can you—"

"No, I cannot explain. And no, I am not being coy; I really don't understand it yet, myself." *I'm not even sure if this has anything to do with Einar's runic spells— the spells that just might relate to the magic Osmod uses—or if there's something even more important to the feeling than that.* "It is as it is," the prince said after a moment, "I'm not mistaken, and I'd appreciate your not saying too many awkward words to Aedh if you can avoid it."

She was silent for a long while, then sighed. "I'll do what I may."

"I know that, love. Ae, but it's a pity these folks are our foes, for they do build beautiful ships. You should see this one, long and lean, with its bright sail and the . . ." He stopped short; the language of Eriu had no word for "rudder." "The great steering-oar," he improvised. "It gives the *Sea Raven* incredible maneuverability."

"Which is how they managed to escape Aedh's attack, even undermanned as you'd made them."

"That, understandably, is a subject I would really rather not discuss here and now."

Sorcha's chuckle sounded a little too amused for his taste. "It would be awkward, yes. But go on, do, about your wonderful new friends and their wonderful ship."

"'Friends' is hardly the word, but yes, the ship is quite splendid. Granted, there's not all that much room aboard; it was definitely built for speed, not comfort. The men even hang their shields along the outer sides to get them out of the way. There is an attempt at a cabin for Jarl Thorkell: a canopy draped over a wooden framework, and that's where I'm supposed to be sleeping as well."

"It sounds charming." Irony dripped from her words.

"That's not exactly the word for it, as Cadwal would argue."

"First Saxons, then Lochlannach. He can't be too happy."

He enjoyed the Tylwyth Teg—or at least one of them— well enough! "It's not just politics. Cadwal, alas, is no better a sailor this time than he was when we left Eriu."

"Och no, not again."

"Och yes. The Lochlannach find it hilarious. Fortunately, it seems that not all of them are immune to the sickness, either, so neither Cadwal nor I have to toss anyone overboard."

"Fortunately," Sorcha agreed. "Ardagh, have you any idea where you're *going?*"

"Not really," he admitted. "South is all I can tell you. I was hardly about to remind them of Eriu, even though we can't be that far from its shores. Though I suspect," the prince added wryly, lowering his voice just in case someone did overhear and understand, "that after that last attempt, Jarl Thorkell is just as happy to leave Eriu for another time. No one has actually said as much, and everyone's bright and cheerful, but there's a feeling underneath all the goodwill that Thorkell had better lead a successful raid this time."

"And will he?" There was a sharp edge to that.

"Not, I assure you, with any help from me."

"At least there's that." Her laugh held very little humor in it. "Sailing south. At this rate, you just may end up back in Wessex."

"Oh, I will," Ardagh promised softly. "Believe me, love, eventually I will. And," he added, thinking of Einar and that cryptic mention of runic spells, "I doubt that Ealdorman Osmod will enjoy my return."

The Accident
Chapter 29

King Egbert of Wessex glanced about at the assembled members of the Witan's inner council, impatience hidden behind the regal mask he'd learned to cultivate so well. But he was thinking as he'd thought all too many times before: What good to be king, what good to have dreams of glory, plans of conquest, when you were pinned so very firmly to the mundane here-and-now? Of course a ruler must always be aware of the details of his land if he meant to keep his throne. Anyone who'd been anywhere near reality in the world of the court knew that. And of course there was a limit to what a ruler could safely delegate away to others.

But do I really need to know about every item sold in Uintacaester's markets or every ear of grain grown in Wessex's fields?

He let his mind wander just a wary bit, toying with the memory of the wayward prince of Cathay, the never quite resolved question of whether that had actually been an attempt at assassination. If not, what? If so, why? Much as he and Osmod would have loved to use it as an excuse to attack Mercia, the Witan had dragged its collective heels.

And unfortunately I have to agree with them.

It was simply too soon for such radical moves; the fact remained, dislike it though he might, that after so short a time as king, he just wasn't secure enough on the throne to successfully muster everyone behind him.

To arms, my people, to arms against the tyrant—now there's a ridiculous image.

Dishearteningly, his spies had brought him absolutely no evidence of a Mercian plot against him, not a plot that included anything as dramatic as assassination, at any rate. The day would come for Mercia, Egbert promised silently; he definitely meant to take advantage of that kingdom's weak ruler. But, alas, not just yet.

He'd resisted the urge to send a message to Aedh of Eriu. There just was no reason for the High King to want him dead, and Egbert was far from ready to stir up anything political in that direction.

Egbert reluctantly returned to the present. Bah, yes, they were still droning on about wheat and sheep. Osmod would surely have told this ealdorman what to do with his grain statistics and that one where he could leave his studies of the wool market, all the while with so charming a smile that neither noble would take offense.

After all, few are they who can take offense with him. Charming and cheerful, that's our Osmod and, the king added with a touch of cynicism, *the amazing part of it is that most of the cheer seems real. As the man himself would say—*

But Osmod wasn't here, was he? Egbert stifled a sigh that would have mingled frustration with a fair amount of anger at himself, and got to his feet. The startled councilmen fell silent, watching him in confusion.

"Enough facts and figures," he said, and forced a cheerful smile of his own. "I wish to see for myself how the land is doing." Egbert started forward, a confused swirling of guards and ealdormen in his wake. "Come, prepare yourselves. We ride."

It didn't take long to organize an expedition; Egbert refused to allow that. Mounted on a properly elegant if smallish horse, he allowed himself a random regal thought as they rode down into Uintacaester's crowded streets: he should see if he couldn't trade with

Charlemagne for some of the larger Frankish steeds, improve the Wessex breed—bah, no, the newly minted Emperor would never part with them.

Ah, look, the surprised crowds were cheering him, and their enthusiasm sounded genuine.

Of course it's genuine. Osmod was right: until I do something unpleasantly regal, like raising their taxes, I am their golden young deity.

Osmod again. Egbert leaned down from his horse to examine the quality of the wool an earnest, red-faced merchant was offering for inspection, and tried to look as though he was genuinely interested.

Osmod. It was ridiculous to become dependent on the ealdorman, on anyone. Ridiculous? Downright perilous.

"Excellent wool," he said sharply, and rode on, leaving the gratefully bowing merchant behind.

It's not as though I truly rely on Osmod, or even trust him all that much, not that ambitious fellow.

Ambitious but charming. Charming to everyone. Sometimes it did seem as though court affairs only ran smoothly—which meant, Egbert admitted, the way he wanted them to run—when the ealdorman was present.

"Yes, yes, those are excellent vegetables," the king agreed with a weather-beaten, beaming farmer. "There's been just enough rain, hasn't there? Ah yes, and I see your hens have been producing nicely; plenty of grain for them to eat."

My, how these little tidbits of personal interest seemed to delight everyone! Those dull statistics droned over by the Witan did have politic uses. He should have done this before, gotten to know the common folk a bit, done his own stint of charming everyone the way Osmod charmed everyone.

Osmod again. The king rode on, trailed by his procession and waving and smiling at the crowds. Odd, how without Osmod's presence, the idea of invasions and expansion didn't seem quite so insistent. Or maybe it was just being down here among the earnest, bustling life of the city. His prosperous, relatively peaceful city.

And yet . . .

Egbert gave a mental shrug. He could only show so much interest in common affairs. The limits of Uinta-caester, of Wessex, would be boring him soon enough; he knew himself. But Osmod was wrong. It made no sense at all to try stirring up things towards war. Not yet. You didn't make any such drastic moves till you were sure of men—in loyalty as well as numbers—of resources and, yes, political stability. There was a ridiculous thought: stability among these his quarrelsome folk. Osmod would say that—

Osmod again. "Enough," Egbert said shortly, turning his horse. "Back to the royal hall."

Dammit, I really have let myself get too dependent on the man.

Easy enough to do. The ealdorman was so—convenient. The only member of the Witan who owned, or at least revealed, more than a token of common sense, he knew how to cut right through the web of court bureaucracy with just a few out-and-out sensible words. Surely it wasn't overly dependent to want someone at court who could take so much of the tedious off the royal shoulders.

Where are you, damn you? Or rather, where is your mind these days? Octa had assured him that the ealdorman had suffered no permanent harm from his illness, and the physician had a respectably high number of cures to his credit. *Don't make a liar of him, Osmod. I may not always trust you fully—but I do need you by my side!*

Osmod sat staring bleakly at the runes, as he stared at them whenever he was awake, ever since that first horrifying revelation.

And, as it had been then, so it was now.

Nothing. Not the slightest trace of Power. Nothing.

Nothing was real, nothing meant anything, nothing . . . dimly, he knew the world remained outside this one room; dimly, he knew that life and the Witan and all of Wessex continued as ever it had. Osmod tried to rouse himself, telling himself that this sudden terrible loss meant nothing; he was still who he'd been, a man with high status at court, great influence on King Egbert of Wessex—

No. Nothing. It meant nothing. Without Power, it all meant . . . nothing.

The softest, most hesitant of coughs cut into his dull despair. "What?"

"My—my lord?"

"Yes! What is it?"

"My lord, it's Bosa."

"I can see that it's Bosa! Now what do you want?"

"It's King Egbert, my lord," the servant said warily. "He sends his greetings and—and wonders when you will be ready to return to court affairs."

When, indeed? This helpless languor was growing worse than tedious; it was getting downright perilous. The longer he waited, the weaker grew his hold over Egbert. He must show the king that he was fully recovered, fully his old, trustworthy, ever so loyal self again.

How? How can I lie so convincingly?

"Yes," Osmod said before Bosa could prod him. "Tell the king that I will be attending his council as usual. Tomorrow. Tell him that. Tomorrow."

"Yes, but—"

"Tomorrow, Bosa. Now, go!"

Tomorrow. Somewhere between then and now, he must regain his Power. Useless to pray to the Lords of Darkness. Even assuming that they were real, that they would listen, they would hardly be the sort to grant a supplicant's prayers.

No. He must regain his lost Power on his own.

Blood. A life. There was the proper path, surely.

But whose life? Something as vitally urgent as this

could hardly be won by that of a mere child or servant.

Someone important, then. But . . . who? And before tomorrow?

Impossible.

"Bosa," Osmod called. "Bosa! Ah, there you are. Tell the king that yes, I will be attending his council today."

"But you said—"

"Today, Bosa."

Of course he was surrounded by well-wishing idiots—and those who were too politic not to seem well-wishing—the moment he stuck his head into the hall. Osmod had expected no less, and played the role of the earnest invalid with all his might: yes, I am still weak, yes, I am so pathetically weary, but yes, I am such a loyal ealdorman I forced myself from my sickbed to attend my king.

Why, look at this: I'm almost a saint, Osmod thought sourly. *Faugh, I'm sweet enough to make myself ill!*

Someone else wasn't quite accepting the act. Osmod glanced from the throng to where Egbert watched, wry skepticism in his eyes. The ealdorman smiled ever so slightly, and saw the king dip his head ever so slightly in return. Egbert was willing to cede that Osmod's illness had been genuine, even if he wasn't agreeing with this "poor, pathetic martyr" performance.

"It's a fine thing to see you up and about again, ealdorman," the king drawled. "Now sit, before you fall."

Osmod sat, trying to ever so delicately pick up the strands of his Powerful influence . . . no. Still not even a spark.

Blood, then, no doubt about it. A life to be given, the life of someone important.

Whose?

For a time, listening to the various Witan members droning on about this inconsequential matter and that, Osmod let his thoughts wander, pondering Egbert's dull-witted mistress. . . . Whatever her name was. Leofrun,

that was it. Leofrun was certainly slow-brained enough
to run into trouble all on her innocent, well-meaning
own.

Ach, no. There was absolutely no way to safely get the
woman alone, no way to safely dispatch her and dispose
of the body.

Who else? Who else? One of the Witan? Now there
was an entertaining thought. Osmod let his gaze rove
over them, settling lightly on this man and that as
though by idle chance. Cuthred, perhaps? Honest as
sunlight, that one, yet bland as an ox. No one would
miss him since no one really noticed he was there. But
then again, that hardly would make him a fitting sacrifice.

What about Eadwig, then? Nothing bland about him:
large as a warrior, florid of face, red of hair, loud of voice.
The court would be a good deal more tranquil without
him.

Alas, no, again. He would never die quietly. No, in
fact, to all of the Witan. Oh, it would be easy enough
to get any of them alone, and there were certainly
enough pompous idiots among the ealdormen who'd
improve the quality of the court by their deaths, but—

But what? What was missing?

Logic, Osmod decided. If he was to gain the optimum
amount of Power out of this, there must be a logical reason for the sacrifice of whomever he chose to—

Wait, now . . . logical. Who would be the most logical person to visit him up in his sickroom? Who had
already shown disconcerting hints of dark suspicions?

"Octa," Osmod murmured, so softly that no one heard.
"Physician Octa. Yes."

Perfect, so perfect. A physician, a healer, a practitioner
of—of goodness. What a perfect offering to the Lords
of Darkness—and how much Power would be in that
goodly blood! Now, Osmod told himself, he merely had
to puzzle out how in the name of those unfeeling and
possibly unreal Lords he was going to manage this. The

murdering of someone so important must look like an accident.

An accident . . . the slipping of a tool . . . no. Hardly anything to do with weaponry, not where a physician was concerned. And Octa was never the sort to accidentally poison himself with one of his own potions. There must be some other way. A fall from a horse—no. Octa almost never rode. A fall, though . . . a fall . . . surely he was on the right path with this—

Ah, the answer was so obvious it practically screamed at him to use it! Osmod smiled, pleased as he'd not been for days. He might be Powerless—for the moment—but that didn't mean he'd lost his cleverness. Oh no, he'd not lost that at all.

Poor me, he thought. *I fear I am about to suffer a most unfortunate relapse.*

Outside, the evening sky was heavy with ever-thickening clouds. Portentous clouds, thought Osmod, lying in bed with the nervous Bosa hovering nearby. Ha, yes, there came the first flash of lightning. He waited, counting off heartbeats . . . yes, there was the first deep rumbling of thunder. The storm was still a goodly way off, but definitely heading this way. Portentous, indeed. And, if the rain came along with the drama, convenient as well.

So. Time to go to work. Osmod moaned, the sound of a man caught in the throes of feverish illness, and stirred restlessly in the bed.

"M-master?" Bosa quavered. "Are you all right?"

No, you idiot. I'm deathly sick. Can't you tell? "I'm . . . not sure. Head . . ."

"Sh-shall I go fetch the physician?"

"No . . ." Osmod murmured. "Be all right . . ." He feigned an attempt to stand, fell back onto the bed with a new groan. "Yes." It was said with apparent reluctance. *A great, strong man, that's me, hating to admit weakness.* "Yes. Must have . . . must have done too much . . . too soon. . . ."

"I—I'll get the physician, it's all right, I'll get Octa."

"Hurry."

Osmod lay there till Bosa was safely away, then sat up, grinning savagely. Yes. Here came the rain. Perfect.

Ah, but here came footsteps on the stairs. Bosa, yes, but followed by someone else. Physician Octa. Osmod lay back again, pretending with all his might to be on the edge of feverish slumber. He heard the physician approach, murmuring to Bosa, and stirred as though too restless to stay asleep, then sat bolt upright, staring at Bosa as though he'd never seen the servant before.

"You! What are you doing here? Begone!"

"M-master? Don't you know me? It's me, Bosa, and—"

"Demon! Begone, I say, ere I call the Church down on your evil head!"

Octa sighed. "The fever's returned. I feared it might. Better leave," he told Bosa. "Your presence is only exciting him."

"But—"

"Don't worry. I can deal with this alone."

"Are you sure . . . ?"

"Of course I—"

"Begone!" Osmod shrieked at Bosa, stumbling to his feet.

"Go," the physician ordered.

Bosa, with a nervous glance back at Osmod, fled. Osmod stood where he was, panting and glaring as though thoroughly out of his mind, all the while listening carefully to the ever-approaching storm, the ever-louder crashes of thunder. He must time this perfectly.

Octa took a cautious step forward, as though trying to approach a wary wild thing. "Do you know who I am?" he asked in a gentle voice.

Forcing back the impulse to shout, *a trusting fool*, Osmod nodded. "Of course. I sent for you. It's important. A matter of utter urgency. Come, you must study this plan with me." He looked back over his shoulder at the physician with a frown. "Come, come!"

Octa, humoring him, moved to his side. "There," Osmod said, pointing, "what do you think of that?"

"I'm afraid I don't see—"

"There! Look there!"

With a sigh, the physician bent to look. Osmod caught up a clothes chest in both arms and, timing his action to the next crash of thunder, brought the chest down with all his might on Octa's head. The physician crumpled, but Osmod was there to catch him before he hit the floor, and neatly pierced Octa's throat with his dagger. Quickly pinching the small wound closed with one hand, Osmod flailed about with the other till he'd found the basin he'd placed within reach.

"For you, Lords of Darkness," he muttered, and let blood fill the basin. Time enough to spill it properly on the ground later. Now Osmod placed his mouth against the wound and drank, ecstatic to feel Octa's life fading into him, flooding him with wild new strength, so much greater, so much more Powerful than any he'd ever absorbed.

Yes, ah yes, ah yes!

Here was Power, here was life, yes, yes, here was all he'd lost, returned in this one fiery rush!

At last, dizzy with satiation, Osmod forced himself to stop. The body could hardly be found with a massive loss of blood, not if this was to look convincing. He staggered to his feet, dragging the body with him, one hand tight over the wound in its throat, timing each pull to each clap of thunder. There, now, there was the stairway, nice and slick with rain.

You're heavy, Octa . . . Osmod thought, panting, *heavier . . . I'd guess . . . than you were in life.*

He lugged the body about to the head of the stairway, waiting, waiting . . . *now!*

With a great shove, Osmod sent the body tumbling down the stairs, then stood at the top of them shouting in feigned horror, shouting and shouting until courtiers came running, bundled against the rain.

"There!" Osmod cried like a man gone beyond hysteria. "There! He—he slipped, I—I saw it, the poor man slipped and fell and cut his throat, there, on that splintered wood, and—and—God help him, is he—"

Bosa had reached the body first. "He's dead," the servant said, staring up at Osmod in wide-eyed horror. "Physician Octa is dead."

Osmod staggered back as though too stunned to stand. But he was thinking, *He's dead. And I—I am alive, I am healed and strong and Powerful—*

I am myself again!

Spells and Raiders
Chapter 30

Cadwal was a huddled mass of woolen *brat*, there on the deck of the *Sea Raven*. Ardagh glanced about at the maze of sleeping Lochlannach (curled up wherever they could find a place, he thought, like so many slumbering beasts), then picked his delicate way through the maze to the mercenary's side. The prince hesitated, not wanting to wake him, but a sepulchral voice Cadwal said in Gaeilge, "I'm not asleep."

"Ah." Crouching by the bundle's side, Ardagh asked softly, so as not to wake the Lochlannach all around him, "Are you feeling any better?"

A baleful eye glinted at him, and the prince sighed. "I withdraw the question."

"Wanted to ask me anything else, did you?"

"Nothing that can't wait till morning." *And hopefully a more seaworthy stomach on your part.* "I hope you know that I did try to keep the Lochlannach from bothering you too much."

"I know. Appreciated." Cadwal groaned faintly. "I'd have fought them over this except I might have survived. You . . . wouldn't be telling King Aedh about this, would you?"

"Tell him what? That his mercenary leader is human?"

"Prince Ardagh . . ."

"Ae, Cadwal, haven't we worse problems than that? No, I will not tell the king you have any such weaknesses. And this one will pass."

309

"Right. When we get to dry land." Cadwal stirred, still wrapped tightly in his *brat*. "Any idea when that will be?"

"No."

Something in his voice must have sounded odd, because Cadwal suddenly sat up, peering at him. "Here, now. You don't look so healthy yourself."

"Ah well, I'm not feeling quite myself, I admit it."

"Och. No insult meant here, but . . . well . . . too much iron, right?"

Ardagh glared, not too happy about having his own weakness discussed, but admitted, "In too confined a space, yes. At least that cursedly solid chunk of iron that's the anchor is overboard till morning."

Was that a wry chuckle from Cadwal? "A fine, heroic pair, aren't we?"

Ardagh found himself grinning in spite of himself. "We are, we are, indeed."

"Tell you what. The first chance we get, we hie ourselves off this hell-ship and away from these barbarians as far as we can run."

"I . . . can't. And don't stare at me as though I'd gone mad." Ardagh dropped his voice still lower. "Cadwal, I may have found a way to fight Osmod on his own terms."

"Oh?"

A world of wariness in that sound. "Listen to me," the prince said in sudden impatience. "I'm not merely talking about taking personal revenge, though I won't deny that won't be satisfying. But there's more to the whole affair than something that finite."

Cadwal frowned. "Something to do with kingdoms, I take it?"

"Clever man." Quickly the prince summarized his thoughts about Osmod and Egbert together forming a military and sorcerous peril to Eriu.

"*Iesu*," Cadwal muttered when he was done. "The way you tell it, the whole thing sounds all too possible. Hell no," he added hastily, seeing Ardagh stiffen slightly. "I didn't mean that the way it came out. The idea of the two of them in alliance—it really does sound like something that could happen. And danger like that . . ." The mercenary's eyes glinted in the darkness. "Neither of us wants to lose our sanctuary, and all that. All right, then. You want any help from me, anything a magickless human can do, that is, you've got it."

"Thank you. Unfortunately, though, the only thing we can do right now is simply be where we are."

"Which brings us back to the first point: Why?"

"I can't be sure, not without a good stretch of time in which to study this, but Einar the self-styled scald just may know some interesting spells—"

"What, that raw-faced boy? He doesn't look as though he could complete a song, let alone cast the simplest—"

"He can't cast a spell at all. That doesn't mean that the runic magics he knows, or claims to know, won't work in the proper . . . ah . . . hands. Runic magic," Ardagh added, "is almost certainly what Osmod is using."

"There's more, isn't there?"

"There is. Cadwal, this isn't anything to which I can say yes or no, but . . . I still *feel* that there's more use to be made of these folk."

Cadwal lay back with a sigh. "Saesnig. Morfren. Tylwyth Teg. And now Lochlannach. God and all you saints up there, if ever I let even the smallest of words of boredom slip my lips, I'll not blame any of you for striking me mute on the spot!"

After a time, his breathing steadied, slowed. *Asleep,* Ardagh thought, *and hopefully finally with a calm stomach.*

The softest of wary sounds made him straighten, then get to his feet. Leaning lightly on the ship's rail, he said over his shoulder, "Jarl Thorkell."

The jarl moved carefully to his side, a nervous sideways glint of eye showing that he was impressed that Ardagh hadn't needed to turn to see who it was. "A pleasant night."

Now Ardagh did turn to him. A pleasant night was

hardly accurate; the wind had died to a faint breeze, and the air was dank and heavy. "You did not come to me to discuss the weather."

"Ah . . . no." Thorkell hesitated a long while, leaning on the rail. "Awkward," he said at last, very softly. "But . . ."

"But you wish me to aid you in something. What?"

"I . . . you . . . you can guess that things have not been too easy for me lately." It was barely more than a wary whisper.

"After the failed raid."

Keen Sidhe night-vision saw the human's face redden. "Exactly," Thorkell said shortly. "I was able to man this ship again, but—"

"But you must have a successful raid or lose status. And so you are exploring new territory, seeing what you can find. What do you want of me, Jarl Thorkell?"

"I'm not ordering you, you understand; I wouldn't do anything that foolish, not with you being . . . what you are. But if you could somehow see your way clear to bringing us to something worthwhile . . ."

"To loot, you mean. I will," Ardagh said with great dignity, "do what I may." *And there, you barbaric seathief, is a vague statement you may take as you will.*

Thorkell, of course, took it as a guarantee of aid. "I knew my luck had turned again," he said, and his teeth flashed in a quick grin.

Ardagh, staring out over the sea, his face a mask of Sidhe calm, said nothing. But his thoughts were far from tranquil. He certainly wasn't about to help the Lochlannach find a target for their piracy. How long, though, before they realized his magic wasn't helping them? It was no easy thing to learn a new form of Power; even with the Language Spell hastening his understanding of Einar's runic spells (always assuming the would-be scald actually knew any), it would take some time to absorb them. And in such a finite, crowded space, just how much time did he have?

*See the mighty Ljos Alfar. See his awesome Power.
Hah.*

King Egbert of Wessex woke in wild alarm, for one
panic-stricken moment sure he was under attack—

No. What had sounded in his sleep like screams of
terror was nothing more than the muffled sobbing of his
mistress, Leofrun, curled up there beside him like a
frightened child.

And like a child, still asleep. Not sure if what he was
feeling was pity or annoyance, Egbert touched her shoulder, shook her gently.

She came awake with a startled shriek.

"Hush, Leofrun. Hush, now. You're safe."

Leofrun fell into his arms, sobbing into his shoulder,
"His eyes! His eyes!"

"*Whose* eyes?"

"*His!* The—the—the—*Octa!*"

Octa! Egbert felt a chill of pure atavistic terror race
through him. Very carefully, he said, "Octa is dead,
Leofrun."

"I know! He—he told me!"

Now Egbert sat bolt upright, pulling Leofrun up with
him. Everyone knew that it was fools and saints who
were visited by the Other World, and Leofrun, poor
innocent, was hardly a saint. What if it really had been
Octa? What if he was using Leofrun as his messenger?

"Stop snivelling, woman," Egbert commanded. "Stop
it!" He waited an impatient moment while Leofrun
struggled to control herself, then asked sharply, "What
did you mean, he told you?"

"It w-was a dream. But it *wasn't* a dream! I mean, I—
I saw him so very clearly. He told me he was dead, he
told me that—that *someone killed him!*"

"That's ridiculous." *Is it? Is it? The dead do sometimes
point out their killers; even the Church doesn't deny such
things can happen. But . . . Octa? He had no enemies!*
"Who would have done such a thing?"

"He—he—he wouldn't tell me."

Egbert let out his breath in a long sigh of relief. "He wouldn't tell you. Octa came all the way back from—from wherever, told you he'd been killed—then wouldn't tell you who had done it."

"Th-that's right."

Her eyes were innocent of any deceit. "Ach, Leofrun," Egbert said with helpless affection, and ruffled her hair as he would have played with a hound's ears. "My poor, dim Leofrun, look at me. Look." He took her head between his hands. "It was a dream. No more than that. Nothing but a dream."

"But . . ."

"Before you kill someone, my dear, you need to have a reason. No one would have had a reason to kill Octa."

"But . . ."

"Think about it, Leofrun. Did anyone hate Octa? Did anyone ever, ever say anything bad about him?"

"No."

"See? A dream. Octa died in an accident. No one killed the poor fellow."

"But . . ."

"Enough." Egbert pulled Leofrun into his arms, not sure if he wanted to comfort her or cast her from his bed. And he felt her lips form a name against his shoulder:

"Osmod."

Egbert drew back, staring. "What?"

"I—I didn't say anything! I didn't!"

Looking into those innocent eyes, the king sighed again. "Of course you didn't. Never mind, Leofrun. I must have been mistaken."

Osmod? Osmod a murderer? God, if he believed that, he was as stupid as Leofrun. "Come here, woman," Egbert commanded, forcing a smile. "There are very pleasant ways to banish dreams."

Giggling, she fell into his arms.

Osmod sat alone in his bedchamber, stolen vitality hot as strong drink within him, and thought of all the work facing him. In the few short days that he'd been ill, Egbert had pulled almost totally free of his control.

My luck, he thought with dark humor. *First an easygoing king with no ambition, now an ambitious king with a will of iron.*

Iron, Osmod reminded himself, rusted.

Yes, but it had been stupid, stupidly vain, to try something as Powerful as attacking Prince Ardagh from such a distance. No wonder he'd fallen ill!

A miracle that I truly didn't burn out my mind! I came close enough to it.

Some quiet divination was another matter; it took more logical interpretation than wild Power. And it would be ideal for edging back into true sorcery.

Osmod had already cleared a space on the floor and placed the white cloth upon it. Now he spread out the runes before him, looking them over for a moment before beginning the divination in earnest.

The prince now, the prince was surely Yew, Oak and Ash, just as the runes had claimed before. All right then, Osmod thought, he'd accept that ridiculous reading as accurate. Of course, then, judging from the way the three runes had fallen, it meant that the prince was alive and . . . mm . . . something to do with water, with ships . . . ah, of course. Sailing. But . . . where? Wondering, Osmod cast the runes again, and frowned. Yew, Ash, Oak, yes, and with them, reversed as if to taunt him, the runes that warned of *Possible danger.*

"Sailing, are you?" Osmod muttered, feeling a sudden savage flame of rage blaze through him. "Here's a hope, Prince Ardagh, that, wherever you may be, you drown!"

But the prince, he reminded himself, struggling for control, was far away, and right now regaining a firm hold over King Egbert was much more important. After a fierce inner battle, Osmod managed to block thoughts of Prince Ardagh from his mind and, with a silent sigh, bent to his work.

Ardagh woke with a savage shock, scrambling to his feet, feeling the deck surging under him, *feeling* the cold burning of iron all around him, finding himself in the middle of a wild storm of shouts and excitement. What— he must have actually drifted off to an uncertain sleep there at the ship's railing, crumpled uncomfortably against the wooden side, and here it was nearly morning and—

A raid! They've spotted smoke—a farm, maybe a village—they're going ashore!

Still dazed by sleep, he nearly fell as the ship was beached with a heavy crunching of sand. Struggling to catch his balance, the prince heard himself trying to protest, one lone voice amid the chaos, hardly knowing why he should care what happened, not to humans, trying to argue that no, they mustn't do this thing. But no one seemed to hear him and all around him were drawn swords, axes, iron in the weapons, in the great lump of the anchor, iron all around him, so close, too close, so much iron, and he—he couldn't bear it and he—and he—

Was suddenly lost in darkness.

Ardagh woke more slowly this time, dizzy, head aching, staring blearily up at Cadwal standing over him like a warrior defending a fallen comrade.

"You all right now?" the mercenary asked.

"Yes. What . . . happened? No, never mind. I remember." The iron-sickness had hit him so swiftly and strongly he hadn't even had the time to be ill. His overwhelmed body had taken the only escape it could. Blinking, Ardagh saw that he was lying in the prow of the *Sea Raven*. "You dragged me here?"

"Thought it was a good idea to get you as far away from the anchor as I could." Cadwal frowned at him as

Ardagh slowly sat up. "You don't know how close I came to getting us both out of here altogether and—*damnio.* Here they come."

Oh, indeed. Like a gang of boys, Ardagh thought, laughing and joking and carrying whatever it was they'd found to steal: someone's pot (iron of course; just what this ship needed, more of that cursed metal), a bolt of cloth, a woman's necklace—plain clay beads, he saw with an unexpected touch of anger, a poor peasant's ornament. Ae, what brave warriors, these! Ardagh struggled to his feet as the Lochlannach came swarming back on board. Thorkell, the prince saw with a jolt, was dragging someone with him—a woman, no, no, a girl, hands bound before her, and Ardagh thought in quick horror of that alien human crime, rape. But she didn't seem to have been harmed more than some scrapes and bruises, not yet.

With a laugh, the jarl dropped his disheveled prize in a heap at Ardagh's feet, then turned to shout at his men, "Oars ready! And—away!"

Not enough wind to fill the sail. The men bent to the oars with goodwill, still joking and laughing, full of cheer.

As the *Sea Raven* bounded back into open sea, the girl at Ardagh's feet stared up at him in shock, eyes wide as she took in his features, so alien amid the Lochlannach. No one much, this youngster, Ardagh thought, save to her people, of course. She was sturdy, with tousled brown braids and a plain brown tunic tied in at the waist with a scrap of rope: a peasant girl from some farmer's holding. But in her eyes was a pure defiance that roused a spark of approval in him.

"Like her?" That was the beaming Thorkell, the essence of joviality. "Not much of a raid, just a farmer's holding, but it's a start. A good omen. She's the best of the loot—and you've earned her."

Confused, Ardagh began a wary, "I—"

"What's this? Modesty? I saw you standing at the rail all night, conjuring this raid for us. Yes, and I saw you collapse from sheer exhaustion!"

Was that what Thorkell thought? Was that what these barbarians believed? That he would actually help them? Hiding his shudder, Ardagh bent to cut the girl's bonds with a slash of his dagger, whispering to her in Gaeilge, "Can you swim?" adding a quick bit of pantomime in case she didn't understand his words.

Eyes suddenly fierce with relief, she nodded. Ardagh pulled her to her feet, caught her up in his arms (trying not to stagger; her solid young body wasn't light) with a shouted incantation that was actually nothing but a Sidhe children's rhyme—and tossed her over the rail. Amid the startled storm of protests, he stood with arms regally folded, seemingly staring straight ahead, but actually keeping a subtle watch on the water. Ah yes, there she was, and swimming to shore as swiftly as a seal. Hopefully there was still a holding to which she could return.

"What are you *doing?*" Thorkell yelped. "If you didn't want the girl, we could still have gotten good slave-money for her!"

Ardagh gave him as coldly sorcerous a stare as ever was on a Sidhe's face, and saw the jarl wince. "It was needful," the prince said without a trace of emotion, and added another vague, but perfectly true statement: "The sea takes what it will."

Put those together and make of them what you can.

"But—oh. Magic."

Several hands flew in warding-off signs at that. Thorkell whirled. "All right, you idiots, enough wasting of time. *Row!*"

Still no wind, but the men had settled into a steady beat that brought the two ships smoothly around a headland—

Ah, look at this. The girl really did reach friends.

Farmers. Fishermen. They had boats, but of course these were nothing to equal the Lochlannach warships. But, the prince thought, a flock of sparrows can drive away a hunting hawk, even, if there are enough of them, kill the predator. And to his somewhat malicious delight, he saw how fiercely the Lochlannach were forced to row to escape this flock.

At last, out in open, empty water once more, Thorkell called a halt. "Thor seems to be playing games with us," he muttered, peering up at the limp sail. "Not a breath of wind now."

Nor was there the slightest breeze for the rest of the day. Ardagh heard the softest of uneasy mutterings from the Lochlannach and knew that they must be wondering if his "sacrifice" of the girl had angered their deity and spoiled their luck. He and Cadwal slept that night, by unspoken agreement, back to back, hands near their weapons.

The morning of the second day found the *Sea Raven* still becalmed, and the mutterings grew louder, with a few definite references to "Dokk Alfar." Thorkell made fervent vows to his namesake deity, promising a downright regal series of offerings if only Thor would relent and send a wind.

The air grew even more still. Not a ripple stirred.

"Guess who they're going to be blaming," Cadwal murmured.

"I know it."

"I'm not up to fighting so many, and we're too far out from land to swim." The mercenary glance at Ardagh. "You wouldn't be having some nice, flashy magic handy, would you?"

"Not really."

Ah well, better to take the offensive while he could. "Would you have a wind?" Ardagh called out boldly.

"Can you bring one?" Thorkell countered.

"The Ljos Alfar can do many things." *As can we all.*

Unfortunately, Ardagh mused, even in the Sidhe Realm, he'd had no great talent for Weather Magic.

Still, better a bluff than a quick toss overboard as a sham or, worse, an evil Dokk Alfar.

The most dramatic place for this farce would surely

be the prow. As Cadwal watched him dubiously and the Lochlannach uneasily got out of his way, Ardagh struck a dramatic pose, one hand steadying himself against the upturned dragon's head, the other held up to the heavens. Taking a great breath, he began to chant in the Sidhe tongue:

"That's right, you mighty stealers of unarmed girls, stare at me! Oh you robbers of peasants and helpless monks, fear my magic! You are nothing but hopeless barbarians, the lot of you. Yes, yes, go on, make your superstitious signs against evil. You are creatures without honor, slayers of the weak and defenseless!"

Well and good and very satisfying in a foolish way, but unless the weather helped out, all the insults he could declaim weren't going to be enough to—

Ardagh's pseudo-magical chant faltered for a moment. *I don't believe this!*

Great dark storm clouds were boiling up on the horizon. Ah, of course! The heavy, still calm had been quite literally the calm before the storm.

And what wonderful timing it has to arrive just now!

As Ardagh continued his chant, shouting out whatever wildness came to mind, the first gusts of wind hit the *Sea Raven,* rocking it fiercely, and men cried out in superstitious terror.

Then the full weight of the storm swept down on them.

A Student of the Runes
Chapter 31

The storm came crashing down on the *Sea Raven* like a living predator, whipping up the sea into a frenzy of waves, winds snatching at the *Sea Raven's* sail, tossing the ship forward like a chip of wood. Ardagh caught Cadwal by the arm and dragged them both down in the prow, which was wet and windblown but the best place to get out of the way of the sailors. Thorkell stood firmly planted at the stern as though the *Sea Raven* was solid as the land, red hair whipping dramatically about his head as he shouted out orders, fighting to be heard above the roar of the storm. Ardagh raised his head, gasping against the force of the wind and the shock of cold seawater slapping at him, and saw the sail stretched to its fullest.

They'd better get it furled before the wind tears it to— ah yes, good work, they've got it now.

No hope to lower the mast, not in this tempest. The best they could do now was simply hope to ride out the storm. Olaf the steersman fought with the rudder as though battling a wild thing, and two others rushed to help him. But with a savage *crack* that sounded even over the storm, the steering oar broke, hurling all three men to the deck. They grabbed desperately at ropes, oars, anything they could find as a great, cold wave broke over the *Sea Raven.* Hands caught two of them; the third man was swept right off the deck into the sea.

Powers, if this flimsy bit of wood goes down, so do we!

But the *Sea Raven* showed no sign of sinking. Helpless before the storm though it was, the ship rode the seas as lightly as a gull.

A rudderless, unguided gull.

Thorkell was shouting something, pointing frantically, there, there! A coastline, a beach, and like it or not, they were being driven towards it.

If the prow shatters, Ardagh thought in new alarm, *so do we!* Cadwal realized the danger, too. They both dove from their shelter to the mast, clinging to it with several of the Lochlannach as the ship—

Hit with enough force to hurl them from their feet, groaning its way up onto the beach . . . and stopped, as neatly as though human hands had guided it. Behind them, the storm raged off as though a sentient entity that was finished with them. The sudden silence seemed almost unnatural, and for a time none of the panting men, draped wherever they had landed, seemed to want to break it.

But then Thorkell said, very, very mildly, not quite looking at Ardagh, "A simple wind would have been enough."

Ardagh got to his feet, managing not to sway, raising a regal eyebrow. "If you use the lightning to heat your food, you can't complain if it burns the forest around you."

"Ah. Yes. Of course." Thorkell closed his eyes, opened them. "Come," he said to his men. "Let's see to the damage."

The Lochlannach climbed wearily overboard, and Ardagh and Cadwal followed, staggering for a moment as their bodies adjusted to land.

"Never could understand that bit about kissing the ground," Cadwal murmured to Ardagh. "Till now."

"At least you didn't get sick."

"Heh. I was too damned scared for that."

The Lochlannach, once they'd caught their collective breath, had begun swarming over the beached ship, calling out their finds. The worst of it—a testament to the skill of the Lochlannach shipbuilders—seemed to be the broken rudder, and Thorkell let out his breath in a slow sigh of relief.

"Not as bad as it could have been, not at all. And Ran seems satisfied with the one sacrifice she claimed."

Ran? Ardagh wondered. *Yet another Lochlannach deity, I'd guess. Presumably a goddess of the sea.*

Thorkell glanced about, hands on hips (and conveniently near sword and dagger hilts). "Forests up there on the ridge. We should be able to find wood for repairs quickly enough."

Assuming, Ardagh thought, and the Lochlannach plainly realized, *that there aren't any local folk just waiting to attack.*

"You, you, and you," Thorkell snapped out, "climb up there and see if you can find out where we've landed. Yes, and if there are any little surprises waiting for us."

As those left behind waited, not a man would meet the prince's eyes; no one uttered so much as a word of blame. After all, he thought, who was going to argue with someone Powerful enough to raise a storm? Even Cadwal, now that he'd caught his breath, wasn't quite looking at Ardagh.

"That storm wasn't my doing," the prince whispered to him.

"Of course not."

"Stop that! I didn't do anything."

"Right."

"Cadwal, I don't have any such Weather Magic! I didn't even when I was back in the Sidhe Realm and—ae, never mind."

For a time the prince stood watching Thorkell carefully not watching the prince.

There must be some use I can make of his suddenly renewed awe of me. . . .

Suddenly inspired, Ardagh moved to Thorkell's side. "This would seem to be a safe time to mention a certain matter. Regarding Eriu."

"Ah?" warily.

"Concerning magic."

Now Thorkell did turn to face the prince. "What are you saying?"

"There is the possibility," Ardagh said, delicately side-stepping untruth, "that such a land is under Otherly protection."

The jarl glanced at him, glanced away. "That explains it. I always suspected that there was something magical about the way the raid was blocked."

"Then you agree. Eriu is protected. It must not be attacked again."

"All right."

The prince, set to argue, opened his mouth, shut it, echoed weakly, "'All right?'"

The jarl shrugged. "Why not? There's just as good picking to be had in Britain. That's not under elven protection, too? No? Fine. Then I'll spread the word at the next Thing, the next great assembly. Can't guarantee that everyone will believe me or listen to me, but that's their problem, not mine."

It took every scrap of Ardagh's Sidhe self-control not to scream, *"All right?" I nearly get myself killed over and over, I go through all this hardship and the whole point of my mission, the whole problem of Lochlannach raids, the whole Darkness-Take-It reason I came to Wessex, is solved with a casual, "All right?"*

Ah well. This spectacular anticlimax was no stranger than anything else that happened among humans. And as the humans put it, take what was given.

"But of course," Thorkell was continuing smoothly, unaware of Ardagh's inner struggle for self-control, "you'll want to travel on with us, not return to Eriu. That's hardly the Ljos Alfar's realm, if the scalds are correct."

"True. But—"

"Well, then, there we are!"

No, there we are not! "Jarl Thorkell, I have done enough. You saw the fury of the storm."

"Of course, and I also saw how you brought us to land as safely as you could. Only lost us the one man—well, you could hardly want to fight Ran's will, I'd think—and the one steering oar; that's amazing control, say what you will."

"Yes, but—"

"And what can *I* say? Of course you'll sail on with us. We'd be cruel to turn you out like some unwanted beggar in this—this wherever we are. No, no, you are our guest! I would not think of abandoning you!"

Which means, "I would not think of abandoning your magic."

"Of course not," the prince agreed without the slightest trace of emotion. "And of course we both understand that none of the Folk can be held for long against their will."

"Against your will! I would never think of such a thing!"

Of course not. And I'm a little green wyvern. "You do realize that when I wish to leave, I shall do so in so complete and sudden a manner that it will seem I've dissolved into the air." *"Seem" being the active word.* "Ah, look," the prince added. "Here come your scouts hurrying down the ridge to meet us."

If Thorkell had wanted to say anything more to his "guest," that was forgotten in the excitement.

"We've landed on a good-sized island," the scouts told Thorkell. "Just which one only the gods know. We could see land to the east that's probably Cymru, and some largish villages to the south that look nice and prosperous. There's one smaller village well within reach. No real sign of defenses to any of them."

"Indeed?" Thorkell said, eying Ardagh thoughtfully. *Wonderful. He thinks I arranged this as well.*

"Well, Jarl Thorkell?" the men clamored. "What say you? They won't be expecting any—"

"No, you idiots! What do you want to do? Attack on foot? Carry off loot and get away *without a seaworthy*

ship? How are you going to do that, eh? How? Going
to *swim* all the way back? Or maybe you were going to
steal some leaky little fishing boats and row and bail your
way back. 'Where's the dragon-ship?' 'Oh, we couldn't
wait for it; we turned ourselves into thralls in our impatience.'"

There were some insulted grumbles at that, but no
real challenges. Thorkell waited a moment, then nodded. "Repairing the *Sea Raven* comes before even the
smallest of raids. Is that understood? No raids till the
ship is repaired! Well?" he added sharply. "This is your
last chance. Anyone want to argue? Anyone?"

No. The Lochlannach stirred uneasily, but not a one
of them said a word. Thorkell strode up and down the
beach like a stallion challenging colts, staring at them,
making sure, Ardagh thought, that he had them properly cowed, then ended up at the prince's side.

"All right, then," the jarl said, satisfied. "Besides," he
added more cheerfully, "there's no need to be in such
a rush. We have an ally none other can claim." His
dramatic gesture swept over Ardagh. "We have none
other than the Power of the Ljos Alfar behind us!"

Ragged cheers.

"So now," Thorkell concluded curtly, "get to work."

With a sly little inward smile, Ardagh thought that the
delay involved in repairing the *Sea Raven* should give
him just enough time to do some serious talking with
Einar the self-styled scald.

Which, as it turned out, was almost ridiculously easy
to arrange. The youngster was, by unspoken consent,
relieved from ship repairs so that he could keep the
magical guest entertained.

*And keep said magical guest from even thinking about
trying to leave.*

Einar, predictably, would much rather have sung his
poems to this new and exotic audience than discuss anything as old-fashioned as runic magics. Fortunately, the
prince thought as the day wore on, the youngster, despite

his lack of any innate magic, really did have a sizeable fund of runic information—as well as, equally fortunately, a passably good voice and quite a clever talent for rhyme and meter.

Even if most of the time I haven't the vaguest idea of what he's saying, or rather, what he means. These folk delight in plays on words . . . what do they call it? Kenning? "The sweat of the sword" for blood and such. Not, he admitted, that Sidhe poetry was so free from intricate double and even triple meanings.

Cadwal was listening to all this as well, or at least pretending to listen. Ardagh and he had secretly agreed that this extra audience made any discussion of rune-spells look more like casual interest and less like any-thing suspicious. The prince could *feel* Cadwal's boredom so strongly that it was almost a tangible presence, but the mercenary sat listening with a rigidly polite smile to what to him, with his knowledge of the Saxon tongue but not that of the Lochlannach, must have been barely understandable.

Of course he's polite. Cadwal's part of Aedh's court. He's used to being politic no matter what!

Ardagh wasn't feeling much happier. He had cast his Language Spell yet again on himself, this time as a magical means of accelerating learning. The spell wasn't totally adaptable to such a use, which meant that he was struggling with a low-level but persistent headache.

"And so," he said, ignoring the nagging little pain, "the runes, if they're to be used magically, *must* be cut on willow staves?"

"Oh no," Einar corrected earnestly. "They can be of bone, like these, or wood, or—or almost anything so long as they're carved by the runecaster himself."

I see." The prince waited patiently till Einar had fin-ished a particularly obscure tale of a Lochlannach rune-caster, then added, "And this rune, what is this?"

"That's Algiz. It's a sort of protection rune. You use

it to invoke the deities' aid, north, south, east, west—
you know."

"Like a Warding."

"Uh, yes, I suppose so. It's the sort of thing that a
runecaster would use in self-defense, according to the
stories. And it's supposed to be *really* useful against . . .
I don't know what the proper term is . . . against magic
recoiling on the caster."

"A magical backlash, you mean."

"Yes. It protects against that."

"*Does* it?" Ardagh said with a smile. "How very interesting. Algiz." *Welcome to my memory, Algiz. I think I'll
find you most useful.* "Go on, Einar. This is quite fascinating. What else can you tell me?"

The slow hours passed, day into night, and Ardagh
continued to take what information he could from the
delighted, flattered youngster. It was complicated
enough, with no guarantee of accuracy save for his own
instinctive little shock of magical recognition with each
new rune. But each rune had its literal meaning, its symbolic meaning, its magical meaning—complicated,
indeed. He couldn't even be totally sure, not without a
chance to test this new learning, that Einar was telling
him enough to make it of any practical use.

And there was a limit to what could be absorbed, even
with the aid of magic. That night, while the Lochlannach
talked and joked about what they'd accomplished, the
prince slept and heard not a word.

But the runes were there in his mind when he woke,
midway through the next day, and with them, a rudimen-
tary understanding of their use. No easy achievement
to comprehend even this much, the prince thought with
a touch of pride; to truly understand a magical system,
one needed to understand the culture that had discovered it, and he could hardly claim to be an expert on
the minds and ways of thinking of either Saxons or
Lochlannach, let alone to be on speaking terms with the
multitude of the latter people's deities.

But I don't need a thorough understanding of either people or their names for the Powers-That-Be to make use of the basic techniques of defense. And attack.

What it was, Ardagh realized, was that as far as he—a Sidhe, a member of an innately magical race—was concerned, the runes, the whole . . . what was the word? . . . the whole *futhark* served to crystallize certain aspects of Existence. This might not be true for humans as well, but the runes were, for him at least, a means to focus his Power in new ways. Being of the Sidhe, of course, also meant that he could absorb meanings and methods and sort them out in his mind with far greater speed than could any human.

It will be interesting to see if these methods still function in my—in the Sidhe Realm.

No. This path of thought was too depressing. Better to concentrate on the here-and-now and see what else could be gleaned from Einar's mind. Better to see if he could, at last, learn enough to combat Osmod. If he couldn't return to his true home, Ardagh told himself, he could at least try to insure the safety of his human sanctuary.

And, he thought with a little shiver of longing, of his love.

Ae, Sorcha, Sorcha, human lives are so short, human emotions run their course so swiftly. Do you still love me, my love? Do you even still remember me?

Human emotions, Osmod mused, were so quick to rouse. So easy to shape. He listened to Ealdorman Cuthred as though truly interested in the plain-faced, plainly dressed man's piteous tale of dishonest servants.

Honest, indeed, our Cuthred, totally, utterly. And totally, utterly dull.

Yet Osmod listened, and every now and then delicately inserted a word, a touch of will, an implication that wasn't quite there that this dishonesty was linked. This dishonesty was part of a plan.

"What plan?" Cuthred said suspiciously.

"Oh, nothing overt, of course. But," Osmod let his voice drop ever so slightly, "I've noted certain signs myself. How better to demoralize a land than to start with its nobility? Nothing overt, as I saw, just small things. Suspicious things. Like that servant of yours—what's his name?"

"The one who stole some coins? Edric. But a few coins—"

"Exactly. Just a few coins. Just a few bolts of inferior cloth or a few ears of spoiled wheat."

A little more will, now, a touch more Power.

"B-but who would be behind such a plot?" Cuthred asked.

Ah, I have you now. "Why, who do you think?" Osmod murmured, and smiled to himself to hear the whispered:

"Mercia."

"Good day, ealdorman," Osmod said, and moved on. One swayed; dozens more to go.

"Ah, there you are, ealdorman."

Osmod, whose thoughts had been elsewhere—he'd only been able to speak with a few of the Witan, not nearly enough and yet he was already weary—just barely kept from starting, bowing and smiling charmingly instead. "King Egbert. What would you, my liege?"

"Come, Osmod. Walk with me a bit."

Do you really think I'd argue? "Of course."

They strolled about the royal enclosure for a time, the king, and therefore Osmod, silent, as casual as though neither had a thing on their minds other than the nice, warm summer day. And then Egbert said suddenly, "Why are you so sure we must attack Mercia?"

Osmod raised a startled brow. "Are you not?" he asked, pretending great daring.

"Oh, eventually," the king began, then cut himself off abruptly, as though he'd already said more than he'd planned.

And so you have, Osmod thought, pleased, *and that means my hold over you is returning nicely.* "Why, then—"

"But why *now,* Osmod? Why so soon?"

"The assassin—"

"May or may not have come from Mercia, may or may not have come from Eriu—may or may not have come from far Cathay for all we know."

"My liege, please." Osmod stopped, turning to face the king with his most winning of smiles. "We both know that the assassin's origin or hiring—"

"Or even if he was, indeed, an assassin."

"Well yes, of course, that, too. But we both know that's not truly the issue."

Egbert snorted and started forward again. "No more than Lord Paris's stealing of Queen Helen was the true issue behind the Trojan War—yes, yes, I learned that tale at Charlemagne's court. But those antique kings were secure upon their thrones, rulers of many years. I am neither. Why risk all now?"

Why? Because I wasted sixteen years of Beortric's dull reign? Because I grow impatient for power and Power both? But he could say nothing of that to the king. Instead Osmod smiled and sighed and lowered his head. "Perhaps I have been too hasty, my liege." *Perhaps my hold over you isn't as strong yet as it needs to be.* "Perhaps I . . ."

"What."

"No, my liege, I—I . . . dare not."

"Don't play games, ealdorman. Say what you would or say nothing."

"Ah. It's just . . . King Offa was a mighty ruler—"

"Granted. King Offa is also dead."

"Yes, but the by-now Emperor Charlemagne is not. And we both know that he and the late king were allies."

"Which he is not with Offa's successor."

"Not yet."

"King Cenwulf is hardly the mighty Offa."

"No, of course not. But that's not stopping him from eying Essex and Kent hungrily."

"Let him. Even if Mercia engulfs them both, I still have enough might to engulf Mercia in turn. But only if I am left alone long enough to win Wessex to me!"

Osmod said nothing. And after a time, Egbert stopped once more. "Look you, do you think I learned nothing in my years at Charlemagne's court? I had more than sufficient time to study how an empire should be forged, how it can be worked together out of all those small and independent units into a successful whole."

"That was done in Frankish lands," Osmod murmured.

Egbert glared. "And can be done here as well."

But then the king caught himself again. "The future is the future," he said flatly. "And no man can claim to read it well."

Not even me, Osmod agreed. *But you admit ambition, Egbert, you admit it secretly to me alone. You trust me as far as a king can trust, and suspect nothing. And with that, my liege, I am, just now, content.*

Just now. There was the Witan to continue to rouse, man by man; the more murmured hatred against Mercia—rather than some quick to burn, quick to fade flame of outrage—the more likely genuine action would be taken. Mercia meant Kent and Essex, indeed most of Britain in a neat little fall of kingdoms. And then . . . oh, no limit to that "and then."

As Osmod bowed and watched his king walk away, he smiled a thin little smile.

I should never have wasted myself on petty sacrifices. Whores. Children. Bah, no wonder I squandered so much time. Killing someone as strong as Octa was the wisest move I ever could have made. And if I'm careful, his strength should stay with me as long as I need it.

Of course, there was still Prince Ardagh to consider. But Prince Ardagh, if the runic readings continued to be as they were, was far from here, not a threat.

Yet.

But I know the limits of his Power. He cannot harm me; I've already seen proof of that.

"And threats," Osmod murmured, amused at his own melodramatics, "can always be . . . removed."

Storm Warnings
Chapter 32

Ardagh stretched wearily. By the end of this, the third day after the Lochlannach shipwreck, the work on the steering oar was nearly complete, the weather had stayed dry, the Lochlannach had hunted and fished without seeing a sign of humanity or a clue as to their exact location, and the prince had gathered more runes to his memory than he would ever have imagined possible.

The accompanying, almost never-ending headache he considered a reasonable exchange.

"Time for us to return to Wessex," he murmured to Cadwal.

The mercenary snorted. "Wonderful choice: Stay with these barbarians or return to the *Saesneg*." But then he added quite seriously, "Are you ready for this?"

"To take on Osmod, you mean? I don't know. In fact, the only way I *will* know is if I succeed."

"No disrespect meant, but—*Iesu*, you don't give a man much assurance."

"What do you want of me, Cadwal? I cannot lie. And I never have understood the human yearning for false hope."

"I'm not yearning for false hope," the mercenary countered. "Just a little bit of the real thing. We're on an island; can't get off unless it's in company with the Lochlannach."

"Oh? What about the villages the scouts sighted?"

"You can't be meaning to walk right into the market square and say, 'Here I am, fresh off a raiders' ship'?"

"Hardly. But if the two of us can't steal away from these folk and past those others . . ."

"There's something very wrong." Cadwal grinned. "Tonight, eh?"

"Tonight," Ardagh agreed. "It's time for the 'Ljos Alfar' to up and disappear."

No way to try his newly won knowledge, not until he could carve the runes. But the night was conveniently dark, lit only by the faint, distant glow of starlight, and Ardagh moved silently out of the Lochlannach camp as easily as ever he'd slipped unseen through the royal fortress of Fremainn, even with the burden of one of the Lochlannach's leather water sacks slung over his back, closely followed by Cadwal, guided by the prince's hand on his arm. Cadwal, too, had a sack slung over his back, this one containing some dried meat and fish. It was not, they'd both wryly agreed, true theft; the Lochlannach could find more than enough fresh supplies to replace what they took.

They're going to think this a magical disappearance, Ardagh thought with a grin, *just as I threatened to Thorkell. Put the fear of the Ljos Alfar into them. Keep them, I trust, from trying to find me again. Ever.*

"That way," Ardagh said in the mercenary's ear. "Follow the coastline."

It wasn't a difficult walk for the most part, not even for Cadwal, for whom the night must have been exceedingly dark, the only real handicap being the need for silence, first to avoid the Lochlannach, then to avoid the villagers. Ardagh paused, considering. Low stone huts, roofs shingled with tile, and a definite smell of new and old fish over all. Good. A fishing village was certain to have the boat they needed.

Yes. There it was, drawn up the beach: one-masted and small enough to be managed easily by two men. Ah, and whatever human owned it was trusting enough to leave the oars aboard.

Cadwal grunted. "I might have known there'd be another boat involved. We're never going to get that launched silently."

"No, we're not."

"And if they have dogs, they're going to be barking their heads off any moment now."

"So they are."

Silence.

"Any idea," the mercenary asked, "how we're going to do this?"

"Yes . . ." Ardagh said slowly. "Ha, yes." He glanced at Cadwal. "Do you think that you can launch that boat by yourself?"

Cadwal shrugged. "Never tried it before, but yes, I'd guess so, if given enough of a diversion for cover."

"That," Ardagh said with a grin, "is my job."

The prince laughed soundlessly in the darkness. It was turning out to be remarkably easy to make an amazing amount of noise without being caught—easy if one had flawless night-vision and could move quickly and quietly enough.

"Here!" he shouted roughly. "You and you, come in this way!" Darting off to a new location, Ardagh yelled in a deeper voice, "No, idiot! No fire arrows, not yet!" And at still another spot, "Attack! Attack!"

One of the oldest tricks in the tales—but by all the Powers, it's working!

Ah yes, here they came, a whole swarm of alarmed, determined humans, spears and knives gripped in their hands, grim anger in their eyes. Ardagh roused the entire village before he was done, sending them off in every direction save the beach.

No time to waste in this hoax. They'd be realizing the trick soon enough, particularly since yes, they did have dogs who would be picking up his intriguing Sidhe scent

soon enough. With a last shout of "They've seen us!"
Ardagh raced silently back to the beach.

Cadwal, swearing under his breath, was struggling with
the boat. Ardagh joined him, and together they shoved
it into the waves and scrambled aboard. At the prince's
hastily gestured commands, Cadwal grabbed the oars,
clumsily rowing them further out while Ardagh struggled
with the lines to unfurl the sail, fighting to remember
long-ago days in the Sidhe Realm when he'd actually tried
his hand at sailing, and done a fairly good job of it, too—

Ha, yes, here we go!

The unfurled sail caught a sudden gust of wind.
Ardagh gestured hastily to Cadwal to ship the oars, wincing as the mercenary splashed them both, then grinned
as the boat obediently dashed over the waves, light as
a bird.

They'd escaped.

"At least we're not out-and-out thieves," Cadwal
muttered, his face faintly green from the boat's motion.
"At least we've given the villagers some repayment by
rousing them; they'll be ready for the Lochlannach."

But Ardagh, trimming the sail, wasn't really listening.
*Be wary, Osmod. Be wary, for what good it will do
you, for I am coming after you at last.*

They came ashore on a rocky little stretch of beach,
landing so roughly that Cadwal nearly went right over
the side onto the rough sand. "We're here," he said dryly,
pulling himself back on board with Ardagh's help. "But
where here may be—somewhere back in Cymru, I'd
guess."

"Probably."

"Now what? It's going to be a long walk to Wessex."

"Now," Ardagh said, leaping lithely down onto the
beach with a crunching of sand, "we go hunting suitable
branches so that I can carve myself a set of runes. After
that, ae-yi, the way things have been going, I'm sure we'll
find some swift and unexpected means of transport!"

"Wonderful. Can't wait."

The prince raised an amused eyebrow at that flat sarcasm, but said only, "Enough speculations. Come, friend Cadwal, let us go hunting branches."

Osmod swept a sly sideways glance over his ealdorman fellow as they strolled together through the royal enclosure. Big, loud and full of bluster, this Eadwig—and usefully weak of will.

" . . . and so," Osmod continued, dipping his head courteously to this lord and that lady as they went, "we must consider not only the insult to the kingdom but the insult to *you* as well."

He put only the smallest trace of emphasis on that "you," knowing that was all he needed, and managed not to smile at his target's sudden frown.

"Insult to *me?*" Eadwig blustered. "How so?"

Look at him, large and florid as some pagan warrior of Wotan. No, no, like an ox from Wotan's feasts. "It's very clear," Osmod said, one man of the world to another. "Any insult to Wessex—and Mercia, by its sly, dishonorable actions has definitely offered insult—any insult to Wessex is an open offense to the Witan—to *you.*"

There, now, that was convoluted enough to nicely confuse Eadwig. The man could only seize upon the most obvious: that his honor had been insulted and must be avenged. Osmod listened to him splutter, and smiled inwardly.

He is mine. "No. We can't act, not quite yet. You understand, ealdorman, of course you understand, that the Witan and the king must be ready to act as one."

Ha, yes, look at this: Eadwig was promising to do his best, and meaning what he said. Not the most politic of tools, maybe, but as useful as any other tool. The work of swaying the Witan, man by man, was going painfully slowly—but by all the Lords of Darkness, it was going well.

No more work with this tool, though, at least not right now. Push too hard, Osmod had already discovered, and his delicate web of a spell tore apart. Excusing himself with a cheerful smile, leaving Eadwig to ponder and try to understand what had just happened (or what he thought had just happened, which was far from the same thing), Osmod returned to his hall.

One more divination, just to be sure things continue going well.

He set the proper Wards then spread the white cloth in his bedchamber. Holding the runes in his hand, Osmod murmured the proper spells, then cast the runes and bent to read what he had cast. . . .

Prince Ardagh. Bah, of course Prince Ardagh! The man seemed determined to thrust himself into every divination. But it hardly mattered, since Prince Ardagh was safely somewhere out at sea—

No. Osmod stared at the runes, then gathered them up and cast them anew. And got an almost identical reading.

He was coming back. Prince Ardagh was coming back to Wessex.

"Damn him, *damn him!*" Osmod gasped, all at once so overwhelmed by a blazing storm of rage that he could barely breathe. No, no, he mustn't let himself lose control, not now, not with the runes still so charged with Power!

Struggling out of the hot red madness, Osmod forced himself, shaking, heart racing, back to some measure of calmness, amazed and terrified at his own overreaction.

And then he knew in a sudden wild flash of comprehension what all this meant, just why he was feeling this all-out-of-proportion rage, why he felt it every time the runes showed him the prince.

It's not just me, but the Lords of Darkness, it has to be the Lords of Darkness or Whatever They represent. They're—Something—is real. He started to his feet, fell back, still too stunned to stand. *It's the Lords of Darkness who hate the prince so terribly, so—so irrationally. No, not irrationally, inhumanly. That's it, almost—almost as though They see the prince as a barrier to Their plans—* which, he prayed, coincided with his own—*no, no, more than that, it's as though They know that Prince Ardagh isn't even human, as though he doesn't even belong in this world!*

Ach, no and no again. That was ridiculous, that was more than ridiculous, that was just too impossible to even consider, and he was not going to let himself keep babbling like some hysterical woman.

But . . . the Darkness . . . a sentient force or forces . . . this explained so much. Osmod, struggling again to rise, sat back down with a jolt as he took in what could only be total truth:

The Lords of Darkness were, indeed, real, and he— ach, he was their vessel. Or maybe vassal? The Lords of Darkness certainly did seem to agree with him that his plans for conquest were well and right—or maybe it was the Darkness itself that had put the ambition into his mind.

No, no, he wasn't going to start wondering like that; such dithering over details led to madness.

Dithering, yes. No wonder I was hesitating so long under Beortric's reign. No wonder it took me such a time to focus my will, my desire. It could not have been an easy thing for the Lords to merge Their so much more than human will with mine.

That stunned him anew. For a moment, Osmod could do nothing more than try to accept that what this all meant was that the Darkness owned him, that the Darkness lorded over him even as he lorded over the common folk, for that one moment it was so terrifying, so alien that the blood thundered in his ears and his breath caught in his chest.

But as suddenly as it had come, the horror was gone. Still sitting where he'd collapsed, Osmod began to laugh, weakly at first, then with genuine humor. Terrifying?

Horrible? Oh no, nothing could be further from terror!
Think of it, think of it! Who else in all the history of
the world had ever had such allies? With Power such
as this behind him, who could possibly ever fail?

Partial Power, Osmod thought with sudden slyness.
After all, if the Lords of Darkness were so almighty, why
oh why couldn't They act directly? If They were so all-
powerful, why did They need a human to act for Them?

*There we have it. Not a slave, not me. An ally, indeed.
They need me and I need them. Fair enough.*

"Let the prince return." It was said both to himself
and to Whatever might be listening. "He has no Power
here. Let Prince Ardagh return. And let him," Osmod
added, this time welcoming a new surge of that hot,
definitely inhuman rage, "let him once and for all, *die!*"

This was, Ardagh thought hopefully, perched halfway
up an oak, legs locked about the trunk and dagger in
hand, the last branch he was going to need for the runes.
He was growing thoroughly weary of playing squirrel,
particularly in this continual gentle drizzle that made the
trees treacherously slippery. Yes, and he was weary of
constantly rousing then quenching his Power all the
while chanting the necessary ritual with each cutting.
This was oak, now, a good, useful, magical tree, and yes,
only one rune left:

> "Hail to thee, oh mighty oak.
> I bid thee give this branch
> And into to send thy strength,
> To bind the might of bright rune . . ."

Which one? Which one? "Algiz!" the prince finished
triumphantly.

He cut the mercifully small branch free with a determined slash of his dagger, *feeling* the little prickle of
Power working right, thinking at the same time with a
touch of Sidhe indignation that a royal blade was never

meant for such menial work as this. Fortunate that its silver alloy was, like the blade of his matching Sidhe sword, remarkably resilient even in this human Realm.

Ae-yi, now to actually carve the runes. The prince scrambled down to the ground, leafy prize in hand. Einar had implied that the carving should ideally be done with the season and phase of moon in mind. Ardagh shrugged. There wasn't much he could do about the former, and as for the latter, ae, well, he'd just have to trust that his Sidhe heritage outweighed any such obstacles.

For a long while the prince lost himself in his carving work, sheltered from the drizzle under the oak's wide branches, unaware of anything but the cutting of the runes into green, slippery wood without cutting his own flesh as well.

This is complicated enough as it is. I don't want to risk adding blood—particularly not my own—to it!

Ah, there. At last. Ardagh wiped his dagger clean, sheathed it, and looked up from his work with a satisfied smile.

"Done?" Cadwal asked.

"Done." Granted, the runes he'd cut were rather unpolished, offending his Sidhe sensibilities by their crudeness, but they were as accurate as his Sidhe memory could make them. "According to Einar," he added, turning the bits of wood over in his hand, "I'm supposed to stain them with something permanent, preferably red paint, but the carvings alone will have to do."

"Now what? Any more ritual?"

Ardagh glanced up from the runes at the brittleness all at once in the human's voice. "Cadwal, I'm sorry," he said suddenly, rather surprising himself. "I never meant to drag you through all this madness."

"Och, well, doesn't look as though either of us had much choice in the matter. But thank you."

"You . . . could leave. Return to Eriu. You'd know better than I about such things, but I'd guess that there are fishing boats along this coast that could be hired."

"What, and miss seeing how all this craziness comes out? Besides," Cadwal continued much more seriously, "if I hadn't come with you, I never would have learned the truth about . . . you know . . . about Gwen. Yes, and sired a—a son, either. And as for Eriu, it's my sanctuary threatened as well as yours, remember." He shrugged. "Who knows? You just may need someone guarding your back while you're battling the sorcerer."

"Ah. Good point."

"Tell you what," the mercenary added with a sudden grin. "When we get back to Eriu, we'll have ourselves a good, rousing drunk."

That startled Ardagh into a genuine laugh. "I must admit that sounds positively splendid." He uncoiled back to his feet, scooping up the runes in both hands. "Right now there is one more ritual to be done: the one that sparks these things into life—or in this hybrid case links them with my Power."

"You sure it will work?"

Ardagh hesitated. "Not at all. But life is, after all, one big experiment, isn't it?"

"Heh."

The prince turned away. This was, for all that he was trying to make it sound reassuringly easy for Cadwal's sake, the most perilous point: the linking of two disparate forces into one. It might well work. But if it didn't, if the two forms of Power tore free—

If that happens, Ardagh told himself with Sidhe pragmatism, *I won't be around to worry about it.*

So be it. He might as well use his native language rather than trying to work with the double strain of unfamiliar magic and a foreign tongue. He was already changing the basic wording as it was. If this added an additional element of peril—

Again, so be it.

Taking a deep breath, emptying his mind of everything but the runes and his own will, Ardagh began his chant.

"I am a staff for rays of runic might.
I shape the might from the depth of the sea
I shape the might from the womb of the earth
I shape the might from the highest heights."

He took a second steadying breath and continued:

"Fiery Fehu flow through me,
Ur shape my rune-might,
Madr unbind the flow of Power,
Rune-might meet in me and blaze
　　　where I will it sent,
Rune-might stream from me,
Rune-might stream to me,
Rune-might work in me!
Rune-might work through me!
Rune-might be mine!"

Ae, Powers, Powers, the wildfire blazing through him! It was agony and fierce delight, light, dark, fire, ice, all in one insane, wondrous rush. Ardagh stood with head thrown back, arms flung up, *feeling* strength flying from sky to earth, from earth to sky, with himself in the midst of it all, the center, the focus, the—

—sense that Something was aware of him, Something of the Darkness and—

—the next clear realization was that he lay crumpled on the ground with not the slightest memory of having fallen, with a panicky Cadwal standing over him, not quite daring to touch him.

"I'm all right," Ardagh gasped out, hearing his voice come out strained and harsh. "Give me . . . give me a moment . . . catch my breath."

"Right. Anything you say."

Slowly the prince's swimming senses cleared. Slowly he came back to himself and left the wildness of the elements behind. And the . . . Darkness? Had that really been a touch of living Darkness he'd sensed? Ardagh

could remember far too well his encounters with the
demon Arridu. Had that one . . . ?

No. Impossible. There was no linking spell or ring or
anything else between that ugly non-Realm and this. The
sudden unexpected blaze of wildfire Power had confused
even Sidhe senses.

*Powers. Just how close did I come to burning out my
mind?* He ached not so much in body as in being, and
the new knowledge of the runes and how to use them
lay like coils of fire along his nerves. Ardagh shuddered,
shuddered again, willing himself back into peace with
himself, sending a tentative wisp of will into his being,
puzzling out what was changed.

Ah. Unfortunately, it wasn't that he had actually gained
any Power; there wasn't that much new Power to be
gained from this Realm. But what he had gained, Ardagh
realized as his mind and body and *self* came back together, was a very real, very new way of using what magic
there was.

It works, he knew without having to test that knowledge. *What Einar taught me works. This strange new
runic weapon is mine.* Granted, he would have to practice its use, get used to the *feel* of it; he wasn't vain
enough to think himself totally proficient overnight. *But
I do, at least, hold the weapon. I am armed against
Osmod at last.*

Old Friends
Chapter 33

Sorcha ni Fothad took a deep breath there in the fields of Fremainn, trying desperately to calm herself, very much aware that King Aedh was watching her, waiting with regal patience. This was the most suitable place for them to meet; king or no, it would not have been proper for them to be closeted together, no matter for what purpose. Aedh also had made it clear that he didn't wish anyone to think Sorcha a spy reporting to her employer.

Knowing the royal consideration for her status didn't make this any simpler to say. "It's true," she managed at last. "I've just come from speaking with him, with Ardagh, and—and—I know this sounds impossible, but he and Cadwal have left the Lochlannach ship after a storm that everyone thinks Ardagh caused but of course he didn't because—"

"Slowly, lass, slowly. You're overwhelming me."

"I—I'm sorry. I was a bit overwhelmed myself." She took another hopefully steadying breath, brushed a straying red braid back over her shoulder, then began again. "Ardagh and Cadwal left Cymru aboard that Lochlannach ship."

"Yes. You've already told me that much."

"Och, of course. But the ship was becalmed, and the raiders called on Ardagh to conjure a wind—"

"Which, I take it, he can't do."

"No."

"A pity," the king said blandly. "It would be so convenient to have him just . . . blow my enemies away. But please, continue. I assume they got their wind." He raised an eyebrow at her reaction. "More than a wind?"

"A good deal more. A storm, one that wrecked them. Ardagh and Cadwal escaped during the rebuilding, and as far as I can tell, are now back in Cymru." She waved a helpless hand. "Something about a stolen fishing boat."

"Cymru. They're *not* planning to return to Wessex and try a second shot at swaying King Egbert, are they?"

Sorcha shivered. "It's far more complicated than that. You see, after the storm, the Lochlannach were in awe of Ardagh."

"I don't blame them! The great and terrible sorcerer who can call down the storm winds—I'd be in awe of such a fellow, too. Perilous game, though: You're only as important as your last—no sacrilege meant," Aedh added with a wry glance heavenward, "miracle."

"Yes, well, Ardagh took advantage of it. And he—they—he—och, let me try this again. Ardagh got the Lochlannach to agree never to attack Eriu again."

That gave Sorcha the doubtful satisfaction of seeing Aedh actually stunned into openmouthed silence. At last he asked, very carefully, "Does he think this . . . ah . . . treaty will hold?"

"For a time, yes. The Lochlannach attitude seemed to be that it was no difficult thing to raid other lands instead."

Aedh let out his breath in a slow sigh. "He asks them to stop raiding us, and they agree. Raiders who have no fear of God or man, he asks them to stop, and they just up and agree." The king shook his head. "Bizarre. God, yes, but I can believe it. It's just bizarre enough to be true." He shook his head again. "Then our peripatetic prince will be heading back to Eriu after all."

"Ah . . . no," Sorcha said, and to her mortification, felt her eyes well up with tears. "He—he really is headed back to Wessex."

"Wessex! Why? If what he says about the Lochlannach is true—yes, yes, I know Prince Ardagh cannot lie. But doesn't he see that if those sea-thieves really are going to leave Eriu untouched, there's no need for a foreign alliance?"

"I don't think that's why he's returning."

"God in heaven," Aedh erupted, *"now* what? A feud. He's started a personal feud. Tell me I'm wrong."

"I—I can't! I d-don't know what he's doing." And now, to Sorcha's horror, the tears did break free. "He—he wouldn't t-tell me."

"Och, lass . . ."

But Sorcha continued fiercely, "If he's doing what I think, if he's trying to—to protect me as if I was a—a— a stupid little girl, I—I'll show him a feud! I—excuse me."

At Aedh's sympathetic wave of a hand, she dashed away.

"Your pardon," Cadwal said, irony behind the words, "but we've been hiking through the forest for," he glanced up at the twilight sky, "nearly two full days now, and I haven't seen any signs of wondrous transport."

Ardagh shot him a wearily angry glare. "As you humans say, 'O ye of little faith.' I may be Sidhe, but even the Sidhe need time to absorb a new magical system." He'd been practicing and practicing again, struggling with the runes, with the whole bizarre system that was so unlike his own, trying to find the way to fuel Sidhe magic through human runes. It was almost working, but almost wasn't going to help him against Osmod. There was also that disconcerting, not-quite-perceptible sense of Darkness watching—no, no, too strong a word. Dimly aware, perhaps.

To the Darkness with *the Darkness!*

Cadwal wasn't exactly cowed by the prince's glare. "And now?" he insisted.

"And now, wait."

There wasn't the slightest guarantee that this would work, any more than any of his other attempts had succeeded. But, Ardagh told himself, the moment one began doubting a spell would work, it was guaranteed to fail. Drawing out the carved sigil known, according to Einar, as Reid, he studied it thoughtfully. The rune literally referred to riding, but it also involved the entire concept of journeying, both actual—which certainly made it applicable here—and spiritual. It also, the humans being as devious in their thinking at times as the Sidhe, involved aspects of control and self-control, and—

And he, Ardagh decided abruptly, was not going to spend all day puzzling over each and every interconnected possibility. He was of the Sidhe, he was an inherently magical being, what he wanted to do took very little Power, and there was not the slightest reason for even this hybrid form of magic to fail him.

Raising the rune aloft in one clenched hand, the prince began a Summoning, focusing his will through the twisted shape of the rune, seeing it glowing in his mind's sight, seeing it as a lure pulling and pulling, feeling the Power building with a small twinge of satisfaction because it was going just the way it should. . . .

Cadwal's startled bark of a laugh snapped Ardagh back to reality. There, half-hidden in leaves, were two shaggy grey shapes, their rough coats glowing in the dim light: wild ponies watching him with ear-pricked equine curiosity and feral wariness.

"Well, they aren't exactly my idea of wondrous transport," the mercenary said with a chuckle, "but they're better than walking. Assuming they let us ride them."

The two ponies had started at Cadwal's voice, and were sidling nervously, nostrils flared, ready to bolt at any moment. "You don't understand," Ardagh whispered to the mercenary, his voice quavering with excitement. "The runic spell worked. Maybe not as fully or as—yes—wondrously as it might. But it did work."

Oh, it had, in more ways than one. There was that

slightest of shadows at the back of his senses. There was also—Ardagh tensed, hardly noticing the wild ponies dashing back into the forest. The magic he'd just cast had been as good as a beacon for some equally magical someone, no, someones: *Sidhe!*

"Down," Ardagh hissed to Cadwal—no time to explain any further—and stalked silently forward, blazing with mingled hope and alarm, wary as a predatory wild thing. Crouching in the underbrush, he parted leaves ever so softly, hardly feeling their prickling. There, now, he could see—

Ardagh froze, staring, heart racing, in that one astonishing moment too stunned to do more than think a dazed, *My . . . lord . . . Iliach. Iliach, here!*

No doubt about it. However Iliach had managed it, that was definitely the scheming Sidhe courtier Ardagh remembered from his brother's court, tall and graceful as ever as he stalked warily through the human Realm. Iliach, fashionable as always, was clad in beautifully cut hunting leathers over elegant spidersilk—sending a pang of pure envy through Ardagh—and his hair was a dramatic blaze of gold against the forest's dark background.

Look at that: Elegant as though he's strolling through a park. But Iliach would never be alone in such a perilous place. There are others nearby; there must be.

He didn't have a doubt as to whom they were hunting. That they hadn't found him already Ardagh attributed to their unfamiliarity with the *feel* of this Realm. It would surely be confusing their sensing of his aura.

What a shame.

The prince waited with predatory patience until Iliach had moved past him, then slipped out of hiding to stand leaning in apparent lazy ease against a tree. A good, sturdy oak, this, and he intended to keep his back safely against its broad trunk. "Looking for me?"

Iliach whirled with a startled hiss, golden hair swirling. But after that second of alarm, he had himself back under Sidhe self-control, revealing his shock only by the slightest widening of his eyes. Still, thought Ardagh, that tiny reaction said volumes.

"Why, my lord," the prince purred, "aren't you glad to see me? Or have I changed so very much?" Gesturing to his worn, disheveled clothing, some of Tylwyth Teg weave, some Lochlannach, he added, forcing his voice to betray none of his inner turmoil, "What, does my appearance alarm you?"

"You . . . are somewhat different than when last I saw you." Iliach admitted in what Ardagh mused was surely a masterpiece of Sidhe understatement.

"And you are exactly the same as when last I saw you, my lord." *Just as sly, just as perfidious.* "Tell me, my lord, what brings you to this outre land?" *And how did you get here? A Portal? A Portal that I can use?* No. Iliach would never be so careless as that. "Surely it wasn't merely from some casual whim. For that matter, how were you able to find me?"

Iliach's smile was a nasty thing. "Oh, distant cousins aided me."

Distant cousins. Tylwyth Teg. *Thank you, Tywthylodd. You've found a nicely devious way to strike back at me, haven't you?* "How charming of them. But surely," the prince continued, putting the barest edge to his voice, "you have not come here alone—ah, no, indeed you have not. Good day to you, my lord Charalian, my lady Tathaniai. You may step out of hiding now." *Are there others, lurking there at the edges of Power's scan? I can't be sure.* "And to what, pray tell, do I owe this visit?"

Lord Iliach glanced ever so subtly at the others, then began, "Prince Ardagh, I shall be blunt."

"What a wonderful change."

"Ah. Prince Ardagh, you have been most sorely misused by your royal brother."

"You've just decided this, have you? After all this while? After you, my lords, my lady, played such a large part in my ousting? Come, come, don't play the hypocrite, Lord Iliach. The role fits you far too prettily."

Ae-yi, look at the anger flash in those elegant blue-green eyes—but just for a moment. "I can't fault you for your bitterness, Prince Ardagh," Iliach said smoothly. "Indeed, it is only to be expected. But . . ." This time the glance he exchanged with the others was a touch longer, a touch more uneasy. "The past is exactly that, and surely the current need overwhelms it."

"Meaning?"

"Prince Ardagh, have you had any communication with our Realm since . . . leaving it?"

"Since being exiled," Ardagh corrected dryly. "And yes, I have. From my brother. Warning me about treacherous nobles. Why do you ask?"

"Enough, Iliach." That was Lady Tathaniai, her face impassive, her eyes as icy-chill as ever. Not a shred of softness in Tathaniai. "Prince Ardagh, blunt we shall be, indeed: Your brother is rapidly proving himself unfit to rule."

"Is he? In what way?"

"There are whispers throughout the Realm of irrational decisions, unfair edicts, suspicion of everyone and everything—the word is even that he plans to put aside his wife."

Karanila! Now, there was shocking news—if, indeed, Ardagh reminded himself with a jolt, it was true. The prince smiled slightly, never moving from the sheltering tree; he'd half forgotten how to play the game of never quite saying truth while ever avoiding falsehood. "Interesting. And how many of you, I wonder," he added, glance sweeping over them all, "are in my brother's employ?"

Not a Sidhe muscle so much as twitched, but that, of course, meant nothing. "So far," Ardagh continued, "you've given me some nice little snips of gossip, but not one word of solid fact."

Lord Charalian sighed as though in genuine regret.

"Facts are difficult things to catch at court, as you know. Suffice it to say, Prince Ardagh, that were one of the blood royal to return, there would be those who would gladly support that one, even as far as . . . one might go."

Ardagh shook his head lazily. "Tsk, you never do learn, do you? I will *not* be a puppet, not of you, not of anyone."

"Yet," Iliach commented, "you would seem to be doing the humans' bidding."

"Such spite, my lord! For shame!" He leaned forward ever so slightly to put a physical emphasis to his words. "I repeat, and this time please do listen fully, for I shall not repeat myself: *I will not be your puppet! And I will not be an oathbreaker to my brother!*" He leaned back against the tree, watching them through half-lidded eyes. No reaction. Well now, he'd expected none. "And why, while we're on the subject, would you ever expect me to trust you or work with you after you betrayed me?"

Iliach looked genuinely surprised at that. "Your pardon, Prince Ardagh, but what has the past to do with the here-and-now?"

"Forgive me. I had almost forgotten how . . ." *devious* . . . "practical our politics can be."

Tathaniai took the smallest step forward, the faintest hint of color in her pale face. "Prince Ardagh, listen to us. It was no easy thing for us to open a Portal into this Realm, particularly in secrecy. We cannot hold it open for much longer; it is too Powerful a thing not to attract attention."

"And you certainly don't want to be trapped here."

Lord Iliach sighed ever so softly, ever so dramatically. "This Realm has changed you. It would be so wrong, so terrible for one of the Sidhe, for a prince of the Sidhe, to be lost to . . . humanity. Come back with us, Prince Ardagh. You need make no promises. Only come back with us to your rightful Realm and then we will have sufficient leisure for more graceful speech."

Oh yes, there would be a good deal of leisure for me in my brother's prisons. If he didn't slay me outright this time around. But Ardagh said nothing, and after an awkward moment, Iliach continued, "Surely you see that we're offering you your only chance to come home. You cannot return on your own. Think of it, Prince Ardagh. Perhaps your mind has been permanently altered so that it may not retain that one vital spell."

Powers, no! But then Ardagh noted Iliach's careful wording and smiled thinly, refusing to show the surge of terror he'd just felt. "Perhaps. Anything may be 'perhaps.'"

But what if he did return with them? What was there to say he couldn't outwit them? Once back in his rightful Realm—

What then? Act against these would-be traitors? Eirithan would thank him sweetly and simply cast him back into exile; his brother had already implied as much in their last meeting. But to act against Eirithan—

Then I really would be an oathbreaker.

"Shoo," he said suddenly, making whisking-away gestures with a languid hand. "Go play somewhere else. I won't join in your games."

"I fear," Iliach said, smiling ever so urbanely, "that you have little choice. This Realm, we've noted, is disgustingly lacking in Power. But there are, after all, three of us—"

"Yes, yes, I know how the rest of that melodramatic line goes, 'and only one of me.' Try me, my lord, if you think me so weak. Try me."

It was bravado. He could feel their threefold Power, and even though it was ridiculously weak in comparison to what any one of them could work in the Sidhe Realm, still, it was, perforce, three times stronger than what he could wield.

Cursed if I'm going to meekly surrender!

Ardagh slipped a hand into the pouch containing his makeshift runes—

Ae, hot! And hot, too, the little amulet he used for far-speech—reacting to the rousing Power, yes, and to the nearby Portal, and for all he knew there would be an out-and-out magical explosion if he tried to even—

"Now I don't know what's going on here," a familiar voice said in Gaeilge, "but I don't think I care for the odds."

Cadwal! "Come join the party, my friend," Ardagh called in relief. "And bring your nice shiny sword!"

"Already have."

The iron blade blazed out, bright as a brand to Sidhe eyes. Ardagh, used to such things by now, never blinked, but his would-be abductors flinched back in alarm, faced for possibly the first time in their long lives by this deadliest of metals. "See, my lords?" the prince drawled. "I have sunk so low. Yes, this human is my friend, and yes, he does bear iron, and yes, I have no fear of it." *As long as it stays in Cadwal's keeping.* "Can you say the same?"

Of course not. And of course they weren't about to admit it. Their faces masks of inhuman rage, the three noble Sidhe spat out, "Live here, then! Live among the humans and rot!"

They turned and fled, managing, Sidhe that they were, to make it look like a graceful, voluntary pace rather than a rout. Ardagh raced after them, suddenly overwhelmed by the need to see the Portal, *feel* it, know if it would somehow miraculously let him pass. There it was, there ahead of him, glistening and shimmering in the night. The three Sidhe leaped into it and were gone, and Ardagh leaped and—

Someone was shaking him. Someone was calling his name. Ardagh forced his eyes open to find himself lying sprawled on the forest floor in the middle of true night, a frantic Cadwal at his side. The prince slowly dragged himself up on one elbow. "What . . . happened?"

"Damned if I know! One moment you were racing

after those—those folk. The next: hell, I don't know how to describe it. There wasn't anything that I could see, but something somehow threw you aside as though you didn't weigh a thing." Cadwal shook his head, clearly remembering. "I was sure you were dead."

"Not quite." Ardagh forced himself dizzily back to his feet, not quite staggering. He warily stretched his arms and winced. "Bruised, definitely, but not broken."

"But *what happened?*"

"Ae, Cadwal. The Portal . . ." But even with his Sidhe will, he couldn't get that all out in one steady breath. "It . . . rejected me. It simply would not let me pass." The bitterness would not let itself be repressed. "It let them go. Those would-be traitors may pass as freely as they will—but I, I who have kept every oath I swore, I cannot!"

Cadwal never flinched, even though, judging from his expression, Ardagh must not have looked even remotely human just then. "I see," the mercenary said after a moment. "That does have a foul reek to it, yes."

His matter-of-fact manner was more comforting than any gushing words of sympathy. "Forgive me," Ardagh told him. "I tend to forget that you're enduring your own exile."

"Hey now, at least I'm still living in my own *world!*"

That struck a sore spot all over again. What if Iliach's half-veiled suggestions were true? What if Eirithan really had lost control of the throne and the land? What then? Civil war? Chaos? Remembering the many eddies and undercurrents of ambition forever swirling in his brother's court, Ardagh shuddered. What of the land? What of the magical heart and fertile soul of the land? There must be a ruler, one ruler, one just, strong will who could guard the land and those upon it. Eirithan just barely fulfilled that role, but if he fell . . .

Not me. It can't be me. Even if it were so, even if I were the one foolhardy enough to take up the burden— I cannot leave this cursed human Realm!

Watching the prince—and probably, Ardagh realized, guessing the gist of his thoughts fairly well—Cadwal pursed his lips thoughtfully. "Tell you what. We get back to Eriu, we really do get good and drunk!"

The deliberate coarseness of that forced a shaken laugh out of Ardagh. "Thank you. I never thought I'd see the time when I'd be gladder of human friendship than of Sidhe, but—thank you."

"Helpful, that's me."

"Don't belittle yourself." Ardagh slipped a wary hand in among the runes. Still almost uncomfortably warm, runes and amulet both. Odd reaction. But then, no one had ever tried mixing Sidhe and runic magic before and—

Powers. He was on the edge of something. Shivering anew, Ardagh thought that if this weird mix of Sidhe magic, runic spell and Eriu amulet could actually produce enough force to be felt, so much force just by accident, then it just might be the key he'd been seeking, the key that would unlock the doorway home. . . .

No, he corrected wearily. Not that easily. This was all very new, very theoretical. He wasn't going to achieve anything without a great deal of wary experimenting. After all, the heat was also a warning of magical wildfire that had almost been released.

And yet, and yet—no. Time enough for serious study when we are back in Eriu. I can wait till then. For . . . there is hope. For the first time in . . . however long, there is hope.

"Still going after Osmod?"

Ardagh, startled back to the present, grinned sharply. "To coin a phrase, my mercenary friend, damned right I am! Powers willing, at least *something* in all this strange adventuring is going to have a satisfying ending!"

Complications
Chapter 34

Alone in his bedchamber with no one to see him—
no one save for innocent Leofrun, and she hardly
counted—Egbert rubbed his hands wearily over his eyes,
then suddenly threw back his head with a cry of alarm
and frustration, hastily choked off.

What was happening? What was the matter with him?
It was one thing to dream of conquest, of glory. Any king
worthy of his throne now and again harbored such
imaginings.

But this was something more. *These* dreams, these so
very aggressive dreams, these visions of war and victory
and domination, had started intruding on his waking life.
They insinuated themselves into his mind whenever he
wasn't on his guard and, Egbert thought, it was only
purest luck that they hadn't actually interfered with his
duties.

So far. And the damned things aren't even enjoyable!

He shuddered. As a boy, Egbert had idly poked into
a great pile of autumn leaves, only to find his stick stabbing into a dead and rotting dog underneath. The sickly
bitter, sickly sweet stench had haunted him for days.

*And these dreams have something of that same falsely
sweet foulness. It's not just the glory of expanding an
empire, no, it's the—the gloating in victims' pain and
misery . . . The dreams couldn't be mine, I couldn't be
conjuring such things!*

Yet who else could he blame? Egbert had done some

discreet investigations, never letting anyone know exactly why. Let them all think this just another level of kingly caution; nothing odd about that since everyone knew there were such things as sorcerers and dark spells. But nothing had come of those inquiries. Who cared, save perhaps the Church, that two of the kitchen help knew a few tiny charms against scalding or that one of the weavers just might be a pagan? No one in the entire royal court was found to be working anything as terrible as sorcery at all, let alone any sorceries aimed against him.

Evident sorceries, at any rate—bah, he was beginning to sound like poor, confused Leofrun.

Egbert ran his hands roughly through his hair, trying to focus his thoughts. God, he couldn't tell a soul about these dreams. That was all a new king needed: *Listen, everyone, I'm being haunted by unpleasant dreams and just may be going slowly mad, but don't worry about it; I can still rule—*

"Bah," he repeated aloud.

A soft hand touched his arm. Egbert sprang to his feet, whirling, snatching blindly for a weapon—

"Leofrun." It was a sigh of relief. "Don't startle me, woman. You know better than that."

"Osmod," she said softly.

"What?"

"Osmod," Leofrun repeated, moving softly to his side, her long, sleep-tousled hair tangled about her naked body: graceful, Leofrun, lovely as a swan-maid for all her dullness of mind. "Osmod is bad."

"Nonsense."

"Osmod," she insisted, "Osmod, Osmod, Osmod."

"Stop that, Leofrun!"

But she continued in blank, stubborn determination, totally oblivious of her nudity, "Osmod, Osmod," until at last, exasperated, Egbert slapped her.

He'd never struck her before. Leofrun stopped as suddenly as if he'd cut the strings of her legs, her mouth half-open, eyes filling with reproachful tears. In another moment, Egbert thought, she'd begin to wail. Or worse, simply stand there and weep without a sound.

Ach, damn. Feeling as though he'd just hurt a child, Egbert sighed soundlessly and pulled her to him. *This is ridiculous. I must find myself a wife. A politically useful wife, yes, but also someone who's sane and sensible! Someone with whom I can have a genuine conversation!*

In the meantime, here was Leofrun. Adoring, stupid, safe Leofrun, her face buried against his chest, her bare body warm against him. Despite his impatience with her, Egbert couldn't resist a little stirring of interest. "I'm sorry," he said to her wild mane of hair. "I won't hurt you again, I won't. But I have troubles enough. I don't need you adding to them with your ridiculous prattle."

Of course she didn't understand one word of that. Leofrun pulled free, wiping her nose with a casual hand, her gaze fixed on him, eyes as wide and blank as those of a cow. Egbert felt his sudden interest fade just as quickly and fought back the sudden urge to strike her again, to shake some sense into that staring face. Useless. She was as she was, and nothing could change her.

"Leofrun," he said with careful patience, "Ealdorman Osmod has done nothing wrong. No, no, listen to me. Listen! He has done nothing wrong. Do you understand that?"

She nodded, but stubborn refusal was in every line of her body, and Egbert sighed and gave it up. "Leave me, Leofrun. Yes, it's all right; I'm not angry with you. Just . . . leave me alone."

The day was bright with sunlight, but Osmod stood hidden in the shadow of the royal hall, watching his fellow ealdormen and working on keeping an aura of *not here* about himself. Which, alas, was not quite as easy as it should have been. This was, he mused, bound to happen sooner or later. As always, the strength he stole in others' blood and lives had begun to drain away. And for a moment Osmod thought with a flash of sullen defiance, *If the Lords of Darkness want me as their agent, why in the name of that Darkness don't They provide me with the proper abilities?*

Because, of course, the Lords of Darkness were neither human nor at all concerned with human wants and needs. And reminding Them of that fact was hardly wise. For a heartbeat he was only human and chilled at the thought of that, at the thought of Their reality and what it meant to him.

And then Osmod grinned in sardonic acceptance. What it meant to him was power and Power both. Things were as they were, and at least the late Physician Octa had been good for a great deal of work, from winning over a fair number of ealdormen to his way of thinking to reestablishing a decent hold on the king's mind.

Not as firm a hold as I'd like. But with the Witan quivering on the edge, almost won, who cares what the king thinks!

Yes, yes, the Witan was already beginning to assemble. Osmod watched as Ealdormen Cuthred and Eadwig, as unlikely a pair of conversationalists as any, stopped to argue. Cuthred, neat and prim as always, was the one shaking his head in disapproval. "No, and no again. It is not wise."

Florid Eadwig threw up his hands in flamboyant disgust. "What sort of man are you? The insult offered by Mercia—"

"Yes, there has been an insult, and yes, we truly must act, I'm not denying that—"

"Now! We must act now!"

"Eadwig, please. This isn't some boyish feud."

"Of course not, dammit, but—"

"Please. We can't just rush madly off to the attack. Before we can even start thinking about marshalling anyone, we must have a plan—"

"Aha, then we *are* in agreement!"

Cuthred blinked. "I never said we weren't."

Eadwig's face brightened with relief. "Ha, of course we need a plan!" He slapped the slender Cuthred on the shoulder, staggering the man. "But at least we're in agreement: Mercia must pay. Hell, we're all in agreement!"

"Except for the commons."

"Who have no say in the matter!"

"And the merchants, who certainly have."

"What are they going to do? Withhold funding? Not if the king raises their taxes!"

"The king," Cuthred muttered darkly. "There's the problem. Will the king himself agree with us?"

Oh, he'll agree, Osmod promised. *Whether he will it or not, King Egbert shall agree.*

But the two ealdormen drew back in surprise as a slight figure drifted up to them, weaving between them like a cat, her rich gown slightly stained, her hair decked with wilting flowers.

"My lady Leofrun!" Eadwig exclaimed. There was, of course, a wordless understanding of her role at court. "Lady, you shouldn't be here."

"She must have slipped her . . . her attendants," Cuthred murmured. "Come, lady, we'll see you safely back to—"

"No," she argued, "no. Osmod. Osmod!"

Eadwig, showing far more patience than Osmod would ever have believed, asked gently, "What about him?"

But Leofrun, glancing frantically from man to man, could only shake her head in confusion. "He—the dead man—Octa is dead."

"Yes, lady, we know that." Eadwig's voice was still remarkably patient. "But thank you for reminding us. Now, come and—"

"No! Don't you see? You don't! Osmod! He—it—don't you see? Not—no!"

"Shh, lady. See? Here are your women now."

"No! You don't understand!"

But the two ealdormen, having handed her over to the frantic ladies, hurried, glad to be free of the embarrassment, on their way.

Yes, Osmod told them, *join the rest of the Witan. The king will be with you shortly. We are almost ready to strike.*

Naturally, someone else was going to have to . . . sacrifice himself for the cause. Himself, Osmod added, or—seeing Leofrun slipping by like a dim-witted ghost, closely trailed by the ladies who were also her guardians—just possibly herself.

No. Leofrun was far too perilous a target.

And yet . . . such complete and utter innocence, for all that she was Egbert's mistress, the innocence of an unspoiled child mixed with the passion of a woman—

Osmod shook his head ruefully at opportunities wasted. As though she'd caught something of his thoughts, Leofrun stopped short, staring at him with the eyes of a deer sighting a wolf. "Lady," Osmod said, and bowed.

But she, ach, she went right on staring; even when her ladies took her gently by the arms and pulled her away, she turned her head to him and kept right on staring.

You know, don't you? Poor innocent, you know exactly who and what I am. And no one will believe you.

Cadwal glanced at the prince as they wove their way through the dense Cymric forest. "You're worried, aren't you?"

"Is it so obvious?"

"It is if you've been living in such close quarters as we've been doing. Not that you've been talking in your sleep," the mercenary added hastily, catching Ardagh's sideways glare, "or any such humanlike thing. But you haven't been talking much while you're awake, either, and what you have been saying isn't more than a word or two."

"Mm."

"Like that. You *are* worried. And . . . well, this is probably none of my affair, but I have a feeling that it's not just about Osmod."

"Meaning?."

"Those Sidhe-folk, they told you something unpleasant, didn't they?" When Ardagh resolutely said nothing, Cadwal pressed on, "Something about your home."

"You are," the prince snapped, "rapidly overstepping the boundaries."

"I was right, then."

"Yes," flatly.

"No shame there, worrying about your homeland. Hell, I've done it often enough, and there's no complications about magic in my case. Well . . . almost none," he added softly, "not counting the Tylwyth Teg."

Cadwal could be stubborn as a hunting hound when the fancy took him. "My brother," Ardagh said in resignation, "may or may not be losing his hold on the throne. The courtiers you saw might or might not have been telling the undistorted truth about that. They certainly went to enough trouble to find me. However, they might also have simply been inventing a tale by which to snare me. And then again, they might or might not, one or all of them, have been sent by my brother to trick me into open betrayal." He glanced sideways at Cadwal. "Does that satisfy your human curiosity?"

"*Dewi Sant*," the mercenary muttered. "And here I thought Eriu's way of governing was complicated. No insult meant, Prince Ardagh, but I'd not be mixed up in your people's politics, no, not for the world's own treasure."

"You're not. Nor am I."

Yet. Or is that to be ever again? Ae, Powers. He had truly never given the safety of the Realm much thought before this. The land was simply *there*, something one took for granted. *Why am I feeling this sudden surge of protectiveness now, when there's nothing to be done about it?*

Hiraeth, he decided at last, *Cadwal's so-evocative Cymreig* hiraeth, *that half-pleasurable pain for what you cannot have again.*

But the runes, clattering softly together in their pouch, reminded him that *hiraeth* someday might be ended for him—no, no "might be" about it, he snapped at himself. He *would* go home. But first he must go back to Wessex.

"Cadwal," the prince said suddenly, "I'm weary of this trudging through the wilderness. And I have, by now, gained as much control over the runes as I'm likely to have."

"Meaning?" Wariness edged the mercenary's voice.

"Meaning that I'm going to try something drastic to return us to Wessex."

Cadwal groaned. "Why don't I like the sound of that?"

"Hush, now. Follow me. I *feel* something nearby, something useful."

And so, Ardagh thought with wry humor, they'd reentered Wessex as much by Sidhe whim as by design. Nothing but Sidhe whim—which had nothing as common as mere logic to it—could explain whatever had possessed him to try using that one small stone circle he'd sensed back in Cymru.

But it had worked. They'd been desperate enough, he and Cadwal both, about seeing this affair safely ended that they'd roused a fair amount of Power. And the Power of the long-dead magician whose bones lay under the Wessex circle had pulled them (though of course he'd never know it, the prince mused) back to his land. Here Ardagh and Cadwal stood, panting and disheveled, on the very spot where they'd disappeared from Saxon sight—however many days ago it had been.

Stood for a moment, at any rate. In the next, Ardagh's trembling legs gave out from under him and he fell,

digging his fingers into the earth in a desperate attempt
to draw some of its Power into his depleted self. And
Cadwal—ae, Cadwal promptly rushed off to be, judging from the greenish shade of his face as he'd run,
thoroughly ill.

After a time, Ardagh managed to sit up, somewhat
restored, to see the mercenary returning, looking shaken
but vastly relieved. "I will never," Cadwal said, "*never*
get used to travelling like that.*"

"Believe me," the prince murmured, "you aren't the
only one." Ardagh snatched out the rune Algiz, clutching
it to him. *You're supposed to be so powerful against
magical backlash—all right, then, do your job!*

There, now. It did work, or his will did, or the sheer
passage of time did, but slowly Ardagh felt strength
flowing back throughout his being.

But he also felt, just for the briefest of instants, that
same odd, alarming sense of Something watching, Something of the Darkness—

No. It, whatever it had been, was gone.

*Assuming this isn't a figment of my admittedly over-
worked imagination, it has to be the use of the runes
that's attracting . . . Whatever it is.* He remembered the
demonic Arridu far too well to be casual about that. *But
I can't* not *use the runes if I'm to stop Osmod.*

Wonderful. Yet another complication.

One with which he'd just have to deal whenever the
situation arose. With a shrug of Sidhe pragmatism,
Ardagh slipped the rune back into its pouch with the
others and struggled to his feet, looking about.

Not a soul in sight, fortunately. But there in the field,
watching him with great curiosity, were two good, stocky
farm ponies, far larger than their scruffy wild cousins,
large enough, in fact, Ardagh thought, to be ridden.

"This won't be elegant," he said to Cadwal, "but I
think that the next stage of our 'wondrous transport' has
arrived.'"

Later, they were able to replace the farm horses with

a merchant's two-horse wagon (leaving the bemused man standing holding the farm horses' makeshift reins and not at all sure what had happened), and the wagon with two good, swift riding horses (leaving the two courtiers standing by a wagon, not at all sure what had happened to *them*).

"Going to have the whole land after us," Cadwal muttered, head half buried over his horse's flapping mane. "Be lucky if we aren't hung as thieves."

"Never mind, never mind. Look."

"Uintacaester."

"Exactly! Ride, Cadwal. We are almost there—" Ardagh cut himself off, staring ahead in sudden alarm. "And," he added sharply, "we must hurry!"

The Return
Chapter 35

Although it was still full day out there, the central fires and wall torches were blazing away here in the Great Hall, casting off light and smoke in equal doses. Add to that the body heat of this agitated mass of Witan members, Egbert thought, and it made for a thick fog of smelly warmth, dulling the senses if not the nose.

Not, unfortunately, dulling the noise, either. The Witan had been at it since morning, arguing back and forth: Yes, we should go to war, no, we can't be hasty, yes, we must strike now, while Mercia's weak, no, we're not yet strong enough, yes, we are. Eadwig held the floor now by sheer volume, orating at full force.

Shut up, Eadwig, Egbert thought wearily, but said nothing.

Why had he allowed this nonsense to go so far? Why had allowed it at all? He could have—should have—said, no, we shall not discuss war with Mercia, and cowed them into obedience by sheer force of will.

Except that lately he hadn't felt very forceful. Those cursed dreams with their taint of darkness. And now this cursed fog of warm, stale air drugging his mind.

If only it was drugging everyone else as well.

No. The king must show no weakness, for all that his head was beginning to pound from the closeness and he could have screamed from sheer boredom. *Don't they see? We are not ready to attack anyone yet, let alone to declare war on another kingdom.*

There it was in all its inelegant truth. Convenient an excuse as the just-might-be-an-assassin prince of Cathay made (and of course that vagueness of "just might" could always be ignored), the collective minds of the Witan were glossing right over the plain, mundane details of supply and funding.

Not heroic enough for them, Egbert thought darkly, *such considerations of merchants and the like.*

Ah yes, the merchants. They supported him, yes, Egbert had no doubt of that, but they didn't know their new king well enough to trust him.

"Oh, do sit down, Eadwig," he said suddenly, forcing out the words through what felt like air turned tangible. "Let another speak."

Eadwig sat, looking as startled as a boy who's unexpectedly received a parental reprimand. *Good,* Egbert thought.

Ha, but now it was Cuthred analyzing point by point, so quietly and pedantically that it would be just a matter of time before he was shouted down. Egbert drew a deep breath, meaning to put an end to this nonsense, then nearly strangled himself trying not to cough on the lungful of heated, smoky air he'd inhaled. It was too cursed difficult to speak in this cursed fog. Easier, far easier, to let the others have their say till, God willing, they finally ran out of words.

The merchants, now . . .

The merchants wouldn't voluntarily hand over their gold to a new king with some glorious project that didn't really concern them. Of course, Egbert mused, it would be easy enough to force them into obedience; all he had to do was raise a few pertinent taxes.

Now? With the city and land so prosperous? Oh, good thinking. Hurt the merchants, hurt the economy, and you hurt your people's trust in you. Hurt that trust and you're just asking for treason to spring up at home while you're off in the field.

God. Here they went again. Two other ealdormen had started arguing as hotly as two small boys. Egbert recognized them after a moment: Cerdric and Aethelred. Members of rival families, families that had been at each others' throats for far longer than either ealdorman had been alive.

Fortunate that I don't allow weapons in here. Though it might stop this farce if one of them took the other's head off.

Aethelred was shouting something about King Cenwulf of Mercia, and Cerdric was shouting right back: He's weak! He's strong! He's not as strong as Offa! He's invaded Kent!

And why, they're both saying without words, haven't I done anything about that last? Kent is, if you reinterpret the law just a convenient bit, part of my territory.

Bah, didn't they see? The invasion of Kent had pretty much decimated Cenwulf's forces, and the man's less than successful forays into stubborn, savage Cymru in imitation of the late Offa weren't helping. The more the Mercian king fought, the more he weakened himself and his land.

And the more time he gives us to prepare.

That was what he should be saying. He should be silencing these idiots. Making himself perfectly, regally clear. Egbert rubbed a hand across a sweaty forehead. If only it wasn't so cursedly warm in here, so warm and—and vague. He could think the words clearly enough, but he just couldn't say them . . . the words just wouldn't leave his mind. . . .

All he could do, Egbert realized, was wait and wait and wait for this seemingly endless ordeal to be done.

He should have expected this, Osmod thought in the few brief moments when he dared take his concentration from the king, from the Witan. Here was the meeting that would finally push his plans forward into action—

Ha, yes. If only. If only. The Witan was hardly one united organism with one mind to be controlled. Osmod watched, half amused, half wildly frustrated, as the debate there in the Great Hall grew more and more frenzied without any result. Too many different folk, too many personal grudges and ambitions, curse them all. They'd been going at it all day now under the lash of his will with barely a break yet, with not a thing resolved. Bah, listen to that storm of eager, angry voices, look at all those fierce, florid faces.

Like a gang of squabbling small boys, the lot of them.

And when oh when was it going to dawn on the idiots, despite his careful proddings, that they were arguing over petty details?

That they were all basically on the same side?

The side of war.

It had dawned on their king some time ago. He was sitting slouched, fingers steepled and a sardonic glint in his eyes, evidently rather enjoying watching the others make fools of themselves. For the moment. Egbert was a patient man—in the way, Osmod mused, that a predator is patient—but there was a limit to even regal forbearance. A fortunate thing, then, that Egbert had not the faintest hint that his will was not *quite* his own.

As long as I don't push too hard, make myself too obvious. After all, he does, deep within, want this war-as-excuse-for-expansion as much as any other. Of course, such *"this is mine just because I want it"* inner desires rarely reached the surface; civilized men rarely yielded to those primitive, deeply rooted impulses. *But with my . . . help, Egbert has no choice, now, does he? Primitive desire for conquest and sophisticated wish for glory—we may be here all night, but by all the powers of Darkness, we'll leave here with an attack on Mercia all planned and ready.*

All night.

No, he mustn't let his thoughts wander like this! Osmod fought to keep the properly concerned, ever-so-worried expression on his face, fought as well to hide his real emotions—

The primary one of which was rapidly growing into full-blown worry. He had depleted so much of his Power in getting this far, in swaying so many minds, and what was left was definitely starting to slide away, bit by tormenting bit. Well and good to interject soothing or sarcastic comments where he thought they'd be most effective, but without the reinforcement of magic behind them, they would quickly become nothing more than suggestions. He must, Osmod knew, take another victim, and soon.

And *yes,* the Darkness burned that in his mind as clearly as a shout, *blood and Power, yes,* giving him a sudden jarring awareness of *Prince Ardagh, of Prince Ardagh here, at the gate, Prince Ardagh—*

Osmod nearly snarled. *Just what do You want me to do about it? I can't take my attention from here— You want the war, don't You? I can't deal with this and the prince both!*

Ach, but he'd already taken his attention from Egbert for an instant too long—or, Osmod thought bitterly, had it torn away—and now the king was surging to his feet, on his face the look of a truly desperate man. "I'm all right," Egbert snapped in response to the sudden storm of worried voices. "Go on. Work this out among you. When you reach a conclusion, then, and only then, let me know."

Damnation.

But there was nothing Osmod could do but bow with the others and watch his king leave the hall. One did *not* find fault with the Lords of Darkness. And at least there was still the Witan on which to work.

For as long as he could. For as long as his Power held out.

Leofrun, royal mistress—though that title meant little to her (except that it meant she could cuddle with Egbert, yes, yes, be nice and warm and play those games that sent funny little fires racing all inside her), Leofrun stood before the Great Hall, stood stubborn as a wooden image to the dismay of her ladies. They were always trying to get her to do what they wanted. None of them knew what mattered, what really, really mattered.

Leofrun whimpered, looking about at the fading day. *This* was what mattered. Soon the sun would be gone. "Night," she whispered. "Night."

"Yes, dear," one of the women agreed. "That's right. Night follows day, you know that. And day follows night."

Leofrun glared at her. They didn't understand; they never understood. Leofrun knew that she wasn't very clever, but at least *she* knew what the night meant:

Dark things. Dark, dark, dark. She wasn't sure exactly what kind of things there were. The priests tried to tell her about devils. They told her that if she didn't act the right way, the devils would carry her off to . . . Leofrun frowned, trying to remember what they always said . . . to "eternal damnation." She wasn't sure what that meant, except that it wouldn't be happy at all. She wasn't sure exactly what acting the right way meant, but Leofrun practiced looking over her shoulder now just to be sure no devils were sneaking up on her.

The devils that were going to carry off Osmod. They were, they were! They would carry him off and—and—

Unless Osmod was a devil, too? Leofrun stared at the Great Hall in sudden new horror. Maybe he *was* a devil! Yes, oh yes, maybe he was! He was just as bad as the ones with horns even though he didn't have any horns, no, or—or cloven hoofs, either! Osmod was a devil, and no one knew, no one but she, and no one would listen to her. Leofrun shivered, and one of the women "tsked" and draped a cloak about her shoulders and pinned it fast.

"Won't you come inside, dear? It's growing late."

Leofrun glared at her just as she had at the others. "No!"

Didn't they understand *anything?* She had to watch. Osmod was in that hall. She had to watch when he came

out, because when he came out, he'd want to kill someone. No one else was going to help her because no one
else believed her. They all thought she was stupid. Well,
maybe she wasn't as smart as some, but that didn't mean
she was *that* stupid! The women all thought themselves
so smart, but she could get away from them any time
she wanted.

She stiffened with a wordless little cry. Egbert! Egbert
was rushing out of the Great Hall, trailed by his guards.
And he looked so very unhappy! Before the ladies could
stop her, Leofrun raced to his side, trying to throw her
arms around him. "Egbert!"

He glanced sharply down at her as though startled to
see her there. "Leofrun. You shouldn't—" He stopped,
changed that to a glare at the ladies and an angry, "You
shouldn't let her—"

"No," Leofrun whimpered. "Not anger. Don't be
angry."

For a moment, his arm went about her, hugging her
to him, for a moment Leofrun was happy and safe and
warm. But then Egbert released her with a sigh. "I'm
not angry at you. I'm just . . . tired, Leofrun. Just tired,
that's all."

Leofrun stared past him at the Great Hall, the hall
that was still blazing with light and noise. "Osmod," she
whispered. That was who had made Egbert tired. Osmod
had hurt Egbert. "Osmod."

This time Egbert's sigh did sound angry. "Don't start
that nonsense again, Leofrun." His hand closed on her
shoulder, not quite gently.

But Leofrun squirmed free, still staring at the hall.
Osmod had hurt Egbert. The devil had hurt Egbert.
"No," she murmured, "no."

Egbert must have thought she was agreeing with
him. "Good," he said, absently ruffling her hair, and
walked on.

But Leofrun stood where she was. "No," she repeated
softly. It would not happen again. The priests were full

of stories about people who had done brave things, even died, for the sake of goodness. And she—no matter what she had to do, Leofrun knew that she was not going to let the devil Osmod hurt anyone ever again.

Ardagh straightened in the saddle of this latest in the succession of "borrowed" horses. Over him towered Uintacaester's ancient walls. In the deepening twilight, they were an ominous grey, like some great crouching beast waiting for its prey.

Ae, what poetic nonsense! Far more important than foolish fancies was the very real psychic fog he sensed swirling about the city. And Ardagh felt a chill settle over him. *I wasn't imagining it, was I? I wasn't imagining that Darkness was watching every time I tried the runes. Foolish me. Here I thought I'd merely be fighting Osmod.*

Did the human know how he was being used? Did he care? From what Ardagh had seen of Osmod, total self-interest and a lack of what humans called morality seemed to be his prime attributes.

But this didn't make sense! It was one thing for Darkness to settle about someone like Osmod, someone who could promise chaos and pain. Why, Ardagh wondered, should the Darkness be so suddenly aware of *him?* The Sidhe had never had any dealings with demonic forces!

Ae, wait. Maybe they hadn't. But he, Ardagh realized with a shock, most certainly had. Even if it hadn't been by his choosing, he had definitely had dealings with Arridu, the late Gervinus's demon ally.

And so it is that the Darkness knows of me, and now the Darkness knows that I'm a threat to Osmod as well. Gervinus, Gervinus, curse your treacherous soul, I thought I was done with you. And wouldn't it please you to see this?

But why hadn't the Darkness already struck? That was obvious enough; It couldn't. If he were reachable, Ardagh thought with sardonic humor, he'd already be

dead. Regardless of human tales of demons, no aspect
of Darkness could enter Reality without a gateway. And
clearly—thank whatever Powers might be involved—
those few drops of his blood that Arridu had stolen, the
blood that might have formed such a gateway, had long
ago lost their potency.

*But what of Osmod? He just might be fool enough to
invite the Darkness in and never see the harm!*

At the prince's angry hiss, Cadwal turned sharply to
him. "What? What?"

"The Darkness is in him and about him, swirling over
the city, waiting for a chance to enter."

The mercenary didn't have to ask who that "he" might
be. "You're not just being poetic, are you?" At Ardagh's
impatient shake of the head, Cadwal continued, "And
a fellow who can see in the night isn't going to be
worried about nice, natural darkness. *Iesu*. You don't
mean we're going to be doing battle against the Prince
of Darkness himself?"

"Don't joke."

"Wasn't." Cadwal paused a heartbeat. "You don't *really*
mean—"

"No. There will be no conventional demonic figures.
But Osmod is playing with more, I think, than either I
or he suspected."

"And where is he? If he's got all that—that dark
Power, why hasn't he already done something about our
being here?"

"I don't know. Something is very obviously distracting him."

"And distracting the . . . uh . . . Darkness as well?"

Ardagh shook his head. No use trying to explain what
wouldn't fit the human tongue. He and Cadwal rode
unchallenged into the city in the midst of a chattering
group of late-arriving merchants. After a moment's
hesitation, the prince turned his horse in the direction
of the royal enclosure. But Cadwal moved his own horse
to block Ardagh's path.

"No insult meant, but what the *hell* are you doing? Marching right into enemy territory?"

"In effect, yes."

"But you—he—"

"Cadwal, please. I cannot afford to wait meekly for him to leave his sanctuary. Trust me on this: I don't dare. In fact, I don't dare wait at all." *Not with that fog of Darkness all around us and threatening to erupt into Reality.*

The mercenary opened his mouth, closed it, caught by the prince's inhumanly steady stare. At last Cadwal shrugged with the casual, resigned manner of one who has fought too many battles to be upset by one more, even one in which he might be badly outmatched. "I keep forgetting. You're not human. At least we have that on our side."

"You still have a choice. You can still leave."

"Hell, man, I've never yet turned my back on a comrade. Even if," Cadwal added with shaky humor, "this time Hell may really be involved. Come on, let's get going before I find some way to talk myself out of this."

Ardagh grinned in spite of himself and reached out to clasp the startled human's hand for a minute. "Comrade, indeed. I'll need someone quite literally to guard my back."

"Uh, right. But," Cadwal added, gesturing with his chin towards the palisade about the royal hall, "getting in there is not going to be easy."

"On the contrary." Even as he spoke, Ardagh was still searching with delicate magical care for Osmod, finding nothing but that unnerving psychic haze of Darkness. "On the contrary," he repeated after a moment, "I suspect that getting into the hall is going to be the easiest part of it all."

A Loving Sacrifice
Chapter 36

Osmod fought down a shout of pure rage. No! He dare not let his emotions overcome him, not now. Grimly, he forced his mind back to self-control, back to total and fierce concentration.

Or almost total concentration. What was going on in this hall was almost too much for even a Powerful mind to bear! Hour after hour, and yet these idiots kept at each other, voices more hoarse perhaps, gestures less frenetic, but with nothing accomplished, nothing!

No. Calmness. Concentrate.

Yes, but again and again he'd almost had them, almost had them all—then again and again had come those savage little surges of distraction shaking his concentration, wasting his already wasted Power, and:

Lords of Darkness, what are You thinking? Osmod cried silently in sudden, irresistible rage. *It's You distracting me, it's You causing the never-ending chaos in this hall. What do You want?*

No answer, of course. And he knew this was a perilous path to be tracing. But Osmod continued savagely, far too worn for caution:

If You do want war, if You do wish Your share of blood and lives—end this! Let me win, let me win—end this stupid farce now and stop tormenting me with "He is here, the prince is here." I know the prince is here, but I am only mortal, like it or not! I can only deal with one war at a time!

At least he could draw a token of Power from what was going on here, enough to keep him from collapsing completely, even if it was as tedious a process as gathering grains of sand to build a beach, and never as potent (or as satisfying, to him and the Darkness both) as the blood-sacrifice. All violent human emotions gave off tiny sparks of energy; the more intense and long-lasting the emotion, the brighter the spark, from the foolish quarrels going on here all the way up to outright war.

War.

Ach, yes, war.

The sudden shock of understanding stabbed through Osmod, sharp as a psychic blade, shaking his concentration yet again, making him quiver because: Of course the Lords of Darkness wanted war; that was why They were so willing to support him, their merely mortal tool, in his merely mortal plans of conquest. They would drink deeply of the blood spilled and the lives lost.

What of it? You knew that.

But would They be so easily sated? There was the heart of it. Osmod felt new shudders race through him despite all his fierce determination. Why hadn't he seen this before? (Had They, perhaps, not wanted him to see it? Had they blinded him to it?) Once the war with Mercia was begun, would They ever let it be stopped? Would the Lords of Darkness ride him as he rode the wills of others, forcing him to force the realm towards more and more terrible carnage—

You idiot! he snapped at himself. *Afraid of war—bah, you sound like a frightened little mouse of a priest!*

There always had been and always would be war; it was the normal state of human life. And most of those lives weren't worth the saving! Bah, yes, look at the lot here. Would the world care if any of them, if all of them, died this very moment? No, no, anyone who worried about the cost or that most absurdly uninterpretable concept, morality, was worthy only of being a victim.

All right, then. Calmness. Calmness. Of course there would be another war, and probably another after it—how else could one conquer other realms? Another war—what of it? This time, Osmod thought, allowing himself a little prickle of pleasure, this time at least, there would also be genuine glory.

Ardagh glanced fiercely about the night-dark royal enclosure, a small, predatory smile on his lips. There were none out here save for the occasional guards, and those were no more than the slightest of nuisances.

"You were right." It was the softest of murmurs from Cadwal.

The prince gave a silent laugh. Of course he'd been right. It hadn't been at all difficult to slip by the guards at the gates, even with the handicap of pulling the human Cadwal into his Sidhe "no one here" illusion; no Sidhe worthy of the name would ever have found it a problem to slide unseen past humans.

High overhead, a wind swept clouds dramatically across the sky, now covering the moon, now letting dramatic flashes of silver flash down, but down here, the air was calm and not unpleasantly cool. Ahead, the great royal hall, alone of all the buildings, still burned with light, torch and firelight blazing from the hall's smoke-holes and out from between cracks in the planking, dazzling Ardagh's night vision. It was more light, surely, than could be explained by feasting courtiers—though the Powers knew there was enough noise for a feast.

Noise that lacks a feast's joviality, though. And . . . Osmod is somewhere in there. I think. It was difficult to accurately pick out even a magical human aura from out of that tangle. *But I'm not in such a tangle of auras. Why, at such a close range, is he still not aware of me? What could be so totally distracting?*

Simple enough to deduce. Since that hall was where the Witan met, what else could it be but something political and controversial? Namely, Osmod's plans for war.

*Let us only hope they keep him enraptured long
enough for me to—*

The prince ducked into hiding against a wooden wall,
Cadwal, almost as quick to react, beside him. "Who is
that?" the mercenary whispered.

A woman, slim as a wraith, wandered aimlessly alone,
her face a pale oval in the night. No servant, Ardagh
thought, not with that rich gown, though no lady would
allow her long hair to fly about in such wild tangles. Her
aura was just as tangled, murky and almost out-and-out
vague, and there was, somehow, the *feel* of a child to
her—

Ah. Children born with weak or distorted minds, just
as those born sickly, didn't live long in the Sidhe Realm;
their own magic destroyed them before they left their
first years. But humans, he knew, were otherwise. There
was a man back in Fremainn, tall and broad-shouldered
as a warrior but with no more intelligence than was to
be found in a human boy of five or six. He was a sweet,
happy fellow despite his lack of intellect, quite content
with doing whatever rough job was given to him.

*I doubt that this wild, pretty creature has ever done
a rough day's work.*

Save, perhaps, in some noble's bed—though bedding
such a woman, the prince thought with a twinge of
distaste, would be almost like bedding a child.

Beside him, Cadwal gave the softest little hiss of
annoyance. "Some half-mad noblewoman. Means her
women will be coming after her and causing a fuss."

Ardagh straightened. "Not quite yet, I think."

The woman was staring right at him, as though her
human eyes could pierce the darkness. With a little
shiver, he realized that she actually could see him, though
not with ordinary sight. The humans did say that their—
ae, what was that pretty euphemism?—their children of
God could see Otherliness more clearly than ordinary
folk. . . .

The woman was coming straight for him, her face

open and trusting as a child's. Ardagh stood frozen, not at all sure what to do. She stopped just before reaching him, staring up at him with wide blue eyes. Dull eyes, yet with a strange glimmer behind the dullness, a wild eeriness that reminded the prince with a jolt of something the would-be scald, Einar, had told him: fey. The look, Ardagh thought uneasily, of those foredoomed.

The woman's voice was soft with wonder. "Are you an angel?" For a moment, Ardagh couldn't find a thing to say, thinking wildly, *I've been called many things, but a holy being, never!* Finding his voice at last, he managed a feeble, "Alas, no."

"But you are here," she insisted. "I prayed, and you are here." Her eyes still full of that eerie mix of dullness and gleaming light, she added without the slightest trace of surprise, "You came for Osmod."

Ardagh heard Cadwal's shocked intake of breath and quickly put a warning hand on the man's arm. "How would you know that, lady?" the prince asked gently. "And who, if I may ask, are you?"

"Leofrun." She said that as easily as a child rattles off her name, adding proudly, "I live with Egbert." The flicker of life suddenly animating her face left no doubt how she meant that. And in that one quick moment, it was not a simpleminded face at all, but that of a woman who loves and knows that she loves.

"And does he love you, too?" the prince murmured.

"Oh. That. No. I don't think so. It doesn't matter. He's the king, you know; he doesn't have time. But he's nice to me," she added, so earnestly that Ardagh heard Cadwal mutter something in Cymreig that could only be a curse on the head of any man who'd misuse so innocent a creature.

Ae, no, not quite innocent. "You hate Osmod."

"Yes, yes, yes." Her expression said, how could he not know that? "He's a devil. You know that, don't you? He's a devil, he kills people. He killed Octa. And—and he tried to hurt Egbert. And I—I—I will not let him. I will not let him hurt Egbert. I will not ever let him hurt Egbert."

Just as love had suddenly animated her face, it now changed her voice to that of a woman who would defend the man she loved with all her being. No matter, Ardagh realized with a little prickle of alarm, how much she had to lose in the process.

Egbert, the prince thought without any irony at all, *you don't deserve her.*

But—Powers, what was that? A chaotic surging of Darkness, of magic—

Osmod!

He had them, Osmod thought, yes, ah yes, he had them almost totally swayed, almost in his hand, the whole noisy Witan, and in another moment they would agree to—

The prince is here!

No, no, he could not listen to that. He had the Witan in hand and all it would take was this one more moment—

Prince Ardagh! Prince Ardagh is—

The moment was lost, control shattered. "No, curse You!" Osmod exploded. "I cannot deal with both at once!"

Damnation! He'd shouted that aloud, and everyone was staring at him. But worse, worse was the cold, deadly, silent voice that might or might not have been real: *Then deal with nothing.*

And—his Power was gone, drained away, leaving him suddenly dazed, suddenly empty, while all around him, the Witan was coming back to its collective senses and losing the irrational lust for war—no! He must find prey, now, quickly, before everything was lost! At least it was night out there; there would be no witnesses. Let the Witan all think he'd been struck by illness or madness, it didn't matter, he'd find some smooth excuse, some explanation, but later, curse them, later. He would find prey, and feed, and return with Power refreshed, grab the Witan and shake them once and for all into doing his will!

With a cursory dip of his head to the others, Osmod fled out into the darkness.

Osmod!

Aware that he had just gone into a predatory crouch, Ardagh straightened ever so slowly, watching the sorcerer slip from the Great Hall. Osmod was looking about with—yes—with predatory wariness.

Hunting, Ardagh realized. *No doubt about it. I haven't sensed his Power because he's worn it down to almost nothingness. He* must *hunt to restore it, he* must *kill.*

Not, the prince added, *if I have any say about it.*

Wait, though. Surrounding Osmod . . . Ardagh blinked, stared with more than physical sight . . . yes. Darkness surrounded the man, swirling about him, that Darkness that had nothing to do with mortal night.

"Stillness," the prince whispered sharply to Cadwal. "Do not move so much as a hair."

I'll not have Cadwal used as a target. But I also will not have Osmod elude us, not now, not after so—

Leofrun! Her face a serene mask, Leofrun was walking away from them, walking seemingly aimlessly towards Osmod.

Just in time, Ardagh clamped his hand down on Cadwal's swordarm, hissing, "No! Do not move!"

"But she—dammit, man," Cadwal whispered fiercely back, "she's walking right into his trap. The poor thing doesn't even know what she's doing!"

Ardagh tightened his grip. "She does." He remembered the look in her eyes: fey, indeed. Fey as only a woman sacrificing herself for love can be.

But not blindly sacrificing. Leofrun meant to take down Osmod as surely as ever wolf stalked deer—and she meant to do it, trusting, avenging innocent that she was, after death, and with Ardagh's aid. Just then, the prince knew with cool, pragmatic Sidhe certainty what she would do and why.

My aid, sweet Leofrun, you shall have. That, I promise you. You shall not die for naught.

Cadwal was struggling to free himself. "But—you can't just—"

"Curse you, human," Ardagh hissed in the man's ear, "be still! Do you think I *want* this? The Darkness is here, real, perilous!" Struggling for words a human would understand, he continued fiercely, "If we move now, if we try to strike while Osmod is Powerless, his blood forms a link with that Darkness!" *Powers, that means I can't simply stab the man; I don't dare spill a drop of his blood.* "Do you see? The Darkness will come *here,* It will defend Its tool and come down on us, and all three of us, you, me, Leofrun, will die, and die for nothing!" Frantic to end the argument before it began, Ardagh nearly shook Cadwal. "Do you see what I'm saying, human? Do you?"

"Let go. I get the point."

No, you don't. Even if this is something one of your faith should see at once: the sacrifice of a willing innocent.

Yes, Osmod would gain Power from her life—but her death, her spilled blood, rather than forming a gateway, would be the surest, strongest bar to the Darkness, banning It from Reality.

That didn't make what was happening easier to witness. Cadwal, swearing steadily under his breath, turned away, but Ardagh, teeth clenched, grimly watched Osmod pull the unresisting Leofrun to him. Ironic, terribly ironic, that he must wait for Osmod to regain Power before he could use Power to destroy the man. But the Sidhe were well acquainted with irony in all its many forms. He watched Osmod slay and feed and totally miss Leofrun's tranquil, triumphant smile. The sorcerer let his victim's body slide to the ground, his eyes misty with satiation, and Ardagh *felt* the new Power surging up within the man. . . .

Now.

The prince took a bold step forward, crying, "Murderer!" With beautiful timing, the clouds parted and a ray of moonlight caught Ardagh in a blaze of silver, so suddenly and dramatically that Osmod recoiled with a startled hiss.

But the sorcerer was only off balance for an instant. "Foolish of you," he snapped, "foolish to return," and tore open what could only be his rune pouch. Magic blazed up about him, and Ardagh snatched out a handful of his own makeshift runes, trying not to remember just how makeshift they were, forcing himself to believe that yes, they had Power, *he* had Power, that yes, this would work. More difficult to believe that this was it, no grand gestures, no dramatic words:

As quickly as this, their battle had begun.

Casting the Runes
Chapter 37

"What is this?" Ealdorman Eadwig thundered. "What in *hell* is going on?"

His voice just barely topped the storm of shouting that was the Witan, confused and alarmed, trying to understand what had just happened.

"What were we saying?"

"What were we thinking?"

"War? Yes, but—"

"We can't—"

"Not now—"

"What—"

"Will you all be quiet!" Eadwig shouted. *"I said: Will you all be quiet!"*

That startled them into momentary silence—and now they could all hear a savage new roar outside the hall. Something slammed against one wall with enough force to make them all start. A voice muttered nervously, "Grendel," and not a few hands moved in pious signs.

"It's not Grendel, you idiot!" Eadwig snapped. "It's the wind, just that. While we've been nattering away in here, the weather must have changed."

"But how long *have* we been in here?" Cuthred wondered.

"Long enough to miss dinner," someone muttered.

"And for what?" asked another voice. "Damned if I know what we've been discussing."

"Same here."

"And here."

An awkward silence fell, leaving one lone voice in the act of concluding, sounding twice as loud in the quiet, " . . . and feels as though we were bewitched."

Silence fell for another tense moment. And then Eadwig gave a harsh bark of a laugh. "That's ridiculous. Who was going to enchant us? King Egbert?"

That started a few nervous laughs. Eadwig snorted. "Enough of this. Won't be the first time we got ensnared in arguing and forgot the hour, yes, and without anything demonic about it."

Wrong choice of words: A few more hands moved in nervous signs at that. "Come," Eadwig said in disgust, "let us—you, yes, and you, what are you doing? Get those doors open!"

"Uh, we're trying, my lord," the guards told him. "The wind—"

"Nonsense." The ealdorman impatiently gestured one of the guards aside and set his own shoulder against a door. Damnation! The wind really was strong! "That is," he said, panting, "one truly hellish storm. Truly hellish."

In the next moment, he realized that was the worst thing he could have said. A stampede of ealdormen rushed forward, pushing at the doors, pushing at each other, nearly trampling each other as they fought in ever-increasing panic to escape the hall that had suddenly become a prison.

"Leofrun!" Egbert groaned and sank to his bed. "Leofrun! Where are you, woman?"

That ridiculous episode in the Great Hall had left him with a pounding head. Leofrun, for all her failings, had a gentle hand and a way of massaging away pain.

Yes, but where was she? Swearing under his breath, Egbert got to his feet. No use bellowing like an ox. Moving to the doorway, he snagged a passing servant. "You. Find the Lady Leofrun. Have her brought to me."

Damned foolishness in the Great Hall, the lot of them

yelling at each other about . . . about what, exactly? War, yes, but . . . ha, no wonder nothing had been resolved, because now that he thought about it with a clear—if aching—head, Egbert could plainly see that there hadn't been any logic to any of the arguments.

What was that all about? Almost as though we'd been bewitched, every one of us.

A sudden roar brought him starkly alert, for that first startled moment thinking *demons*, then relaxing with a wan laugh. Wind. Nothing more terrible than wind. God help him, he was getting as fanciful as a woman. As Leofrun.

Where *was* Leofrun? Egbert moved impatiently to the doorway again, just in time to meet a group—a gaggle, he thought unkindly—of nervously chattering ladies. Leofrun's ladies, Egbert recognized, and held up a brusque hand for silence. He'd long ago given up threats of punishment; Leofrun could, for all her slow wit, be sly as any fox in escaping her ladies when she wished. "What now?" he asked. "Where has she gotten to this time?"

Some snivelling, some nervous, humorless titters. "She—she's not anywhere in the hall, King Egbert," they managed at last.

"Are you sure?" Leofrun sometimes played at hiding. Like a child, Egbert thought, just like a child. *And what*, his mind asked, unbidden, *does that make you?* "Have you looked in all the corners?"

"We looked everywhere," one woman said miserably. "The Lady Leofrun is out there. Outside. Somewhere."

"In that storm?" Swearing, Egbert called for his heaviest cloak. This time he was going to retrieve the woman himself. And this time, Egbert promised himself, Leofrun, like an erring child, would truly learn how to repent.

Ae, yes! In this first wild blaze of Power against Power, Ardagh knew with a surge of emotion that was almost joy that this time he and Osmod could strike at each other. This time their magics could kill.

Would kill, he corrected with blunt Sidhe honesty. Only one of them would see the new day.

But how fine it felt, how wondrously fine, to be testing his strength not with some mundane sword but with Power! Even though it was nowhere near the glory he had known in his homeland, even though this weak, hybrid magic squirmed and twisted in his mind, struggling to tear itself apart—ae, it was so very *right* to meet his foe like this!

Oh yes. A Sidhe trying to use a magic foreign to him and a human trying to use his limited Power in combat when he's surely never had to fight a sorcerous duel before: That should, the prince thought wryly, *make the odds somewhere about even.*

He'd heard some of the ridiculous tales the humans enjoyed, of magical duels full of wonders and flashes of fire. There would be little here for any watching human to see (watching Cadwal, yes, but the others, Witan and king—where were they?). The sudden crash of Power against Power created a savage whirling of wind all about Ardagh and Osmod, a sorcerous gale strong as a wall cutting them off from Reality, sealing them in its heart, in a circle of more than natural stillness surrounded by all that shrieking savagery.

Let it rage, Ardagh thought. *It keeps us safe from interference.* He turned his will to shutting out the storm and all its fury from his mind, blocking it, blocking, till he could see only the runes, hear only them whispering their names to him, till he could *feel* only the meaning they held—

No, no, the *meanings!* Ae yes, all at once the whole swarm of them came swirling into his mind, wild as the storm, an endless tangle of possibilities that, were this not in the midst of combat, would have fascinated him. But he couldn't afford confusion just now! Yes, and was the human overwhelmed by this every time he cast a rune-spell? How could he deal with the endless range of meanings? Some were literal, some figurative, some even so symbolic he couldn't read them—how could Osmod endure?

How? Because, curse it, the human was only that: human. Osmod would see only what he wanted, the shallowest, most obvious of interpretations. And if he could do it . . . Ardagh forced himself away from the web of endless possibilities, narrowed his thinking as best he could to pick only *one* thread of meaning from the snarl, follow only that *one* meaning out of many, and—

Heat! Terrible, angry heat surged over him—ha, Osmod really was seeing only the obvious, for this was surely Thurs he cast: Thurs or Thorn, as these folk called it, Thorn or even Thurisaz, easy names for the very heart of cosmic destruction, the rune of fire, demonic fire, the Powerful force of chaos.

You idiot! Ardagh raged. *You'd use the lightning to spark your candle—you really do want to end this duel quickly.*

Oh yes, Thurs could end it quickly—for both of them, and probably most of the royal enclosure. But there were other sides to Thurs, just as for the other runes, and Ardagh hastily expanded his mental focus, welcoming the swarm of meanings, hunting for Thurs in all its aspects. Powers, this wasn't an easy way of magic, so cursedly complex, wasteful of Power. He was dimly aware of his body's panting, but he could still find: yes, here was something, Thurs as the wild creative force of sex, of life, and Ardagh grinned as the killing fire turned to a much more pleasant heat.

Too pleasant. This had all taken only a few seconds of real time, but with a great wrenching of will, Ardagh pulled his mind from sudden hot, joyous thoughts of Sorcha, controlling himself as no human could, very well aware that Osmod was about to strike again. And very well aware, too, that there had to be a counterbalance for the fire that was Thurs.

Yes! He struck back at Osmod with Is, Isa, ice and self-protection in one, cooling the fire, the sorcery, cooling the will, Osmod's will, dazing the human, befogging his senses. Yes, ah yes, and now, if only he could find—

No. The force of Is hadn't held long enough; he simply didn't have the experience for that. Osmod might not have a Sidhe's Power, but he was certainly more skilled in the use of runes. Stunned, confused though he was, he could still strike back with another all too Powerful rune:

Hagall, the prince realized, *Haegl or whatever they call it here:* Hail in all its essence of destructive force. *Powers, he does mean to destroy us both!*

But the rune must have other sides, just like the others, and if he could only find them . . . find them quickly, because every second warding off something as fierce as Hagall was draining his strength to the point of danger. . . .

Yes! With a great psychic effort, Ardagh twisted the rune's meaning about from negative to positive, menace to protection against that very menace, not even trying to tap into the greater sense of cosmic shielding.

But before the prince could find a rune for counterbalanced attack, Osmod struck again, frantic with haste. This time, to Ardagh's shock, it was with a rune he didn't recognize, one that clearly wasn't used by the Lochlannach though his Sidhe senses caught the Saxon name, Daeg, and his Sidhe senses knew this was being cast in its most terrible aspect, the force of sheer, horrifying change.

Osmod, you madman! You'll destroy us both, and the city with us!

There had to be a safer side to this, but he didn't know the rune, he didn't know how to deal with it. Desperately prodding his wearying mind for a weapon, Ardagh seized upon the only rune he could find that was even remotely related: Ar, Ger, Jera, he couldn't remember which was the Lochlannach name, which the Saxon, but it was the rune symbolic of the changing of the year, the normal, sane changing, relentless and hopeful. Nothing of wild chaos here—

—and Daeg slid harmlessly away, its magic blunted, leaving the prince staggering and breathless with relief and the sudden uneasy return to balance.

Whatever made me think I could win a duel like this? Foreign, so damnably foreign I don't know how to take the offensive.

Instead, he was letting Osmod, merely human Osmod, drive him figuratively back and back, helpless to do more than just defend.

Oh, you great dolt! Ardagh snapped at himself in a sudden blaze of fury. *Of course you can't win a duel like this, never like this! You're letting Osmod set the rules, and you're actually playing by them. Think, curse you!*

Ae, yes. "You're weary, aren't you?" the prince called out suddenly over the roar of the wind, and *felt* the wall of Osmod's concentration shiver slightly. "Of course you're weary." Ardagh fought to hide the tired quiver in his own voice. "This is such a magic-weak Realm. We both know that. So very magic-weak. No wonder you tried to end our duel quickly. You knew you must end it before you just . . . fell over from exhaustion!"

Ha, that stung! "I am strong enough," Osmod snapped. "And you are a fool to try besting me."

"Oh, I was," Ardagh agreed smoothly. "I was a fool to think I could win a game you controlled. But it doesn't matter now. You never could wield much Power, could you?"

"What nonsense are you—"

"Of course you couldn't." *Keep him off balance; don't give him a chance to think of the runes or he'll have us fighting into mutual collapse.* "That's why you had to steal life force. For Power. Oh, and of course to appease your masters." He smiled at Osmod's quick, hastily suppressed start. "Yes, I know about the Darkness." *Which is why I can't kill you with a blade. I cannot risk your blood opening a gateway.* "You've been very clever at it, killing in the midst of all these folk with none suspecting."

"Oh please. You can't expect me to confess to that."

"Have I said anything about confessions? Tell me, Osmod, how many lives has it been? What, can't you remember?" *No, you really can't, can you? And that bothers you not at all.* "Come, how many lives *have* you stolen?"

"Not as many as I shall." For a heart-stopping moment, the Darkness itself swirled about Osmod, for a moment Darkness burned coldly from his eyes. "Pretty words, Prince Ardagh. But I will not be lulled by them!"

Power surged up about him again, but to Ardagh's immense relief, the Darkness faded, unable to find an opening. And this wasn't quite as strong a blaze of magic as before. "I was right," the prince exclaimed. "You really don't have much Power left. Not even with the blood-force you stole from Leofrun."

Leofrun! There was the way out of this, so obvious it all but screamed in his face. *Powers, yes, Leofrun and her sacrifice. Leofrun and justice.* He'd been going about this all wrong. Not desperate defense or blind attack, no, but one specific attack: Justice.

Ignoring the battle runes, the glyphs for fire, ice, death, Ardagh hunted through his mind till he'd found Reid, Rad, the heart of rightful choice, of honor, and Tyr, Teiwaz, the very essence of justice. He cast them both together, even though the strain of it blazed through his head, cast them both with all his weary will.

Fire hit him, so suddenly he nearly screamed. Even as he was hurling Tyr and Reid at Osmod, Osmod was hurling Thurs's fury at him, and if there weren't any physical flames, the savage, all-engulfing pain was still very real.

"No," Ardagh gasped out, and "no," again, willing,

There is no fire, no pain: I do not acknowledge them. There is no pain! There was nothing but the two runes Reid and Tyr, honor and justice, honor and justice, honor and

Leofrun. Soft and silent as fog, she moved to Osmod's side, her face tranquil, her eyes dreamy. Soft and silent as fog, she enfolded him in her arms. Ardagh gasped in relief as the fire vanished. He saw the shock in Osmod's eyes as he struggled against fog that yielded yet would not disperse. But he also *felt* the Darkness rousing and swirling all about, hunting for the smallest crack into Reality.

Act, a chill, indifferent nonvoice told him. *Or act not.*

It hardly mattered to the Darkness. There was, It told him without words, no way for It to lose and he to win. Leofrun couldn't hold back the Night, not alone, not even she, innocent, willing sacrifice though she'd been. If she fell, the Darkness would tear her being into mist, and there would be the gateway. Ardagh could never overcome Osmod's magic in time to save her, but if he killed with a blade, blood would be shed—and there would be the gateway. And he, finite, useless creature, could do nothing for there was no justice, no hope, only endless . . . indifference.

A cold, clear flame of purest rage blazed up in Ardagh. *Kill Osmod? So I shall—but not on Your terms, old Darkness, never on yours!*

He was Sidhe, born of magic, born of music and pitiless honor. He was Sidhe and *yes, there is justice* and *yes, there is hope.* Wild with that pure, pure rage, the prince cried out, "I claim Avenger's Right through she who was Leofrun! I claim Avenger's Right for all the lives you stole! Hear me, Osmod! Hear me!"

And the prince cried out a spell that was a wild new mingling of runic and Sidhe Power. It was shaped without thought, shaped by fiercest instinct, shaped with all the savage blaze of will within him as he hurled it straight at Osmod:

"May you be consumed as is
    the wood upon the fire,
May you shrink as does
    the frost beneath the sun,
May you fail as water in a drought,
May you fall as helpless as a withered grain.
You are Smallness,
You are Weakness,
You are Powerless!
You are Nothing!
You are Nothing!
You are Nothing!"

Osmod fought back. Strangling, choking, Osmod
fought with all the desperate strength of a man in flames.
His Power surging up with one last blinding blaze, too
much, far too much—all at once far more than any one
mortal frame could hold. Ardagh *felt* Osmod's heart tear
itself apart as the spell engulfed him, saw Osmod scream,
the sound drowned out by the roar of the wind. Wide-
eyed with horror, the sorcerer stumbled to his knees,
still struggling to rise, still struggling to live even as his
body died. With a sudden roar of thunder, the whirl of
Powerful wind was gone.

And Osmod's life went with it.

The Morning After
Chapter 38

The savage wind was suddenly gone, so suddenly that
Cadwal, who'd been helplessly pressed back against a
wall, staggered forward with a startled grunt. *Iesu,* almost
morning. The sorcerous battle had gone on for nigh all
the night.

Never would have believed I'd have thought about
something like that. Or seen it, for that matter. What-
ever it was I saw.

Look there, that crumpled form was the sorcerer
Osmod, lying close by his victim, that poor innocent,
whatever her name had—Leofrun, that was it. No doubt
about whether she was dead, God have mercy on her.
As for the other: After a battle, you checked the foe first,
made sure he wasn't going to spring up behind your back
while you were examining your own wounded. Cadwal
approached as warily as he would someone feigning
death on a battlefield, but one touch of his hand to the
man's wrist and one glance at the staring eyes told the
story clear enough: The man's heart had given out during
the battle and slain him.

And not surprising, since it was magic putting the strain
on it. Iesu, *there I go again, thinking that so calmly.*

Och, but the prince! To Cadwal's relief, Prince Ardagh
was very much still alive and looked to be unhurt but,
judging from the way he'd dragged himself wearily up
on one elbow without even glancing up, was in no condition to get any farther.

Hell of a place for him to collapse. And what do I do if he passes out altogether? Sling him over my shoulder and run for it?

Just as Cadwal reached the prince's side, the doors of the Great Hall burst open, releasing a horde of wild-eyed ealdormen. *Like so many frightened calves out of a barn,* Cadwal thought, and drew his sword, holding it in the casual "not quite a threat yet not quite not one, either" manner he'd long ago learned was more effective than any outright menace.

And look, here came King Egbert, disheveled as though he, too, had been caught by the wind. Cadwal saw his eyes widen at the sight of the three fallen bodies, two of them dead, then caught a flash of genuine pain on the royal face at the realization that one of the dead was Leofrun.

Sure enough: "Leofrun," the king breathed. Of course, Cadwal thought, it wasn't properly regal for him to go and check the bodies himself; instead, Egbert gestured to one of the attending servants.

"Don't bother," Cadwal said laconically. "They're dead, the both of them." He saw renewed pain in the king's eyes, and thought with a touch of surprise, *So he did care something about her after all.*

But the crowd was just now noticing the third figure, Prince Ardagh, and to his disgust, Cadwal heard words like "treason" and "murderer" being bandied about.

"Och, stop that nonsense!" he snapped, pitching his voice to ring out as though these were nothing but raw new recruits. Into the startled silence he'd created, Cadwal continued, "He didn't murder anyone. You want to know who killed the poor lass, look at the knife at that one's side." His jerk of the head took in Osmod's corpse. "Blood on it, blood on him, not a drop on the prince here."

Of course they turned, of course they looked. And of course they couldn't miss seeing that truth. Egbert stared at Cadwal, eyes cold and exceedingly regal. "What happened here?"

Was he expected to cringe? *I'm in the service of the High King of all Eriu, you arrogant Saesneg. I'm not going to be overawed by the likes of you.* "What happened," Cadwal drawled, "is that your late ealdorman over there was leading a secret life. As a sorcerer."

He had the satisfaction of seeing the king actually recoil. "What madness is this?"

Cadwal shrugged. "Only madness was maybe on his part. Look you, there's your poor lass lying dead as his victim. And if I were you, I'd start checking back to see who else at your court met a mysterious death or just out-and-out disappeared."

"Physician Octa," someone murmured, and Cadwal saw the king wince. "Octa," Egbert echoed, "yes. My poor Leofrun . . . you really were telling the truth, weren't you? You were telling the truth about Osmod, and none of us would listen."

Cadwal remembered the prince's words about magical persuasion and nodded. "Right. And I'll wager the lot of you that you're suddenly finding your minds a good deal clearer than they've been in days." He met the king's eyes and saw it as blatant truth. Egbert was suddenly realizing exactly what had been happening to him.

Which isn't necessarily a good thing for the prince and me. Kings don't like the folks who point out their failings, and Egbert isn't going to like our presence reminding him that he'd put his trust in that bastart *Osmod.*

But before Cadwal could say anything nice and noncommittal, Prince Ardagh was struggling to his feet, pale with exhaustion but somehow managing to stand proudly straight of back. "I am not a traitor, King Egbert." His voice was faint but steady. "I am neither oathbreaker nor assassin. You know that, King Egbert. Swear to it."

"I don't see what—"

"Swear to it."

There was just the barest hint of . . . what? Cadwal

wondered. Not anything as easily defined as menace. Just a matter-of-fact, *You will do this.*

"Of course you aren't an assassin," the king said suddenly, his sharp sweep of a hand saying, it's not important.

Leave it, Cadwal pleaded silently to the prince. *Don't push this any further.*

But: "Swear to it," Prince Ardagh repeated, staring directly at the king.

Few humans, Cadwal thought, could meet the steady gaze of a Sidhe. Even one who was half-dead on his feet. "Prince Ardagh," Egbert said in an angry rush, "you are no assassin, traitor nor oathbreaker, as far as it is in my knowledge; I swear to this. Your honor, Prince Ardagh, is clean. Now do not press this matter any further. There is . . ." His voice faltered as his glance rested on, flinched away from, Leofrun's body. "There is much to be done."

"And we," Cadwal cut in as urbanely as he could, "will not be disturbing you any longer." Ah yes, that sounded properly elegant. "If you will but grant us horses, we shall be returning to Eriu this very day." *Before you decide to see that we, your embarrassingly awkward guests, meet with some sort of "accident."*

For a long moment, he was sure that the king was going to refuse. But just when Cadwal was wondering if there was any possible way for one swordsman and one bone-weary Sidhe to fight their way free, Egbert waved a brusque hand. "Granted. You are free to take your leave."

Ardagh stood in starlight, leaning lightly on the rail of the ship taking him back to Eriu and still feeling very fragile. This was, according to Cadwal, the first time he'd been truly conscious since they'd left Uintacaester.

I'll have to accept his word for it, since I don't remember a thing. That was, as Cadwal would put it so delicately, one hell of a duel with Osmod.

He shuddered, thinking about it. In the Sidhe Realm,

such a duel would have been over with elegant swift-
ness. Here . . . all night. All night to finally put an end
to Osmod—and nearly to himself as well, from sheer
exhaustion. At least, Ardagh thought wryly, Cadwal had
assured him that the journey here had been most wonderfully uneventful.

Ae, Cadwal. I owe him a great deal.

Ha, here was the man now, looking wan and uncertain.

"Ships," the mercenary muttered.

Ardagh chuckled. "I won't ask you, then, how you're
feeling."

"How I'm feeling," Cadwal said shortly, "is that once
I get my feet back on solid land, I am never, ever leaving
it again." He glanced balefully at the prince. "Glad to
see at least one of us is healthy again."

"Mostly. Ae, we make a fine pair. The triumphant heroes
returning," with heavy irony, "home."

"At least we *have* one," the mercenary countered. "Even
if it's not our own."

He staggered away before the prince could find a
retort. Ardagh grinned ruefully and returned to looking
out over the peaceful water. He shifted his weight slightly
to match the ship's roll, and the runes still in their pouch
at his side clicked together as though reminding him of
their presence. Them, and the possibility of new magics.

And the possibility, too, of renewed interest from the
Darkness.

No. He wouldn't worry about possibilities of any sort,
not right now.

Save, perhaps, for one? Ardagh thought with a sudden shiver of wistfulness, *Sorcha.* It seemed impossible
that all this long, convoluted journey had taken such a
short stretch of human time, a few of their months, no
more. But it would hardly have seemed brief for her.

*Does she still worry about me? Does she still think
of me? Does she—ah Powers, does she even still love me?*

He'd been too weary lately to even try contacting her, but all at once Ardagh couldn't bear to wait any longer. No one was close enough to overhear, so he took out the small amulet and began his call.

"Ardagh!" Sorcha answered so suddenly and fiercely that Ardagh started and nearly dropped the amulet.

"Sorcha, I—"

"Where were you? Where in the name of—where the *hell* were you? And where are you now?"

"Right now, love, I'm on a ship headed back to Eriu."

There was a long silence on her part. Then Sorcha murmured in a voice that wasn't quite steady, "God be praised. God and whatever Powers kept you safe be praised. But where were you? Surely not in Uintacaester all this while!"

"Actually . . . yes. I . . . let's just say that things were rather hectic. After that, I was just too weary—"

"Stop that!"

"What—"

"Don't you think I've seen you do this before? Whenever you don't want to talk about something, you rush right by it in a torrent of smooth words. And by the time we humans catch up, we've forgotten the original subject."

"There isn't . . ."

"Ha, you can't continue, can you? You can't tell a lie. Ardagh, please, *what happened?*"

"Osmod," he said in brusque surrender, "turned out to be a sorcerer. We fought. I won. Sorcha, that's past—"

"A sorcerer!" Her voice sharpened. "You knew this from the first, didn't you? Telling me just that you didn't like the man, that he wasn't trustworthy or whatever other excuse you used—you knew what he was!"

"Sorcha, it's over. No need to be afraid."

"I'm not afraid, dammit, I'm furious! Why didn't you tell me the truth? Why weren't you honest with me?"

Why, indeed? "I didn't want to worry you," Ardagh heard himself say lamely.

"And instead you treated me like—like a half-wit who couldn't bear to hear the truth!"

Ardagh winced, remembering Leofrun. "Never that."

"What, then? You would never have been so—so—so *condescending* to a woman of the Sidhe, would you? Well, would you?"

"No, of course not. But you—"

"But I am just a human? Is that it?"

"It wasn't—"

"Wasn't it? Why were you shielding me, then? What, no answer? Come, come, be brave, my Sidhe love: *Why were you shielding me?*"

"Because," Ardagh admitted angrily, "I was most stupidly trying to act like a human for your sake!"

"For *my* sake? Och, Ardagh, do you think I'm so stupid I can't accept you for what you are? Och, *Ardagh!*"

With that, Sorcha broke contact. Ardagh stood clutching the amulet, trying to steady his breathing and calm himself. Sorcha, ae Sorcha . . . what had she just told him, there between the hot words? That Sidhe and human could never, ever hope for happiness between them? Was that it? Was it?

He came rigidly alert, staring, all at once sensing *Darkness, Darkness here.* "Osmod!"

The sorcerer stood in the air before him, a lean grey flame no longer bearing even the most remote resemblance to the urbane courtier he'd been in life. Eyes wide and wild with hate beyond the merely human stared at Ardagh. "Osmod, indeed." It was a chill whisper. "Or what is left of Osmod. You have not won, my enemy. You are not free of me."

"Oh now, this is too much, this is just too much. Don't you even have the good taste to stay dead?"

"You are not free of me," the ghost insisted.

Like hell I'm not! All his frustration and anger burst free, and Ardagh erupted, "Am I not? Ghost, you never have understood who and what I am. I am not human, ghost, I am Sidhe, of the Folk of Faerie. And as one of the Sidhe, I have no fear of ghosts—most surely not of you! I ban you, Osmod, I bar you from the waking world, the dreaming world, from all the living worlds. My will is strong, and I deny you! I forbid you the right to haunt me or any other! Now, go to Hell," he finished, and meant it quite literally. "Go to Hell and keep Gervinus company!"

No drama to it; Osmod was simply gone, between one second and the next, and the night was once more tranquil and undisturbed.

Ardagh looked up at the great earthen mound and wooden palisade that was Fremainn and felt a wild confusion of emotions: relief, yes, that his journey was done, but . . .

Sorcha, he thought. *To what have I returned?*

They were through the great gates before he could hesitate.

There on the grassy slope of the royal enclosure waited King Aedh and what looked like all the court, a gaudy rainbow of bright *brats* and tunics. But Ardagh found himself hunting for one figure, his heart pounding so fiercely he thought he would fall from his horse there in front of them all, because she wasn't there, she wasn't. . . .

She was. Sorcha was there. Sorcha was waiting for him. And all at once the last of his fatigue seemed to fly from Ardagh. He leaped from his horse, racing to his love, catching her in his arms, their lips meeting in a kiss so fierce it was nearly a mutual assault, the two of them heedless of the good-humored cheers around them.

At last they had to draw back a little if they were to breathe. "I thought I'd lost your love," Ardagh murmured in Sorcha's ear.

"Och, Ardagh. Never." She drew back slightly to study him. "You really were afraid of that."

"Yes."

"Ah. Human and Sidhe: We really don't always under-stand each other's way of thinking, do we?"

"It would seem not." Half-afraid of the answer, he added, "Is that . . . is that a problem for you?"

Sorcha laughed, brushing his cheek with a quick, tender hand. "They do say that every romance needs its share of mystery and surprise."

"And of chaos and—"

"And fierce arguments, yes, and," she added with a sly quirk of an eyebrow, "fiercer reconciliations."

He had to laugh at that, but Sorcha poked him sharply in the ribs. "I really was angry with you, though, no joke about that."

"Nor do I blame you. I had no intention of patron-izing you, I hope you can accept that. And I certainly won't belittle you again."

"I know." Her voice was smug. "I know." Sorcha smiled up at him, her eyes warm. "And never mind the past. It's enough that you've come home to me."

Home? Ardagh wondered. Not exactly. There were still so many questions left unanswered. Why, for one thing, was the Darkness so interested in him? What was truly happening in the Sidhe Realm? And oh, by all the Pow-ers, would he ever find his way back there?

But Sorcha was warm and loving in his arms. And for the moment, Ardagh told himself, for the moment Fremainn was home enough.

Afterword

Although this is, naturally, a work of fiction, a good deal of it is based on fact.

In the year 799 A.D., a horrendous storm really did sweep across Ireland; the *Annals of the Irish Kingdoms* describes the devastation. That year, the historic King Aedh did fight a battle—possibly two—against the King of Leinster, who did enter a monastery after his defeat. The chronicles of the time make it unclear whether the battle came before or after the storm; I have chosen to make it afterwards, giving Leinster the motive of trying to strike while the High King's guard was down. And yes, the historic Fothad mac Ailin really did proclaim his poem, which is quoted in part in Chapter Two, against involving the clergy.

In the English land of Wessex, King Beortric, who had, indeed, wed Edburga, daughter of the powerful Offa of Mercia, did have a favorite, Worr (Asser, chronicler of the life of King Alfred, says tactfully only that Worr was "very dear to the king"), and did rule for an untroubled sixteen years before dying unexpectedly; rumors suggested poison, and named Edburga as the murderer, deliberate on the part of Worr, accidental on the part of Beortric—particularly since she fled to France shortly after. Edburga, incidentally, came to a bad end; put in charge of a nunnery, she was expelled for "lewd" behavior and ended up a beggar on the streets of Paris.

Egbert did spend the years of Beortric's reign in exile,

mostly in Charlemagne's court. Since it seems unlikely that even an easygoing ruler like Beortric would allow an adult rival to live, and since Egbert is described as being fairly young when taking the Wessex throne, I have made him a child-exile. The year of his accession to the throne is in doubt: some sources say 800, some 802 A.D. I have taken the author's privilege and chosen 800.

Egbert did, by the way, go on to conquer a good deal of what is now England, though he never did take on the Welsh Celts.

Osmod is fiction. The Saxon blood-drinking cult is not.

The author makes no claims for the validity or usability of the rune-magics in this book, Saxon or Norse or, for that matter, that of any other magics in this book. This is, after all, a work of fiction!

Anyone looking for Neolithic circles near modern Winchester is going to be sadly disappointed. However, there are several hundred circles in Britain, most two to three thousand years old, for the curious tourist to investigate. While the majority are stone, there are a few, like the famous Woodhenge near the even more famous Stonehenge, that were made of wood. Archaeologists excavating Woodhenge uncovered perhaps the only human sacrifice to be found buried within a circle; I've taken the liberty of creating a second such site—and sacrifice.

Just as the Sidhe are said to be the Irish Folk, so the Tylwyth Teg are the Faerie Folk of Wales. They are said to take the occasional changeling—and the occasional human lovers.

Yes, Viking raiders would sometimes put ashore in isolated spots to cook themselves some hot meals! And raids on Ireland really did drop off to practically none from 800 to about 830 A.D., after the end of Aedh's reign.

On the naming of names: Eriu is an ancient name for Ireland; Gaeilge is the language (we call it Gaelic). Cymru was—and is—the proper name for Wales, while Cymreig is the language. Uintacaester is the Saxon name for Winchester, based on the Celtic name "Uinta" and the Roman suffix "caster" or city. The modern city has pretty much covered up the remnants of the Saxon/ Roman city. Hamwic, or Hamwih, which was a major trading site of the Saxon era, is now mostly buried under modern Southampton. The Lochlannach are, of course, the Vikings; Lochlannach is the Irish Gaelic word for them.

For the linguistic purists: There really wasn't a Gaelic word for "rudder" until the Viking invasion.

There are many books available on the culture of the Vikings ca. 800 A.D., fewer about the Irish or Saxons of that period, and almost too many often contradictory books on runes. Some of the books consulted for this story include:

Aswynn, Freya. *Leaves of Yggdrasil*. St. Paul: Llewellyn Publications, 1992.

Blair, Peter Hunter. *An Introduction to Anglo-Saxon England*. Cambridge: The Cambridge University Press, 1956.

Campbell, James, ed. *The Anglo-Saxons*. London and New York: Penguin Books, 1991.

Chickering, Howell D., Jr., trans. *Beowulf: A Dual-Language Edition*. New York: Anchor Books, a division of Bantam Doubleday Dell Publishing Group, 1977.

Davies, John. *A History of Wales*. London and New York: Penguin Books, 1994.

Davies, Wendy. *Wales in the Early Middle Ages*. Leicester: Leicester University Press, 1982.

Donovan, John O., trans. *Annals of the Kingdom of Ireland*, 7 volumes. New York: AMS Press, 1966.

Fell, Christine. *Women in Anglo-Saxon England*. Oxford and New York: Basil Blackwell Ltd., 1986. Originally published by British Museum Publications Ltd., 1984.

Hagen, Ann. *A Handbook of Anglo-Saxon Food: Processing and Consumption*. Norfolk: Anglo-Saxon Books, 1992.

————. *A Second Handbook of Anglo-Saxon Food & Drink: Production & Distribution*. Norfolk: Anglo-Saxon Books, 1995.

Harrison, Mark. *Viking Hersir: 793–1066 A.D.* London: Osprey Publications, 1993.

Heath, Ian. *The Vikings*. London: Osprey Publications, 1985.

Hill, David. *An Atlas of Anglo-Saxon England*. Toronto and Buffalo: University of Toronto Press, 1981.

Ingram, The Reverend James, trans. *The Saxon Chronicle: AD 1 to AD 1154*. London: Studio Editions Ltd., 1993. Originally published in 1823 by Longman, Hurst, Rees, Orme and Brown.

Jackson, Robert. *Dark Age Britain: What to See and Where*. Cambridge: Patrick Stephens Ltd., 1984.

Keynes, Simon and Michael Lapridge. *Alfred the Great: Asser's Life of King Alfred and Other Contemporary Sources*. London and New York: Penguin Books, 1983.

Laing, Lloyd and Jennifer. *Anglo-Saxon England*. London: Routledge & Kegan Paul Ltd., 1979.

Linsell, Tony. *Anglo-Saxon Mythology, Migration & Magic*. Pinner: Anglo-Saxon Books, 1994.

Quennell, Marjorie and C.H.B. *Everyday Life in Roman and Anglo-Saxon Times*. London: B.T. Batsford Ltd., 1959.

Roesdahl, Else. Translated by Susan M. Margeson and Kirsten Williams. *The Vikings*. London and New York: Penguin Books, 1991.

Simpson, Jacqueline. *Everyday Life in the Viking Age*. London: Carousel Books, 1971.

Thorsson, Edred. *At the Well of Wyrd: A Handbook of Runic Divination*. York Beach: Samuel Weiser, Inc., 1988.

————. *Futhark: A Handbook of Rune Magic*. York Beach: Samuel Weiser, Inc., 1984.

Tryckare, Tre. *The Viking*. New York: Crescent Books, 1972.

Walker, David. *Medieval Wales*. Cambridge: Cambridge University Press, 1990.

Welch, Martin. *Discovering Anglo-Saxon England.* University Park: The Pennsylvania State University Press, 1992.

Whitlock, Ralph. *The Warrior Kings of Saxon England.* New York: Barnes & Noble Books, 1993.

Wiseman, John. *The SAS Survival Handbook.* London: Colins Harvill, 1986.

Wood, Margaret. *The English Medieval House.* London: J. M. Dent & Sons Ltd., 1965.

Wood, Michael. *In Search of the Dark Ages.* New York and Oxford: Facts on File Publications, 1987.